REGENERATION

Also by Stacey Berg

Dissension

REGENERATION

An Echo Hunter 367 Novel

STACEY BERG

HARPER
VOYAGER
IMPULSE

An Imprint of HarperCollinsPublishers

This is a work of fiction. Names, characters, places, and incidents are products of the author's imagination or are used fictitiously and are not to be construed as real. Any resemblance to actual events, locales, organizations, or persons, living or dead, is entirely coincidental.

Excerpt from *Dissension* copyright © 2016 by Stacey Berg.

Digital Edition MARCH 2017 ISBN: 978-0-06-246614-3

Print Edition ISBN: 978-0-06-246615-0

Harper Voyager, the Harper Voyager logo, and Harper Voyager Impulse are trademarks of HarperCollins Publishers.

HarperCollins is a registered trademark of HarperCollins Publishers in the United States of America and other countries.

FIRST EDITION

17 18 19 20 21   HDC   10 9 8 7 6 5 4 3 2 1

For Mary, who makes the world new every day

CHAPTER 1

Echo Hunter 367 studied the dying woman in the desert with grudging admiration. The woman had walked long past what might reasonably be expected, if that lurching stagger could be called a walk. When she couldn't walk anymore, she had crawled, and after that she had dragged herself along, fingers clawing through sand until they clutched some purchase, body scraping over rocks and debris, heedless of the damage. Now and then she made a noise, a purely animal grunt of effort or pain, but she forced herself onward, all the way until the end.

I smell the water.

Desperate as the woman was, she had still been cautious. Though an incalculable distance from any familiar place, she still recognized danger: the wind-borne sand that scoured exposed skin clean to the bone, the predators that stalked patiently in the shadows for prey too weak to flee. The cliff edge that a careless girl could slip over, body suspended in space for the briefest moment before her hands tore through the thornbush, then the long hard fall.

Echo jerked back from that imagined edge. It was her last purposeful movement. From some great height, she watched herself collapse in the sand. One grasping hand, nails torn, knuckles bloody, landed only a few meters from the spring's cool water, but she never knew it. For a little while her body twitched in irregular spasms, then those too stilled. Only her lips moved, cracking into a bloody smile. "Lia," she whispered. "Lia." Then she fell into the dark.

For a long time there was no sound except water trickling in a death rattle over stones.

Then the high whine of engines scattered the circling predators.

Pain returned first, of course. Every inch of skin burned, blistered by sun or rubbed raw by the sand that had worked its way inside the desert-proof clothing. Her muscles ached from too long an effort with no fuel and insufficient water, and her head pounded without mercy. Even the movement of air in and out of her lungs hurt, as if she had inhaled fire. But that pain meant she was breathing, and if she was breathing, she still had to fight. With enormous effort she dragged open her eyes, only to meet a blinding brightness.

She made a sound and tasted hot salt as her lips cracked open again. "Shh," a soft voice said. "Shh." Something cool, smelling of resin and water, settled over her eyes, shielding them from the glare. A cloth dabbed at her mouth, then a finger smoothed ointment over her lips, softening them so they wouldn't split further when she was finally able to speak. *Lia*, she thought, letting herself rest in that gentle strength until the pain subsided into manageable inputs. Then she began to take stock.

She lay on something soft, not the rock that had made her bed for so many weeks, although her abused flesh still ached at every pressure point. The air felt cool but still, unlike the probing desert wind, and it carried, beyond the herbal tang, a scent rich and round, unlike the silica sharpness of sand she'd grown so accustomed to. Filtered through the cloth over her eyes, the light seemed diffuse, too dim for the sun. Indoors, then, and not a temporary shelter, but a place with thick walls, and a bed, and someone with sufficient resources to retrieve a dying woman from the desert, and a reason to do so. But what that reason might be eluded her. The Church would never rescue a failure.

Unless the Saint commanded it.

She mustered all her strength and dragged the cloth from her eyes. She blinked away grit until the blurred oval hovering above her took on distinct features, the soft line of the cheek, the gently curving lips. *Lia*, she thought again, and in her weakness tears washed the vision away. She wiped her eyes with a trembling hand.

And stared into the face of an utter stranger.

"**W**ho are you?" the woman who was not Lia asked, in an accent that was strange but understandable.

She knew the answer, she realized, though a moment ago she could not have said. A hunter. Echo Hunter 367, if specificity were required. Once she had been interchangeable with all the others. Now—everything came back at once: the city, the rebellion, her mission. The Saint. There were recent gaps, stretches of time where her mind had simply not captured any information, but that was unsurprising given the length and desperation of her journey. What was surprising was that she had survived; she had not expected to. Had not particularly wanted to.

But she had her duty. Instead of answering the woman's question, she croaked through a still-parched throat, "What is this place?"

The woman pursed her lips thoughtfully. They didn't look much like Lia's, now that Echo could see more clearly. They were thinner, in a narrow face that was tanned from sun, though not nearly so dark as a hunter's, with a slightly crooked nose and eyes that were plain and brown as any ordinary cityen's. "The dispensary. I'm the physic this turn. Khyn." The woman's eyebrows lifted. They were plain and brown too, like the hair that she wore in a simple braid tucked behind one shoulder. A few strands had come loose and stuck damply down the side of her neck. "I usually just see cuts and broken bones, and every now and then someone gets sick. Little things. Nothing like what happened to you. Whatever that was."

Since that wasn't a question, there was no obligation to answer. Echo looked past the woman, studying as much of her surroundings as she could see without having to turn her head. Only part of one wall was visible from this angle; aside from a shuttered window, it was entirely lined with built-in shelves and cabinets that were made of metal and wood, and even some thinly plated glass. Most of the drawers were marked with labels that looked machine-written rather than hand-copied, and on paper that might not have been used for something else first. The lettering was too small to read from here; those details could wait for later. The room was lit by three parallel light tubes much like those in a Church laboratory, and an unseen fan, humming just above cityen hearing, moved enough air to keep the temperature comfortably cool. Power to spare, then.

Power meant a Saint to keep it running.

Echo breathed through a stabbing pain.

A med, or something like one; a laboratory; a Saint—she had found another Church. Another city.

Until now she had not believed it possible. For four hundred annuals since the Fall, the city—her city—had thought itself orphaned by the catastrophe. The great array of dishes in the desert had listened, hunters had searched, most never returning; but none, ever, had found a sign of other survivors.

She wondered briefly if this were a hallucination, a final wish as her body failed in some desolate waste. If so, there might be no way to tell. But then she knew: her last dream would not be of duty, however much it should be.

Lia.

She worked to steady her breath. It took a little time.

"I need to see the Patri," Echo demanded.

The woman's brow furrowed. "You need to rest. I've given you some fluid"—she gestured, and only now did Echo notice the pricking of the thin tube inserted into her left forearm—"but it's too soon for you to eat." She rolled her chair forward to pinch the back of Echo's hand gently. When she let go, the skin made a little tent that stood up for a few seconds before slipping back into place. "You're still awfully dry, but it's safer to fix it slowly. I'm sorry; you must feel terrible."

"Fine," Echo said, "I'm fine," but darkness was gathering in the corners of her vision again. "The Patri— I have to see him. I have a message."

"I'll take it. Just tell me, and then you can rest."

Echo shook her head. "The Patri," she insisted, or tried to, but the tiny movement had shaken her thoughts loose. The woman leaned forward again to do something with the tube, and the shadows rolled nearer, then closed over Echo altogether.

The woman, Khyn, was still watching her when she awoke again. This time Echo had the sense to keep quiet, only slitting her eyes to evaluate the situation before blurting further questions. In the windowless room she could not judge the passing of time, but it must not have been very long: loose strands of Khyn's braid still clung to her neck, and the chair sat at the exact same angle to the bed. In Echo's experience cityens seldom could keep themselves still very long. That made them different from the patient predators of the desert, though no less dangerous.

Nor was Khyn the only other person in the room, though Echo thought they had been alone before. She couldn't see the others, but she heard them breathing, faster than seemed normal, two or three of them over by the far wall where the door must be. One door, a shuttered window; not ideal in her current condition, but then, she hadn't come this far only to try to escape. She was here for their help, if she could persuade them to provide it. The people by the door—male, most likely, from the smell, though it wasn't always easy to tell—fidgeted; she heard the tiny squeak of leather as a boot shifted. They were anxious, watching her, and why not? Even if they didn't recognize what she was, they must have been surprised to find a stranger in the desert. Shocked, more like: Echo had seen no sign of any other human in the many weeks since she had left the city in search of other survivors. She had traveled west as far as she could, choosing that direction for no reason other than to know that the sun touched the city—Lia—before it reached her. Then the great rift in the earth had forced her north for so long that she wondered if she had truly reached the edge of the world. By the time she found a way down the cliffs and across the barren bottomlands, she was near the end of her strength, and she'd spent the last of that climbing out the other side.

She wondered how they had found her.

That was unimportant now. What mattered was her mission, and to accomplish that she had to gain their trust. She moved her limbs deliberately, like a restless sleeper awakening, then allowed her eyes to open fully and turned her head. It didn't hurt quite as badly as before.

"She's awake," Khyn called to the strangers. "Wait, give her some room to breathe, will you? She might still be delirious."

"We'll see." A male face, bearded and not at the moment friendly, pushed itself into Echo's vision. "Who are you? What's your name?"

Delirious might be useful. "The desert—the desert—"

"We know you were in the desert. Who was with you? Were you looking for something?"

"So hot," she muttered. "The sun—find shelter, I need to, I—"

"You're safe here," Khyn said, shooting a glare at the man. "Can you tell us anything about yourself? What's the last thing you remember?"

"I'm not . . ." She let her voice trail off, then grow stronger. "I'm not sure." Then, as if seeing her surroundings for the first time, she widened her eyes. "Where am I?"

"Safe," Khyn repeated. "You're in the preserve. We just need to figure some things out. Now try to think: can you remember how you ended up in the desert?"

The young hunter Gem, wishing her luck, had dropped her at the limit of the aircar's reach. What would that better version of herself think now? "I—I don't know," Echo said. She wiped her mouth. "So dry. Do you have water?"

"Plenty. Hand me that container, Birn, would you?"

The bearded man complied with a frown as Khyn slid an arm around Echo's shoulders. "Here, let's see if you can sit up." Echo let herself lean into the wiry arm; in truth, she wasn't completely certain she could rise unassisted. It was better once her feet were on the floor and the cool liquid was running down her throat. The water was flavorless beyond a faint metallic taste. Filtered, maybe even distilled. And Khyn said they had plenty of it. The source must be secure.

"She's well enough," Birn said. "The team will want to see her."

Khyn nodded. "When's Stigir going to be ready?"

"Late meal. He's with the stewards."

"Again? He goes in and out too much. It's not good for him."

"He knows what he's doing. He sent the vektere out searching again; he wanted the stewards to be aware."

The man by the door spoke for the first time. "If anyone else were out there, we'd've found them. We followed her trail hours back, until it was wind scrubbed. She was alone."

Hours. How long had she been unconscious? That gap was dangerous. If she had really been delirious, if she had spoken—but they didn't know her name, or whether she had companions, or where she had come from. Even if her mind had rambled, she couldn't have given anything important away. "I'll tell you whatever I can," she offered. "Now, if the Patri is ready."

The three of them exchanged glances in a way she didn't like. "Let me know when Stigir's in," Khyn said. "I'll bring her to the team."

"We can question her now," Birn said.

"When Stigir's back. The whole team should be there."

The man scowled; Khyn met it with a little shrug.

"Fine," he said at last. "Jole, you stay here and watch. Call me if anything changes."

When he was out the door Khyn said, "Don't let Birn upset you. He's just arguing because it was my idea. Once you talk to the team it will be fine."

Echo doubted that. Birn reminded her of someone else, a boy she had known once, and made into an enemy. It wasn't his looks, but that suspicion, the instant dislike he had taken to a stranger in his people's midst . . . She let the last sip of water wash her mouth before swallowing reluctantly.

Khyn took the empty container from her. "Let me get you some more." She returned with it and watched, smiling, as Echo drank. "Do you think you can stand for a few minutes? You'll feel better if we clean you up a bit." Khyn helped her into an alcove where indulgently warm water flowed at the turn of a handle, then into someone else's clothes. The cloth was soft, pleasant against her stinging skin. "We'll clean yours and give them back to you later. If there's anything left of them."

"Thank you," Echo said, settling back into the bed. Even that small effort had exhausted her. Just as she let her eyes drift closed, Khyn asked, "Who's Lia?"

Saints.

"Don't worry. I won't tell Birn. Or even Stigir. I know that tone of voice when I hear it, even if it comes from someone talking half out of her head." Khyn hesitated. "You were alone when they found you. If there's somewhere else we should be looking . . ." For a body, Echo knew she meant.

"No one came with me." Only in her heart, where Lia's voice still sang wordlessly. For a time, in those first days, she had thought it was real, like the Saint's thoughts that the priests interpreted through the patterns on their control boards in the sanctuary. When she listened to it, she saw Lia's golden eyes, felt Lia's arms holding her with that strength so different from a hunter's, tasted her lips, full and soft as they had been in that one night . . . With time and distance the voice had faded, until now it was only an echo of something that might have never been. That made it no less real, to her.

"It sounded like she was important to you."

"It doesn't matter now. She's gone."

"Dead?"

The word was a stab of pain, like a stunwand charge firing through her nerves. Her silence was answer enough.

"I'm sorry." Khyn's fingers interlaced in her lap. "Try to sleep. Stigir won't be back for a while, and you need the rest. I won't give you anything this time, I promise."

Echo almost wished she would. She was certain that sleep would evade her, as it so often did; or worse, bring with it the dreams. But this time when she closed her eyes, the shadows found her on their own, and took her nowhere except the dark.

CHAPTER 2

The first thing Echo noticed about the compound, even before Khyn led her outside, was how it smelled. The dispensary, like every medical area Echo had been in, was notable mainly for the lack of odor, the impression that something offensive had recently been scrubbed away. But the outside air bore innumerable scents. Some, like the residue of wood smoke and the oily metal of machinery, were familiar; but others were harder to place. There was resin as from newly sawn wood, only stronger; a muskiness close to but not exactly bovine; and beneath all that, a rich smell like the desert after one of its infrequent rains, but rounder, deeper. It was cool here, too; not the sharp cold of the desert nights in winter, but a long chill that emanated from the ground, the way the rocky tunnels that burrowed beneath the Church were always cold. Echo inhaled deeply as the outer door opened.

The first thing she saw was the trees.

She knew trees, of course; they grew in the city, here and there where roots could tap a water source, usually along the old buried aqueducts; but those were tough, straggling things, with twisted trunks and scant needle-like foliage. In the Church compound the priests had a small orchard, where they grew medicinal fruits and taught young hunters about harvests; the cityens lately had started plantings of their own. What stood before her now was something else altogether: a vast stand of closely spaced trunks with arching branches, and broad green leaves so dense that only glimpses of the cloudy sky showed in between them. The tallest towered high above; others rose more modestly to twice or three times her height. They spread across the hillside beyond the compound of low-slung buildings like the one she and Khyn, followed by the silent Jole, had just exited.

Distant air currents started a wave of motion that rolled down the hillside, carrying with it a swirl of fallen leaves. Now she recognized the scent that had eluded her: decaying organic matter, tons of it, layering the ground beneath the trees. She wondered what it would feel like to walk on that, instead of rocky dust and sand.

Then she felt a chill, not only from the breeze

plucking at her shirt. They'd brought her much farther from the desert than she'd realized.

The second thing she saw was the door built into the hillside.

It was as tall as the magnificent Church doors, and just as wide, its two panels dividing an arch set right into the rock. There must be an enormous excavated space beneath the hill to justify such an entrance. Light glinted off metal as the clouds shifted.

"Storm coming," Khyn said, with a hint of unease. "Let's go." She offered a supporting arm; after a fractional hesitation, Echo took it.

The whole compound was only the size of a few city blocks. Echo counted eighteen buildings, though there could be more hidden among the trees. They looked old, but not decrepit; the few windows glinted with intact glass, and doorways and rooflines maintained proper angles. The regular spacing and identical sturdy construction of concrete and metal suggested that all had been built at once, utterly unlike the chaotic destruction and reclamation evident throughout the city. This whole place must have been planned, though its purpose was not yet evident.

The sun was low beneath the trees, casting long shadows as Khyn led Echo along a street completely free of debris. Only a few other people were about, moving purposefully between the buildings. She heard the whine of engines somewhere distant, an aircar by the sound of it. If that was how they'd brought her in, she could be many days on foot from the last place she remembered walking. That might make it more challenging to get out.

On the other hand, she knew how to fly an aircar.

Others noticed them crossing the compound and stopped where they were, and some came out from the buildings to watch as well. A few began to follow, making Echo's back tickle between her shoulder blades, but none came too close, and Khyn seemed unconcerned. Echo kept walking, pretending not to notice. Khyn took her to the building with a metal number 1 affixed next to the door. A man stood there in the unmistakable attitude of a sentry. He was dressed like Khyn—like everyone Echo had seen—in serviceable woven shirt and trousers, not much different to the eye from what hunters wore in the city, what Echo wore now, though her long trek had worn the practically indestructible fabric to rags. Echo wondered if the forebears had bequeathed these people all the same miracles they'd granted the city.

And what the people did with them, if they had.

"Hallo, Nik," Khyn said. "Is the team ready?"

The man nodded. His shirt was marked with a V, as was Jole's, Echo noted now. Vektere, the man Birn had said. Guards, plainly enough. On his belt Jole wore a short baton that might be a kind of stunwand, but that didn't mean he carried nothing more deadly; hunters only showed their weapons when a display would be useful. And she was weak, still, alarmingly breathless after the short walk from the dispensary.

"All gathered," Nik said. He looked at Echo with open curiosity. "A stranger! Never thought I'd see that. Lucky for you we were looking for Ully. No sign of him yet," he added at Khyn's questioning look. "But don't worry. You know Stigir will never let us give up."

Another guard accompanied them down the hall. This building was important enough for security, or Stigir was; or maybe it was just because of Echo. All the hall doors were shut, though the place felt active, not derelict and abandoned like so many passages in the subterranean bowels of the Church.

The fourth door on the left stood open, and a dozen faces looked up in unison as Khyn led Echo inside. It was like entering a classroom of young hunters ready for a lesson, though this room had a long central table rather than desks, and the window looked onto the distant stand of trees, rather than the sanctuary with its ever-turning dish atop the spire. Were the priests still listening for her? Echo wondered with a sudden emptiness beneath her breastbone. Or had they given up long ago, when the relays in the desert could no longer trace her signal across the impossible distance? She dismissed the distraction impatiently; she had no time for such childish thoughts.

"Welcome," said the man sitting at the far end of the table. He was dressed like the rest, with no decoration of rank on his person, not even the V, but there was gray in his hair and neatly trimmed beard, and a clearness to his gaze. "Please, have a seat." Echo didn't like having her back to the door, but there were only two empty chairs, and Khyn had already moved to the other one. Just as well: in the seat next to that was Birn, glaring in Echo's direction. A few of the other men and women wore frowns as well, but more perplexed than angry. The leader, though, gave her the friendly smile of a man comfortable that she posed no threat. He didn't recognize her for a hunter, then. Hardly surprising, given her sorry state.

"I'm Stigir," he said, "Prime this turn. You've already met Khyn and Birn, of course. This is Yilva, the controller lead; Rohan, from foresters; Jax, herders . . ." Some of the designations made sense; others were unfamiliar. Echo made note of those to ask Khyn about later. For now she only nodded to each team member in turn. Stigir smiled. "I'm sorry we haven't given you much time to recover, but we're too eager to hear your story to wait. You might start with your name; we'd like to have something to call you other than 'the stranger we found in the desert.'" The smile grew wry, the way they did when cityens shared a joke about themselves. "You might guess that we've been saying that quite a lot."

She shaped a smile back. "Echo." That should be sufficient; they all seemed to go by a single name.

There were murmurs of greeting, and a few more smiles, and she asked Stigir, "Are you the Patri?"

The murmurs turned to confusion. Khyn said, "You used that word before. We don't know what you mean."

"Leader," Echo said. Perhaps she had come among cityens after all, and Stigir was no more than the head of one clave. "I am happy to answer your questions as best I can, but forgive my weakness. If you have one who is in charge, please, take me to him. Then I can tell you all at once."

The woman Yilva frowned. She appeared to be older than Stigir by a good many annuals, but she sat straight-backed in her chair, and her eyes were still clear. Right now they were narrowed in suspicion. "Are you trying to delay us from finding out why you came here? Because we will, don't make any mistake about that."

"Yilva—" Khyn began, but the woman cut her off.

"She's a stranger, preservers' sake. Listen to the way she talks. Who knows what she wants?"

Birn nodded agreement. "Now she's even seen the—"

"*Birn,*" Stigir said, just sharply enough. Whatever Birn had been about to give away he bit back. Too bad. Echo was certain it had to do with those doors built into the hill.

"I meant no insult," she said. "If I violate your customs, it is through ignorance, not intention. As for delay, I have no reason for that. If you are the leader, I will report to you."

Stigir made a gesture that took in everyone at the table. "The team leads together. I'm Prime this turn though, so if it makes you more comfortable, you may speak directly to me."

"Very well." She took a breath as if to compose her thoughts. In truth, she had rehearsed this moment many times in her journey, though not once had she ever expected it to come. *Lia*, she thought to the woman far away in the Church's sanctuary. *Do you know what I'm about to do?* But no answering voice crossed the wastes between them. She focused on the man in front of her. "Since you found me in the desert, you must know that I come from far away. How far, I am honestly not certain. I traveled for many days that I remember, and some that I do not. As for *why*"—this was the tricky part. She did not want to lie to them— there was no reason for that—yet she could not give too much away until she understood better what they would do with the information. Even the friendliest cityens could make a deadly enemy, as she'd learned to her regret. "I come from the city. One of many, in the past, we know; but in all ages since the Fall, we have stood alone. We have listened, and watched, and searched, to no avail. But now—" her own pulse quickened at the sound of the words—"I have found you."

There was one still moment, then everyone starting talking at once. Yilva exclaimed, and Birn replied with equal vehemence, the exchange too quick for Echo to follow through their accent; but the sense was clear enough as Birn's hand chopped in her direction. If it came to that, she would need to be very quick. In her current condition, and unarmed, she could not overcome twelve of them. She was not even certain that she could defeat one man in a test of strength. But it wouldn't be a test of sheer strength, and she had little doubt that she could damage Birn enough that he would be no threat to her for quite some time.

What the rest of them would do then was a different matter. They were already off balance, disconcerted by their sudden shift from magnanimous rescuers to targets of an outsider's attention. Even Stigir stared at her with eyes gone wide. But Khyn only looked at Echo, then into the middle distance, contemplating something beyond the room's blank wall.

Stigir rapped his fist against the table, then did it again, harder. Finally the babble died down. When he spoke, his tone was still mild, but his brows had drawn together in consternation. He might be their leader, but he gave away far more than the Patri ever had, at least to her. "You were looking for *us*?"

That was what disturbed them, more than the mere presence of a stranger. They had something they thought was of value, and they thought she was after it. That could be both dangerous and useful. She considered a show of strength, then decided not to encourage their fears. Not yet. Instead she spread her palms in a gesture of apology. "For anyone. I would have failed. But luckily for me, you found me first."

It seemed to reassure them. They leaned back in their chairs, postures relaxing. Even Birn's glower subsided. "Well," Stigir said. "You certainly have given us a shock. We suspected that there might be other places where some survived, yes, but to know for sure—please, tell us more about this city you come from."

She had a sudden memory of sitting before another man, telling another story to gain his confidence. But this time her goal was not to neutralize a threat. Most of what she said now would be true. She had prepared it with special care. She spoke for some time about cityens and claves, the day to day life of a society once little more than a remnant of a lost civilization, now beginning, against nearly impossible odds, to grow and even thrive. She talked about the stads where enough grain could be grown to feed almost everyone, and fabricators like the young man Exey, who every day invented new and better ways to perform the necessary tasks of survival. She told them how more babies were born now than died, and most of them intact, at which they exchanged sharp glances with each other, but didn't interrupt her.

Of the rebellion that had nearly cast it all back

down into the dark, and her own bitter role in that, she said nothing.

At length her throat, still raw from the desert and utterly unaccustomed to so much talk, gave out, and when Stigir asked the first question, she produced only a hoarse squawking noise. "Here," Khyn said, reaching into a low cabinet against the wall and handing her a flask. She sniffed from cautious habit, but it was only more water, surprisingly cold. She drank it all in one breath and nodded her readiness to go on.

"Explain again, please, about the Church."

"It is like your 'team': the leadership of the city. Those whose wisdom makes them suitable to decide larger things, oversee the use of resources, and so on. The Patri is the head, like you." They did not need to know about hunters or defenses.

"And you're a member of this Church?"

The question awoke the old ache, like a new wrenching of a half-healed joint. Every answer anywhere near the truth was too complicated to make sense here. She only said, "The Church knew my intention, yes."

"What intention exactly was that?" Birn demanded. "What did you think you would find?"

"I had no expectations," she admitted. "My plan was simple: to search, as long and far as I could, and if there was any other city, any at all in the world, to find it. Many like me have gone before, but none has ever returned."

"No wonder, if they tried to cross the desert," Yilva said. "You couldn't expect to survive."

"I nearly didn't. Yet thanks to Khyn—to all of you—here I am."

"What kind of people would let you take that on yourself?" Khyn asked, appalled. "Didn't they care what would happen to you?" *We take care of each other here*, another woman had said once. Now, as then, Echo had no answer.

"Desperate ones," Birn said. His palm hit the table, hard. "She hasn't told us the half of it. What would make anyone send their people in search of total strangers? What would make anyone *go*?" His question drew nods of agreement, and measuring looks in her direction.

"It is not unreasonable," Stigir said, "to ask again what you want from us. Please, answer carefully."

She was tired, and her bones hurt, and suddenly she was in no more mood for caution. She looked at the team around the table, meeting their eyes each in turn. "Have you truly never wondered? Have you never even wished that you might find other survivors, beyond whatever boundaries mark your holdings?"

Stigir said, "Such things are none of our concern. Like you, we have our own task. And I must tell you: there is nothing more important to us."

"What is this task?"

Stigir didn't answer right away. He barely glanced

around the table, but Echo saw the way he took in every subtle message sent by way of expression or posture, from Khyn's elbows-on-table curiosity to Yilva's tightly folded arms. She felt an instant's longing for that intimacy, the work of a team long together, and well led. But she had not shared such a thing since long before she'd left the city.

The silent consultation led Stigir to a decision. "We are Preservers," he said, and now she heard the word as a name. "But that is a discussion for another time. You must be exhausted. We've kept you too long tonight, after everything you've been through. You've given us a great deal to think about, and it isn't our habit to be hasty. Be patient, please, and meanwhile, be welcome."

Khyn took her back to the dispensary. It was almost dark; soft glowlights lit the walkways at close intervals. They were set to continuous-on, and nearly every bulb burned full, unlike the haphazard arrangement of lightstrings in the city. Even the door built into the mountain was outlined brightly against the dark mass of the rock. If they meant that to be secret, it was not through camouflage. Everything Echo had seen here was in better repair than in the city, or even the Church. "Your Saint must be strong," she said to Khyn.

The physic looked sideways at her. "That's another word we don't understand."

"You have lights, and fans, and"—Echo lifted the

flask she carried, which had been refilled yet again—"a way to make things cold. Who controls all the power?"

Khyn's expression cleared. "Ah—stewards. Yes, it's an especially good group this turn. It's procedural to assign the most experienced for winter. You never know what the weather will do." None of that made sense, but before Echo could ask, Khyn continued, "I thought a storm was coming, but I guess not."

Echo drew a slow breath through her nose. Beneath the animal and machine scents the breeze carried a faint hint of silica, harsher than the others, and more familiar. "How far are we from the desert?"

Khyn hesitated, then shrugged. "It's not a secret. A hundred and fifty kils, maybe a little less. Why?"

"The upper wind is moving fast. Your storm will come."

"How do you know that?"

I can smell it, Echo almost said. She caught herself just in time. "I could be wrong."

Khyn stopped. "Something tells me you're not wrong very often."

Only when it matters most. Echo stared up at the darkening sky. Against all the artificial light, only the brightest stars poked through. At least they were in their proper positions. At this very moment a hunter in the Churchyard might be looking up, seeing the same patterns in the sky, and against it, the dark outline of the spire, the dish turning, the beacon calling into the night, the Saint—

Enough. Echo had told these people the truth: she had a mission, and no higher duty than to fulfill it. She must not be distracted by her own weakness. It was past time to stop thinking about what she had left behind and focus on what she had been sent to do. "This place is nothing like the city," she said. "I would like to see more. Nothing, of course, that isn't permitted to strangers."

"We don't *have* strangers," Khyn said wryly. "Forty thousand cityens, you said? We might not be a tenth that many. Someone knows everyone. But Stigir had a point: just this morning you couldn't even walk. You've kept the water down, so we're going to try some soup, and then a good night's sleep, and we'll figure out what comes after that tomorrow."

Echo's stomach rumbled in reflex. For days she had considered that she was more likely to make a meal for something else than to eat again herself. Soup would be a kind of victory. And Khyn was right: she needed to recover her strength. There was much she had to learn about this Preserve. "All meds sound the same," she said.

"It's hard to go wrong with food and sleep. Come on, Echo. Let's get you settled in." Khyn glanced up at the distant doors. "Seems like you're going to be with us for a while."

CHAPTER 3

A clattering noise woke her in a surge of panic before she remembered that she no longer lay dying in the wastes. The softness brushing against her face was a blanket, not an aerial predator's feathers; and the eyes that stared intently at her from a few feet away belonged not to a drooling canid but to a human child.

A little girl, seven or eight annuals, squatting just outside the open door of the room Echo had been given. A bowl sat on the floor in front of her, and she was stirring whatever it contained with a vigorous clang of metal on metal. "Did I wake you up? I'm sorry. Khyn told me to be quiet. I try to follow instructions, but it doesn't always work. The fostri say I'm ob-sti-nate," she added, sounding out the syllables with care. "But I remembered to bring you your breakfast, didn't I? I hope you'll tell them."

Echo sat up slowly. Things still hurt, but not enough to matter. And these people let a child within reach. "I will make a full report. Is it more soup?"

"That would be a funny breakfast. Here, try it."

The girl slid the bowl across the threshold. Its outline glowed blue in Echo's peripheral vision for a fraction of a second. Ah. They might not realize she could see that part of the spectrum. The forceshield must be calibrated to let objects through but not the living. It probably wasn't set to lethal, or they would have warned her; they were too eager to question her to lose her to an accident so soon. Unless they were just careless. Retrieving the bowl, she touched her tongue to the spoon. "It's good," she said, and it was, though she didn't know *what* it was. Some kind of thickened milk or very thin cheese, only tangy, more sour than the bovine milk cityens consumed. "Did you make it?"

"Of course not! I'm too little. I heard them say you were strange."

At this age juvenile hunters knew a great deal more than how to make their own breakfast. And cityen children—Echo had only known a few. But they too were utterly unlike this child, who studied her unabashedly with wide brown eyes while she twirled the end of a braid that looked very much like Khyn's. She was dressed like Khyn too, in trousers and rolled-sleeved shirt, though the girl's had acquired an impressive state of disarray. Nonetheless, she might be informative.

"What is strange about me?" Echo asked.

"Well, for one thing, you talk funny. Like the way you say soup. It comes all out of your back teeth. See, when I say it, my lips go all round, like this. Soup, soup, soup." The girl bounced on her heels with every word, causing a substantial amount of hair, long since escaped from the braid, to flop across her face.

"I do see," Echo said. "But you can't."

The girl brushed her eyes clear. "Now I can. That's another thing. Your hair is all curled. Everyone else's is flat. Why do you make yours like that?"

Echo touched hair grown much longer than hunter custom. This didn't seem like the time to discuss denas and the selection of advantageous traits, so Echo said instead, "I am relatively certain that your— fostri, did you call them?—were not referring to my hair. What else did they say?"

"Well, they probably wouldn't want me to tell. If they knew I was listening, that is. But they can't not want me to tell if they didn't know I heard, right?" It seemed improper to encourage such convoluted reasoning, so Echo remained silent while the girl persuaded herself. "I don't see why it would be a secret anyway. They said where you come from there's a whole herd of children, and their fostri keep making more and more, just like our capri do. But that can't be true, can it? Because if we got too many capri they would eat all the grasses, then all the little trees, and then we wouldn't have any grasses or trees, and then we'd have to start over again from the special seeds inside the mountain, only we're not allowed to because we're supposed to preserve them until something gets born. I forget what. So we keep the best capri to make more, and eat the extra ones. That's what the fostri say. But I don't like to." The child's eyes grew huge, and a hand flew to cover her mouth. "Do you eat the extra children?"

Memory flashed as vivid as the child in front of her now. A girl's body falling at the feet of her batchmates in the dark Churchyard. Another, tumbling over a cliff. "No. We do not." Echo forced her lips into a shape she hoped would reassure the girl before her. "Especially not the ones who bring us breakfast. What is your name?"

The girl stared, then broke out in a peal of laughter. "Netje. You really *are* strange. Echo, that's what I heard them call you."

"You may as well. Now then, Netje, tell me more about these capri."

The girl prattled happily about herd creatures that sounded more or less like bovines, but with horns, and rather more animated, if the girl's description was accurate and Echo's limited prior experience was representative. Echo provided an encouraging sound from time to time, asking after the capri's food supply and avoiding darker questions about how the herd

was managed, and all the while pondering a population that limited its own growth, and special seeds
preserved within a mountain.

"Netje!" Khyn's call interrupted both the child's
streaming words and Echo's line of thought. The
physic came around the corner and stopped, hands
on her hips. "I told you not to wake Echo! You were
just supposed to bring her meal for later. Have you
been here chattering this whole time?"

The girl jumped to her feet in fair imitation of
Khyn's posture, only with her little fists balled up.
"I did bring her meal. And she talked to *me*. I wasn't
bothering her at all. Was I, Echo?"

"No, you were not. Neither were you obstinate."

"See, I told you, Khyn. And I'll take the bowl back
and wash it, you don't even have to remind me." Echo
ran the spoon around the inside of the rim, licking
off the last drops before sliding the bowl towards
Netje. "Thank you," the girl said, but Echo noted
how careful she was to keep her hands on her side of
the invisible barrier as Echo passed it back. However
she'd learned that lesson, it had made a lasting impression. Then she pranced off, braid bouncing from
shoulder to shoulder.

Khyn shook her head. "That girl is a trial. She has
more energy than I know what to do with."

"She is yours?" The Church bred hunters in
batches, of course, but cityens raised the children
they bore, most of the time. And Netje resembled

Khyn, more than just the mimicry of the braid and clothes.

"This turn. Her birth mother's a steward. Normally she would have waited until Netje was older, but we were short-handed. You were kind to indulge her. Sometimes I pretend I'm still asleep."

Echo suppressed a small stab of guilt. "She seems very knowledgeable about the capri."

Khyn grinned. "She spends enough time with them. They're better listeners than most of us."

"May I see them? If Netje's description is accurate, we do not have anything exactly like them in the city."

She took a step forward, purposely sudden, and Khyn raised a hand hastily to a spot on the door jamb at shoulder level, where the switch for the forceshield must be concealed. Echo heard a tiny click. "Sorry," Khyn said, reddening. "I thought it would disturb you less than a guard. You still need to rest."

"I feel well enough." In truth, her head was beginning to ache again, and her ankle throbbed where the old injury had never had time to fully heal. But those were minor annoyances.

Khyn rolled the end of her braid in her fingers. "You recover quickly. Two days ago you were more than half dead."

"Your care was expert."

"I didn't do that much. And this wasn't the first time you've run into trouble, is it? You have a lot of scars."

Echo decided the capri could wait. If these people learned too soon that she was a hunter—what that meant—it would only make them suspect her motives. "Perhaps you are right. I would welcome more rest." That was not entirely untruthful; she lay back on the comfortable bed with a sigh.

Khyn grinned wryly. "If only Netje listened as well as you." But before she left, she clicked the forceshield on again.

Lia's face shaped itself in the darkness behind Echo's eyes. It was like remembering the dead, only worse, for back in the city Lia's body lived—the Saint's body, now. Lia was gone, lost the moment the crown had gone on, binding her to the city forever . . . Sleep was a long while in coming, and this time it brought the dream: the cliff, the crumbling edge. Echo's hands losing their grip. As always she jerked herself awake just before the falling body hit bottom. By now she could do it without flailing beneath the covers, with hardly any sound other than a quick-drawn breath.

Khyn stood in the doorway, watching. It was impossible to know what she had seen; her expression seemed faintly troubled, but then she smiled and said, "Do you feel up to some real food? We're having a celebration. They found Ully this morning!"

"The one you were searching for when you found me?"

Khyn's smile broadened. "Stigir never gives up. He kept the vektere out looking, even though no one else had any hope. Turns out Ully was just the other side of the mountain, but he'd twisted his knee and couldn't get back. Come on, this will be a special meal."

Khyn took her to a long, narrow building at the far end of the compound. Unlike the sturdy, squat construction of the rest, this one was a fragile jewel, made all of clear glass panels set into metal frames. As soon as she entered, Echo understood the place's purpose: the late sunlight rebounded off the panels, trapping the heat inside; the central aisle of paving stones led through rows and rows of plants and trees, all growing in containers, the different types clustered together in patchwork shades of green. She recognized pomme, and one type of eating greens; the rest were unfamiliar. The heavy air smelled rich and wet; droplets condensed on the panels and tracked down into the dirt. Echo loosened her collar.

A long table had been set up down the aisle; the hint of smoke and roasting meat wafted in from the far door. A dozen or more Preservers sat at the table already, some wearing the V and others, like Khyn, in clothing bare of insignia. At the other end people gathered in a happy crowd around a man who sat with a bandaged leg up on a chair; he was telling a story, gesturing broadly with the cup he held while they laughed and clapped his shoulders.

"Still at it, I see," Khyn said.

The Preservers nearby shifted on the benches to

make space for Khyn and Echo. "Ully was always good with a story," one said, grinning. "Now he's got one worth telling." He turned to Echo. "You must, too. We were hoping Khyn would bring you. We want to hear everything."

"I brought her to enjoy herself," Khyn said a bit sharply. Echo wondered if that were really the only reason. Some interrogations could be more subtle than others. Relenting, Khyn grinned at the man. "I couldn't let her miss a glasshouse meal. Winter's close; who knows how many more chances we'll get. Echo, this is Dorin." One by one, she introduced the others around the table; they nodded and smiled, studying Echo with frank curiosity. Again she noted the resemblance among them, like cityens all of one family.

Someone passed a heaping platter. "You're timing's perfect. Capri's just off the spit." Khyn, apparently not sharing Netje's aversion, took a generous portion; Echo shook her head and accepted a bowl of greens, steaming and slightly sulfurous, instead. She took a small helping of what appeared to be cheese, soft and far milder-smelling than the musky kind she was used to. There was bread too, still warm from wherever they baked it, with a chewy crust and fine insides; she fingered a crumb, wondering where they milled the flour. All at once she found herself thinking of a different table, another woman sitting next to her. She swallowed a bite with difficulty and set her utensil down, letting the meaningless talk wash over her.

"Here." One of the Preservers slid a cup along the table. If she were a cityen, she would be young to wear the V on her shirt. Hunters were a different matter. The girl's eyes were wide, her expression eager, though she kept her voice low as she said, "Fermentate, but I'll get you water if you'd rather."

"Fermentate is fine." Echo normally disliked the sense-dulling properties of ferm, but the sour effervescence eased her throat.

"I'm Taavi." It seemed unlikely, given the small population, that there were twenty in this young woman's annual. Perhaps the vektere were borne randomly, rather than in batches as hunters were. "Did you really walk across the desert? I didn't think anyone could survive there."

It was always useful to know what limitations potential adversaries set for themselves. "Your people must have some experience with it; they recovered me successfully." A pleasant sound wafted in with the smoke, someone outside playing a stringbox, or something like it.

Taavi shrugged. "The vektere patrol all the periphery, but we don't go very far into the desert. It's too big a strain on the aircars, all that dust in the engines. Mostly we just keep an eye to be sure no one's wandered too far from the Preserve. Or gets stranded somewhere, like Ully. The real work is west: the forest turns wild, and sometimes the big predators get too close. Crister got killed this spring, defending a forester from one." She swirled her ferm, looking away. "I'll have a turn out there soon. I hope I do okay."

Juvenile hunters knew their capabilities long before their first independent assignment. Those who were not ready did not survive their teaching exercises.

Sometimes they didn't survive their teachers.

"Are you adequately prepared?"

"My training's gone all right, I guess." Taavi tapped the letter embroidered on her shirt. "Birn gave me the V. But so far I've only worked close in. The periphery—that's different."

Echo's fingers tightened around the cup. It seemed inappropriate to send the girl out with such a lack of confidence; fear as much as rashness could lead to deadly error. She said, "If you are uncertain, you must seek additional instruction."

Taavi's eyes shone. "Are you a vektere?"

"We do not have vektere in the city." Echo hesitated, then decided the opportunity was worth the risk. "I have gained some experience in my explorations, however. Perhaps we could share what we have learned."

"That would be—" Taavi broke off as Birn approached, frowning.

"Aren't you due on patrol, Taavi?"

"In a few minutes." Taavi rose reluctantly. "Another time, Echo, I hope."

"I look forward to it."

"I don't know what you really want," Birn said after the young vektere was out of hearing, "but you're not going to get it from us, no matter who you try your story on. We're not fools."

Echo sipped her ferm. "I will keep that in mind."

"You do that." Birn took a seat elsewhere at the table, but his gaze never strayed far. She felt the weight of it on her even when the stringbox player moved inside and the Preservers moved tables aside to clear a space at the end of the glasshouse. Khyn rose, extending a hand to Echo.

"Do your people dance?"

The harvest fest, the musicians there. Lia, laughing as they took their places. Echo's hands sliding to rest on Lia's waist, feeling the flesh and bone beneath the soft-spun cloth. Then the two of them skipping sideways down the line, under the raised arms of the other couples, until they got to the start, where they broke apart to clap the beat for the next pair coming. And later, another kind of dance, and music of their own making.

It took Echo a moment to catch her breath. When she did, Khyn was still standing there, hand out, smiling. "No," Echo said.

The next morning Khyn took her to see the capri. Fortunately she had taken Echo's abrupt response as a sign of fatigue. Echo still chastised herself for the loss of control; she must not squander Khyn's goodwill.

A vektere approached as they left the dispensary, but Khyn said, "It's all right. She's my responsibility," and the man let them go. A hunter might do the same, and follow unsuspected behind. Or the interaction might have been planned, to see what Echo would do if she thought she was free. If so, they would be disappointed; she intended only to gather information. At least for now.

The capri enclosure sat on the far side of the compound, in an unpaved area with no buildings other than the simple shelter built for the animals. The surrounding fence was made of rough poles split from the trunks of moderate-size trees. On one post was mounted a small box, with a red pull handle and metal mesh over a round opening, and wires running down until they disappeared into the ground. An alarm of some kind, perhaps. A pile of extra fence posts lay neatly stacked behind the shelter, where the flat area of the compound began a gentle slope uphill. Trees marched upward in orderly rows, obviously planted and maintained for a purpose, like the priests' orchard in the Church compound. Higher up, the trees looked older, wilder. The thick growth hid the cavern doors from view.

The young capri were wild as well. Netje's description had been surprisingly accurate. The creatures were much smaller than the juvenile bovines Echo had seen in the city, and they bounced across their pen on stiff legs that propelled them over or on top of every obstacle they encountered, including each other, which then precipitated another round of energetic hopping about. The smallest one, startled by some invisible force, leapt straight in the air, came down on a bale of dried grasses. It discovered that it now occupied the highest ground, which it proceeded to defend with stubby horns from all the other capri, until all at once it realized that it was tired, and curled atop its perch in a fuzzy bundle and went to sleep. "That one's Netje's pet." Khyn laughed. "Sometimes she leads it around on a string. Reminds you of her, doesn't it?"

"All young animals have certain characteristics in common," Echo agreed.

Khyn leaned her elbows atop the fence. The pose was casual, but the muscles in her forearm worked as she picked at a splinter in the rail. Her fingers were long, well-formed. Echo watched them while Khyn debated her response. "I wouldn't be the best judge of that," she said at last. "Netje might have mentioned that there aren't many other children." Perhaps it was an attempt to gain Echo's trust, confiding something that she might already know from the child, or would soon observe for herself.

"Your population is small. If you do not need many replacements, a large number of children is not required."

The splinter broke off. "Is that the way your people think of children? Like some kind of replacement part?"

I wanted you to see it, Lia had said, flush from the happiness of helping a cityen deliver her first child. It had been her way of showing Echo that there might be something different from the harsh upbringing she had known. And before that, when Echo herself had been no more than Netje's age, her old teacher Tana had said, "Cityens love their children." But even then Echo had known that not every child lived happily.

"We don't eat them," she said.

"What?"

"Netje wondered what we did with the extras. She is familiar with the concept of limited resources."

Khyn snorted. "Not from any experience of her own. All that girl has to do is give that big smile and flip her hair around, and she gets whatever she wants. No one can resist. I bet she even tried it on you, didn't she? You're right, though; it wouldn't make sense for us to have too many. I just wish . . ." Her fingers drummed on the rail. "I'm sorry, I'm going on like Netje myself. Have you had your fill of capri? Let's walk up the hill a bit. Just let me know if you get too tired."

A wide path led from the enclosure up into the

stand of trees. It was unpaved, but the dirt was packed down, firm enough to accommodate the carts whose narrow tracks had been captured in what was now dried mud. That must be how they hauled things up and down the mountain, since aircars could not be piloted among the trees. Echo wondered how many of the craft they had: she had not heard another since the day she had first awakened. Maybe they were no longer flying since they'd found Ully. In the city only a few aircars still functioned, though perhaps some had been restored since she'd left, as the new Saint gave the city the strength to rebuild after the rebellion. Lia, healing her people.

The path passed through the center of the grove. The morning sun filtered through the leaves in a dappled pattern, creating shadows that swayed with the breeze. Echo's senses came alert; any number of small predators could hide themselves here. Nonetheless, the grove was pleasant, the ground soft underfoot compared with the sandy rock of the desert, the shivering of the leaves a musical hiss. The trees bore fist-size fruits, smooth and red. Khyn reached up to pluck one, sniffing its stem end before offering it to Echo. "Pomme? It's pretty close to ripe."

Echo's fingers laced together behind her back. "No. Thank you."

"Your loss." Khyn made short work of the fruit, crunching her way through it in a few bites. She shoved the core into a pocket. "The capri love them."

They walked on, and the trees changed, the fruits they bore more orange than red, and yielding to the touch. "Fersk," Khyn said. "I like them even better, but they're fussy; they don't like the cold. I don't think they grew naturally here, before. Go ahead, try one."

The fruit was warm from the sun. Its scent was sweet, and the taste was sweet too when Echo bit into the unexpectedly soft flesh. She leaned forward so the juice would drip to the ground instead of dribbling down her chin. Soon there was nothing left but the single hard, pocked seed. "Do you save them to make a new one?" Khyn shook her head, and Echo flicked the seed away, then wiped a prickly bit of fuzz from her lip.

They walked on through the grove. All the trees bore fruits, the type changing at regular intervals. Not all the stands were equally successful; in some places, the branches thinned, in others, the fruit hung small and sparse. It was a test, Echo surmised, to see what kinds did best. But that seemed odd: if the whole grove were given over to pommes they'd be able to harvest more than she had ever seen at the city's markets; and she knew they could be kept a long time, especially in the cooler part of the year. She chose not to ask: Khyn appeared distracted, her attention turned inward, as if she struggled with some decision. Better for Echo to stay silent; cityens in that mood sometimes offered important information unexpectedly.

Not much farther on, the path narrowed, the

packed earth changing to softer ground, a blanket of decayed leaves broken by the occasional root or stone. It got markedly steeper, too. No wheel had left an imprint here, and the bootprints became sparse enough for Echo to distinguish one from another. She saw occasional animal tracks too, larger versions of the incurved crescents the young capri made in their pen. She wondered if any of them belonged to the predators Taavi had mentioned, but that seemed unlikely; Khyn led her along with no apparent concern, and there was no sign that the vektere had followed.

The trees changed here as well. Wide leaves gave way to thin, flattened spikes growing densely along branches that bore woody, wide-scaled fruits. Echo bit into one experimentally and spat out splinters, drawing a small laugh from Khyn. "You can eat the seeds," she said, "but it's not worth the trouble to pick them out."

Echo weighed the cone in her hand. The parts did not fit: plenty of water, and so much food that they could disregard an inconvenient source, and indulge in crops whose yield was doubtful; Netje had spoken of culling the capri to control their numbers. Yet despite all that, the human population was small. And there were not many children.

Maybe it wasn't only because they didn't need replacements.

Echo looked back the way they'd come. It was these needle-covered trees that gave off the scent she had picked up all the way down in the compound. The resiny bite was much stronger up close, especially now with the branches waving in the rising wind. The same branches blocked the buildings below from view, but the angle of the sun and a rough idea of the time they'd walked told her where she was with respect to the main compound. She started off through a space in the trees, the way a person might who didn't realized she'd missed the trail. The outcropping—and the great door carved into it—should be there, across the bow of the hill.

"Not that way," Khyn said at once.

"I am not too fatigued."

"Well, I am." Khyn forced another laugh. "I don't know what I was thinking, bringing you all the way up here, especially in this wind. That storm must be coming after all. Let's go back."

Echo returned to the path. Just on the edge she stumbled, grabbing at a branch for balance; it broke partway through with a sharp crack. Khyn reached for her; Echo left the branch hanging and let Khyn pull her up. Then, instead of letting go, Khyn linked an arm through Echo's, offering support that was not unwelcome. The walk down was faster than up, but by the time they got to the grove Echo's legs were aching, and she was glad to stop for a drink from the flask Khyn carried. Her body recovered quickly, but it had been pushed close to its limits in the desert. "Sure you don't want to try a pomme?" Khyn asked, taking another herself. "No? Put a few in your pocket anyway; the capri will be thrilled." Echo obeyed, aware again of the tension running beneath the light-hearted tone.

"Hold out your hand like this," Khyn said as they stood at the rail of the enclosure. The capri bounced over, butting each other with their stubby horns as they fought over the bits of pomme, even though the bale of grasses was barely half consumed. They were more skittish with Echo, no doubt confused by her unfamiliar smell. The tiny one, showing the fierce-ness small things often needed to survive, hopped stiff-legged near, then back a few times before it finally worked up its courage to lip the fruit from her outstretched palm. Its muzzle was soft and dry. "They like you," Khyn said.

"They like the pommes."

"That too. You say you don't have capri in your city?"

Echo shook her head. "Bovines. They are some-what similar, but much larger and less agile. Until recently they were raised primarily for milk, but now the cityens consume the meat as well. It is nutritious, but far less efficient a food source than grain." She realized she had seen no fields. "Where do you produce the grasses for them?"

"On the other side of the compound. The ground runs flat for a long way; it's an easy place to grow the things that need sun."

They were nearly out of pomme. The little capri, emboldened by its previous success, butted Echo's hip between the fence rails. It was strong for its size; if capri grew as big as bovines they would be dangerous. She pulled her pocket inside out, searching for a last bit of fruit to give it. The loose fabric flapped in the breeze, sending the capri straight up in the air. It landed splay-footed, eyeing her with disapproval. Khyn tossed a pomme core its way; the little capri caught it at the top of its arc and skittered away. "You spoil them," Echo said.

"There's more fruit than we can use," Khyn replied with a shrug.

Echo decided it was time to push. "I do not understand. Your soil is rich; the trees are obviously cultivated, and the capri are well nourished. In the city these conditions would favor expansion of the population, yet there are relatively few of you. Do you not wish to grow?"

"It's not that simple," Khyn muttered, which in Echo's experience meant that she could not, or did not want to, explain. She stared at the fence rail, gaze unfocused. Echo waited. Then Khyn straightened. "All right. Maybe you can help somehow. Preservers know we need it." She made a gesture that took in more than just the capri. "This place was already here before the catastrophic years—what you call the Fall. The stewards then did everything they could to save it, make sure it survived. I can't imagine what it must have been like, seeing the whole world going to pieces around you, wondering if anything you did mattered at all . . . I don't know how they kept enough hope to plan for any kind of future. What they did surely seemed the only way then; I can't blame them. But things are changing. You're here, aren't you? Maybe we need to change too, if we want to keep going. Even Netje challenges what doesn't make sense to her, and we're not children anymore, to blindly follow the plan the first stewards left us. The team needs to realize— What's wrong?"

Echo forced her fists to unclench. She breathed through the pain, counting the passage of air through her nostrils, one, two, three, one, two, three, focusing on the simple drill until the buzzing in her ears cleared and it was Khyn's voice she heard, not Lia's, and she stood in front of a pen of frolicking capri, not in the burning sanctuary in the last moments of the rebellion. Of Lia's life.

Before she could speak, a squawking noise came from the red-handled box. Netje's breathless shout blared through the wire mesh. "Khyn, Khyn, it's Marget! The baby is coming!"

"It can't be! She isn't due for—" Khyn broke off with an unfamiliar curse. "Come on," she said, and started away at a run.

A small group of people, all strangers, crammed into the dispensary, surrounding the woman who lay grimacing on the bed. Khyn elbowed her way through. "Someone find Stigir. The rest of you get out of my way. *Out*. You too, Echo. And take Netje away. She doesn't need to see this. Or hear," she added, as Marget groaned with the pain of another contraction.

Echo maneuvered everyone else out the door and slammed it behind them. She knelt by the head of the bed while Khyn began her examination. "What happened?" Khyn asked. "When did the contractions start?"

"I was in the Vault," the woman said through clenched teeth. "Checking the cooling unit. I wasn't doing anything, just looking, and all at once—" She broke off with another groan.

"Breathe," Echo commanded.

"I told you to leave," Khyn said.

"I may be of use." She caught the woman's shoulders as her back arched against the cramping pain.

Khyn's lips thinned, but she didn't argue. "Was there blood?" she asked Marget.

"A little. Not too much. It's too early, it can't be coming yet. I did everything you said, I can't—" Another spasm doubled her off the bed, and Echo strove to hold her without causing more damage. Khyn moved quickly, inserting a tube like the one she'd put in Echo's arm, squeezing something through it from a small vial she grabbed from the cabinet. Marget's voice trailed into an incoherent muttering and her struggles diminished, though the muscles still rippled and clenched across her abdomen. Khyn made another injection, then began her examination. Marget's body jerked wildly. Khyn's face went still, and then Echo saw the spreading stain.

"Push," Khyn said. "Marget, wake up and push."

"I can't," the woman moaned. "It's too soon, please, Khyn, you have to stop it!"

"It's too late, it can't be stopped. The baby's not— I'm sorry, Marget, so sorry. You have to push. You have to get it out."

"I won't lose this one, I can't. It's your fault! Get away from me! Get away!" A flailing leg struck Khyn, knocking her back. Echo switched her grip on the woman's shoulders and swung across the bed, pinning the woman down.

"Listen to me," she ordered. Marget's head swung wildly in negation, and Echo shook her shoulders hard. "*Listen*. If you do not push, you will die. I will count. One, two, three—now!"

It was over soon. Marget lay sleeping, face pale but breathing steady as Khyn's medicines took effect; but the small form bundled in the blanket had never breathed at all, not even to cry one futile protest. Echo had glimpsed the malformed head, the gray misshapen mass leaking out the back, before Khyn hid the remains from sight, fussing over Marget's bandages, which didn't need it, rearranging the tools Echo had cleaned, checking Marget again, and finally collapsing back in her chair, face in her hands. She made no sound, but Echo saw her shoulders shake. Lia had felt this same helpless anger, faced with the suffering of the cityens she cared for. Perhaps all meds did.

But Lia had been more than a med.

"You bear no responsibility," Echo said. "The baby must have been malformed from the beginning. You could not have changed the outcome."

"They have to listen to me now," Khyn said in a trembling voice. "They don't have any choice."

Echo pulled a chair next to her. "What do you wish them to do?"

"I don't know why they're so stubborn. None of this has to happen. None of it."

"The woman will live," Echo said. "She may still be able to bear."

"And risk another one of *those*? I wouldn't let her, even if she wanted to. She might not make it next time."

"You are a capable med."

Khyn opened red-rimmed eyes. "You were a big help. Have you had training, or are babies so common in your city that everybody can deliver them?"

"More common than here, it appears. It was not always so; I knew a man, born many annuals before me, who remembered when few children survived. To him each one was precious. But now so many cityens bear successfully that they sometimes need help to provide for them."

Khyn gave a short laugh. "More babies than you know what to do with. I envy you."

Echo thought of the abandoned children she had found in the desert. "It can cause its own difficulties."

"I'd like to have them." Khyn leaned back in the chair, covering her eyes with a forearm.

The door opened a crack, and Netje slipped through, alone. "Is Marget all right?" Somehow she managed to keep her voice to a whisper.

"She will take time to recover," Echo said equally softly. Khyn did not look up.

"What about the baby?"

"It is dead."

Netje's huge eyes flooded. "Was it a boy or girl?"

"I did not look." She had been busy with Marget at the time, but it seemed a paltry excuse now.

"I want to see."

Echo unwrapped the tiny body wordlessly. Netje reached out with a trembling hand to stroke the down-covered arm. The tears ran down her face, but she ignored them, only petting the boy over and over, as if she could comfort both of them that way.

There was a disturbance in the hall. Echo reached for the weapon she wasn't carrying, grasped instead, with a shiver of memory, the sharpest instrument from Khyn's tray. Khyn's head jerked up. "What—" But it was only Yilva and Birn.

"Netje, child, what are you doing here? Go outside, right now." Glaring at Echo, Yilva guided the girl through the door with a firm hand. She took the baby from Echo. Peering over her shoulder, Birn shuddered, but Yilva gave the body a long unflinching look. Then she smoothed the cover back, caressing it lightly, her old face lined with sorrow. "Marget's all right?"

"I told them to get Stigir. Where is he?"

Birn said, "With the stewards. Preservers, when he finds out . . ." He glanced at the small bundle, wiping his mouth. Then he focused on Echo. "What's *she* doing here?"

"Be glad she was. Otherwise Marget might not have . . ." Khyn stared down at the sleeping woman. "She said it was my fault, and she was right. I'm not going to let happen one more time. We have to refresh the line."

"Don't start all that again," Birn said. "You know it's not your fault, and so will Marget, when she wakes up. There are others still carrying; we'll know more when the season is over. There's nothing to change the team's decision."

"The team isn't the one delivering dead monsters." Khyn's voice climbed in frustration. "What else is there to know? This is the third child that died this year. And two last year. And what's wrong with them—" Khyn took the blanket-wrapped body in her arms. "It isn't fair. We wouldn't let it happen to the capri. I'm not going to let it keep happening to these poor children."

"The stock is limited," Birn said. "You know that as well as I do. We'd use it up if we took some every time we have a hard year."

"It's not just one year," Khyn insisted. "The line is failing."

Echo went cold. She heard it again, the long-ago conversation that was never meant to reach her ears. "The line is failing," the Patri had said. "There will be more to cull." How many times since then she had believed herself an example of that failure, she could not count.

"I know it's hard," Birn said. He wrapped an arm around Khyn's shoulder, pulling her close. "But remember what we're here for. The stewards will find a way. Just be patient for a little while longer."

Khyn tugged out of his grasp. "We have to open the Vault before it's too late."

Birn's face hardened. "You used to have better sense."

"You used to be more reasonable." She looked from Birn to Yilva. "I'm going to see Stigir. Come if you want, or not. It's your choice."

"We'll go with you," Birn said. "But the team isn't going to listen. You're making a big mistake." But as he spoke, it was Echo's face he fixed on.

CHAPTER 4

Echo lay on her bed, listening to the wind roar down the mountain. By the movement of shadow across the high slit of a window, more than three hours had passed since Khyn had gone off to confront the team. "Stay here," Birn had ordered when Echo made to accompany them. Echo had heard the tiny click of the switch on the other side. Birn didn't bother to warn her not to hurt herself trying to break through the forceshield. Maybe he assumed she'd listen to him and stay put.

Maybe he had vektere waiting, in case she didn't.

She thought about the dead baby, and Khyn's argument with Yilva and Birn. The Patri shared Khyn's fear, on a larger scale: it would not take many bad annuals to send the cityen population spiraling into a downfall from which the city might not recover.

And as for the hunters, and the Saint . . . Refresh the line, Khyn had said. The burden of maintaining the city had consumed the Saint before Lia after only a few annuals. Lia was different—but even the thought of the same thing happening to her made Echo's gut twist. If Khyn really knew how to do what she suggested . . . Frowning at the ceiling, Echo reexamined the facts she had and determined that they were insufficient. Until she acquired more, she had nothing to report.

Nothing? She could almost hear Lia's laughter, see the golden eyes alight. *You've walked across the desert and found a whole new city that's nothing like our own. They have funny little not-bovines, and a kind of fruit that isn't a pomme. Bring yourself home and tell me all about it!*

For an instant Lia felt so real that Echo could smell her skin as it warmed under the sun on a market day, feel the softness of her body the night they lay together. She almost reached out, to trace the fine crinkled lines at the corner of her eye again—

But Lia was gone.

Echo lay alone, adrift in this faraway place where even the wind smelled strange, sounded strange too as it soughed its way through trees grown greener and denser than she'd ever seen, like the desert in bloom a hundred times over. She counted her breaths, in and out until her heartbeat steadied. The Church remained, and when she returned she would make her report to the Patri, who would parse it for meanings no hunter could hope to see. He would turn the problem over in his quick mind and probe for details she had acquired without realizing, and then he would commune with the Saint, for the Saint preserved the Church, the Church, the city. So it had been, and so it would always be.

And Echo, when he was finished with her, would sit alone in the sanctuary, and bow her head, and listen for Lia's voice in the silence that filled her heart.

Her eyes drifted closed. The wind increased; she heard an occasional distant thump as small pieces of debris struck outside, and the rolling boom of thunder. She was nearly asleep when the cry brought her back fully awake.

She held perfectly still, eyes closed, listening. The sound had been distant, wrong, something that didn't belong. Not Marget in the other room; someone outside, calling from far away. All Echo heard now was the wind, but she knew she had not imagined it. After a moment it came again, fainter this time, but the high, tremulous wail could only belong to a child.

She rose from the bed. "Is anyone there?" she called down the hall. There was no answer. Echo tested the forceshield with a fingertip. It sparked and popped, but the discomfort was tolerable. Still she hesitated. They thought the shield would hold her; she lost a significant advantage if they discovered it could not. Maybe she could pretend the power had failed. Then the cry came again, thin and desperate, and she thrust her arm through the barrier, ignoring the pain while she felt for the hidden switch. The forceshield dropped. Shaking out her tingling hand, Echo ran for the outer door. Birn had left no guard; perversely, she wished he had not underestimated her at such an inconvenient time.

A quick glance down the main walkway told her no help was in immediate reach. The wind swirled, but she could manage it. She had been caught once in a desert windstorm. She had only survived by climbing down a ruined shaft, where she clung for hours to the rusted iron ladder, her body sheltered by a fallen beam while debris pelted past her, splashing into the pit far below. Every time something struck her the ladder creaked and bent a little more. When she had crawled back out on shaking arms, she found the sand blown smooth as far as she could see, the trackless distance marked only by the drifts of sand against jutting rock, and the carcass of some less fortunate predator scoured clean to the pink-white bones. Here in the Preserve, the biggest danger would be flying debris.

She turned her head slowly back and forth, listening. *Call again*, she urged the lost child silently. But it had already been longer than the interval between the other cries. She was on the verge of going for help after all when she heard it again, a shriek of rage or despair woven into the wind. Netje's voice, she was sure. What would bring the girl out into this storm?

Echo sprinted for the capri pen. A rail had come down in back, leaving a gap the animals could squeeze through, but most of them, with the stolid good sense of herd animals, were huddled together in the safety of the enclosure. Netje was not with them. Echo circled around to the gap. Crescent tracks led straight up the path to the grove. So did a child's small bootprints.

Echo yanked the red handle on the post-mounted box but heard nothing, not even static.

She ran up the path at the best pace she could manage. It was raining now, the huge drops pelting so thick that she constantly had to wipe her eyes. In the desert the rare rains like this could fill the veins of a dead riverbed so fast that anything foolish enough to be caught there had no chance of survival. She didn't know the mountains, but already water streamed ankle-deep on the path, and the mud began to suck at her boots. The tracks led her through the grove and up the trail on the other side. Soon the water would erase them, but she didn't need them anymore; the awful sound ahead was beacon enough.

A fallen tree pinned the little capri right across its middle. Its front legs scrambled madly, digging deep into the mud, but its back half lay flaccid and still. Its pathetic bleating cries scraped across Echo's nerves like stunner fire. Netje knelt beside it, tugging at the tree with all her strength. Her arms and face were lined with scratches that bled into the rain and turned her tears pale pink, and she was screaming louder than the capri. Echo hauled her up by the arm and set her down beside the path. "Hold on to that tree and don't let go," Echo shouted above the wind and noise.

"We have to save it!"

Echo gripped a branch, dug in her heels, and pulled. The mud gave no purchase; her boots carved twin tracks as she slid forward, but the tree did not budge. She tried again, and the branch she was holding broke, sending her sprawling. Once more she tried and failed. The water was knee-deep on the path now, sucking at her legs with frightening strength. The capri flailed, its back half completely submerged, front legs churning the water to muddy froth as it strained to keep its nostrils above the flood. "We have to go," she yelled at Netje.

The girl let go of the tree and flung herself forward, not towards Echo but across the path. She grabbed the capri's head, lifting it as high as she could. White showed all around its eyes, and its muzzle frothed pink. "I won't leave it! It will drown!"

"So will we! Come on."

Echo reached, but the girl jerked away. The movement sent her off balance and she stumbled, losing her grip on the capri. Its head dropped beneath the water. "No!" Netje screamed, and then cried out again as a flailing hoof caught her across the chest, knocking her back into the trees.

Echo leapt forward. She lifted the animal's head

clear with one arm and wrapped the other around its chest, clamping it tight to her body. She pulled, and the capri screamed again, hideously, but it did not even begin to slide free. She felt the trembling all through its small desperate body. She shifted her grip on its head, feeling for the nubby horn. When she had the best purchase she was going to get, she took one deep breath and twisted with all her strength. The *snap* was audible even above the storm. With a last bleating sigh, the animal went limp against her. She let it slip under the water and reached for Netje.

The girl punched Echo in the chest with both fists. "Get away from me!"

"We must go now." Echo wrapped an arm around Netje as she had around the capri, pinning both her arms. The girl tried to knee her, and she used the opening to scoop both legs up with her other arm. After that there was nothing the child could do; she struggled another moment, then went limp except for the sobs that shook her entire body. Echo turned down the hill.

A gust greater than the others shook the forest. There was sharp *crack*, and a tree came down in a cacophony of creaks and lesser cracks, landing atop the limb that had felled the capri, completely blocking the path. No going back that way. Even carrying Netje, Echo might be able to pick her way downhill without a trail, but it would be time-consuming, and she was anxious to find a sturdy shelter out of the way of further falling trees. Echo peered ahead through the driving rain. This was about as far as she had come with Khyn, and that meant—yes. The branch she had broken on purpose on her walk with Khyn still hung in place, by some minor miracle; it swung back and forth but the wind had not ripped it free. She'd estimated the doors in the hillside to be no more than a few hundred paces ahead, and she set out that way now, following the curve of the hill and hoping her guess was good.

By the time she saw the entrance, her legs were aching with effort and her back burned out of proportion to the girl's slight weight. The weakness frightened her; even a hunter's body could be pushed past full recovery, and she had used hers ill over recent months. And she wasn't young, as hunters counted themselves, though their lives were shortened more often by violence than frailty. It shouldn't matter to her, past the basic urge for survival and the need to fulfill a mission; but as she struggled forward she yearned body-deep to live long enough to look on Lia one last time. Then she remembered that it would not be Lia she saw. The doors loomed, and for an instant it was the Church before her, and she held a different child, a boy she had nearly died to save, and she reached a shaking hand to the panel that would taste her traitor's blood and burn her for her crimes.

In the next moment her vision cleared, and she remembered where she was. The doors she stood before were metal, not the massive iron-wrapped wood that guarded the Church; and they bore some kind of design, obscured now by the sheeting rain. She pounded a fist hard against them; above the wind and thunder she couldn't tell if anyone might hear. Nothing happened. She cast around for a rock to bang and then saw what she should have from the first: the panel wired alongside the door. She pounded that too, and stood gaping as the metal slid quietly back into the rock.

She expected a cavern, some ancient fortress carved into the native rock; but instead found herself in a medium-size room, white walled and well lit, exactly like the rooms in the dispensary below. It held only a few chairs and tables, a long rack of hooks where occupants had hung their outer clothes, and two startled vektere who jumped to their feet as she stumbled through, bringing a swirl of wind-driven rain with her.

"Preservers help us! Get inside!" One of the vektere ran for the door; the wind and rain cut off abruptly. The other stood staring, hand on his baton. "What in the world were you doing out in that? You could have been— Who are you?"

Echo ignored him, laying Netje on a table and stripping off her soaked clothes. The girl had long since gone ominously quiet, and her skin was pale and chill. "Get something to dry her with." Shocked though he was, the man had the sense not to argue.

He grabbed something soft off a hook and began to chafe some warmth back into the child's body. She started to shiver, a good sign, and her skin regained some color.

"That's Netje!" the other vektere, a woman, exclaimed. "What happened?"

"She was caught in the storm. She is uninjured, only cold." The words came out shaking, and Echo realized that she was shivering too, now that the heat of exertion had passed. She wrapped her arms around herself and shifted from foot to foot, making a puddle of muddy bootprints on the floor. "Send for Khyn."

But the woman was staring at her. "You're the one they found outside."

The other vektere's head snapped up. "The stranger!" His hands forgot their task. Echo took a small step forward. The vektere stood closer together than they should. She raised her hands as if to rub her arms, a position from which she could easily defend herself, but the pair made no move against her. Instead the woman only asked, "What were you doing out there with her? What are you doing *here*?"

"I will explain, but please, see to the child first. Find Khyn."

"Thank the Preservers, she's here already. I'll get her. Hald, you stay with Netje."

Things moved quickly after that. The woman ran out, not through the big door but across the room; Echo caught a glimpse of a long hallway that must lead back into the mountain. Others entered as she left, workers and a few more vektere, crowding the ante-room and asking all their questions at the same time. She explained briefly while she helped Hald, and a minute later Khyn came running in. Echo moved out of her way, watching until she was satisfied that Netje was sufficiently revived, then dropped into a chair where she sat trying to get warm.

A rolling boom sounded outside, and the lights flickered, going out for the space of a breath. When they came back they were dimmer, and the illumina-tion unsteady. "It's surges from the storm," Khyn said. "The stewards will balance them." Her lips thinned. "Stigir's still in the link." The words made no sense, but Khyn was correct; in a minute the lights came back on full, and stayed that way even as the thunder rumbled beyond the door.

Khyn demanded to hear the story for herself while she examined Netje, who by now was sitting up, though she still seemed dazed. This time Echo pro-vided more detail. "The capri could not be saved, so—"

"She killed it!" Netje shrieked. "She killed my capri!"

"It would have drowned," Echo said.

Khyn tucked a blanket around the girl. "Netje, just go to sleep, you'll feel much better when—"

"She killed it! She broke its neck!"

The Preservers eyed Echo as if they could see her doing it. With Netje safe they were going to start thinking about what to do with her. This was the place she was not supposed to see, let alone enter, that held something so valuable that someone had built rooms deep within a mountain to protect it. It would be a waste not to learn what it was. She made a vague gesture that she hoped seemed like an apology.

"Let me see your hands," Khyn said sharply, reaching to pull them into the light. Most of the bleeding had stopped by now, but the palms were bruised and swollen, striped with shallow cuts where the branch had torn through. Khyn drew a quick breath of dismay. "Why didn't you tell me?"

Echo flexed her fingers. "It is nothing serious."

Khyn scowled at her. "You're worse than the vektere. They're always trying to prove how tough they are. Hald, bring that kit over here, would you, and some water. And see if someone can find another blanket."

Khyn's touch was light and steady, but it took a long time to dig all the splinters out. Eventually it was done, everything clean and dry, an ointment smeared on the cuts to lessen the sting and clean bandages wrapped around like gloves with the fingers cut out. "Better?" Khyn asked, but her smile seemed forced, and when Echo tried to meet her eyes, she busied herself instead with her pack.

Hald pressed a switch, and the main door slid open a crack. The wind whistled through, carrying a swirl of wet leaves. "It's raining too hard to take you down now. We'll all sleep up here tonight and sort things out in the morning."

The vektere laid down blankets and passed around food procured from somewhere within the back rooms, individual portions of something minced, then rolled thin and dried, that tasted mostly like pomme. Echo chewed a few bites and slipped the rest into a pocket against later need. She could manage easily enough until morning. Netje woke briefly to ask, "Are we camping?" which made everyone laugh, until the girl caught sight of Echo and let out a wail of dismay. "Make her go away!"

Echo rose on stiff legs. "I will sleep over there where I will not disturb you." The room was warm enough, and she had slept many times on surfaces less comfortable than the smooth floor, hard though it was. She curled up the way any predator would, back to the corner and a head pillowed on one arm. And she watched the inner door, waiting.

Khyn came over after settling the child, a blanket around her shoulders and an extra that she passed to Echo. "Netje will be fine in the morning. I wish I could say the same for the rest of us." She settled onto the floor with a sigh. In the hours since she'd left the dispensary, her anger had worn into a kind of sorrowful determination. "I dread telling Stigir about the baby."

"It was his," Echo said in a flash of clarity.

Khyn nodded miserably. "His heart will break,

but that's the whole point. We have to stop this. We have the seed, now we need to—" She broke off with a guilty glance towards the inner doors.

And all at once Echo understood exactly what Khyn wanted to do. The explanation had been in front of her the entire time. Netje looked much like Khyn, though the med said the child was not hers; and Echo had noted the resemblance among the others. And there were so few of them—not just children, but any Preservers. Generations ago the city had gone through the same bottleneck. Without sufficient variability in the breeding pairs, few off-spring survived. The Church had managed to guide the cityens through it, and out the other side. It had been close; only the wisdom of the forebears had kept humanity from falling over the cliff. Echo had been taught all this, the better to help her serve. Yet she had still managed to misunderstand, because it was not what she expected to find.

It was happening all over again here.

And now Echo knew what the Preservers meant to hide from her. "The seed for your line is stored in the Vault."

Khyn glanced around the room. Netje slept in her corner; the workers who were trapped here for the night shifted and mumbled on their blankets as they too fell into sleep. The vektere had divided themselves into shifts, a pair back at the outer door while all the others rested. No one seemed particularly interested in Khyn and Echo. Khyn lowered her voice anyway. "The team doesn't want you to know this, but I need your help. I have to make them see reason, before it's too late." She leaned so close that Echo could feel her breath as she spoke. "*All* the seed is stored in the Vault. Us, the capri, the trees—all of it. That's what the Preserve is for. And the time has come for us to use it."

One of the vektere at the door glanced over, attention drawn to their voices; Echo could not risk questioning Khyn further while he watched. Instead she let her eyes drift closed as if exhaustion overcame her. After a few hours, she awoke as planned. Everyone still slept except the two vektere on duty, and even they were dozing. She stifled a flash of disapproval; they were not hunters. She rose and padded across the room with well-trained silence. The inner door gave with only a tiny click; the vektere didn't turn. She slipped through and closed it softly.

Door after identical door lined the long hallway. They were not simple panels, but heavy hatches rimmed with some kind of rubbery material, and closed with long levers marked "Lock" and a quarter turn away, "Open" in large raised lettering. Beside each door a dial was mounted on the wall, a half circle of numbers with an arrow swung nearly all the way to the left, and each door bore a small window, fogged with interior cold. She squinted through one and saw racks upon racks of small boxes, marked with numbers and letters that looked like some kind of coordinate scheme.

Inside those boxes would be the seeds of everything that had existed before the Fall. The Church thought these treasures lost forever. What the priests could make of them . . . She thought of the laboratory in the bowels of the Church, and the pink blob of eggs beneath the magnifier lens, all that was left of a girl named Ela.

A girl Echo had murdered.

Perhaps even now the nuns bore a batch of Ela's successors. If they grew, and if Echo lived long enough to see them, she would recognize herself in all the hard young faces.

Her hand was on the lever when she noticed the red lamp above the door. Some kind of alarm, probably, and she did not want to be discovered just yet. Reluctantly she turned away.

The hall dead-ended at another door, this one closed not with a hatch but with a smaller version of the panel set into the mountainside. Now she could see the design clearly, though it made no sense: a pair of twisted ladders, joined at the ends to make a circle that split into precise halves when she approached.

She stepped through and came up short, the breath stopped in her throat.

For a long moment her mind refused to process what she saw. This room was larger than the others, and comfortably warm. The soft lighting came from tubes shielded to diffuse the glare. That only emphasized the bright patterns playing across the panels set at regular intervals in an open circle edging the room, panels like those the priests sat by in the Church sanctuary. People monitored these panels too, but Echo barely noticed them, all her attention focused on what lay at the center of the room. In the sanctuary, wires ran from the panels to the altar and the Saint's copper crown, then snaked high up the spire, spiraling the Saint's thoughts into the web that controlled power, light, the forcewall that protected the city. Here, wires connected the panels too, but not to an altar. Six couches faced each other in a circle like the petals of a flower, and in each lay a body, the cables passing from them to a column that blossomed with colored lights at the center of the circle.

Six couches. Six bodies.

Six Saints.

Even as she struggled to believe what she saw, Echo knew she had found a treasure far greater than any seed. The survival of the entire city hung on the one woman in a generation made to ascend as Saint. Without her, systems faltered: aircars crashed for lack of a beacon to guide them; the forcewall fell. Cityens died. And the Saint line had been failing; each life flickering briefer than the one before, until it seemed that the city itself would lose the battle against the dark.

Until Lia, the Saint who had been not made, but born. Echo closed her eyes against the image of the body shrouded on the altar, the crown spinning her essence away in the fine tendrils that sustained everything but her own life.

Six Saints, to preserve this one small outpost.

Echo opened her eyes again to find the men and women at the panels staring back at her, as amazed as she was. Someone, quicker than the rest, slammed a button and a whooping started in the hall.

And then Echo felt her knees give way as one of the Saints sat up, removing his glittering crown.

CHAPTER 5

Vektere poured into the room, grabbing her arms and wrestling her to her knees, but she didn't even try to resist. "The Vault," Stigir murmured, lifting the crown from his head like a cityen taking off a hat. His gaze, oddly distant, passed over Echo without recognition, as if he were seeing something else entirely. "There's been an alarm. Is everything—" He broke off with a wince, hand to his head.

One of the people monitoring the panels—Echo couldn't think of them as priests, not in this room so far removed from the Church—spun on her stool. "Careful, Stigir, that wasn't an orderly extraction!"

Khyn pushed into the room past the vektere holding Echo. "Run the sequence again, Smilla, manual extraction. Quickly Stigir, before you hurt yourself."

Stigir nodded vaguely and let her settle the crown

on his head again. The moment it was in place his eyes went blank, his features slack, his mind suddenly absent as if it had never inhabited the flesh. Smilla returned to her station, fingers dancing over small buttons inlaid on the surface beneath her screen, the panel lights reflected in miniature in her dark eyes. "Ready," she told her companions. "Start the procedure again at step seven." They worked in silent concentration for a moment until the woman was satisfied with what she saw. Then she hit a last key, and the complex pattern on her screen contracted to a single pulsing dot.

Stigir opened his eyes slowly. Khyn removed the crown and helped him sit, a hand supporting him until he returned from wherever he'd gone. "Ah, that's better. Thanks." He swung his feet to the floor, leaving the crown beside him on the couch as if it were nothing.

"You're not a Saint," Echo said stupidly. Her mind kept seeing the sanctuary, its dim lights and ancient wired panels and the dark altar where the woman married to the City must live out whatever strange existence she led, sacrificed to save them all. Echo could not grasp this: a whole group of Saints lying in comfortable chairs, a man joining and leaving that irreversible union like a cityen going in and out of his habitation. It was not possible. It had never been possible in the history of the Church.

Stigir murmured, "We still don't know what you

mean by that. There are quite a few things about you we don't understand." Then he snapped fully awake. "What is she doing here?"

The lights dimmed fractionally. The woman at the panel adjusted a dial, bringing them back to full strength, and said, "Would you mind taking this conversation outside? You're distracting the stewards."

"Come," Stigir said, pushing himself to wobbly feet. Khyn held his arm until he caught his balance. The ones pinning Echo's arms dragged her up and didn't let go.

She let them lead her out while her thoughts rushed ahead. The Church had always taught—had always believed—that only a specially bred mind could take on the burden of Sainthood. Even Lia, born a cityen, carried the denas that made it possible for her to wear the Saint's crown. Despite her fresh strength, the burden would wear her away, too, one day. But if there were a way to spread that burden, to ensure that if one Saint failed others could take up the load . . . The Patri had to know.

And if a Saint could remove her crown . . .

Echo's concentration focused to a single point. She had to bring this information to the Patri. Nothing else mattered now.

The front room buzzed with activity. Echo smelled rain and wet dirt; a new group of vektere, Birn and the young woman Taavi among them, rushed in through the open door. Birn ran to Stigir as

Khyn helped him to a chair. "Yilva had just sent us to check on the Vault when we heard the alarm. What happened? Are you all right?"

"Give him a minute," Khyn said. "He just came out of the link." She knelt by Stigir, laying fingertips on his wrist. "These short cycles aren't good for you. Your nervous system needs time to make the adjustment in both directions, before it gets so tangled up it can't make them at all."

Stigir rubbed his temple with his free hand. The crown had left marks, red indentations encircling his forehead. "It just takes a few minutes to get used to being me again. I wanted to update the stewards on everything that's happened since we found—what were you doing in the Vault?"

Echo jerked her attention back from the room at the end of the hall. From what she had seen there. Every instinct screamed to return to the city *now*. To do that, she had to gain the Preservers' trust. Or failing that . . . "I had to relieve myself," she said.

Birn jabbed an angry finger at her. "She's seen what's inside."

"I saw nothing but boxes kept in cold," Echo said, flicking a warning glance at Khyn.

"Then why did you break in here? I told you to stay in the dispensary."

"So what if she did see? She isn't our enemy, Birn." Khyn gestured at the child collapsed on a pile of blankets in the corner. Even the alarm hadn't awakened her from her exhausted sleep. "She risked her life to save Netje. The little fool ran into the storm trying to catch a capri that got loose. If Echo hadn't gone after her, I don't know what would have—" Her voice caught. She looked at Echo, brow creasing as she thought of something for the first time. "How did you know?"

At that, the vektere murmured among themselves. Soon it would occur to them to wonder how she'd gotten through the forceshield, too. Now more than ever it was important not to frighten them. She must persuade them that the Church would be an ally, not a threat.

"The wind carried her voice."

Birn's face darkened with suspicion. "No one else heard anything. How did you—"

"This all can wait," Khyn said. "There's something more important. Stigir, I'm so sorry to have to tell you this. While you were in the link, Marget . . . the baby came."

A hushed silence fell in the anteroom.

"That can't be," Stigir said, forehead furrowing. "It isn't her time, she's carrying until the equinox at least."

"Marget is all right, but the baby . . . There was nothing I could do." Khyn clasped his limp hand in both of hers. "I'm so sorry."

He stared at her, uncomprehending. Then his face changed, the way a man's did when he realized the wound he had sustained was mortal. He made no sound, but he dropped his face into his hands, shoulders shaking.

Khyn began to weep too. "We can't let this keep happening. We know how to fix it. We just need to make up our minds. Please, Stigir."

Birn laid a helpless hand on Stigir's shoulder. "How can you trouble him with this now?" Khyn began to protest, and he added, "You're not the only one who cares. Leave him alone."

Stigir raised his tear-streaked face. His voice was heavy, but he was composing himself already, a steadiness that reminded Echo of the Patri, for all Stigir claimed no such title. "It's all right, Birn. She has a right to ask." His shoulders rose and fell. "Tomorrow. The team will decide tomorrow."

It was Khyn's victory, but Echo's heart pounded. She knew that tomorrow might bring her one chance to persuade the Preservers to bring their tech to the city.

CHAPTER 6

"Will the team listen?" Echo asked. No one had slept any more last night; they had returned down the mountain at first light. Khyn was pacing the dispensary with the restless energy of exhaustion.

"Stigir's always fair. Too fair, sometimes. If he thinks he might want something for his own benefit, he'll go against it just in case."

"Perhaps it would help if I speak of the city's children." Echo ignored a twist of guilt. She was not ready to reveal her plan, but she needed Khyn to get her in position to implement it.

Khyn scowled out the window. "It's Birn I'm worried about. Even if he didn't have any other reason, he'd be against opening the Vault just because I'm for it."

Echo had enough experience with cityens to guess why. "You and he were formerly paired?"

Khyn gave a startled laugh. "Me and Birn? Pre-servers, no. Stigir and I . . . Birn was always jealous. It was a long time ago, but he never forgave me, even though it was already over between them. Not that it mattered in the long run. Stigir's true love is the Pre-serve. That's more important to him than any of us."

The words burrowed into the hollow place behind Echo's breastbone. "But he does not have to choose. He is able to come and go from the link at will."

"Of course. The stewards take turns in the link, otherwise they get too worn out. It's a big burden." She gave Echo a puzzled look. "Isn't that what your Saints do?"

Echo thought of the wizened body of the old Saint, dying. The crown settling over Lia's head, and the moment of astonishment in her eyes, before they closed forever. "Something like it." A tiny spark of a thing she did not want to name for fear of extinguish-ing it tried to catch in her heart. "What is the longest a steward can stay in the link before the damage is permanent?"

Khyn shrugged. "I wouldn't want to find out. A few weeks is hard enough on them. Even somebody really talented, like Stigir."

"Is that how the stewards are chosen? By talent?"

"How else? It's like the vektere, or Netje with the capri. I tried the link once, but I didn't like it. Turns out I'm much better at taking care of the stewards than joining the link myself."

Surprise jolted through Echo. Before she could stop herself, she asked, "What was it like?"

"There's a sort of shock when the interface connects." Khyn grimaced. "The room goes away, and then it's like a long, long fall— What's wrong?"

The shutters were open. A few raindrops still streaked the window. Echo focused on one's slow slide down until she was sure her expression was under control. "I did not realize one could simply . . . try on the link, that's all."

"It mostly takes concentration," Khyn said. "You would probably be good at it."

Echo saw in her mind the altar at the center of the sanctuary, and the crown that would destroy any who donned it except the true Saint. "I doubt it," she said.

Soon after, Taavi came to the dispensary. "Are you ready, Khyn? The rest of the team is gathering."

"It's about time. Come on, Echo."

Taavi shifted from one foot to the other. "Stigir didn't say about Echo."

"*I* say." And when Taavi still hesitated, Khyn added, "If it's Birn you're worried about, remember, I have equal right when it comes to the team."

The young vektere gave an uncomfortable nod.

As they walked, Taavi kept looking sidelong at Echo, her expression not hostile but somehow troubled. She seemed about to speak once or twice but changed her mind, until finally, arriving at some decision, she slowed, glancing up the mountain. "All the vektere have heard how you saved Netje."

"I am glad I was able."

Taavi stared down at the muddy toes of her boots. In a low voice she said, "I was the one stationed closest to the capri enclosure, and I heard nothing. It would have been my fault."

From another hunter that would have been a fair assessment. But this girl had none of a hunter's advantages. Yet her failure would weigh on her until she questioned every decision, every instinct.

Echo knew that burden all too well. She said, "It is also a fault to allow one error to assume undue significance. The next time you will know to position yourself better."

After a moment, Taavi's face cleared. She said nothing, but when she resumed her pace, her step seem lighter.

"That was kind," Khyn murmured, looking after the vektere.

Echo couldn't tell if the note in her voice was surprise.

Word must have traveled ahead that Echo was coming with Khyn. A small phalanx of vektere surrounded them at the door of the team building. For the first time, some of them were armed with more than batons: hands hovered close to slim black boxes on their belts, stunners or something worse. Echo had revealed too much in rescuing Netje when they could not; or perhaps it was only because she had been inside the Vault. Khyn frowned, but said nothing.

The vektere nearest gestured towards the door. Echo paused. It might be a trap. Likely she could wrest the guard's weapon from him, and if she used him as a shield, she could probably break through their formation. Then it would only be matter of out-racing them in the long dash to the aircar yard.

If the black weapons could not strike from a distance.

And if escaping alone did not mean utter failure.

She let out a long breath and followed Khyn inside.

Raised voices carried through the closed team-room door. Birn, close to shouting, and Yilva, lower but no less urgent. The grim-faced vektere exchanged glances. "Birn got here first," Khyn said, her expression darkening. "I'll have to make them see reason."

The faces around the table gave Echo little hope of that. More than a few looked as grim as the vektere. Birn shot a glare at Echo, but Stigir, lips pressed thin, shook his head. "She has seen the Vault. If she hasn't guessed already, she will soon." Khyn stared at the floor, guilt plain on her face; Echo wondered if Stigir was really deceived or just protecting her. The Prime looked one by one at his team. "We face a critical decision. Khyn?"

"It's what I've been telling the team all along.

You've seen the numbers, but you don't realize what they mean, because it's happening so slowly."

"We've heard it from you before," Birn said. "Remember the cold winter a few years ago, when the bearing women all got sick? You said the same thing, but the next spring there were a dozen babies. It was all fine."

"That was as many in one year as even I remember," Yilva added. "We're not like the capri. It's always been rare for us to bear."

"That's the problem. In Echo's city many women can bear. Isn't that right?" Echo nodded, saying nothing. Better to let them get as far as they would go on their own. Then she could give the last push.

"The Preserve full of children . . ." Longing filled Stigir's soft voice.

"It won't be," Khyn said. "We won't have any children at all if we don't do something soon. I've been doing the calculations over and over, trying to find another explanation, but there isn't one. Our numbers are falling, far past normal fluctuations." She turned an aching look on Stigir. "Surely you of all of us understand."

His eyes were shadowed. "We must not use the seed for our own benefit."

"The whole purpose of the Vault was to keep the seed for when it was needed. I'm telling you, we need it now. Four hundred years is too long; Netje's generation will be near the last if we don't refresh the line.

I know we need to guard the seed until the time is right, but if we aren't willing to use it to save the Preserve, then when will we be?"

The anguished question hung in the air. Then everyone started talking at once, spitting out numbers, reinterpreting the data; some of the team seemed to support Khyn, others to think her concerns were premature. Echo only listened, waiting. When the arguments wore down and Stigir leaned forward to speak, she knew it was nearly time.

Stigir steepled his fingers, and his voice took on the ritual tone of a man repeating a story he had heard many times before. "The Vault exists to preserve the future. *We* exist to preserve the future. Four hundred years ago, when the catastrophe loomed over the world, the first Preservers knew what would happen. They sacrificed everything, devoting their lives to protect this great treasure. They withdrew from the world, and," he added with a touch of bitterness, "the world forgot about them. But they knew their duty, as every generation down to us has known. We do not merely save ourselves. One day, when the world is ready to be reborn, we will open the Vault. Until that day we will preserve."

"That day has come." Echo rose, ignoring the instant suspicion of the vektere around her. Everything depended on this. She spread her feet, drew herself taller. Let them see, for the first time, the sinewy hunter strength against which they could not hope to measure. The calm hunter arrogance that dismissed any attempt to try. The vektere understood first: she smelled the hormones surging into their blood as they recognized the predator they faced. She met their eyes, each one by one, so they would be sure. The black weapons came out, plain answer to the danger. The team saw too, dismay dawning. Fear.

Even Khyn looked stunned.

Echo let the moment stretch out. Then she smiled and turned her hands palm up, the threat running out of her like sand through her fingers. "If I wished you harm, I could have done it by now. I do not. I was sent to seek help, and to offer it."

"We have seen how you help." That was Yilva. "There's a coldness in you that even the vektere don't want. We have our own ways."

"And they have served you well. But the time comes for change. Khyn knows it. I believe the rest of you do as well. When your women bear no more young, when you have no vektere or stewards to replace the ones you lose—then it will be too late. Khyn offers you one alternative. I give you another." Khyn made a tiny sound of betrayal; Echo ignored it. "Come with me to the city. We once faced the same challenge as you. Though we have no vault, no seed such as you preserve, we overcame. Now let us help you. You have very little to lose."

The Preservers' faces fixed on her with shock, and no little consternation. The team all began speaking at once, a babble of conflicting voices, some touched with excitement, others, like Birn's and Yilva's, dark with warning. Echo watched with intense concentration, noting especially those whose gazes drifted far away, seeing possibilities they never had before. Khyn, Taavi, a few others. A flicker of that hope even passed across Stigir's face. She felt its tentative stir inside her as well. If Preservers came to the city, if the priests in the sanctuary obtained the interface technology . . .

Birn's hand slammed the table, and everyone jumped. "It's a trick. She wants us to give up the Vault."

"No. I do not." What Echo wanted was infinitely more important.

The argument started again, but Stigir motioned them all to silence. "We must not act in haste with respect to the seed, not when the stakes are so high. And as for the other, there is a great deal to think about. Let us take it under consideration, separately and together, until we are certain, however long it takes. That is the wisest course."

Khyn threw up her hands in exasperation. "Is that all you have to say? You won't open the Vault, you won't look outside, you're afraid to do anything but—"

Stigir rose, his expression closing. "Our ways have served us for four hundred years, while the rest of the world drove itself to ruin. Where others chose division, violence"—his glance cut at Echo—"the Preserve kept itself apart. We stand outside the world. We will rejoin it when it is ready. Not before."

"How," Echo asked softly, "will you know when that is, if you refuse to look?"

Hope stirred again in Stigir's eyes. Echo held her breath. *It's time for everything to change.* Lia's words, from long ago. For a moment Stigir seemed to see that future—that vision Lia had died for—then his gaze fell again on the hunter standing before him.

"My decision is made," he said.

CHAPTER 7

"I thought I could make him understand." Khyn stood with her head bowed, hands clasping her elbows. The vektere had brought them back to the dispensary and left again, but Echo heard the pacing in the hall. "Maybe it was too soon after the baby; he just isn't thinking straight yet . . ." Khyn's voice trailed off. When she raised her eyes, her face was set in determination. "The only thing that matters now is finding a way to continue the line. Whatever I have to do. What about you? Now that you've seen what fools we are, you probably can't wait to get out of here."

New footsteps marched toward the dispensary, too far off for Khyn to hear, but Echo knew what they meant.

"I'm just sorry you came all this way for nothing. I wish—"

The door clanged open. "Come with us," Jole ordered without preamble. He had three men with him, and Saints knew how many out in the corridor. They all had batons in their hands, and the small black boxes on their belts; whatever they were, Echo had no doubt that they were fully charged. She stayed where she was, sitting on the bed, arms wrapping her knees.

"Now wait one minute," Khyn began.

"Sorry, Khyn. Birn's orders." Echo wondered how much Stigir knew about those orders.

"Then I'm coming too."

Jole shook his head. "You stay here."

Khyn's expression went still. "What's going on, Jole?"

"I wouldn't argue about it. Birn's angry enough with you as it is." He turned to Echo, expression grim. "Let's go."

Hunters would kill her outright. The vektere would squirm at that, but a simple return to where they'd found her would be enough. Neither served Echo's needs. Still hugging her knees, she licked her lips. "Where are you taking me?" She let her voice shake shamefully.

Jole loomed above her. "You'll find out soon enough. Don't make it any worse."

She pushed herself off the bed with difficulty, then gasped as her knees gave out, sending her stumbling towards him. Instinctively he reached to catch her.

Letting her weight continue to drop, she grabbed him with one hand on his wrist and the other gripping his arm just above the elbow. As she sank, she slipped a foot behind him, then straightening with all the strength in her legs and hips, she levered him right over her shoulder. As he cartwheeled past, she stripped the baton from his flailing hand. He landed on his back with an agonized *whoosh* and lay still.

The other three men, briefly frozen in shock, sprang back to life, fumbling for the black weapons. One brought his up, touching a button; a red light flashed and she threw herself aside. Smoke stung her nostrils; glancing back, she saw where the light had charred a hole in the wooden cabinet. She whipped Jole's baton through a long arc; the men jumped back to avoid its sting. Now they were on either side of her, unable to fire for fear of hitting each other. Khyn, both hands over her mouth, was backed against one wall. "Stay there," Echo snapped, all the attention she could spare.

The man on Echo's left kept edging around, trying to get behind her, while his friends kept her busy with their batons. She stepped forward, and the man on the left, suddenly finding himself in position to grab her from behind, made his move. As he reached she ducked, curling tight on bent legs, then shot a booted foot backwards into his knee. There was a crunching sound and he went down, screaming. His weapon bounced off into a corner.

The two remaining vektere exchanged glances. Now they did what they should have from the beginning, circling slowly, trying to get a clear line of fire. She feinted forward, stabbing with the baton like a knife, but they were smart enough not to take that bait. Now they were nearly on either side of her. She pushed to the right, trying to keep between them and Khyn, before one of them got the clever idea of using the physic as a shield. "You can't get us both," the taller one snarled.

The man with the knee had gone from screaming to a half-conscious whine that sounded like a failing aircar engine. Jole still hadn't moved, but his wheezing breath was steadying. She had to finish this soon. She stopped still, raising her hands. "Maybe you're right. I give up."

And in the moment they froze, perplexed, she flung the baton straight into the face of the man on her right. The charged end struck with a loud pop, and he went down in a heap. Echo was already diving at his partner. She knifed her left hand at his wrist in a sweeping strike that knocked the black weapon from his grip. He was very quick, spinning away before she could hit him again, and nearly catching her with the baton in his other hand as she jerked back out of reach. Now he had the initiative; he lunged forward, taking advantage of his long legs to thrust himself inside her circle of defense.

She arched away and the baton ripped through her

shirt, barely missing her chest. With no flesh to carry the current, the device did not discharge; the smell of hot metal singed her nostrils. The tip curved back at her as the vektere tried to catch her with a backhand move. She blocked, barely, and followed through with a stiff hand thrust at his eyes. As he ducked back, she hooked a foot behind his front heel, sweeping inward with a sharp movement and catching his leg as her foot kicked it up into reach. She hopped towards him, preparing to yank the leg up and flip him onto his back—and her weak ankle gave with a stab of white hot pain.

She heard herself cry out as she fell. All she could do was throw her body into his knees as she went down. Both of them hit the floor. He scythed the baton towards her; still rolling, she caught his wrist and jerked hard as she drove her shoulder into his. She felt the joint give with a pop, snatched the baton from his loosened grip, and slammed it back around and into his chest. His whole body went rigid as the shock froze his muscles, then he collapsed in a sprawl across the floor.

Echo panted on hands and knees while her mind tried to force her body to move. The whole fight had taken perhaps three minutes. Anyone nearby would have heard the noise. There must not be any vektere left in the hall—fools—or the alarm would have been raised by now.

A hand touched her shoulder. She struck backwards with an elbow, barely checking the blow as she recognized the white, tear-streaked face behind her. "Saints! I told you to stay back!"

"Are you hurt?" Khyn tried to help her up. Echo shook her off, climbing to her feet and testing the ankle gingerly. It would hold her weight, but she wouldn't be outrunning anyone. She limped over to the door.

"Let's go," she told Khyn, in the exact tone Jole had used. Khyn heard it; doubt crept into her eyes. Echo forced an apologetic smile, gesturing at the fallen vektere. Then, because she wasn't sure if any of them could hear, she added, "What's the shortest way over the mountain?"

"South," Khyn said. "But—"

"Come with me."

The corridor was empty. If they were lucky, they could slip out of the compound without being seen. The twilight shadows would help. Luckier still, and the vektere they'd left behind would send the others hunting south after phantom prey.

Echo didn't believe in luck.

Khyn wore a brittle smile. It was mostly shock, Echo knew. She hoped it didn't wear off too soon. "Where are we going?" Khyn whispered. Echo slipped the baton up her sleeve without answering.

The few people out in the compound wouldn't have found it unusual for a pair of Preservers to leave the dispensary building and saunter casually in the general direction of the glasshouse. If they'd been particularly observant, they might have noted that the saunter was a little bit *too* casual, and one of the pair in particular kept glancing over her shoulder, as if she expected a friend to join them any time. "Stop that," Echo ordered.

"I can't help it. They'll be out after us any minute."

"We'll be gone."

"Where? Surely not into the forest. The vektere would find us sooner or later—if not them, the predators. But if we try to cross the fields into the desert, they'll be able to track us from an aircar . . ."

"Shh." The shock was indeed wearing off. The questions were admirably logical for someone with no experience—and no clear idea of Echo's capabilities. Khyn would be starting to wonder whether fleeing from the Preserve was her best choice. As angry as the others would be, she'd still have hope of persuading them eventually. A year, even two—if the women failed to bear, the questions would bubble up again. The stranger who'd roiled the Preserve's tranquility would be long gone; people would remember how sensible Khyn had always been. Stigir would be fair, Birn and Yilva would listen to him . . . It all made perfect sense. Echo hoped Khyn didn't think of it. Her ankle throbbed, and it would be a long way to carry an unconscious body.

They were coming up on the gap between the walkway and the team building. The glasshouse glowed like a jewel at the end of the path. Shadowy figures moved inside. The wiry notes of a stringbox drifted into the night with a pleasant melancholy. The Preservers were so like cityens: even facing a threat to their very existence, they would ignore it as best they could to take pleasure in what they had.

If they didn't— Echo's thoughts were interrupted by footsteps behind them on the path. Walking, not running; no one shouting for help. Khyn didn't hear yet. If they could make it to the path into the trees before their follower recognized them— "Khyn!" Netje exclaimed.

Saints. *Send her away*, Echo silently urged Khyn. She would not allow the girl to cause their capture.

"Netje! Preservers' sakes, child, what are you doing out at this hour?"

"Why didn't you come to the capri pen today? We were supposed to check—" She broke off at the sight of Echo. "What's *she* doing here? I thought Birn was mad at her." The crossed arms and stony glare made it clear that Birn wasn't alone in his feeling.

"That's silly, Netje. Why would Birn be mad at Echo?"

"I don't know. I kept asking but no one would tell me anything, not even why you didn't come to the pen. But then I heard some vektere talking." She broke into a proud smile. Then her expression grew cloudy again. "I was real quiet, and they kind of forgot I was there. They said he doesn't like it that some people want to go outside. I don't understand why that's so bad. *You* always tell *me* to go outside." She paused. "They said you and Stigir are having a fight."

"We must hurry," Echo murmured. Every nerve thrummed. Any minute, someone would come down the path.

Khyn gave Netje a tremulous smile. "Don't worry about what the vektere say, sweetheart. Now, listen. I'm sorry I forgot about the capri. We'll go tomorrow, as soon as things settle down a bit. Okay?"

Netje's face puckered in preparation for further argument. Time to put a stop to this. Echo stepped forward. Netje shrank back, a young animal's instinctive recognition of a predator. Her shoulders lifted, prelude to a scream.

Khyn caught Netje in a tight hug. The air went out of the girl in a muffled *oof.* "Good girl. Taavi's probably on patrol near the dispensary. If you go straight there, you can take her to check the capri now, before it gets too dark." She squeezed once more, then released her. "Go on."

Finally the girl nodded. Fists jammed in her pockets, she shambled back the way she had come, glancing at them once or twice over her shoulder.

Stupid, stupid to let her go.

Echo stood frozen until Netje disappeared around the curve in the path.

Then she grabbed Khyn's arm and started to run. The girl might not meet anyone on her way to the dispensary. The Preservers in the glasshouse might not look out. It couldn't be far now, three or four minutes if Khyn could keep up the pace . . . "How far can your aircars go?"

"Aircars?" Khyn gasped. "So that's—"

"*How far?*"

"I don't know! The vektere fly them. I've never been past the edge of the Preserve."

"Can they cross the rift?"

Khyn stumbled, tiring already. "The rift! Preservers keep us! How far away is your city?"

That was not the immediate problem. Echo pulled Khyn along. The clearing was just ahead, a flat, open space with a small structure at one end and light posts set around the perimeter. By now it was nearly full dark. Only a few of the lamps were on, creating irregular pools of light, but it was more than enough for a hunter to see by.

There were three aircars, and no visible guards. Of course not. The Preservers thought their enemies were all natural: weather, predators, the dissolution of the line. None of those would be huddled in the shadows, furiously planning an escape. Still, there should be at least a watchman, proof against mischance or a vektere who'd had too much ferm.

On a night where everything had fallen her way, the absence of such a precaution seemed one stroke too lucky.

If it was a trap—well, sometimes traps sprung

back at those who set them. She dismissed the concern she could do nothing about and studied the aircars. They were like and unlike the ones she knew from the Church, the same stub-winged, triangular shape; but these were bigger, boxy; designed originally perhaps for cargo carriage rather than long distance patrols. Still, at least one of them had had the range to find her in the desert. She looked for signs of dust and sand, but the storm had washed them clean. Baked-on mud around the landing struts showed her which one had flown most recently; she hoped that meant the vektere trusted its reliability.

She hoped the stewards could not bring an aircar down with a thought.

The hatch was open. Echo pushed Khyn ahead of her up the ladder and said, "Stay here."

"Where are you going?" Khyn's voice slid up towards panic, as if she feared the aircar might take off on its own.

"I'll be back in a minute." She ran to the other two aircars. There wasn't time to be thorough, but she could buy them an hour, maybe more, depending on the vektere's skill with repairs.

She had just jumped down from the third aircar's hatch when the voice behind her said, "Stop there, Echo. Now raise your hands and turn slowly. No, don't come any closer."

Taavi had been better trained than she gave herself credit for. The young vektere stood at the proper distance, black weapon ready but not within easy reach of her quarry. All she needed to do was shout. Or maybe the vektere in the dispensary had been found by now, alarm already raised. But if not, then Taavi wouldn't know that Khyn was already inside the aircar. Echo glanced around the perimeter for others, saw no one.

She hadn't seen Taavi either.

It didn't matter now. Taavi was the immediate threat; she had to be neutralized. Echo inhaled, sending a wave of strength to muscles still aching from their previous effort. It would be a long step on the bad ankle. Taavi took in her torn clothes, the bruises. Her mouth crooked. "I didn't like the orders Birn gave the vektere," she said. Then she lowered the weapon and turned her head away.

Echo's elbow caught her behind the ear with precisely judged force. Echo made no move to catch her as her body crumpled to the ground. The scrapes would only make Taavi's story more believable, if the vektere thought to check. She felt a pang of guilt. When Taavi woke and learned that Echo had taken Khyn . . .

A few seconds later Echo sat at the aircar's controls. "Hurry," Khyn urged, unaware of what had passed outside. Echo ignored her, studying the dials and switches for a few precious seconds. There, lift and direction, and there the distance meter, all familiar enough. That button would be power—

Saints. Maybe they were really going to make it.

She punched the button. Relief surged through her with the vibration of the engines, quickly modulating to a victorious hum. The aircar lifted, gaining forward speed. The moon rising behind the mountain cast long shadows across the fields, dark arrows pointing east. Somewhere that way lay her city, her Church. And her Saint, waiting, sleeping in her crown on the altar.

And beside Echo, face pale in the control panels' light, sat a woman who knew how to help stewards out of the link.

CHAPTER 8

The aircar whined through the darkening sky. Echo pointed the nose north, though her whole being strained to fly east, towards the city. She didn't know what tracking mechanisms the Preservers might have. The fighting hormones still coursed through her blood, heightening her senses uselessly. The pilot's compartment offered only a forward view. Anything could be looming behind, ready to blast them into a thousand bloody bits. She stabbed at the panel that should indicate objects around her; the round screen lit up with a sweep arm rotating in a slow circle, an even green glow brightening and fading behind it as it turned through the quadrants. No tell-tale dots flashed on the dial; she hoped that meant no pursuit. Even so she pushed the engines to their screaming limit with her heart pounding and the seat pressing hard into her back. She forced herself to count slow breaths, one after another after another.

When she got to a hundred, she eased off the power; the engines quieted to a pulsing hum. Then she tested the controls, going through them systematically until she had an adequate understanding of the aircar's function. It was a cargo vessel, she thought, built for long distances and high reliability; it had no weapons or defense capability that she could ascertain. The Church's aircars had been designed for the bitter war that preceded the Fall. Those few that remained, these hundreds of annuals later, no longer had functional weapons, but the predatory lines still showed.

She ran through a series of exercises to dissipate the fighting hormones, saving vital energy for a time it would be needed. Gradually her pulse and breathing returned to normal. She became aware of a small sound inside the aircar, not mechanical: Khyn weeping softly, her face turned away.

"Are you injured?" Echo's eyes swept over her; she saw no blood or obvious deformity.

"N-no."

"There is no sign of pursuit. For the time being, at least, we are safe." That was not precisely true: the Preservers could be anywhere, and there was no way to know how long the aircar's power would last; but there was no point worrying Khyn about conditions that could not be changed.

"That's good." Khyn's voice trembled, more than the engines' vibrations accounted for. She wiped her nose with the back of her hand. "Sorry to act like a silly child. I've never fled for my life before, that's all."

The children Echo knew didn't weep. And the Preservers had not directly threatened Khyn, though perhaps, having defied Stigir, she found it easier to imagine they had. Nonetheless Echo said, "It is a natural reaction to the stress."

"You're the one who did the fighting, but I don't see you falling apart." Then her voice changed, as she remembered: "The vektere—you were limping, I saw. I'll check whether there's a medkit somewhere on board."

"That isn't necessary. It is an old injury." She glanced at the physic. "Do you know how to pilot this aircar?"

"Useless on both counts," Khyn said, attempting a small laugh that mostly failed.

Echo concealed her disappointment. A second pilot would let them stay airborne that much longer. But she only said, "You performed adequately when it was required."

There was a small silence. "Thank you."

"Rest. I will wake you when I need assistance."

"I doubt I could sleep that long." Then Khyn did laugh, tremulous but warm. "If I had to run for my life, I'm glad I picked you to do it with, Echo."

Echo said nothing. After a little while Khyn's

breathing settled and her face slackened. Echo concentrated on the controls, glancing at Khyn from time to time.

Only after she was certain Khyn was well and truly asleep did she change course towards the city.

Hours later the pull of fatigue became inescapable. She could go a long time without sleep, but it was folly to fly at night over unfamiliar territory with her vision limited and reflexes slowing. The digits on a display blurred. She rubbed her eyes, trying to clear them—then realized that it was not her sight but the numbers spinning, too fast to follow. The aircar was suddenly at three times the altitude, too high, much too high—she shoved the yoke forward to drive the craft down, then leveled at what should be a safer height. She read the dial again, scanning for the ground below, not understanding what the instruments told her, and then her heart leapt against her chest as a solid rock face loomed straight ahead. She jerked back on the controls, yanking the nose into a steep climb, and the straining aircar skimmed barely over the edge. Hands shaking, Echo let the craft settle beside a jumble of rock and exhaled a long breath. They had just crossed the enormous rift—and she had nearly flown them into the far wall.

The turbulence had jerked Khyn dazed from sleep. "What's wrong? Have we run out of power?"

"Not if I read the gauges correctly. I must sleep for a few hours."

Khyn scanned the dark sky anxiously through her window. "Any sign of them?"

"No. The rocks will shield us from all but direct view. Keep watch through that window. Wake me if you see anything. Anything at all."

She was hunting a child again up a cliffside trail in the dark rain. She called over and over, but the child, fearing a predator pursued, kept running just ahead. Echo heard her gasping for air, then a sharper cry, cut off all at once. She ran harder, fighting against the flood. The child would be swept away, over the edge.

Struggling over the last rise, she caught sight of a figure writhing beneath a fallen tree. No, not a tree: a flash of lightning lit not branches, but a pyramid of bones. Where was the child? There was no sound now but the rushing of the water and an animal's desperate bleating, that even as she pushed forward turned into a bubbling scream as the water rose over the velvet nostrils.

She tore at the bones. They knew her too well; each move she made only locked them into a tighter trap. And now she knew them too: the bones of her dead. Ela. Tana. Another girl she had hunted once, and dragged back to be sacrificed on the Church's altar. The trapped animal, pinned through and through, kept screaming. She couldn't bear it. She took its face between her hands and snapped its neck. In the instant that it died the lightning flashed again, actinic white, and the face she held was not the animal's but Lia's, Lia's neck that she had snapped, and the rising flood was not water, but something thick, hot and sticky as it filled her mouth, her eyes—

She jerked awake with a sound like the animal had made. Rolling onto an elbow, she wiped her face. Her hand came away wet. Sweat, she told herself. Sweat. Not blood. She hadn't killed anyone.

Not tonight.

Khyn, head pillowed on the passenger seat, was watching her with eyes that reflected moonlight. "Maybe you'll find your Lia again one day."

But even in her dreams, Lia was gone.

Two days later the aircar limped perilously a bare hundred meters above the desert sand. The sun should lend it power, but there was something wrong with the panels, or perhaps it was just her ignorance of the systems. Echo nursed it along as best she could, alternating engines and cutting power until it barely maintained navigable speed. Once she misjudged; the craft stalled, falling like a stone until she slammed the engines back on full and pulled them up with crash alarms blaring. Khyn didn't made a sound, but the padding on her armrests still showed the marks where she had gripped it. From then on she mostly stared out the window, eyes fixed to the horizon, never looking down.

Now Echo flew as close to the ground as she dared. That it comforted Khyn was foolish, she knew; the fall would kill them just the same; but the engines strained less, and they needed all the distance they could get. She kept one eye on the desert floor all the time, the other fixed on the dial at the left edge of the instrument panel. She did not understand every readout, but that one she was certain would show the homing beacon, the signal the Saint sent out from the mast atop the cathedral spire. Though hunters used it as a guide in the desert, it wasn't meant for them. Instead, it was the Church's signal to the world, the city's plea to any who might have survived the Fall. Come to us, it said. Join us in the fight to survive. In four hundred annuals, no one had ever answered.

Until now.

The white line dragging itself across the black dial stayed stubbornly flat. They were traveling in the right general direction, the sun showed that; but it was hard to estimate the distances. Even at its slowest, the aircar far outpaced the progress Echo had made on foot. In the vastness of the desert, it would be easy to miss the city altogether. When she had left, returning had been far from the forefront of her thoughts.

The white line glowed and died, glowed and died. The engines coughed along, every catch making Echo's gut clench in fear of their last breath. If the craft did not intersect the beacon soon, it would be too late. She tapped the dial, as if that would make a difference. The line winked lazily, mocking her. Frustration blurred her vision. She scrubbed at her eyes, creating sparks behind the closed lids.

That was what she thought the first blip was, a spark. She didn't even bother to hope. Then she saw it again, and a third time, the line peaking and falling each time it swept across over the left side of the dial. It pulsed like a heart, stronger and stronger with every beat. *Lia*, she thought, and pressed her palm to the dial. She felt nothing but cold glass.

Her other hand reached to punch the engines into a last dash straight for the city. Then she made herself see sense. It was one thing to bring back a single Preserver, with her knowledge of the link technology and the secrets of the Vault. It would be something else entirely to lead a pursuing force straight to the Church.

Lifting her eyes from the dial, Echo fixed the line in her mind: the flattened boulder not far ahead, a skeletal thornbush, the distant weathered outcropping. Then, too gradually for Khyn to notice, she swept the aircar in a wide half turn, changing their heading away from the city. To make certain, she flew even lower, letting the engine exhaust mark the desert in a trail a clever pursuer would find.

After a little while Khyn stirred in her seat. "We've changed direction. Have you seen something?"

That was far enough.

Echo dropped the aircar to the sand, but she didn't kill the engines. She hit the button to pop the hatch. "Get out," she ordered Khyn.

"What?"

"Wait for me here. I won't be long."

"Where are you going?"

"Just do as I tell you. Stand over by those rocks."

Biting her lip, Khyn clambered down the ladder. On the last rung she stopped, clinging to the rails. "Don't leave me here. Please, don't leave me."

Echo didn't answer. Khyn, white-faced, stared at her hopelessly, then dropped the last little distance to the ground. Echo pulled the hatch to, but didn't latch it. She nudged the controls, and the aircar coughed uncertainly into the air, barely making forward speed. A canyon gaped just ahead, nothing compared to the great rift, but still a long, long way to fall.

She crouched on the pilot's seat, one hand on the controls while the other held the hatch handle against the rush of turbulent air. She cut the power even further, peering over the aircar's nose, estimating speed and distance second by second. She would only get one chance.

The ground disappeared from view. She jerked the craft sharply left and killed the engines. Uncoiling her legs with all her strength, she exploded through the hatch at the instant the aircar fell, two landing struts on the hatch side hitting sand, the other two hanging over the cliff's edge.

The aircar tilted violently away from her as she leapt. Her bad foot caught on the last rung of the ladder, and for a moment she was being pulled up, swinging through the air as the craft began a slow roll into the abyss. With a desperate jerk she pulled the foot free, cartwheeling away from the aircar towards the rocky ground. The impact slammed the breath from her lungs, but if she made any sound, it was drowned out by the screaming protest of metal across rock as the aircar slid over the edge and tumbled into the canyon. She heard it bang once, twice against the cliff wall, then a final hollow *boom* as it hit the rock below.

Flat on her back, she listened as the echoes died away. Finally she dragged herself to her feet and limped cautiously to the scarred edge. The rock showed fresh gouges as if a giant hand had clawed the cliff, searching for some hold to save it from the fall. Crushed metal lay scattered across the floor of the canyon. She saw no fire, but a small column of smoke drifted gently down the canyon, and the smell of burnt polymer stung her nose even from this height.

No one could have survived that crash. That was what she hoped any pursuers finding the site would believe. It had been close enough to the truth for her. She had nearly made a fatal mistake.

She hoped she wasn't making another one with Khyn.

By the standards of the desert it was not a particularly difficult journey, though she had to keep her boot laced tight to brace her purple and swollen ankle. The ache was constant enough that she almost didn't notice it anymore. Khyn was so furious at Echo for not explaining about the aircar that she didn't speak at all the first day, but soon she had no energy left for anger. The hardest part was finding the landmarks that had been so obvious from the air, and even after that there was nothing to do but trudge to the next waypoint Echo lined up, and then the next. The huge desert canids tracked them all the time, patiently waiting for signs of weakness; they howled mournfully to each other in the endless dark while Echo and Khyn tried to sleep atop whatever jumble of rock raised them highest above the desert floor.

Once Echo found bones, and a few scraps of cloth. The bones were scattered, and most bore tooth marks, but the jagged crack spiraling through one long femur looked to have been made while the leg still bore weight. Echo rubbed a bit of cloth between her fingers: Church fabric, from a uniform like the one she wore. Now she knew what had happened to her batchmate Criya, sent to tend the arrays in Echo's place, when the Patri first had his suspicions of her.

"I hope if I'm ever lost they send you to look for me," Criya had said once.

"What is that?" Khyn asked, looking over Echo's shoulder.

"Nothing important." Echo pocketed the scrap of cloth. The remains were useless, the soft parts long ago consumed, the precious eggs lost to the Church. She kicked the bones away.

When they finally found the first array, the metal dishes glinting in the sand, her breath quickened with eagerness. For the first time she could almost envision success: she would bring Khyn to the Patri, fulfillment of his great dream to find other survivors. A quick sketch of what she had encountered, and his sharp mind would fill in every detail. He would know what to make of the Preservers, and how to persuade them to rejoin the world.

He would know what the linking tech meant for the Saint.

Almost home to you now . . . But Lia would not be there to meet her, only the Saint. It would have to be enough.

Then Echo put those imaginings out of her mind. This was in many ways the most dangerous part of a mission, when success seemed likely and the focus on survival flagged. She must not grow careless. If the Preservers had found a way to track Khyn and her this far, they might work out the location of the city yet. It was much too soon for that.

She kept pushing, and they made acceptable progress. The tiny animals that scampered among the rocks provided sufficient, if not plentiful, food, and Echo knew where to find ancient cisterns that still held water, buried among the ruins. Even so the journey had been hard on Khyn, though she did not complain. The sun had burnt her light skin despite the head covering Echo had fashioned for her, and she had to force herself to choke down the strong-tasting meat. Dirt darkened her hair, and the braid had long since matted and frayed. Though they slept at night against rocks that retained the sun's heat for hours, Khyn still shivered with the cold; after the first night, Echo had positioned her facing the warm stone and lain close against her, lending her own protection against the probing breezes. It was strange to feel the softness of another body against hers, and while Khyn shifted and snuggled closer, Echo lay awake long into the night. They kept the habit, though as they got closer to the city the rock gave way to jumbled ruins, and it was not only the air that put a chill in Khyn. "What happened to all the people?" she asked, and Echo saw her trying to visualize the city this must have been.

"The Fall," Echo said.

"I know, but I never imagined . . . They all just *died*. Preservers help us, no wonder they built the Vault. They saw this coming . . ." As had the forebears had who made the Church and hunters, Echo thought, but did not say. And the Saint. The Saint whose thoughts Echo still could not hear, though she listened with all her heart as the physical distance decreased.

Now, after a last walk that had begun well before dawn, they stood at the forcewall. Echo had brought them to the northern edge of the city, where the wall was farthest from habitation. The instant they crossed, the priests' panels would detect them, but the distance would give them some little more time to be prepared. She did not know what welcome the hunters would have.

She also did not know for certain whether Khyn could cross. The bones of some small creature the forcewall had not recognized as human lay scattered at the base. She saw the tooth marks where scavengers had taken their share. "What's wrong?" Khyn asked, not seeing the barrier as Echo could, the faint haze shimmering in the air.

"We're there."

Khyn's head jerked up. "The city?" She looked around, confused, seeing only more ruins around them.

"The forcewall. It will be another hour before we encounter any cityens. I hope."

"What do you mean, you hope?" Khyn's expression darkened as she eyed Echo with new suspicion.

"We want to be found by hun—my friends," Echo said. She lifted a hand to the forcewall, feeling the familiar tingle. Somewhere far away, this inanimate flow of molecules connected to a mind that had once been human, a woman whose cheek her palm had cradled. Her body yearned to feel that touch again.

It never would.

Echo withdrew her hand. "Put one finger here. Just one."

Khyn raised her hand hesitantly, chewing on her lip. Her fingertip brushed lightly at the barrier. It rippled with a *zzzt*, and she jerked her hand back. Echo grabbed it, flipping the fingers up to examine them. No burn marks, no charred flesh. And evidently Khyn's heart had not been stopped. "Does it hurt?"

"It tickles," Khyn said. "Is it supposed to do that?"

"Yes." Still Echo hesitated. She could leave Khyn here, find hunters, try to persuade the priests to drop the shield for the instant it would take to bring her through . . . Who knew how long that argument would be? Even close in like this, the desert was dangerous. And there still could be Preservers somewhere on their trail.

"Oh, no," Khyn said. "I know that look. You're not leaving me alone again." Before Echo could stop her, she leapt through the barrier. On the other side she stood, rubbing her arms, a surprised grin lighting her weary face. "I'm in the city now. I wonder if any Preserver has ever stood here?"

Echo stepped across. "Not that I know."

Khyn fell in beside her. "Where are all the people?"

"It's early yet." She had timed their arrival for dawn, when the streets would still be empty. If they were intercepted by hunters, the likelihood of an accident was small, but the edges of the city attracted cityens whose ability to reason clearly was limited, or whose intentions towards defenseless travelers were suspect. The latter might not recognize her for a hunter, tattered as she was and with her hair grown out, and the odds of an unfortunate encounter were less in the daylight that such predators avoided.

Khyn's nose wrinkled. "I smell something—oily, like an aircar or something." She glanced around nervously. "If they got here before us somehow—could they fly through that forceshield? Or over it?"

"Not without the Church knowing. And I would have heard them. That's the river."

"Your water smells like that?" Khyn was clearly reconsidering whether the small desert creatures were the worst sustenance she would be forced to consume.

"We don't drink from it."

"Thank the Preservers." They walked in silence for a few minutes, picking their way through the rubble. Before long a path emerged, where fallen debris had been dragged aside to clear a way where one person could walk, then two abreast, and then the path merged into an old road, wide enough to pull a cart along if you had anything worth transporting. Here the rubble had been reshaped into habitation, at least of a sort, stones piled together to form walls, ancient sheets of metal set atop for roofing, even the occasional translucent polymer across a gap in the stone to let in a little light.

No one in the Preserve lived like this. Khyn looked around, face sober as the strangeness of the place she'd been brought to sank in. She seemed about to say something, then changed her mind, only kept walking with the same dogged patience she'd shown in the desert.

They were no longer alone on the road. The city stirred as the sun rose, cityens emerging from habitations that grew more substantial with every block, the streets passable, rubble long ago reclaimed for better uses. People moved with purpose, going about whatever business they had today. Khyn kept slowing, staring wide-eyed at everyone who went by. "Look at them," she said in wonder. "So many! I didn't really believe . . ." Echo nudged her along before her odd behavior drew too much attention. The cityens gave a wide berth to the two ragged strangers, but offered nothing other than suspicious looks. It was just as well; Echo could not imagine the cityens' reactions if they discovered a true stranger in their midst.

Four hundred annuals. It would shake the city to its stones.

The hunters would show up soon. They had to know she was here by now.

Most of the people were headed south towards the oldest part of the city, many with baskets or large bags slung over their shoulders, some even pulling handcarts. Perhaps it was a market day. The taint of the river's sludge had faded; Echo smelled cooking oil now, and bovines whose musk was somehow rounder and slower than the sharp scent of the capri, and floating gently above the rest, the warm aroma of baking bread.

Memory sliced through her, so quick and sharp that it took a moment to register the pain. Not far from here she had sat at a table among cityens like these, sharing platters of greens, watching as Lia, golden eyed, laughing, reached for another piece of bread while Milse grinned and bragged about the new mill, and Loro glowered, and the Warder smiled benignly, no hint of the rebellion he plotted darkening his gaze. The market these cityens headed to was where Lia had handed her that pomme, an unexpected gift in the small quiet space before the blood. It all seemed so real, so present: surely if she took the turn ahead, followed the numbers down into the Ward, she would find the clinic still standing, Lia caring for the endless stream of cityens who came to her for help—

No. Lia was gone. There was only the Saint.

In the desert, the Preserve, it had all seemed distant, the past so far away it could hardly touch her. In the soft indifference of hopelessness, she could choose among the memories, imagine what she wished with no reality to call it a lie.

Now every landmark, every crunch of rubble beneath a boot, every familiar smell brought back the bitter truth.

Echo kept her feet moving, one in front of the other, concentrating on the simple task the way hunters were taught to do when there was no choice but to go on, however impossible that seemed. The pain in her ankle helped. She focused on the way it changed through the process of each step, the sharp stab as her weight landed, grinding protest as the sinews stretched to propel her forward, throbbing heaviness as the foot swung through air to begin the cycle again. A simple pain, easy to understand and manage.

"It must feel good to be home," Khyn said.

Echo could not answer.

They kept walking, right through the center of the city. In the months Echo had been away it had recovered, the fresh damage from the rebellion fading with the other scars. Streets Echo remembered as blocked by rubble were passable now, and here and there an abandoned building showed signs of rehabilitation. The old Saint had been weak, the city dying. Lia's ascension had saved them all.

And still no hunters came.

Echo's belly tightened. By the time she had left, the city had regained a fragile balance: the Church still guiding, with the new, strong Saint at its heart; but the cityens now closer to equal partners, no longer obedient children following the Patri's instructions without question. Nor were the cityens entirely united: the squabbling had already begun, from the wealthy North clave to the restlessly energetic Bend, to the Ward, where the rebellion had started. The cityens in the streets now carried that tension in their shoulders, the quick, purposeful rhythm of their steps. "That's as they did?" Echo heard one ask another in the slow drawl of a cityen from North.

"It is, Saint curse them for't," his friend replied. "And if not the Saint, I know a man as has a friend, and that friend no love of Wardmen. We'll have our justice, that we will."

"The hunters won't like that," the first man said.

"You see as any hunters come round here?"

"No, but . . ." The conversation faded as the men passed, but Echo's worry did not. Why *were* there no hunters patrolling here? True, there had never been many, and far fewer in recent annuals as the line stretched farther and farther from the template, but not to see any, even on this road leading west from the center, towards the Church where it stood guard as it had since long before the Fall—

Khyn stopped so suddenly that Echo almost walked into her.

"Preservers keep us," she said reverently.

The Church's metal spire flamed in the rising sun. The mast rose high above the stone tower, its sun-charging panels stretched out like a man's arms spread wide, turning in a slow, all-encompassing embrace. The dish at the very top of the mast sent out its signal as it had for all the empty centuries since the Fall. The mast's wires pierced the stone, running invisibly down the tower; but Echo knew where they led, each connected to a panel inside the sanctuary, where the priests waited for a reply to their endless question: *is anyone there?* They could scarcely guess that the answer stood only a mile from them on the road, sunburned and thirsty. Echo wondered how they would like it.

Khyn turned to face Echo, the light reflected in her face. "Is that the Church?" A few cityens came down the road, one pulling a cart; Echo drew Khyn out of their way.

"We'll be there soon. You'll be able to—"

Too late, her mind processed what her eyes had just seen. The cityen with the cart, whose face had been so carefully averted. The hunched posture had been a touch too contrived, the cloak too artfully arranged to disguise the uniform beneath. And the boot, just visible beneath the hem, the better-kept match of the ones that Echo herself still wore—

She shoved Khyn away, drawing a startled cry, but the fight was already over. Before she had a chance to turn, the stunner whined up through its charge, then there was an instant of white hot fire in her nerves, and then everything went black.

CHAPTER 9

She climbed out of the dark reluctantly. The familiar ache weighted her muscles; the light stabbed through her closed eyelids. Her body recognized from feel the dimensions of a hunter's cell in the domiciles, perhaps even the one that used to be hers. Someone sat still at the end of the pallet, watching. Echo opened her eyes a cautious slit, knowing what she would see: the face above her like a mirror of her younger self, unlined, untroubled by doubt or fear. If the girl were lucky, those would not come to her, even later.

No, not a girl anymore: it was a woman who spoke, amused irony in her tone as she said, "We find ourselves in this position too often, Echo Hunter 367."

"Gem Hunter 378," Echo croaked. Her head ached too. "It was not necessary to stun me."

"You were approaching the Church with an unknown person, after a long absence. You might have been under duress."

That didn't even deserve an answer. "What have you done with her?"

"She is with the priests. You can imagine the stir her passage through the forcewall created. A true stranger—yet again you have succeeded against all odds. Even the hunters were surprised. Have no fear; she is safe."

The Preservers had treated Echo well, in similar circumstances. She did not wish to consider what it said that she would suspect the Church of worse. "What did the forcewall show?"

Gem's expression was unreadable. "The priests did not share details. Apparently the Saint became— agitated."

"Li—the Saint." Echo struggled upright. She was not bound; Gem's arrogance hadn't changed. "Is all well with her?"

"She is strong."

Take me to her, Echo nearly demanded. She wanted nothing more than to rest in the sanctuary, kneel by the altar and listen, beneath the quiet murmurings of the priests at their panels, the small beeps and hums of the mechanisms that ran the Church and therefore the city, for the whisper of the Saint speaking only to her, that Echo could hear only with her heart. Or not: for even here the silence rang inside her, and the fear swelled again that it would never be broken.

She jerked her attention back to her duty. "The beacon—Gem, the signal must be stopped at once. I may have been followed."

"The possibility occurred to us," Gem said. "There has been no sign of pursuit, however."

"With the beacon off they're unlikely to find their way here. Even so, we must be prepared."

"I did not say the beacon was off."

"I do not have time for your riddles, Gem Hunter 378. I must see the Patri."

Her assessment had been incorrect after all: a thin line settled between Gem's brows as she glanced past the door. Not merely riddles, then. "There have been many—changes—while you were away. Some more welcome than others. I am told to let you see for yourself." The words, and Gem's reticence, gave Echo a twist of unease.

That faded as they emerged into the sun. It was still morning; the Church compound was busy as usual before the full heat of the day. The nuns who had been pregnant last summer had borne while Echo was away, and strolled or sat in the shade with the babies at their breasts, the tiny 390s whose only duty now was to grow and thrive. That would change soon enough. Hunters only a few annuals older were practicing to one side, wobbling through the most basic patterns of punch, block, kick, while a dozen or so more mature juveniles danced through the freeform drill, striking and throwing each other with barely pulled blows. For an instant Echo thought she saw her old teacher Tana among the supervising hunters—before she remembered that Tana was dead, and at Gem's hand.

She wondered if Gem had nightmares. She did not wish hers on the girl.

"The Patri is waiting," Gem said.

It seemed strange, after all that had happened, to stand at his door again. He had exiled her once, in fury at her disobedience, then readmitted her when she returned with Lia, the first Saint since the Fall to be born among men rather than made by the priests. It was that fresh strength that had saved the city, when the old Saint failed and the cityens' rebellion threatened the end of everything.

Lia's—the Saint's—sacrifice had been willing. Because of it, the Patri had forgiven Echo.

She would never forgive herself.

Gem knocked on the Patri's door. There was conversation within, a brief delay. Then Echo was ushered in.

A man, white haired and pale eyed, sat at the desk, surrounded as always by the stacks of prints passed down by the forebears. His thin fingers laced together as he leaned forward in the big chair. Behind him, a hunter stood guard, framed against the window. In her shock, Echo barely noticed her, though there had never been guards before.

"Jozef!" she exclaimed, finding the name in memory. He had been a laboratory priest, one of those who worked in the underground rooms where hunters were made, and sometimes a Saint. She saw again his hands directing delicate instruments that poked and prodded the treasure beneath the magnifier, processing Ela's eggs after Echo murdered her in the desert. His duty, as she had had hers. She was wrong to hold it against him.

He studied her, humorless and dour as she remembered. "You will call me Patri now. Vanyi named me before he died."

It was the first time in her life she had heard the Patri's given name. For that man, other than the Saint the center of the Church, and therefore of the world, any name beyond the title would have been superfluous. "Yes, Patri," she said to the priest who sat in his chair. Her voice came out thin, squeezed by the swelling in her throat. "My service to the Church in all things." She focused on a point beyond his shoulder, where the window provided a glimpse of the sanctuary. "I must make my report to you."

"Make it brief. I have urgent matters to attend to."

She clenched her jaw to keep her mouth from hanging open. More urgent than her return with a stranger? In the desert she had rehearsed this moment over and over, only with the Patri she knew. With this man, who sat tapping his thumbs together in an impatient rhythm, she scarcely knew where to begin. "There is *another city*! What the Patri always hoped for—we are not alone. There are not many cityens, but they have much natural wealth. Their technology is in some ways better preserved than ours; they grow a large variety of trees and crops . . . and they have saved seed, from before the Fall, including for their own line." It was the superficial report of a juvenile, but he had instructed her to be brief. She said again stupidly, "There is another city! What we have dreamed of for so long—we have found it at last."

"That was Vanyi's dream. I am Patri now. Believe me, I find enough trouble in this city without searching elsewhere for more."

Such an answer made no sense. Perhaps he was testing her. She took a deep breath. "Then I regret one more piece of news I bring: I may have been followed, by men of ill intent towards me if not the Church. I took precautions, but you must turn the homing beacon off, in case they were able to overcome them."

Jozef showed his teeth in the grimace that passed for his smile. "I am aware of the circumstances. The woman Khyn was forthcoming with the hunters. They have prepared."

Khyn's description of the vektere would be all the warning the hunters needed. Nonetheless Echo said, "They have energy weapons, more advanced than ours. They are neither as strong nor as well trained as hunters, but in sufficient numbers, with such weapons—"

She broke off as the hunter by the window stepped forward. Nyree, one of the 365s. Beyond reproach, that batch; strong and focused and unquestioningly confident of their own competence. Nyree stood with her arms crossed, weight balanced lightly on her toes, seeming to look down on Echo, though there could be no real difference in their heights. "Yes. And you may have led them to our doorstep."

Echo straightened her shoulders. "The risk was justified. Patri, I have additional information to report. It pertains to the—" She broke off. She could not say it aloud, not in front of Nyree. If the hunters found out—let alone the cityens—the shock would rattle the Church. "I beg you, Patri, might I speak with you privately?"

Nyree frowned. "I advise against, Patri. Until we are sure of her state of mind, we should not leave her alone with you. And what would a returning hunter report that is unsuitable for others to hear?"

Sensible precaution, from a hunter's point of view. Echo had no time for it. "My mind is perfectly clear. As for my report—it is for the Patri to determine who should hear."

Jozef looked at her a moment, then nodded. Scowling, Nyree walked around the desk. "I will be just outside."

"Well?" Jozef prompted, pale eyes regarding her with mild curiosity.

"The Preservers—certain of their leaders at least— they enter a kind of link to their systems. Like the Saint's to the Church. And Patri"—she wet her lips and continued—"they can leave it as well."

He tapped his thumbs together. "What is that to us?"

She blinked. The Patri—the old Patri—would have understood instantly. "They do this to ease the strain on those who control their systems. The woman I brought is familiar with the process. I thought perhaps . . . the burden on the Saint, controlling the whole Church, the whole city, alone . . . The Preservers could help us learn how to . . ." Her voice ran dry.

"Priest Dalto is questioning the woman now. If there is evidence of anything immediately useful he will inform me." She was wrong; he was not entirely without humor. She saw a flash of it now, sharp and bitter, in the curl of his lip. "When I was a priest, I might have indulged myself. As it is, however, I have more pressing duties. The city's problems do not solve themselves. This stranger only complicates things." He reached for one of the prints. "If you will excuse me."

"My service to the Church in all things, Patri," she said after a moment; but he was already engrossed in the print and made no reply.

Echo stood beside Gem in the yard. Nothing had changed—the hunters still drilled, the nuns still nursed their young—but everything seemed out of focus, as if she saw it through a broken lens. *There is another city.* The world might as well start turning the other direction. How could Jozef not care? She glanced back over her shoulder.

"Why did the Patri choose him?"

Gem shrugged. "The hunters were not consulted."

"Of course not, but . . ." She stopped herself there. The question itself was close to blasphemy; that Gem did not reprimand her for it was no credit to the younger hunter. It did no good to compound both their errors. The sanctuary, there across the yard, called to her. The Saint would know the answer, if Echo could ask. But that also was perilous ground.

Following her gaze, Gem frowned, the tiny line appearing again between her eyes. And then to Echo's surprise she said, "We have a few minutes to spare. I was not expecting your interview with the Patri to be so brief."

The priests monitoring the panels glanced up at Echo's entrance, then returned to their work. Her presence or absence was nothing to them. Their boards hummed quietly; lights flashed in patterns unreadable to a hunter, the only reflection of whatever passed for thought in the Saint's mind as her awareness spun out across the city. The Patri—the old Patri—had said that even he could not understand all the patterns said. Echo made her way past the tangle of wires and machinery to the altar. She forced herself to look. What she saw made her legs tremble, as always. She knelt, the stone cold beneath her knees.

Lia lay as still as death, her arms crossed over a metallic blanket, the crown of wires glittering on her brow. Echo had placed it there, with her own hands.

She would as soon have cut them off. But Lia, far braver, had accepted her duty, almost gladly, for her sacrifice had saved the city. The old Saint had been weak, dying, her body beneath the shroud withered, flesh sunken against the bone as the city consumed her, though she had been young and strong only a few annuals before. Echo dreaded the day she must see that happen to Lia. Yet it had not: the shining cloth lay lightly over the still-smooth curve of her breast, and her lips, parted slightly as in sleep, were full and soft. Echo put a fingertip to her own lips, remembering. Though Lia's eyes were closed, she looked as if she might waken any moment, rise and put off the crown with the smile that had made Echo's heart beat fast long before she knew why.

She had sat here too, hours on end, in the first days after Lia's ascension, only dimly aware that around her the Church pulsed with the new Saint's power. Erratic systems functioned smoothly for the first time in annuals; others that had failed came back online. Meanwhile the cityens, shocked back to sense by the violence that had nearly engulfed them, turned their energies to rebuilding what the rebellion had shattered, and more. Echo hadn't cared about any of it. She only sat, rent by grief, wrapped in the emptiness that was all she had left.

Then, in that silence, she had heard it. Not words as men spoke, but a voice nonetheless, a presence inside her mind, twinning with her heartbeat. It whispered to her in Lia's voice, and told her she was not alone. It had been enough to let her live.

And then it had faded.

Echo made herself breathe through the pain, as she did each time she came here. It never went away, but one day it might wane, she hoped, like the other old wounds that could mostly be ignored, only recalled when an ill-advised movement or the weather brought on the ache again. One day she might kneel here and see only the Saint, and not Lia.

She did not think so.

Already she knew the wrongness of the hopes kindled in the Preserve. They had been borne of distance and weakness, and a kind of forgetting. Now that Echo knelt again in the sanctuary, the vaulted ceilings arching high above, the vast and echoing space suggesting something much greater than mere men could conceive, she remembered why Lia had chosen as she had. Why there was no gainsaying that choice.

But what if there had been another way?

What if there still was?

Lia . . .

And then the Saint moved.

At first Echo thought it was the wateriness of her vision. She wiped her eyes, angry. She would not dishonor Lia by looking away. Then she saw it again: the faint twitch of a hand, a spasm of curled fingers, as someone dreaming of falling over a cliff might grasp for an invisible rope.

Echo rose to warn the priests, but there was no need. A high-pitched beeping interrupted the steady hum of their machines, and the pattern of the panel lights changed, yellows and a bit of red flashing in rapid sequence. "What is the matter?" she asked, staring at the screens without comprehension.

"Power fluctuation," a priest said, fingers stabbing at buttons. The beeping continued. Another priest called out from his station, something about a circuit, and the rest sprang into action, hands jabbing at switches and dials. Echo felt a surge of fighting hormones as her body reacted to the danger, but there was nothing here that she could face. Her fists clenched uselessly at her sides.

"Help her," she demanded.

Ignoring her, the priest studied his panel narrow-eyed. "Stepan, control the outputs. Three clicks. Better. Two more . . . Good. And look: that switched the beacon off. Finally." The exchange of orders and reports went on another moment, then the beeping changed to a lower tone, slowing. Echo glanced back at the altar. The Saint lay still.

"What happened?"

The priest wiped his face on his sleeve. "Something disturbed the systems. It happens, we don't know . . ." His voice trailed off into worried silence as he focused again on his screen. Echo dared not return to the altar. Instead, heart still pounding, she rejoined Gem in the yard.

"Is something amiss?" Gem asked.

When the old Saint was failing the Patri—Vanyi—had forbidden the least hint of discussion, keeping the secret from all but a few. Echo did not know what rules Jozef had imposed. But this was Gem, who had seen the old Saint die, and Lia ascend. "There was an alarm," Echo said. "Something about outputs. And then the beacon turned off."

Gem glanced at the spire, saying nothing, but the line was back between her brows.

The stewards in the Preserve knew how to balance their systems. "I want to see Khyn."

"We all do. She is still with the priests, however."

That was a good sign, Echo told herself. Jozef might be preoccupied with other matters, but the priests would pursue their questioning until they learned everything they could about the workings of the Preserve. That would mean understanding how the stewards controlled the systems. Khyn would be eager to provide the information in exchange for the help she sought for her people. But she would be frightened as well, alone among strangers in a place stranger than she could imagine. It would reassure her to see Echo's familiar face. Echo took a step towards the priests' domicile.

Gem said, "You must report to the hunters first. Come." After a moment's hesitation, Echo followed.

Another surprise awaited at the refectory. Priests sat together off to one side, and hunters in their usual corner, while the nuns occupied the long center tables as always. A group of very young hunters ate with them, probably being taught table customs, but it was not the juveniles who caught Echo's eye. Instead, it was what she had never expected to see: cityens mixed among the nuns, women and a few men conspicuous in their city garb. The conversation was even louder than she remembered, punctuated by laughter and some small amount of argument. A pair of older hunters stood nearby, not eating but watching, their postures attentive but not particularly concerned.

"We permit them entry for morning meal," Gem said, following her glance. "A compromise after the last tithe. The Patri saw no reason to keep the new nuns from their families, if they choose to see them. Also, the cityens insisted."

So simple a change. Yet the tithe had been the focus of the cityens' unrest, anger at the Church for taking their daughters triggering the broader rebellion that had briefly, and nearly catastrophically, pitted hunters against the cityens they were made to protect. Echo remembered the boy Loro's rage over the sister he had lost annuals ago. What if he had been allowed to visit her, see the care and attention lavished on the girls who would bear the next generation of hunters and priests? "Which Patri?" she asked Gem.

"There is only one. Come, take a plate."

The choices seemed narrow after the bounty of the Preservers' glasshouse. Echo took grains, and the greens she favored. She wondered what Khyn thought of the food.

The hunters at their table tracked her progress as she approached. Among them sat Brit Hunter 364, Indine, a 362, and Ava, a batchmate of Gem's. She slid aside as Echo pulled up a stool, and no wonder: that batch had seen its share of losses, and many of them could be laid to Echo's account, one way or another. "Gem has asked for my report."

A flicker of glances. Indine said, "Nyree will wish to hear it as well."

Brit's expression was bland. "Nyree is not present. And the Patri has not forbidden us to know." Her words relayed only the fact, and her tone suggested nothing beyond. Yet Echo imagined that she heard something else. *Us*, she thought. A group of hunters thinking of themselves as *us*.

Gem said, "You were gone a long time, Echo; be succinct."

"I know how to compose a report, Gem Hunter 378. I trained you when you were young." Saints, she sounded like Tana. Suddenly the few annuals between her and Gem felt like a hundred. "Nonetheless your advice is sound." It was, as well, difficult to follow, with all that had happened at the Preserve and after; she omitted much that would only be of interest to the priests, and concentrated on what the hunters would need to know to defend the city should it come to that. They listened intently, only interrupting to clarify a detail now and then. The chatter from the nuns' table rose and fell; she kept her voice beneath it, cautious habit. "If the vektere find the aircar," she concluded, "they should assume we died in the wreck. I covered our trail from there."

"A hunter would not assume," Brit said.

"No," Echo admitted. She thought of the men she had overcome in the dispensary, and Taavi. "But they are not hunters, by nature or training. They are closer to cityens, if cityens were more like one another."

"The cityens are less alike than ever," Gem said. "They are still angry at each other. Especially at the Ward. It has taken some effort to keep the peace."

"We underestimated them," Ava said, perhaps thinking of the mob that had nearly trapped her in the city at the start of the rebellion.

"But we defeated them in the end," Indine said. "It was not so difficult."

Echo could not keep the sharpness from her tone. "Only because of the new Saint. Without her who knows what might have happened?"

Indine shrugged. "That is a matter for the Patri."

"What is, Indine?" asked a voice from a few steps away. Nyree. Echo wondered who was guarding Jozef now, or if Nyree had only been there because of Echo.

"We were discussing the Saint," Brit said. Her tone was pleasant enough, but though Nyree stood with a plate in one hand and a beverage in the other, she did not slide over to make room at the table.

"I'm glad to hear that you know what matters are best left to the Patri."

Brit said, "We all know a hunter's place, Nyree."

Nyree looked at Echo. "Some of us might not."

Echo rose abruptly. "Take my seat. I'm finished."

"I have not heard your report."

"You heard what I told the Patri. I have given the details to the others here; if you have additional questions after consulting with them, I will be happy to answer."

Nyree's expression tightened. "Be available in case I send for you."

Echo felt a surge of annoyance, beyond what the words deserved. "The Patri did not inform me that I am under your orders."

"He has delegated matters concerning the hunters to me." Nyree stared at Echo a moment more, then took a place farther along the table.

"We have always reported directly to the Patri," Echo said, trying to keep the dismay from her tone.

Indine shrugged again. "Patri Jozef finds this less burdensome."

Before Echo could ask more, another group of juveniles clattered in for their meal. There, among them—pottery crashed, and the chatter in the refectory died to silence. Then there was a familiar howl of rage, and a tumbling ball of fists and kicking feet rolled across the floor as a fight erupted within the new arrivals. One of the watching hunters laughed and waded into the mess, unwinding arms and legs until she held one child, red-faced and spitting, by the collar while another bled copiously from the nose. The nuns cooed and clucked in sympathy, and the visiting cityens looked on aghast.

The hunter, still laughing, shook the girl she held. "Indine, I thought you were keeping an eye on—" She broke off with a grunt, clutching her knee. The child, seizing her chance with commendable speed, tore free.

And launched herself at Echo.

Echo barely had time to brace herself before the small body barreled into her. The girl's arms grabbed both her legs in what might have been a good take-down if their sizes were more evenly matched. Instead, Echo reached down and grabbed the girl under the arms, swinging her up off the floor. The girl clung with both legs around Echo's waist and her arms now tightly wrapping her neck. Echo crooked her chin into her shoulder to protect her airway against the grip. Then they stood like that, hugging hard, Echo's cheek close against the girl's, while the nuns chittered away and the hunters watched with expressions ranging from amusement to, in Indine's case, outright disapproval.

"Okay?" Echo whispered when she managed to catch a breath. The girl nodded against her cheek. She was considerably heavier than she had been months ago, when Echo had found the children half starved in the desert, and there was new muscle in her arms. "Where's your brother?"

"W' the priests. Likes 'em. S'okay too." The small body shuddered against hers. "They said you weren't coming back."

Some of them might have hoped not. "There is never a guarantee." Echo thought suddenly of Netje. The girl must be bereft. She wondered what the vektere had told her. What Taavi thought, now that she knew Khyn was gone. "You do not need me now."

The girl clung tighter. With a last squeeze, Echo set her down. The girl wiped a grimy hand beneath her nose, her tears already past. "Your escape maneuver was excellent," Echo said, loud enough for those around to hear. "However," she added, as Cara limped over, "you must be certain your opponent is disabled before you turn your back. I'm sure Cara will spar with you later if you wish. Now you may return to your exercise."

Cara laid a hand on the girl's shoulder, not too roughly. "It's Indine's turn for sparring. Come Fury, we'll try to get through the meal without eating any cityens."

"Fury?" Echo looked at Indine, who shook her head.

"I was against the experiment altogether. Gem named her."

Gem, when Echo had never seen the need.

"It seemed apt," Gem said.

"Too much so," Indine said. "She is not a hunter, and it is a mistake to try to make her one. She picks up fighting skills easily, but she has not learned to control her temper. And she hates cityens. Every time she's around them it leads to some sort of outburst."

"She has reason to," Echo said, remembering the barren desert existence the girl and her brother had chosen over the abuse they had known in the city.

"That may be, but if she does not learn her place soon, she will be of no service to the Church."

A juvenile hunter who could not serve would be culled. What would happen to the girl, who was neither hunter nor cityen? "You cannot judge her as you do the others, Indine. Give her time."

"We are made to serve," Indine said. "If *she* was not—" This time her shrug was eloquent. "You should have thought of that before you brought her to the Church."

CHAPTER 10

Echo stalked out of the refectory without waiting for the priests to give the teachings for the day. She felt an unreasonable anger at the girl. Fury. In the desert camp she had absorbed Echo's makeshift lessons with intent concentration. She'd been nearly as quick to learn as a hunter child would be, stealthy, patient, particularly skilled at the sharp strike that finished her prey cleanly. Why should she not be an equally apt student now? She knew the importance of the task.

Echo could not spare time to assist her now. She had left Khyn alone with the priests too long already. Their interrogation would be more fruitful with Echo present to assure her that all was well. Echo marched towards the priests' domicile. Above ground it was just an ancient building, hewn stone and narrow windows; the priests lived here in quarters more generous than the hunters' spartan cells. Below, in a warren of tunnels and crypts built long before the Fall, lay the laboratories where the priests did their work to keep the Church alive. It was the central truth of all life since the Fall: without the Saint the Church would die; without the Church, the city.

But now Echo had found the Preservers.

In the hot and dusty Church compound, the Preserve already seemed like a fading dream.

A juvenile hunter only a few annuals older than Fury stood watch at the domicile entry. The duty was a mere formality, hot and miserable even in this season, and generally only assigned when a juvenile required time to contemplate a poor performance in some exercise. This girl's blackened eye and swollen cheek suggested the area of deficiency. Echo herself had rarely stood here. But then, her failures had not come in training. Unexpectedly, the girl blocked her way. "I am required to secure approval for all entries today," she said.

Echo swallowed an intemperate reply. The girl was here for training; she would make a contribution. "What is your name?"

"Deann Hunter 382."

"What was the error for which you earned this duty, Deann?"

"I did not defend my position adequately in a simulated cityen attack. As a result, the Church was overrun." The girl stared straight ahead. Even at eight annuals, the magnitude of her failure weighed on her. Echo looked more closely. It was common for hunters to suffer injuries in training, but this girl had been struck hard more than once in the face. The simulated cityens had been enthusiastic.

"What batch portrayed the cityens?"

"The 380s."

"You must have been outweighed significantly then. Were you outnumbered as well?" The girl nodded. "Did you surrender?"

"No!" Deann practically squeaked in outrage. "I fought the best I could until they knocked me out."

"And yet your position fell. Have you devised a more successful strategy in retrospect?"

"Not yet," the girl admitted forlornly.

"Then I shall assist you." Deann's eyes widened with hope, at least the one that wasn't swollen nearly shut. "When facing a superior opponent," Echo continued, "a tactical retreat can lead to victory."

"But I was ordered to hold my post at all costs. Would it not be disobedient to leave?"

"Yes. But if that task was impossible to complete, a reassessment might be more appropriate than a wasted death. You could be more valuable alive. But you must be completely certain that the ordered outcome is impossible to achieve; otherwise your action is merely cowardice. And even if you decide correctly, you must still accept the consequences of your disobe-

dience." The girl frowned, trying to reconcile conflicting imperatives. The concept was likely beyond
her comprehension at this age, but the lesson would
stick with her. To be certain, Echo added, "Now,
Deann, we will practice. You have been assigned to
defend that door, is that correct?"

"Yes, that is correct."

"I intend to enter."

Deann assumed a fighting crouch. "I must not let
you."

Echo crossed her arms. "I am a full-grown hunter,
unimpeded by significant injury, and you lack the advantage of surprise. Do you think you can defeat me?"

"I will try my best," the girl said stoutly.

Echo sighed. "Indine must be your primary in-
structor. You will only recapitulate your earlier mistake. Do you know *why* you've been assigned to guard
this door?"

"Yes. The priests wish not to be disturbed."

The lesson in not giving away information unnec-
essarily would have to wait for later. "If you attempt
to fight me, I will overpower you, and then I will disturb them anyway. What other choices do you have?"

"I could try to enter ahead of you and give warning. Maybe I could even block the door from inside."

"That is a better plan," Echo said. She threw a
punch at the girl's injured cheek, just slow enough to
be sure Deann could block it. The counter came faster
than Echo expected; the girl almost hit her as Echo

took a long step past her and spun. Her injured ankle protested, but she still ended up between Deann and the door. "However, its likelihood of success against a more experienced opponent is small. No, a counterattack will not work either; I will be inside the building before you can complete your move." Deann froze on one leg, the other cocked midair in preparation for the aborted kick. "Now what?"

The girl's features worked. Echo hoped that she wasn't going to cry; she found herself wishing Deann at least a small success. Suddenly the juvenile whirled, taking off at a run across the yard. "I will return with reinforcements!" she called back over her shoulder.

Echo laughed, surprising herself, then felt a wash of melancholy. If she survived long enough, Deann would recognize another lesson buried in today's encounter. But by then she would be used to being used.

Echo strode down the stairs to the lower levels, making no attempt to conceal her approach. Before the Fall, the underground warren had connected the compound's buildings, but now the tunnels were impassable much beyond the sturdy foundations of the domicile. Debris entombed the contents, and perhaps some of the occupants, of many of those ancient rooms. There was still more space than the Church required. The hunters had a work area at one end, but it was towards the priests' laboratories that she turned now. There was no need for guards down here. Instead she found herself face to face with a young priest armed only with a broom. Plaster dust whitened his already light hair, and his face was streaked with grime. Perhaps he was performing some kind of priestly penitence. "What was your error?" she asked.

He eyed her askance. "May I help you?"

"I have been sent for the Preserver woman." He did not challenge her, but led her down the long hall. Doors stood open here and there, the priests inside working with the intense concentration of hunters. A few rooms held desks instead of equipment, just like the hunters' classroom in their domicile. Young priests, no more than boys, sat with their heads bent in silence over prints. One had dark hair, striking amidst the fair; and the small hands gripping his print were still tanned with sun. His face, fuller than it had been, was touched with wonder at whatever he read. Echo's breath caught. Perhaps he heard; he looked up, meeting her eyes.

She had not seen him since the long and agonizing night she had carried him, near to death, to the Church. She took a step towards him, feeling acutely her failure to have his name to call. His expression froze; then he dropped his gaze back to the print and refused to look up again. Bewildered, she spun on her heel and rejoined the priest in the hall.

She heard Khyn's voice, tight with frustration or fear, before the young priest opened the door. "If you let me look at the systems, maybe I can explain it better."

"In good time," a male voice said patiently.

"It will be easier to show you. And then you have to— Echo!"

Khyn flung herself at Echo, much as the child Fury had. "I kept asking for you, but they said I had to talk to them first."

"I know," Echo said, nodding over Khyn's shoulder at the man leading the questioning. She knew him, Dalto, a sanctuary priest. "Are you well?"

"Fine, yes. They just have so many questions." Khyn straightened. "I want to see this Saint of yours. And then I want to ask some questions of my own."

"I will accompany you to the sanctuary."

Dalto raised a pale eyebrow at her presumption, but before he could complain, Gem arrived. Perhaps Nyree had set her as another kind of guard. Her practiced glance took in Echo, the priests, Khyn with her arm still wrapped around Echo's waist. "Echo Hunter 367. That explains why Deann needed reinforcements. Indine was displeased." So, for some reason, was Gem, despite the lightness of her tone.

"She performed adequately. I shall speak with Indine."

"It is Deann's problem." Gem turned to Dalto. "I will join you as well. With your permission."

Dalto smiled thinly. "Your service is appreciated."

At the threshold of the sanctuary Khyn stopped still. "Look at it!" she said, voice hushed. She squinted, trying to adjust to the dimness. Light angling though the rose window tinted the walls high up; the priests' flickering boards provided the only other illumination. Shadow swallowed everything else, except the platform where the Saint lay in her glittering shroud. "This tech is *ancient*."

"It has served since the Fall," Dalto said, a trace of stiffness in his tone.

"Longer than that from the looks of it. It's a miracle that you've managed to preserve it. Your skills must be incredible. Wait until Stigir—" Her voice broke off as she remembered that she wouldn't be reporting to Stigir any time soon. Echo knew that feeling from her own bitter experience, the habitual internal dialog, the sudden dropping sensation in the gut that came with the realization of exile. Khyn closed her eyes briefly, then busied herself studying the panels. Gem stood by the altar, her gaze fixed on the Saint, her expression unreadable. Echo wondered with a peculiar twinge how often the young hunter had watched here in the long months of Echo's absence.

A priest turned in his seat to address Dalto. "Good news. We were finally able to turn off the beacon. I still have no explanation for the delay, but the command was finally accepted."

"What about the power fluctuations?"

"Still present intermittently. The one this morning was stronger than any we've seen. That was when the beacon finally shut down. We think something in the system may have reset itself, but it is difficult to be certain. The patterns are so irregular compared with the old Saint—and so strong, the panels have difficulty compensating. But I suppose too much power is a better problem than not enough."

Dalto grimaced. "Try to damp the surges as best you can. I fear a burnout of the panels. If that happened . . ."

Khyn eyed the tangle of wires that connected one board to another and the boards to the Saint's crown. Her gaze traced the thick cable winding from there up the wall, where it passed outside to the spire with its charge panels and rotating dish. "One steward to run the whole city? Incredible. The power it takes— and the strain. They must be a mess when they come out of the link."

The pulse pounded in Echo's throat. The priests at the boards glanced up in puzzlement. Dalto must not have shared all he'd learned yet. "Come out?" one asked. "What do you mean?"

Khyn's confusion matched theirs. "You know. Remove the interface, detach themselves from the circuits. Whatever you call it when they leave the link."

"There is only one Saint," a priest said.

"One at a time, I see that. Preservers. It's amazing. How long is a turn?"

There was a long pause.

Echo said, "The Saint is married to the Church forever."

Khyn's face stilled. "Forever?" She stared at the body on the altar. "That's impossible."

"It is true," Dalto said.

"But that would be . . . Preservers help us. I can't even imagine . . ." Khyn turned to Echo in appeal or accusation. "How could anyone ever agree to that?"

A body slipping over the edge. A hand grasping at empty space. "The Saint is made to serve," Dalto said briskly into the silence. "But this is not what we came to discuss. You said that your priests—controllers," he amended, "can modulate the inputs. Can you show us what you mean, please?"

Khyn looked from the altar to the boards and back, then swallowed. She studied the priest's panel, then reached over his shoulder to tap on the glass. When she spoke, her voice was almost normal. "This is the readout for your input channel?"

The priest cast a questioning look at Dalto.

"The Patri desires her opinion."

Echo wondered how directly Jozef had expressed his desires. There was more than a trace of excitement in Dalto's voice, though his features were composed as always.

The priest said to Khyn, "That channel shows power coming from the mast. The primary feed is coordinated through Stepan's board"—a priest a few seats away nodded—"but the signal shows here."

"There are still gaps," Dalto added. "The connections should be self-healing, but that one was missing

from the beginning. The defect is on the Saint side."
Echo drew a sharp breath to protest, but he contin-
ued, "It is a miracle that she was able to marry the
Church at all."

"Which one is the signal from the dish?"

"Incoming here. This dark strip—that would be
the outgoing beacon, but it's off now."

"Keep it that way," Khyn said, voice tightening. "If
Birn and the others are still trying to track us down,
they could follow it straight here."

"The signal does not carry all the way to the Preserve," Echo said. Surprise or dismay flashed through
Khyn's eyes, only partly replaced by relief.

"In any event," Gem added, "we have taken precautions."

Khyn forced a smile, then turned back to the
priest. "So when you talk about damping the power
fluctuations . . ."

The conversation quickly outstripped Echo's limited comprehension. Hunters learned what was necessary for their duties: how to maintain weapons, fly
an aircar. The sanctuary was the priests' domain.
Even the Saint was not required to understand,
only to serve. Unlike the hunters, who were bred in
batches, priests made one Saint in a generation. It
required a special mind, made to be exactly like the
very first woman who had put on the crown, or the
Church would reject her, destroying her instantly, as

the forcewall rejected intruders. Echo wandered to the altar, again stood studying the Saint's empty face. *The priests did not make you*, Echo thought fiercely. She still did not understand how it was possible. Small bits of denas, the Patri had said, scattered among the city-ens and only recombining now, to create a Saint not made, but born.

Gem came to stand beside her. The younger hunter gazed down at the Saint. "Her courage was admirable. Even though she was not raised to know her duty, she accepted it when she had to."

"She always knew. Just not that she was the Saint."

"I only met her at the end, but I trust your judgment." Echo looked up quickly, but saw no mockery in Gem's expression. Gem continued, "I come to the sanctuary often, and sometimes I overhear the priests. I cannot be certain, but I believe that there is more than the matter of occasional power fluctuations."

Echo's gut contracted in fear. "She cannot possibly be failing so soon. The lights, the power—her strength shows everywhere."

"Yes. You can see it all over the city. But I think that the priests in some way—fear her. That they cannot control her as they wish. The beacon, for example."

"How could the Saint reject the priests' inputs? Why would she?"

Gem lifted a shoulder. "For the first, I know no better than you. Perhaps it is not possible. For the second—no one knows what her thoughts are like, not even the priests. Or if she even has them. I only find it interesting, Echo Hunter 367, that the beacon would not switch off despite all the priests' efforts. And then you returned to the sanctuary, and it did."

CHAPTER 11

Gem left Echo alone with the Saint while Khyn answered the priests' steady flow of questions. Echo should have many questions of her own, about the hunters, the city, all that had happened in her absence, but for now all she could do was sit here, mind oddly empty. That changed abruptly when she heard the sound of worried voices. She leapt up, afraid of another power fluctuation, but it was not the priests, who worked with Khyn unnoticing. Instead Gem returned from wherever she had been, her face so expressionless that Echo knew at once something was wrong. "What is it?"

"Come quickly." Echo hesitated, glancing at Khyn. "Do not worry, the priests will not let her out of their sight." Gem took Echo across the yard to the hunters' work area. Nyree and Brit were already there. Lying like a dead thing on the table before them was a small device that Echo recognized immediately, though it was broken into pieces. The simple grip looked intact, but the chamber and tube had been separated, apparently by the same force that had peeled one end of the tube open like the petals of a flower. A few small gears had fallen free of their housing. Her hand stole to her arm, which still bore the scar, a puckered reminder of how near she had come to death.

Others had not been so lucky. Echo had seen it herself, hunters cut down by projectile weapons while she watched in helpless horror. The battle had carried all the way to the Church, the ragged cityen army fueled by ferm and panic and long-pent rage; the hunters driven by desperation to kill those they had been created to protect. Crop-powder explosions had shaken the walls; the air in the Churchyard had been thick with stinging smoke. So close, the cliff-edge of another Fall, and from this one, the city might have slipped irrecoverably into the dark. It would have been, if not for Lia, the end of all the world they knew. So very thin, that margin of survival.

"What is that thing doing here?" Echo asked, voice harsh.

"I found it next to the body of a cityen near the Bend," Brit said. "It appears that he was fatally injured when it exploded."

"The weapons are unreliable," Gem added. "The tech is simple, but the details are difficult to master."

Echo scowled at the scraps of metal. "The Church intended to confiscate the remaining projectile weapons after the rebellion. Was this not accomplished?"

"Do not lecture us like juveniles," Nyree said. She opened one of the storage cabinets where the hunters kept their static wands and projtrodes. It now held shelf after shelf of devices similar to the one on the table; they had been sorted into groups of those most like each other.

"It would not be possible to find them all," Echo allowed. "But why would a cityen carry one against the Church's order? Was he from the Bend?" That clave had always been the most difficult for the hunters to control, with its warren of tight alleys and ancient buildings that provided plenty of places for small prey to go to ground. Yet it was the Ward that had rebelled.

"The face was unrecognizable," Nyree said. "But that is not our concern." She turned to Gem. "Explain."

Gem picked up the chamber section of the weapon. "It is damaged, but not too badly. Look closely."

Echo took the device reluctantly. The grip was made of metal, probably melted and poured into a simple mold. The attached chamber was big enough to hold a spoonful or so of the explosive crop powder. She could still smell the acrid stench the powder left when it burned. There was a sparking device, connected to a short lever—no, two levers. In fact, now

Echo could see— "It can fire multiple projectiles simultaneously?"

Gem nodded. "I have made a study of these weapons." Somehow Echo was not surprised. "This is the third one of its type we have discovered in the past few weeks. Nothing similar was recovered before that."

Gut tightening, Echo looked at the other hunters. "The Patri thinks someone is making new ones."

"The Patri has not yet formed an opinion," Nyree said. "But it seems the most obvious conclusion."

Weapons like this had made fools believe they could take on the Church. "Surely they have not forgotten."

"Those who have will be reminded," Nyree said. "You spent many weeks in the city. Perhaps you know more about the weapons than you reported. Such as where to find the makers."

Echo set the parts down with a clank. "No," she said, voice sharper than it ought to be. "But I know someone who might."

Exey's voice floated up from the workshop below. Echo slipped silently down the stairs, Nyree close behind her. "Yes, my friends," Exey was saying below, "I'm sure it works. I'm the best fabricator in the city. Well, one of them. I know you Northers have a man who's not so bad himself, but he's a bit picky about whose chits he takes. No, let's not argue about that again, this is neutral ground, you know. And since we're getting along so well today, I'll give you all the same deal, and I promise it's better than you'd find any place else, not that anyone else could make one of these . . ." Echo remembered the stair that creaked and stepped over, leaving Nyree to tread on it and give their presence away. The tumbling stream of words dammed up abruptly at the sound. It didn't matter: there was no way out but up the steps. And cityens with clean consciences had nothing to fear.

The cityens, a woman and two men besides Exey, backed against the workbench as the hunters entered the brightly lit shop. The well-dressed man must be the Norther; he nodded smoothly at the hunters. The others might or might not be innocent, but it wasn't fear Echo saw in their faces. Or rather, there was fear, but something else, too, that tightened their jaws and compressed their lips even as their eyes widened. Nyree, sensing it too, took a wide step left, so that no one could engage both hunters at once, if anyone was foolish enough to consider a fight. But they weren't fools, though the man was close enough that he spat on the floor. Exey raised a forestalling hand. "Esteemed hunters. To what do we owe—*you!*"

"Out," Echo ordered the others, then, as the man who had spat reached to take something off the table, "No, leave that."

"It's paid!" the man objected. "Hunters, same as

always. Take whatever you want. That's not the peace we agreed to." His lips worked as if he might spit again. Instead he swallowed as Nyree stepped closer.

The cityen woman grabbed him by the arm. "Come on, Merrone. Don't argue with them. The Saint knows who's in the right, that's all as matters. We'll take it up with the council."

"Good idea," Nyree said. "Now leave us." They fled up the stairs. The Norther followed at a calmer pace, a nail in his boot clicking on every stair.

Exey was staring at Echo. "I thought you were dead," he said, pale as if he had seen her lifeless body rising. His face was thinner than it had been before, and a few strands of gray wove their way through his long hair. He still wore it pulled back; the decorative clasp, all golden filigree, glinted when he jerked his gaze away. "I *hoped*."

Nyree picked up the object on the table, a small box with a thick cable entering at one end and several smaller wires coming out the other. Exey must have been demonstrating when they interrupted; delicate tools and a small glowbulb were laid out neatly on the tabletop. "What is this?"

"Charge splitter," he said.

"What do you do with it?"

"Split charges." Nyree's eyes narrowed, and he added impatiently, "From a sun panel. It lets you send power more than one way at a time." His eyes bored into Echo. "What do you want?"

"We have reason to believe that cityens are still making projectile weapons."

"That's nothing to do with me. You know how I feel about those things. At least I thought you did. Maybe I was wrong. I was wrong about you in everything else, wasn't I? To imagine that I thought you were trying to save her, that I thought you ever cared for her—"

Echo took one step forward before she could stop herself.

"Ask your questions," Exey said. "Or are you going to break my arm this time just for entertainment?"

"I didn't think you were making them. Who is?"

"I wouldn't know."

"Would you know where?"

His lips pressed together in a thin line. "This isn't a game to me. Those weapons started it all. Benders killing Wardmen, Wardmen killing hunters, and hunters—the whole thing was a mess. My friends died, on both sides. Lia—but you would have taken her anyway, wouldn't you? That's all you came here for, from the very beginning."

Nyree, perched on a corner of the table, was watching with interest. Echo made herself speak calmly. "I don't want it to start again, Exey." She pulled the pieces of the broken weapon from her pocket. "Take a look at this."

Disgust fought with curiosity on his expressive face. Curiosity won: he studied the parts with grim fascination, using a magnifying glass for a better view of the sparker, squinting to sight through the exploded tube, finally sniffing gingerly at the chamber. "Shoddy workmanship." He swept the parts together and dropped them back in her hand. "But I have no idea whose."

Echo believed him. He was right; she remembered the anguish on his face the first time he had described projectile weapons to her. He had given the information to her for free, hoping she would tell the Church, hoping the Church would stop the coming battle. The Church hadn't, but Lia had.

"Speak of this to no one," Nyree said. She stood, tossing Exey the charge splitter in the same graceful motion. He made no effort to catch it. Pieces tinkled across the concrete floor. Shaking her head, Nyree took the steps two at a time, disappearing out of sight.

"Come see her," Echo said suddenly.

"For *what?*" The pain in his voice lanced through her.

"She isn't dead, Exey."

"That would only make it worse. You would know, if you cared."

She drew a long breath. "If you think of anything we should know, send word."

Echo was almost at the landing when Exey called out. "It was made from scrap parts, but the metal is too soft. They'll probably figure that out. Look for a smithy that can work harder blends. There can't be that many."

She nodded and turned to leave. "Echo. Would she recognize me?"

She thought again of the still face, the silence, where there used to be a voice whispering her name. Exey's liquid eyes held hers, pleading. "I don't know," she said.

Sunset stretched in a forbidding red line across the horizon by the time they got back to the Church. Echo was tired, this walk on top of the long desert journey. Her ankle ached, and she had foolishly expended extra effort not to let Nyree see her limp. The spire cast a sharp shadow down the great steps, the tip pricking Echo's heart, where Exey's question burned. "We must report to the Patri about the smithies," she said reluctantly.

"He requires facts, not mere speculation. Besides, the information may not be accurate. The hunters must investigate first."

"You can tell them, then. My presence is not required." Her heart ached too. Seeing Exey had brought back too many memories.

"Is there something you wish to avoid reporting?"

"You were there the whole time, Nyree. It was a simple interrogation. I have no doubt that you can summarize it accurately."

Nyree only raised an eyebrow. "You stayed behind to talk with the fabricator. What did you discuss?"

Echo's face burned with the heat still radiating from the sunbaked stone. "Nothing important."

"I shall report that then. I hope for your sake it is accurate."

Echo slapped her palm against the access panel.

CHAPTER 12

She slipped into the sanctuary so silently that the priests at the panels took no notice. Neither did Khyn, who sat slumped on a stool, fatigue evident in the line of her shoulders, the droop of her head. It had been a long day for her too. Echo found a place in the shadows by the altar. The rose window floated disembodied against the darkness of the vault; the metallic shroud over the Saint's body seemed to glow faintly. An illusion, Echo knew, like so many things that seemed true. She stood with her eyes closed, trying to still the chaos of her roiling thoughts.

Would she recognize me? Exey had asked.

No one could say. No one knew what the Saint thought, if the patterns that moved in that great mind could even be considered thought. She might recognize Echo, as she might know any hunter, or none. Echo's breathing quickened. She struggled to control it. A hunter must not fall prey to her hopes or fears. The ancient catechism taught the most basic truth of the world: the Saint preserved the Church, the Church the city. Hunters in their turn had only one duty: to serve the Church in any way required, exactly as required. Over and over Echo had told herself that that was what she had done in bringing Lia to this altar, setting the crown upon her head. Serve, that the city might be preserved. Just as she served by bringing Khyn to the city, in hope of helping the Saint.

But she had not done that for the Saint alone.

Do you know me? she asked into the emptiness.

There was no answer. There could not be. Gem was right: Lia had known her duty. Long before Echo met her she had been a healer, tending all who needed her. When she had learned she was to be sacrificed as the new Saint, fear had not deterred her for even a moment. The tears she had shed were for Echo, not herself.

And now there was only the Saint.

Lia . . .

A whining sound jolted her nerves. "Another surge!" a priest said. Echo hurried closer, where she could see over the priests' shoulders to the panels. Lights flashed; she saw the disruption of the pattern, a spike where none belonged. "Look at that."

"Let me see," Dalto ordered. The priest quickly

yielded his place. "Yes, coming from the input side again. Decrease that channel. I'll redirect the excess power."

"Storage is full," the priest warned. "It can't go there."

"I know. I'll bleed it through the mast." Dalto's fingers danced over the panel, and the alarm quieted. In a moment the lights steadied, functions returning to normal. Or so Echo hoped. "Can you read the panels?" she whispered from behind Khyn.

Khyn jumped. "Preservers! How long have you been there?"

"Can you?"

"Some. It looks like they've got it under control." Khyn's eyes tracked the cable leading from the altar up into the vault, where it disappeared on its way to the mast. "I hope no one was standing on the roof when he diverted the power up there."

Echo leaned closer to the boards. "What caused the surge?" she demanded, pulse racing.

Dalto's gaze flicked to her. "What are you doing here?"

This morning she had spoken to Lia in her mind, then imagined that the Saint moved. And then, the surge in the system, and the homing beacon shutting off. And now . . . "The priest said it came from the input side. Does that mean someone—something within the sanctuary?"

Dalto shook his head, impatient at her ignorance.

"That would be impossible. All the input comes from the Saint—her thoughts, her commands. Our panels only redirect them."

Khyn's eyebrows lifted. "You don't initiate the circuits? Preservers keep us. No wonder you have surges."

"We have alternate outputs for the power stream. In the past they were always enough. This Saint—the connections are not yet seamless. I thought they would close themselves in time, as the Church and Saint adjusted to each other, but it has not happened yet."

"Are the surges dangerous?" Fear pierced Echo. The Saint at risk, whatever the cause . . .

"They stress the systems." Dalto rolled up a cuff that had come undone as he worked. He said to Khyn, "I have work to do here. A room has been prepared for you in the domicile; Echo can take you. We'll talk further in the morning." With that, he turned back to his panel.

The last rays of sun cast their shadows tall against the stone wall of the cathedral as Echo and Khyn crossed the dusty compound. People were still about: nuns chattering in small groups, priests scurrying towards their domicile like tiny desert animals headed for their burrow. One or two stopped short, seeing a woman dressed in hunter clothing who on second look was clearly not a hunter. Echo discouraged them with a glance. She wanted to talk to Khyn alone. Stress on the systems, Dalto said, and the old Saint had withered so quickly. But stewards knew how to balance surges . . .

"Look," Khyn said, voice hushed. Her trembling finger pointed at the group of 388s chasing each other around the side yard, watched by a few nuns who likely hoped the small hunters would exhaust themselves before nightfall.

"There will be time later to observe the juveniles."

Khyn tore her gaze from the children reluctantly. "Just seeing so many at once . . ." She wobbled, then steadied. "Do you think we could find something to eat? The priests didn't stop for a midday meal."

Echo curbed her impatience. It was only a small delay, and both of them required nutrition. "There might still be something left in the refectory." Gem had said the cityens only came for the morning meal.

Khyn looked over the nondescript grains and wilted greens remaining from the evening meal, took a portion of bread instead, then sniffed the block of overripe cheese. Her nose wrinkled. "It's bovine," Echo said.

Khyn smiled wanly. "I'll have to risk it. Do you by chance have any ferm?"

"Just water."

"Too bad. I could use some after a day like this. Preservers keep us, I can't believe we only got here this morning. I'm not sure I really believe we're here at all. A whole new city . . . Do you want to join your friends?"

Nyree and a younger hunter whose name Echo could not recall occupied a corner table, though their plates had already been cleared. Hunters rarely sat idle, but they could wait with still patience as long as required to track their prey. The pair were looking towards Echo and Khyn with unconcealed anticipation. It was not Echo's responsibility to satisfy it. "Let's go outside." She led Khyn to one of the rough-hewn tables near the side yard, where the juveniles sometimes took meals. The nuns supervising the 388s nearby nudged each other in surprise, but at Echo's firm nod turned their attention back to the children. The table's last occupant had been practicing crude weapon making: the surface was strewn with wood shavings, and a few stripped sticks, ends fashioned into points, lay scattered about. Echo brushed them aside.

Khyn watched the juveniles wrestle as she ate. She shook her head in bemusement at either the rough play or the density of the bread. Echo made herself wait until Khyn swallowed a few bites and paused for water before finally asking, "Dalto seemed pleased. What were you able to tell them?"

The Preserver dragged her attention back from the children. "I was mostly trying to understand. Your systems and ours are so different. It's like someone took the same idea in opposite directions. Though why anyone would ever imagine doing it this way . . ."

"The forebears made the Saint to save the city." Those men and women who had foreseen the Fall had sacrificed everything to ensure the survival of some remnant of humanity, in the desperate hope of rebuilding a world they would never see. Even the Patri—Vanyi—had found himself wanting in comparison with them. That there might have been another way—it was blasphemy even to consider such a thing.

It was impossible.

Khyn pulled the hard crust off her bread and poked at the middle. "The priests seem pretty worried about this particular saint. The things they asked—and then the way they acted with that surge just now . . . Has there been any kind of trouble with them before?"

Echo's mouth went dry despite the water. "Did they say there's something wrong with—" She broke off as the pair of hunters emerged from the refectory and bore down on them. "Nyree. And . . ." Echo pulled the name from a dim recollection of a long-ago classroom, a quiet girl, one she had liked. "Marin Hunter 373?"

"I am honored that you remember, Echo Hunter 367."

Echo doubted that. Marin stood closer to Nyree than hunters usually did, unless for a tactical reason, which there was none of here. Echo saw the way their bodies instinctively adjusted to each other as they moved, the awareness that they shared beneath a conscious level. Hunters could pair as they chose when needs demanded, but Echo's estimation of the girl dropped a little. "Is there something you require?"

Nyree slid onto the bench next to Khyn, while Marin positioned herself between them and the nuns. "Only a chance to spend more time with our visitor. Our initial meeting was brief. You can imagine how interested we all are."

"I've been with your priests all day," Khyn said with a smile, but her voice had gone tight. "I really don't think I'm up to any more questions tonight."

"Everyone knows how tedious the priests can be," Nyree agreed. "I suppose the Preserve must have something like them."

Khyn shrugged. "Not exactly."

"In what manner are they different?"

"I have already reported my observations," Echo said sharply.

"There is nothing wrong with my memory, Echo Hunter 367. I merely wish to verify what you have told us."

"Besides," Marin added, "most of us did not believe that there could truly be another city, let alone that we might speak to a cityen from one."

"Then you should have had greater trust in the Patri."

"Even Patri Jozef was surprised." Marin gazed at Khyn with frank curiosity. "I know that you have already reported to the priests, but if you do not mind too much, please—tell us what it is like there."

Khyn took a sip, then stared into her cup. Whatever she tasted in the water made her mouth turn down. "I wouldn't know where to start."

"Begin at the beginning," Marin said, as she would to a juvenile, but it was not unfriendly. "Describe the surroundings."

Khyn laughed weakly. "They aren't anything like this, that's for sure. There are trees, for one thing, a whole forest; and plenty of water, too, from all the precipitation. And it's not nearly so windy, except in storms," she added, as the breeze pushed a handful of wood shavings along the table.

"The wind here is seasonal," Marin said. "The priests teach us that this area was forested once. Is it true that trees grow so close together that you cannot see the sky?"

"Well . . . I've never been where you can't see the sky at all. But sometimes it's only patches between the branches. When it's cold and frozen precipitate layers on, it can get dark." At that moment, the nuns in the sideyard broke into a peal of laughter. "Quiet, too."

Marin's eyes swept the dusty compound, but she was seeing something else. "I should like to experience such a thing."

"Never mind that." Nyree leaned in closer. "Tell us about your priests. And your hunters."

Khyn met Nyree's gaze with surprising strength. "I told *your* priests: we don't have hunters."

"Surely you have some need to protect yourselves?"

"Of course we do. There are predators, especially in the wild part of the forest; and every now and then someone drinks too much ferm. But hunters . . ." Khyn looked from Nyree to Marin, and finally to Echo. The little frown returned. "Maybe your city has worse problems than we do."

"Yet you came. Perhaps Echo Hunter 367 gave you an inaccurate report."

"She was clear enough." Echo could not be certain whether the trace of anger in Khyn's tone was directed entirely at Nyree. "And I'm sure she can answer your questions better than I can. I'm sorry, but I'm just so tired."

"Only a few more—"

"You heard her, Nyree," Echo said. "The priests will not be pleased if she is too fatigued to function tomorrow. Their questions are more important than yours."

"Perhaps so." Nyree picked up one of the shaved sticks, testing the point on her fingertip. "I believe this is the work of the feral child, Fury. Another stranger you brought to us, Echo. She has a talent for making ordinary things into weapons. It is a useful reminder." Nyree stood, tossing the stick away. "I look forward to our discussions."

"I don't," Khyn muttered when the hunters were gone. "That older one, Nyree—she was part of the group that caught us in the city. I think. At first I thought you were twins. But you all look so alike—more than we do, even." She gave Echo a tired smile. "Of course I'd know you, even without the long hair. But the rest of them—you told us you don't have a Vault. How does it work, if you don't all come from the same seed?"

If Echo explained, Khyn would want to know where the eggs came from. She might, remembering the drowning capri, wonder about Echo's role in obtaining them. Learn about Ela, dying at the base of a cliff. *You came for me*, the girl had said. *I knew you would*. It might make her think twice about sharing information with the priests. "I cannot describe the process properly." That, at least, was true. "The priests can tell you more, after you have answered their questions." She glanced at the darkening sky. "What I told Nyree was true: you must rest now."

No one stood guard at the domicile entry this evening; Deann's penance must be complete. The quarters assigned to Khyn were more than adequate, a priest's room with a bed large enough for two or three to share if necessary, a chair, and a water tap of its own. Hunters' austere cells seemed barren by comparison, though that was nothing to those who spent half their lives patrolling the desert. Khyn sat on the edge of the bed, hands folded between her knees.

"Do you require something else?" Echo asked.

"No, everything's fine. It's just—" Khyn cast her eyes down, refusing to meet Echo's gaze. "It's funny. In the desert, somehow I was never really scared. Only that time I thought you were leaving me. But now that I'm here . . ."

"The compound is well protected. It is safe to sleep without a guard."

"No canids or anything?" Khyn tried to smile, but her lips trembled.

"They cannot cross the forcewall. And hunters patrol at night."

"That woman Nyree is scarier than a canid."

"She would not harm you against the Patri's orders."

"That's comforting. I think." Now Khyn's voice trembled too. "I'm sorry, Echo. I'm just so tired. We hardly slept at all last night, and then all the questions, and it's just—just so *strange* here . . ." She buried her face in her hands, shoulders shaking. Echo waited. Tears were a useful outlet for strong emotion, and they passed quickly. More quickly, often, than the pain that caused them. After a few minutes Khyn raised her face. "Sorry," she said again. "You must think I'm an idiot. You never seemed frightened in the Preserve, and you were more lost than I am. I chose to come here. There's nothing for me to cry about."

That was a reasonable assessment, but in Echo's

experience, cityens expected a different response. She considered. "The cheese is not very good."

Khyn's laugh worked a bit better this time. She scrubbed her damp face with her sleeve. "I agree with you there." She hesitated, fiddling with her braid, then said, "I know I don't really need a guard, but I would . . . I would sleep better if you stayed with me like before."

It was a simple enough request, though it had obviously cost Khyn something to make it. There was no sense compromising her dignity further. "Very well." Echo stretched out next to her on the wide bed. The mattress was softer than the one in her cell; the thick walls blocked sound efficiently. The temperature was neutral, though Khyn rolled close against her side as if she still felt the desert chill.

Echo could sleep in virtually any conditions that a mission required; these were a luxury. Yet she lay open-eyed for a long time after Khyn's breathing smoothed into a quiet rhythm, and it seemed, in this room so close to the heart of the Church, that she found herself much farther away than she should.

CHAPTER 13

Gem intercepted her as she emerged from the domicile in the morning. Khyn was still asleep, and Echo had chosen not to wake her for the morning meal, judging that the extra rest was more important. The priests could obtain food for her later. "I've been looking for you." The younger hunter's irritation seemed disproportionate to the offense. "The cityens' council demanded a meeting with the Patri. He wants you there."

"Demanded?"

"Since the rebellion they are unconscionably bold."

Echo hurried with her across the yard. The wind had picked up; dust and bits of dried plant material rolled around them in erratic eddies. "The council was not named when I left. Is the membership settled?"

"From the Bend there is a man who runs a trade shop, and a purveyor of ferm. From North it's the man who supervises their portion of the grain supplies, and the metalsmith Tren. You know him." Echo did. His smithy was not far off, in an area where juvenile hunters often trained. Echo saw by the crook of Gem's mouth that she too was remembering the time Echo had taken her there with her batchmates, on an exercise meant to be innocuous. Impossible to believe that was less than an annual ago. It felt like a lifetime.

"Who represents the Ward?" Echo tried to make her interest seem casual. That clave, where Echo had posed as a cityen, had been Lia's home. It had also been the heart of the rebellion, and suffered much of the worst destruction. Echo had caused some of that herself. The Warder, though his actions had triggered the battle, had repented and died trying to stop the fighting. She didn't know who might be left.

"A former fighter who barely speaks, and a woman who never seems to stop. The hunters were concerned about admitting the man. However, the Patri concurred with the cityens that activities associated with the rebellion must be forgiven for the truce to take hold." That man would need to walk carefully. Hunters had long memories, and forgiveness did not enter into their calculations, truce or not.

"How did the Patri choose them?"

"The cityens chose. The Patri deemed it the most

expedient way, given the lack of evidence for one method or another."

Gem's neutral tone suggested no judgment of her own, but Echo's breath caught. In the aftermath of the rebellion, little could have been more important than regaining uncontested control of the city. For Jozef not to decide such a matter . . . *He is the Patri now*, she reminded herself, tamping down the spark of unease.

The council members were already in the large room near the Patri's office, seated around a rectangular table. They had been talking heatedly among themselves, but fell quiet as Echo and Gem took places against opposite walls, standard procedure when there might be trouble in a closed space. Echo recognized the Ward councilors immediately: Teller, a sour-faced man who despised everyone not from the Ward, and Tralene. Memory stabbed at Echo: Tralene, heavy with child, weeping in the Ward's clinic, and Lia, gentle as always, telling her that this baby was going to be all right. Tralene's belly was flat now, and her young face bore new lines about the mouth and eyes. She and Teller sat a little apart from the other cityens at the table.

Echo recognized the metalsmith Tren too, and next to him sat the man who must be the grain supervisor. A few bits of chaff still clung to his clothes, which otherwise looked newly woven. Even the impractical white shirt was barely stained, the elbows unpatched as yet. The Benders, unfamiliar men, could afford no such luxury, but Echo smelled soap, and the younger man's long curls were still damp. It was odd how fastidious Benders could be, considering that the rest of the cityens viewed the Bend's ancient alleys as the least savory part of the city. A pompous Norther would just as soon never set foot in the Bend.

But one of them had been at Exey's shop. Perhaps Echo did not know now what was normal among the cityens. She studied the councilors one by one, estimating strengths and weaknesses from the way they sat, whether they fidgeted or were still, the nuances of their expressions. Such was ingrained hunter habit; she knew Gem would be doing the same.

The cityens studied them more covertly. The resemblance among hunters always confused them, though unlike Khyn, they were well used to it. Echo wondered if any of them realized which one she was. Then Teller's gaze narrowed, and he sat forward abruptly. She met his eyes, seeing the spark of recognition before he leaned back in his chair, face hard with resentment, three fingers tapping on the table-top over and over. A twisted scar ran up his forearm and disappeared into his sleeve. Echo could still see the marks along its length where Lia had placed the stitches.

When she looked up, Gem was watching her, expressionless.

Finally Jozef appeared, Nyree at his shoulder. The

Patri slid into the chair at the end of the table. Nyree, arms crossed, stood with her back to the door. Now the hunters were triangulated, the room entirely under their control. They would not even need to look at each other if sudden action were indicated. So easy, despite all that had passed, to reestablish the familiar patterns.

Echo had not fit into them since long before she had left the city. She didn't think she would again soon.

The Patri said, "I apologize for the delay, cityens. How may I serve?"

The councilors avoided each other's eyes, and the Patri's too. The wait had given them too much time to think; they were more nervous than bold now. Finally Tralene said, "Thank you for agreeing to see us, Patri. We know that you have many responsibilities. We talked among ourselves first; we didn't want to disturb you for nothing, but there is a matter we felt could not wait for our scheduled day next seven. You see, we heard—that is, there was someone who said he'd seen—"

Jozef raised a hand to deflect the stream of words. "As you say, I have much work, and unfortunately little time. Be direct with me, please. What is this urgent matter?"

There was another hesitation. Then the grain supervisor from North said, "It's like as this. Some say as there's been a stranger brought to the Church. A rumor, Patri, like as not, but I said as we should come to you."

So soon. One of the cityens on the road must have noticed Khyn as they entered the city. The old Patri would have found a way to turn this complication to his advantage: announce fulfillment of a legacy, declare the rebirth of the city. Everyone would have believed.

Jozef tapped his thumbs together. The councilors' eyes clung to him. Echo had seen that kind of dread in a sick person's eyes, when he waited to hear his fate. Then the Patri said, "It is true, Kennit. But there is no cause for alarm. She is a single woman, from a small outpost far away. We knew such a thing was possible." It was as if he said, *it might rain*, or, *the crop could be better than expected*.

The man licked his lips. "A stranger? What is it as she's wanting with us?"

"It is the other way around. We. . . invited. . . her here, so that we can learn more about this other place, and whether it might offer anything of use to the city. It is only conversation, of so little consequence that I did not think it necessary to inform you before our scheduled day." He let the mild rebuke hang in the air.

"A *stranger*," Tralene said, amazement in her voice. "I know we always hoped—but to happen now—may we see her, Patri? Talk with her?"

"There will be time for that later. She only just arrived, as perhaps you also heard. Be patient, please."

Teller's fingers drummed the three-beat rhythm again, then stilled. "Won't be so easy. People hear, they're going to want to know as all it means."

"I'm only asking you to wait until we've finished our assessment. If anything important comes of it, I will share it with you immediately."

"North will do that, then," Tren said with a ponderous nod.

"Can wait forever, as I see," Kennit added. "The Church has always been help enough, North knows that, if not some." He cast an oblique glance at the Wardmen. Teller glowered, but Tralene laid a hand on his scarred arm, and he subsided. The Benders only stared, first at each other, then at the Patri, seeming unable to speak at all.

It was a worrisome division, Echo thought: which cityens would treat the arrival of a stranger as of no practical difference in their lives, and which would see a pivot on which their whole future might change. Waiting gave them too much time to think about it.

"We're in agreement, then," Jozef said. He considered a moment, then said, "I have a more immediate problem to discuss with you, and perhaps it is best that this also not wait for our scheduled day. A man was found dead last night, killed by a projectile weapon. That's the third one since the truce. The hunters will get to the bottom of it, of course, but if any of you has useful information, I would welcome it."

The dry tone suggested nothing beyond the facts, but it didn't have to. Weapons, and hunters searching the city for them—if the Patri meant to distract the councilors from Khyn, he had made a good choice. After a moment, one of the Benders found his voice. "Man's name was Wold. Kind who got in a little bit of trouble now and then, but not so you'd think he'd be killed for it." Gem had said the man was killed by his own malfunctioning weapon. Interesting that the cityens didn't seem to know that.

Kennit smoothed his sleeves. "Seems as trouble always finds those as make it, Silton."

"Seems as those who can buy their way away from trouble don't know that they're talking about," Teller said before the Bender could answer. "Of course if North didn't try to keep more than your share—"

"Like you've kept from the grain stores? You Wardmen think as we don't know about that? Harvest came in, the claves' portions are all put up separate like we agreed, sure enough. Problem is, the portions aren't divided as it seems they should be. Seems as some wanted more than what they're owed."

"The amounts were agreed to in advance," the Patri said. "And what does all this have to do with the dead man?"

"Respectfully, Patri, point is it's not the agreement as caused the trouble," Kennit said. "More the keeping to it. Could be the same with the weapons.

Maybe some still haven't learned all that lesson as they should." His heavy-lidded gaze at the Warders left no doubt who he meant.

"We gave up our weapons in the truce," Tralene said with a shudder. "And glad to see them go."

Silton, the Bender, glared at her. "Who killed Wold then? Somebody's still got them. Could be as just some troublemakers in the fringes, but Wardmen didn't think weapons were so horrible when you were using them against the other claves before."

"We always did! It was only a few had them, and most of them gone now"—Tralene's breath caught for a moment before she continued—"and those that aren't are sorrier than you can know." She didn't look at Teller; he didn't look sorry.

Tren studied the backs of his callused hands. They were crisscrossed with shiny burn scars. "Going to be searching the smithies I'd say. Be honored if you'd as start with mine, Patri."

"Was me, I'd look in every habitation in the Ward," Kennit muttered.

"And free to do it," Tralene said sharply. "As for the grain, if someone shows we've stored more than our share, we'll give it back. I'm only asking don't make the children go hungry in the winter."

There was a little silence. Echo waited for the Patri to break it with an order, but instead he let it go on. Then the shopkeeper from the Bend said, "Could be a mistake with the portions. Seen that sort of thing happen in the shop with someone counting chits. Maybe just recounting would settle things. Have a hunter help us watch." Heads nodded all around the table. Even Kennit made no objection, though his look was as sour as Teller's.

Silence fell again. Something still bothered them, and none wanted to be the first to say.

"If there is nothing else?" the Patri said.

"Fine," Teller snapped. "If the rest of you won't, I'll ask: what about the Saint, then?"

Echo felt her pulse skip. "The Saint?" Jozef's voice thinned across the word.

Teller said, "Ward might not have all the fancy shops as in North or fabricators like the Bend, but we still got our power lines and our mill. Three times yesterday the lights went out. Came right back on, but that's a thing shouldn't happen. Makes people worried. They seen too much of that when the old Saint was sick."

Jozef waved a dismissive hand. "The Saint is strong. There is power to spare, so much that we have to divert the flow to storage now and then. That's what happened yesterday. You needn't concern yourselves about the Saint."

Tralene's lips moved silently, forming a name. "She's well, then, Patri?"

Jozef frowned. "The systems are functioning fully.

Now, cityens, if there is really nothing else?" The councilors, dismissed, filed out of the room, but Echo stopped Tralene with a hand on her arm.

"Your child. How is he?"

"You're the one who was Lia's friend, aren't you? I never would have thought . . ." Tralene's voice trailed off. Then she smiled softly. "He's a sturdy boy, like his da. Thanks to Lia. If she hadn't taken care of me, when I was so sick carrying him . . . But now she's taking care of all of us, isn't she. I hope she knows how we're grateful."

"Come on, Tralene," Teller said with a scowl.

Nyree led the councilors away, and Gem went in the middle of the group. Echo waited in the hall to bring up the rear, all proper procedure. But Kennit hung back, delaying to speak to the Patri alone. He kept his voice too low for a cityen to hear, but Echo's sharp ears had no difficulty picking up the words. "About the stranger. Patri, we know as your decisions are always for the best. But it seems as that this is not the time to welcome such a one. With all the things as going on already, last we need is new to stir up trouble."

"I told you, Kennit, there's no reason to be alarmed. The hunters have increased their patrols just in case. The city is safe."

"Respectfully, Patri, remember as what happened before. Hunters almost weren't enough. Something happens again, you'd be needing cityen help. North will serve, you know we will. Only it's just, with Wardmen so erratic, it's as may be they explode any time. The stranger might just be the thing as sets them off. Or the Saint. They claim she was a woman from the Ward, I hear some say, not a proper Saint as the Church makes and that's as why the lights go out."

A surge of anger burned through Echo. *Not a proper Saint,* when Lia had sacrificed everything—

But the Patri replied with no more than a hint of irritation. "The cityens needn't worry so much about the Saint, Kennit. The Church preserves the city, that's what's important. Do you understand me? Good. Make sure the rest of your clave does too."

"Yes, Patri." It might be relief in Kennit's voice. "North's as grateful for your strong hand. Church as it's always been."

Echo blocked the Norther's path as he exited the room. "It is blasphemy to question the Saint."

Kennit managed to meet her eyes. "I heard as the Patri said, esteemed hunter." He brushed past her without waiting for her reply.

"Echo," the Patri called from within. The old Patri would have known she had overheard his conversation. Did Jozef?

"How may I serve?"

"You lived among the cityens. What did you think?"

She started where the ground was surest. "Obviously the claves still harbor resentments against each other. That could be beneficial, if it discourages them from unifying in any potential . . . disagreement . . . with the Church."

"Another rebellion, you mean. I don't see how fighting among the claves would be much better. Do you think the councilors were telling all they knew?"

"On the grain count I believe they all thought they spoke truly, though they could not all be correct. But about the weapons . . . I am not certain."

Jozef's fingers steepled, and he rested his chin on them, his eyes narrowing like a priest contemplating a print whose meaning was unclear. "I find it difficult to be certain of anything with them. If I give them some leeway to manage their own affairs, it may help prevent further outbursts. Or so the prints I am studying suggest. I do not pretend to understand the way cityens think." Jozef laughed without mirth. "Vanyi did me no favors when he dragged me out of the laboratory. The magnifiers make it possible to see clearly. One simply gathers evidence and then arrives at a conclusion. What else did you observe?"

Here the footing was less certain. She remembered again Vanyi's secrecy about the dying Saint. Perhaps this Patri too feared the rumor of weakness as much as the weakness itself. "About the Saint—they *were* frightened, even Teller. Your words reassured them."

"They were true. She is the strongest Saint in a hundred annuals." Jozef laughed again, short and bitter. "Vanyi expected that to be the solution to every problem. He was wrong about many things."

An unreasoning anger mixed with the dread his words brought. "Forgive me, Patri, but the priests seem barely able to control the surges."

"It is a matter of adjusting the inputs. They will find a way."

"Has Khyn's information been useful, then?"

Jozef's eyes narrowed. "That is a matter for the priests. You heard what I told Kennit." He had known, then. It was a lesson to keep in mind. "There's no need for so much concern about the Saint."

"But Patri, surely, nothing is more important—"

He stopped her with a sharp gesture. "My ways may appear different from Vanyi's, but I am the Patri now, as much as he ever was. I require the same obedience you gave to him. Remember that, Echo Hunter 367."

The old Patri's voice would have thundered across the yard. Jozef's was thin as the edge of one of his instruments, that would cut and be gone before you felt the pain. "My service to the Church in all things," Echo said, chilled.

The pale eyes rested on her. "As it must be."

CHAPTER 14

Echo could not follow Dalto and Khyn's discussion of the sanctuary systems. She lacked the technical expertise, of course, but more than that, she struggled to pay attention. The altar tugged all the time at her, insistent as a voice she could not quite hear trying to tell her something of surpassing importance. She only wanted to sit and listen. Yet the silence, the emptiness inside as she gazed at the Saint, was unbearable. "Lia," she whispered to the shadows, but then the quiet was pierced by another alarm, and a flurry of action from the priests as they brought it under control again. She swallowed her questions. *Dalto said the surges could not originate from within.*

Khyn was not faring much better. The weight of exile pressed on her, and everything from the food to the wind seemed to remind her of how far she was from any familiar place. The cityens in the refectory stared and pointed, and though many seemed only curious, not all the looks were friendly. Echo did her best to keep Khyn apart from them, fearing that any sign of hostility would make Khyn think twice about disclosing the Preserve's capabilities. During one lull in the sanctuary work, Echo brought her to the small grove behind the priests' domicile, where hunters rarely wandered. It was deserted at midday, too hot for the priests to find comfortable, though for a hunter even this sparse shade was pleasant. The trees had been watered this morning; the smell of moisture baking slowly from the earth contrasted with the flinty sharpness everywhere else in the compound. Someone had missed a late pomme, a surprising oversight; it hung withered from a branch, the sweetness gone sickly with rot.

Khyn wiped sweat from her face. "I understand what they're asking, but your systems are so different I can barely explain . . ." She broke off, brows drawing together. They did that more often than not, and lines of tension narrowed her eyes in a constant, worried squint. "You said they would be able to help with the Preserver line. Why won't they tell me anything?"

Because they have no need. Echo felt a guilty relief that Khyn did not have a better grasp of tactics. Far better that the priests first obtain all the information she could provide. If they were still reticent after that, Echo would do what she could to persuade them;

she owed Khyn that, at least. But if what Khyn knew was inadequate to help them deal with the surges . . . Echo began to regret the thoroughness with which she had covered their trail from the Preserve. "You must tell them everything you can."

Khyn laughed shortly. "Or what? They'll set Nyree on me?" Then, when Echo didn't answer, her face paled. "I'm trying. You know I am, don't you?"

Khyn wept again that night, hard sobs that shook the bed stand, until Echo finally did as she must and wrapped her arms around her. If Khyn felt the tension in the shoulder she buried her face against, she gave no sign, and finally, breath still faintly stuttering, she fell into a deep sleep. Echo slept too, and dreamed of being pushed over the edge of a cliff, and as her body flailed against air she looked back and saw that it was herself who had done the pushing.

Echo stared at the mast burning atop the spire. *You go there from weakness,* she chastised herself; *it is time to serve as a hunter again.* Swallowing her resentment, she sought Nyree, who merely said, "I will assign you if I think of something suitable."

Yet there was no shortage of work that needed doing; the hunters were stretched thin. Most of them, those who were not occupied teaching the juveniles or guarding the Church compound, were out patrolling the city. They went in twos or threes, more for the cityens' safety than their own: a misguided cityen might fantasize himself the match of a single hunter, and if he were armed, or unlucky, the hunter might have to injure him, or worse, to protect herself. But a group of hunters together was too formidable to be challenged.

Unless the cityens doing it meant to start a war.

She heard Kennit's warning again: the city might explode at any time. In the rebellion, the old Saint had suffered the most: consumed by the attempt to protect the city from itself, devoured by the violence . . . And now the new Saint on the altar, but the same fate waiting.

A haze filled the air. For an instant Echo's pulse sped as if battle had come to the Church again, but it was only dust, kicked up by another gust of wind. She blinked, and her eyes cleared, revealing a group of small hunters marching across the yard, Indine in their wake. It appeared to be a formation drill, simple enough, but one of the girls was struggling mightily, too fast on the turn and not close enough to the others. As Echo approached, Indine called the group to a halt.

Fury stomped impatiently in place. Then, seeing Echo, she cut out of her line, throwing herself gleefully at her. "Caught th' hunter," she said, a game the smallest juveniles practiced. Fury was too old for it.

"Get back to your batch," Echo ordered, conscious of the juveniles and other hunters watching. Scowling, the girl returned to her place, where she stood, arms crossed and hips askew. Disheveled, a pointed stick thrust through her belt, she looked more like the cityens from the fringes than a hunter. Indine sighed. "You are a bad influence, Echo Hunter 367."

"She'll learn. Where are you taking them?"

"North clave. Gem is overseeing the recounting of the grain allocation; we will join her in the inspection."

"I shall accompany you."

Indine raised an eyebrow. "Have you no other duty?"

"I am free at this time," Echo answered stiffly.

By the time they got to the granary, Echo was reconsidering her decision. Fury had scuffled twice with the 384s around her. She was probably an annual or so older than they, no way to know, but they were hunters, already stronger and quicker despite their size disadvantage; and blood now dripped steadily from her nose although she defiantly refused to wipe it off, or cry. The 384 whose fist had caused that was still rubbing a swelling knuckle. "That is why," Echo advised as she fished cloth from a pack, "it is better to use your elbow when striking a hard part of the body such as the head. Wrap your hand with this. Fury, clean your face. You will distress the cityens."

The granary occupied the front part of a building that had been old even before the Fall, though not so ancient as those farther south in the Ward. Built of hewn stone, it took up most of a block. The front wall, perhaps four stories high, had been graced with huge arched windows, long since bricked in; more recently, irregular openings had been cut in the brick and covered with haphazard bits of glass to let in some light. The floor inside was another kind of stone, off-white and still polished smooth after all these annuals. Fluted columns supported the ceiling, and arched openings echoing the windows led to other rooms, almost as large; some of those were still full of debris. A tumble of what looked like huge stone bones spilled through one archway. A ribcage large enough to hold three hunters captive lay upside down, the shape bound together by metal straps; next to it, a chain of vertebrae strung on wire extended in a long tail past the pelvis they were attached to. Discarded nearby, a triangular head the size of a grown man's torso had been reassembled from pieces each no bigger than Echo's palm. She ran a finger over the glued joints, wondering what odd impulse had moved cityens before the Fall to spend so much effort to so little purpose.

Dismissing the distraction, she turned her attention back to the main hall, which currently held storage sacks of grain stacked in head-high piles, the supervisor, Kennit, and a handful of other cityens, and Gem, chalking numbers in front of each pile. She had already marked a table full of smaller sacks, the kind distributed to individuals. "You overcounted that one," Kennit said. Then he caught sight of Echo, and his expression, already dissatisfied, turned down-right sour.

"I don't believe so," Gem said mildly. "But if you wish we can re-stack all the bags." The workers groaned at the prospect.

"The 384s will assist," Indine said. She took a seat on the curve of what appeared to be a giant shoulder blade, leaving the juveniles to work out an acceptable plan on their own. It did not take too long. Soon three of them had scrambled to the top of the first pile and were sliding sacks almost as big as themselves over the edge, where the other girls wrestled them into a single layer across the floor. They quickly realized that working in pairs was more efficient; that left Fury, predictably, without a partner.

Echo lifted her chin at another pile of sacks. Fury scrambled to the top and began shoving them down to Echo, who caught them without difficulty and slid them across the floor towards the 384s. Indine shook her head. Kennit stood cross-armed, glaring at Echo. Other than that, the work was not unpleasant, Echo's muscles flexing and contracting in rhythm against Gem's steady counting and the squeak of chalk on the stone.

A man poked his head in the door. "Kennit, you in here?" he called, breaking the rhythm. "We need to talk. Some of the men are as planning—"

"Not now," Kennit said sharply. "I'm busy, Div, even you can see."

"Is there something we can assist you with, cityen?" Gem asked, still squatting with her chalk poised to make another mark.

Div shook his head. Echo had seen him before, she thought as she paused to listen, but not in North. "I didn't expect as there'd be hunters here. No need to interrupt. Kennit, I'll see you later. No rush," he added, retreating hastily. His left heel made a metallic tap against the stone.

Exey's shop. That's where Echo had seen him. She wondered what he'd been about to say that Kennit didn't want hunters to hear.

A sack hit the floor and burst as Fury, inattentive, dropped it where Echo had been. Grain flew everywhere. Kennit sputtered; Indine motioned Fury down from the pile and handed her a broom. "Make sure not to let any go to waste," she ordered.

Gem watched the girl sullenly sweeping. "She is not a hunter."

"You are always too quick to judge," Echo said, but she felt a sinking in her belly.

"What favor is it to her to try to make her something she is not?" Echo did not answer, and Gem turned back to her counting with a shrug. Her initial tally proved to be correct, and so, when the rest of the piles were counted and stacked again, was North's grain allotment.

"Wouldn't need hunters checking if the Church passed it all out as used to be. Best you count the other claves twice over," Kennit grumbled, wiping his face. "Might be they've hidden part away where nor Church nor other councilors can find it, and then they say as we got more than we deserved."

"In any event you have enough. I shall inform the Patri that the matter is settled to your satisfaction," Gem said, and went to assist Indine and the 384s with the last few sacks.

"Informing him as isn't all that's needed," the councilor muttered under his breath.

"Was there something you meant to say?" Once cityens would never have dared criticize the Patri where there was the slightest chance a hunter might overhear. But Kennit looked more irritated than afraid.

"Wardmen won't be stopped by counting and council meetings, all I meant. They need a proper lesson."

"That is for the Church to decide, not you."

"Always was, before. Church as it should be, that's what North as wants. Now if you'll excuse me, esteemed hunter, I'll help finish up here. You have as better to do than deal with me."

The 384s trudged along in tired silence, even Fury too subdued to instigate any mischief. It was just as well: North in general was safe, and the cityens living here were used to hunters and unlikely to be alarmed by their exercises. Nonetheless, dusk was approaching, and though the lightstrings triggered by their passage were brighter and closer together than Echo remembered, night in the city would never be without its dangers. And Echo was still troubled by Kennit's attitude. Church as it should be, as if North were the judge of that. It was a small provocation, but those were in some ways more alarming than a single challenge that could be dealt with decisively. The rebellion had broken the city into pieces, like the stone head in the granary, and there was no pattern to show how it could be glued back together.

Her attention jerked to a sudden brightness: lightstrings flashing on in response to motion down a side alley, at the same time voices rose in heated argument. She didn't have to check to know that Indine and Gem also noticed; they were already detaching themselves from the file of juveniles, taking up positions between them and the disturbance. The words were hard to make out, but the tone suggested too much ferm and nowhere near enough good sense. "Nothing to do with us," Echo said. She flexed her sore ankle, working out the stiffness just in case.

Indine nodded towards the juveniles, whose fatigue had been replaced by eager interest. "It is an opportunity."

"Indeed," Gem said, teeth flashing, but Echo's gut tightened at the thought of Fury confronting cityens.

"I do not think we should engage them needlessly."

"She has to learn," Indine said. In a moment she had given the girls their instructions, and they were striding down the alley in well-rehearsed formation. Indine, Gem, and Echo followed, keeping to the shadows. Echo told herself she should not be so anxious. The juveniles would have practiced such a scenario many times in their training, and there was virtually no altercation among cityens, short of rebellion, that three mature hunters could not control.

A half dozen men stood in the pool of light, four of them faced off against the other two. By the state of their clothing there had been some pushing and shoving, but no real harm had been done; everyone was still upright, and though as expected they stank of ferm, Echo did not smell blood. They were still cursing and spouting nonsense when the 384 leading the exercise stepped into the light. "Is there a problem, cityens?"

The men spun in comic startlement that was amplified by their expressions when they saw how small their challenger was. "Who's that as wants to know?" one of the four slurred, shambling forward.

The girl hooked her thumbs in her belt. "Flo Hunter 384," she said with calm authority.

"Well, esteemed Flo Hunter, it's like as this. Those Wardmen there as wanted to pass, and we were just explaining how they aren't welcome in our clave. Soon as they go back, there's the end of any problems."

"Problem is they stole our chits!" one of the Ward-men exclaimed, outraged.

"Fee for safe passage," the first man said. "Shouldn't've come this way."

"The streets are free to all," Flo said. "Give them back their chits, cityen." Her high voice betrayed only the slightest uncertainty, but it was enough for the men to start to smile.

"I'm thinking you're too small to make me," the Norther said, and lurched towards her. It was no contest at all. His wildly swinging punch sailed over Flo's head as she dropped to scythe her extended leg into his ankle, and then she had him facedown, a knee in the small of his back. Fury leapt from hiding to assist her, small hands pressing the cityen's cheek into the dirt with only a little more force than necessary. And before his fellows could come to his aid, the other 384s emerged from the shadows, a pair for each of the remaining men. It was more than enough for them to reconsider their plans.

Still hidden, Indine rose from her crouch beside Echo and Gem with a barely audible exhalation. Flo had never been in real danger, though neither she nor the men knew that. The 384 yanked a pouch off her prisoner's belt and tossed it at the others' feet. "Sort out your chits and go home," Flo ordered, releasing her hold on the man. At her nod, Fury let him go as well. Echo let out her own sigh of relief.

The man's friends, grumbling, pulled him upright. One of the Wardmen, seizing the chance, snatched up the pouch, then he and his friend were pounding down the alleyway. "Hey, that's as mine!" the purseless man shouted, as his companions took off in pursuit. He took a few limping steps and stopped, cursing. "You gave them all my chits!"

"Leave them to it," Indine, still hidden in the shadows, ordered the 384s in disgust. "They are too foolish to deserve further assistance from us tonight."

And then Echo heard the familiar metallic click.

"Drop!" she shouted, but it was already too late. The man had Flo by the arm, the projectile weapon to her head. Thank the Saints, the girl had the sense not to struggle as the man drew her back, away from the hunters.

"Let her go, cityen," Echo ordered. Indine appeared to her right, only a few steps away. If they had to charge, he would not be able to hit them both. But Flo would have no chance.

"You two stay away," he snarled, then, to the 384s, "That's as all of you, too." The girls stopped dead still in a loose half circle with him and Flo at the center.

"You have had too much ferm, cityen," Indine said in a conversational tone. On Echo's other side, a shadow moved within the deeper shadows. Indine continued, "We know that these things happen, do we not, Echo Hunter 367?"

"We have seen it before," Echo agreed. It did not

matter what they said, as long as it kept the man's eyes on them. "If you set the weapon down, cityen, nothing else will come of it, other than an aching head in the morning. Tell us, where did you find that?"

"Scum part with anything for a few chits," he mumbled, voice beginning to shake.

"Which scum?" Echo asked in her most encouraging voice. *Be ready*, she told Flo with her eyes. The girl swallowed hard.

"Think I'm stupid? That's as not—" Some instinct must have warned the man. As Gem emerged from the shadows behind him, he turned, presenting a perfect target.

But not for Gem.

Fury darted forward, the eye-blink strike of a desert predator. A thin whine, not even a scream, and Flo tore herself free. The projectile weapon fell harmlessly as the cityen crumpled. The butt of the pointed stick impaling the cityen's eye socket stared balefully at nothing. His body twitched once, twice, then stilled.

"Dead," Fury pronounced with satisfaction. The other hunters, adults and juveniles alike, stood speechless.

"You warned him his head would ache in the morning," Gem said into the stunned silence.

"It is not amusing," Indine said, glaring at Fury. "We needed to know where he acquired the weapon."

Gem stepped over the body to retrieve the device. "We know who he would have called scum."

CHAPTER 15

"It's not right, what it's not." Teller didn't quite dare raise his voice, but Echo could almost taste the anger burning in his belly. His hard tone was more than enough to draw Nyree's ire. "You speak to the Patri, cityen. Do not forget your place."

Teller wasn't too stupid to be afraid; his pupils dilated, but he managed to meet Nyree's stare. The air in the Patri's office was hot and still; Echo smelled Teller's fear as much as she saw it. "I'd be saying the same to anyone. We did some things as was wrong, we know that now, but we made amends, same as the Church demanded. Shouldn't still be paying, then. Shouldn't have our men rousted and our shops and trades shut down on some drunken Norther's word. And he's the one as had the weapon!"

"He paid for his crime," Jozef said. Hunters had

made certain that the man's attack on a child was the focus of reporting on the incident. That the child had been a hunter, and the exact circumstances of the man's death, were details the cityens did not require.

"Why not North, then? The whole Ward is punished, and we've done nothing." Teller's fingers drummed a rhythm of frustration on the table. Tralene laid a hand on his arm; he subsided, scowling.

"The man told the hunters his weapon came from the Ward," the Patri said.

"His exact word was 'scum,'" Nyree added.

"Is that what you think of us?" The lines on Tralene's face seemed deeper today, etched by a resigned sorrow.

"We are not saying you were directly involved," Echo began, but Nyree cut her off.

"Direct or not makes no difference. The Norther had a weapon that came from the Ward. It is your responsibility."

"Respectfully, there's no proof of that," Tralene said, looking past Nyree to the Patri. Her voice shook, but only a little, and underneath was some of Teller's hardness. It called to mind the Warder, who had led the rebellion. Echo had thought him weak, a foolish old man, until the moment he drew his weapon against the Church.

"Then prove your innocence," Nyree said. "Find out who is making the weapons and report to us."

"How are we supposed to do what all your hunters can't?" Teller made to stand; Echo pushed him back into his seat before Nyree could do it. He jerked away from her hand.

"We would tell you, if we knew," Tralene said. "After everything that happened—I swear by the Saint."

She turned to Echo. "You believe us, don't you? You were with us. You know that's an oath we could never go against."

Any answer was a trap. Echo did believe Tralene; the woman would never betray Lia, even in something as trivial as an oath. Teller was another matter. He had been in the Warder's inner circle. Echo remembered the projectile weapon in his hand, the fervent gleam in his eye. If she said so, it would give Nyree all the excuse she needed to declare the Ward guilty. But a defense from Echo would hardly help the Ward in Nyree's eyes. And she did not know what the Patri thought—did not even know, she realized with a lurch in her belly, how much the old Patri had revealed to him about her part in the rebellion. In bringing Lia to become the Saint.

Everyone was watching her, waiting. *You were with us.* It was not only the Wardmen being judged. "Our service to the Saint in all things," she said at last. Then, with a presumptuousness that drew a quick breath of outrage from Nyree: "Remember that when you swear by her. The Church will not act without evidence. But you must be very certain that you honor your oath."

"We're thankful for all the Saint does," Tralene said. "And the Church. Patri, I'm telling you as plain as I know how: we aren't the ones making this trouble, whatever anyone may believe."

"It is not a matter of belief." The Patri's estimating gaze remained on Echo an uncomfortable moment longer before finally moving to the Warders. His thumbs tapped each other, then stilled. "However, you may take this as a fact: the Ward will regret it if the evidence proves you're lying."

"If the Saint could hear, she wouldn't like it," Teller muttered as Echo escorted them out. "Church always squeezing the Ward, and her one of us."

Echo yanked him to a halt in the shadow of the wall. "Don't give them any excuses, Teller."

Tralene pulled him away without another word, leaving Echo alone with dark memories of the Ward, and the rebellion, and the smoke-filled sanctuary where so many things had come to an end.

She dreamed again of the cliff, and falling into a bottomless dark. When she jerked herself awake it was still dark, only a little light from the hall leaking in under the door. In the dimness Khyn's eyes shone softly as the Preserver watched her, head pillowed on her arm, close enough that Echo could feel the small currents her breath made in the air between them. "Have I disturbed your sleep?" Echo asked.

"No." A ghost of her old smile touched Khyn's lips. "There's everything else for that. But you're different here, somehow. Not just because you've cut your hair either. In the Preserve when I watched you sleep— you were a stranger there, far from home, but nothing really bothered you. Even in the desert . . . But here something worries you all the time." Khyn took a breath, two, then said, "You hoped you would find your friend Lia when we got here, didn't you?"

Echo studied the ceiling. She could just make out a lighter patch where the plaster had been repaired recently. Another sign of recovery, owed to the new Saint. "I told you, she is gone."

Khyn touched her shoulder lightly. "I'm sorry."

"Go back to sleep. You require a clear mind for your work with the priests."

Khyn did, after a time; but Echo stared at the irregular borders of the plaster until her eyes blurred and the spot seemed to take on shapes, a cloud, a map, a face that looked down at her and judged. It seemed a long time before dawn turned it back into nothing more than a repaired crack in an old building.

Fury sat at the domicile door. She jumped to her feet when Echo emerged with Khyn, straightening her shoulders and staring straight ahead with red-rimmed eyes. Echo paused. "You've been assigned guard duty?"

The girl nodded, kicking at the dust.

"Guard duty?" Khyn said. "She's younger than Netje." The lines around Khyn's mouth whitened.

Echo knew that thrust of memory, the exile's fear that home would be forever out of reach.

"The assignment is for her benefit." A twist of her own fear shivered through Echo's belly. The cityens might not know what Fury had done, but the hunters did. If Flo had not survived, Fury would not be standing here. Echo's voice came out harsh. "Have you identified your error?" Fury only scowled. "Think harder, then." Echo turned on her heel.

Khyn glanced back, frowning. "That's not like you. What did she do?"

Echo did not answer.

The refectory was packed, even the hunters' corner crowded. Nyree caught Echo's eye, baring her teeth as she indicated the two unoccupied stools next to her and Marin. Echo searched the tables, hoping to find another option, while Khyn dawdled over her selection before settling on bread and cheese again. "I guess I'm getting accustomed to it," she said, lifting her plate with an anxious little smile. That fled when she saw where Echo was looking. "On the other hand, I'm not very hungry. Maybe we can come back later."

It would not do to show weakness. Scanning the room again, Echo saw Brit, Gem, and Indine at a table together, leaving one empty space. "Go sit with them. I will join Nyree." The prospect did no more for her appetite than it had for Khyn's.

Khyn started towards the other hunters with a

combination of reluctance and relief. Then, as Echo made for Nyree's table, Brit rose, gesturing for Echo to take her seat. Echo veered that way, inappropriately relieved herself.

"I have finished my meal," Brit said as Echo set her tray down. Nyree, watching, scowled. "I am only waiting for teachings."

Gem was frowning almost as darkly as Nyree. "If you do not require your cell, you should ask that it be reassigned," she told Echo.

"I was not aware that cells were in short supply." Echo looked over the tables, counting heads. Then she realized: "If I displaced you upon my return, you may have the cell back. I do not care which one I am assigned."

Gem's face flushed, though the fans turned steadily and the refectory seemed no warmer than usual. "That is not what I meant." She cast a glance at Khyn, who reddened as well. They all ate in silence for a time. Then Gem cleared her throat. "I do not recall seeing wind this strong so early in the season."

"Your experience is limited," Indine said, poking a stray grain back into place on her plate. "Echo remembers the 377 winter well, I am sure."

"Orla, Ren and Shiel were killed in a windstorm that season. The aircar crashed when the beacon failed." Echo's utensil made a metallic squeal as she scraped the last grains from her bowl. "That would not happen with the new Saint. The beacon's transmission is strong—at least it was before it was turned off."

"How far out were you when you acquired it?" Gem asked.

"Approximately three days by aircar, if we could fly them that far."

"That is a very long way past the arrays."

Echo had done the calculation more than once. *At least halfway to the Preserve. I could find it again. I could bring more help for Li—for the Saint.*

"Much farther than your estimate," Indine said to Gem. "It is fortunate that Nyree did not accept your suggestion about patrols. It would have been a waste of effort."

"I disagree. A hunter is a valuable resource."

Indine harrumphed. "Echo returned on her own in the end."

Echo stared at Gem. Before she could compose a question, Khyn said, "Those hunters who died—they were friends of yours?" She had peeled the crusts off her bread as usual; now she fiddled with the pieces, stacking them one on top of the other. At least she had not wasted any of the cheese. "That must have been hard."

"They were batchmates."

"Batch—oh." Khyn sat up, meal forgotten. She looked from Echo to Indine to Gem. "I see. I see." Her forefinger traced an eager pattern on the table. "From what little I could get the priests to tell me so far I was thinking—but of course it makes sense, if you don't get your seed from a Vault. And if we can figure out a way to do it with the Preserver line, even Birn couldn't . . ." Her expression changed. "The vektere would be here already if they were coming, wouldn't they?"

"I believe so, yes." An aircar could have covered the distance Khyn and Echo had traveled on foot three times over by now. But sometimes lying in wait, letting your prey grow careless, was a better strategy.

Khyn let out a long sigh. "That's a relief," she said, but the sound in her voice was not all gladness.

"Perhaps," Brit said with a glance at Echo, "they will welcome your return one day if you bring them something of sufficient value."

"I don't know. They must be so angry with me." Khyn seemed about to say something else, then reconsidered, eyes downcast.

Gem swept the discarded crusts into her palm. "Perhaps not. It is likely that they believe that Echo abducted you."

Khyn swung on Echo, eyes wide. "Is that true?" Her voice rose, the way cityens' did when they felt some strong emotion. "You never told me! How could you—"

"Quiet," Brit murmured, but it was too late. Nyree, attracted by the commotion, had left her table and was coming this way, Marin at her side. Perhaps she had not heard Khyn's words.

"Echo Hunter 367 has always kept secrets." Nyree's teeth glinted. "Even from the Patri. Haven't you, Echo?"

"What I shared with the Patri is between me and him." Let Nyree figure out which Patri she meant.

"For example, I am aware," Nyree continued coolly, "that you have not shared everything that happened when the new Saint ascended. But I have heard rumors." Her glance flicked from Indine to Brit to Gem, then back to Echo. "I have heard that it was never your intention to bring us the Saint."

"No doubt he shared what he felt you deserved to know." Nyree had no quick retort; for a moment Echo felt a childish triumph. Then her chest constricted. Indine, Brit, Gem—they had witnessed Echo's weakness in the sanctuary that day, and her shame. They had seen her admit things no hunter should know. Reveal things no hunter should *feel*. They were looking at her now, and she knew they were remembering, the same as she was. If Nyree found out . . . The old fear rose again, only now it was not just for herself. The Saint needed her. She said stiffly, "I am a hunter, Nyree. I serve as the Church requires."

"It is not enough to say so. Service requires obedience. The *Church* requires—"

Brit interrupted with a gesture towards the front of the room. "The Church requires silence at this moment. Priest Dalto is giving teachings."

Dalto's instructions were brief and efficient. The wind was expected to worsen; the nuns and smaller juveniles were reminded to stay within reach of shelter. Meanwhile, the pipes had been repaired so that it was no longer necessary to hand-carry water to the hunter domicile, and a new set of sun-charger panels would be tested when the weather improved.

"Good news," Indine murmured, and the others nodded. Of the Saint, Dalto shared nothing, for none was entitled to know; but Echo thought about the unsolved power surges, and the band around her chest grew tighter. She slipped away from the table before Dalto finished answering questions.

Khyn caught her just outside the door. "You did it on purpose, didn't you?" Echo traced back the conversation, trying to guess which offense she meant, but Khyn continued, "The vektere heard you order me out of the dispensary. Then no one saw us together except Netje, and when they heard her story they would have assumed you made me say what I did. But why didn't you tell me? I've been sick to death, knowing what they must think of me . . ." She broke off, choked, but this time no tears followed.

It is not their judgment that troubles you, Echo thought, but she felt a pang of guilt. She had had her own reasons for not revealing that aspect of their escape. "I regret causing you additional distress. You acted to help the Preserve. That is what should matter to them in the end."

"I know, but . . . Don't you care about what your friends think of you?"

It seemed so long ago that she had sat before the old Patri, fear chilling her bones, knowing for certain, *he is going to have me culled.* Because he judged her weak. Unsound. And now there was a new Patri, who hardly knew her at all, and Nyree. Her stomach fluttered. "Of course. A certain amount of trust in each other is necessary for us to fulfill our functions."

"That isn't all it is," Khyn said, her voice grown wistful. "At least to us." Then her face firmed with a new determination. "But you're right about one thing: I did come to help the Preserve. It's time to get Dalto to tell me more."

A hunter would have been withholding information all along in order to gain leverage. Echo feared that Khyn would finally think of it, now that she realized her people might welcome her back. The priests must get everything they needed first. "The best way to do that is to keep assisting him with the Saint."

"We'll see." Khyn pursed her lips. "What did Nyree mean about you bringing them the Saint?"

"The story does not matter now."

"Another secret?" The breeze plucked a strand of Khyn's hair from her braid; she pushed it out of her eyes. "Well, whatever it was, I'm sure you were doing what you thought best. You don't let much get in your way."

Chairs scraped inside, voices rising as teachings

came to an end. A group of juveniles burst out of the refectory towards freedom, leaving the door swinging on protesting hinges. And there, close by, stood Gem.

Echo hovered by Khyn and Dalto long enough to assure herself that Khyn was still, at least for now, cooperative. Then she sat beside the Saint, watching her as Lia used to watch the cityens she cared for when they slept, or cityens watched over their children. That made her think of Fury and her brother. No one had watched over them. They had survived a long time on their own in the desert before she found them. It was marginally to Echo's credit that she had thought it best to deliver them to the Church. The boy seemed to be doing well enough with the priests. But Fury . . . Perhaps, if they decided she was no hunter, they might not bother to cull her. Simply turning her out would be sufficient. What would happen to her then, a child with no place among Church or cityens . . . It would not matter at all, when that end came, that Echo had meant well by bringing her here. Lia had said it a long time ago: *what you do matters more than what you think.*

Echo stared at the expressionless mask that was the Saint's face. Lia had never looked like that in life. Maybe it was only because the eyes were closed, those luminous golden eyes that had always held a hint of sorrow, even when Lia smiled, or laughed, or looked up from the circle of Echo's arm, contented as if she could have lain there forever . . .

Light filtered down from the rose window above the loft. A haze hung in the air, dust, perhaps, blown in from the yard outside. She blinked hard; it didn't help.

A footstep sounded behind her, so soft that a cityen would not have heard it. "What do you see when you sit here?" Gem asked. She had known Lia, briefly, had hunted her and Echo into the desert and brought them to the Church, when Echo in her weakness sought to flee. To the rest of the hunters—the rest of the Church—she had always been the Saint. It made the figure on the altar seem all the lonelier.

In Echo's silence Gem continued, "I asked the Patri the same thing once. He had no answer either. By then he had become quite weak; he hardly spoke at all, and sometimes when he did, his mind wandered. Once he even called me Echo." Her lips twitched. "He came here often. He seemed comforted when he looked on her." Echo felt a faint surprise that Gem even recognized the feeling; it was impossible to imagine her ever needing comfort. But the line between her brows was there again. "I was here the last time, watching. He may not have been aware."

"You spied on the Patri?" It was outrageous, even for Gem.

The young hunter lifted a shoulder without embarrassment. "I assisted him to the altar, then withdrew. I thought he forgot I was there. But I have wondered, since. He spoke to the Saint, but I am not certain his words were directed only at her. He said, 'I served the Church, but one must serve the Saint. So it must be. We are all made to serve.' It made little sense to me at the time. But now sometimes I think . . . Perhaps he meant me to hear. Or rather, you. It was the day he called me Echo." Gem regarded the figure on the altar a moment more, then left as quietly as she had come.

The Saint blurred in Echo's vision. Too many questions tried to form themselves at once, congealing in a painful lump in her throat, crowding speech from her tongue.

How may I serve? It should be the only question a hunter could ask. But in the bottomless silence of the sanctuary, Echo could only wonder, *how may I serve you?*

It was not the Church she spoke to. Not the Saint.

Lia. Oh, Saints, Lia. I cannot let you go—not if there might be a way—I cannot.

Blasphemy.

But it was not. She knew that old weakness in herself, that she could not put aside her doubt and do as she should. The old Patri, the Saint before Lia—they had used it against her, set in motion the plot that had led her to Lia. That had made her bring Lia to the altar. But now she knew the truth. She saw it happening again, her own hands placing the crown on Lia's head, her own arms holding her until the thought, the consciousness, all that was *Lia* leapt away from her, into the vast city-mind that was the Saint's . . . It should have been over then, and yet . . . *I love you*, she said again, as she had in the last moment of Lia's life, and felt again the pain that seared her heart.

An alarm shrieked, jolting her out of the memory. Echo whirled to see priests stabbing at their boards. The panels flashed, a panicked pattern it took no skill to read. "Divert the power, quickly!" a priest cried, voice rising like the alarm.

"Storage is still full, I can't put it there!"

"Bleed it through the mast," Dalto ordered. Khyn stood beside him, the boards' reflected light flashing in her wide eyes.

"I am! It might not be enough!"

"Disconnect the secondary." Dalto spoke as calmly as a hunter, but the fingers gripping the edge of the panel showed white around the knuckles.

"But that will—"

"Create an outage in the city power lines. I know. Only for a moment. I'll reroute from here. Ready? One, two, three—now!"

The alarm stopped shouting as abruptly as if someone had cut its throat. Echo's heart pounded with fear, but the tense lines of the priests' backs gradually relaxed. "It worked," Khyn breathed.

Dalto sat back with a sigh. "I've set the excess current to alternate between the mast and the storage sink. The fluctuations will stress the system, but it should hold for now. We're going to have to find a better solution soon. If we don't, and these surges keep happening . . ."

"What caused that?" Echo demanded.

"If we knew that, we would stop it." He rubbed his jaw, trying to release muscles that had clenched tight.

But Echo could hardly breathe. Before, she had spoken to Lia in her mind, imagined that the Saint moved. And then, the surge in the system, and the homing beacon shutting off. And now— "Are you certain nothing from within could trigger it?"

"I told you before, the systems don't work that way." Dalto's eyes narrowed; she clamped down on her fear before his suspicion could fully form. After a moment he turned to Khyn. "How do your controllers handle excess power?"

Khyn leaned over Dalto's shoulder to peer at his board. "I wish Stigir were here. He could explain it so much better, but . . . With the stewards the input starts out divided, then it all combines into one final flow. I wonder if you could do the same in the opposite direction? Split the output power into different streams?"

"Split it instead of alternating it . . ." Dalto's fingertip traced the pattern on his board, then tapped a place where the filigreed lines intersected. "This would be the place. What kind of device do you use?"

"The stewards do it from within the link." Khyn's

lips pursed. "Could you make another interface if you wanted to?"

Dalto recoiled. "Only the Saint can wear the crown. The Church would reject anyone else instantly." He glanced into the shadows surrounding the altar. "But we have to think of something. We cannot afford too many more episodes like that. The danger to the Saint . . . Rerouting the power is only temporary, one way or the other. We have to find out what's causing the imbalances."

There was more conversation then, the priests and Dalto, Khyn . . . Echo's mind registered none of it. *Breathe*, she told herself. *See the boards? They are stable. The Saint is stable. Dalto will find a way to stop the surges. Khyn will help him. If not Khyn . . .* The pattern shone on Dalto's screen, pulsing ever so slightly, gold against the green. The power flow, Echo thought. Somehow it looked familiar. And it was beautiful, the filigree of lines and curves, as if the forebears who designed it had tried, despite their desperation, to bequeath some remnant of grace to those who followed . . . Hunters eschewed ornament, the better to blend unnoticed into any background, but cityens liked decoration, some of them even weaving colored threads into their recycled polymer, simply for the enjoyment. They made shiny baubles from the ubiquitous discarded metals and wore them in the ears, in their hair—

In their hair. That was where Echo had seen that

pattern before: in a hairclasp, glinting in the bright light of a workroom . . .

She slipped out of the sanctuary before anyone could ask where she was going.

It was a relief to face a concrete problem. Search, capture, retrieve . . . It took no understanding of the boards, no thought more complex than where her prey might hide. It did take some time to accomplish. Exey was not in his workshop; neither was he at his young brother's habitation in the Bend, the second place she stopped. "I haven't seen him in a few days," the young man said, dandling his baby on his knee; it burbled and blew happy spit bubbles. "I was worried because of the trouble with the Ward—*he's* not in any trouble, is he?"

"If you see him, tell him I was looking."

"I will," the boy promised. "I remember you helped our Lia when Lialy was born. We'll always be grateful." The baby gave Echo a wide one-toothed smile, as if it could understand. She made her mouth shape a curve in response. Perhaps the baby would think it was real.

The boy bit his lip. "You sure he's not in trouble?"

"I need his help."

He bounced the infant up and down. "There is this one place . . ."

The remains of these dead buildings stood taller

than any habitation in the city. Though constructed by men, they seemed to have grown themselves, stone and metal trees stretching towards the sun like the forest in the Preserve. Before the Fall, the priests said, this had been the center of the city; but it had been all but abandoned for hundreds of annuals. Only those too unfit to make their way in the claves, like the vagrants who lived on the city's edge, lived here now; and only the occasional young cityen or hunter bent on exploration visited.

When this building had collapsed in on itself, the debris had made a kind of ladder inside the shaft that cored the tower. Echo wedged herself up level by level, her way lit by daylight sifting in where doors had fallen away. It was not a difficult climb for a hunter, except for the pain in her ankle; for a cityen it would be challenging but doable for the young and agile. Indeed, she saw the signs of passages both old and recent, candle stubs stuck on flat spots, rusted containers that had probably held the adventurers' food or water.

Or ferm. Her nose wrinkled at the yeasty scent gone sour. That meant it had been spilled recently, but not just now. There was light coming from above, dim, artificial. She moved more cautiously, in case she was surprising someone other than Exey. After another ten feet of climb, she came to an opening. The sill was covered with trails of dripped wax where people had set their candles down to boost themselves through. A lightstick, still glowing, was wedged into a crevice.

She pulled herself up and over in one movement, conscious that it left her framed in the doorway. The vestibule the shaft opened into was bisected by a hall. One end was blocked, but the other was clear. The smell of ferm was stronger in that direction, and so was the light. She padded that way silently.

The light, and smell, were coming from a room at the end of the hall, near the building's outer shell. She heard something now too, a faint scratching noise. Crouching beside the door, she paused a moment to let her eyes adjust to the brightness, then snaked a look. Then, with a sigh, she rose and rapped on the doorframe to announce herself.

Exey fell backwards out of his squat, knocking over the small jar sitting next to him. The liquid inside splashed across the floor, adding to the stink. He snatched up the print he had been working on before the spreading puddle of ferm could reach it. The scratching sound had been his stylus over the surface. The mineral scent of ink pierced the sourness of the ferm. It brought a sharp stroke of memory: Lia, taking her careful notes on blank print that Exey had made, while Echo sat across the table watching her.

"Saints!" Exey said, glaring at her. "Can you fly, on top of everything else?"

She plucked the sheet from his fingers. "What are you working on up here?" The print was covered with all manner of sketching: a diagram of something that looked like the grain mill; a simple lock and key; fine lines woven into an oval like the clasp he wore in his hair, with a cable leading from one end. The pigment still gleamed where he'd been adding to the lock and key. Exey snatched the print back, fanning it through the air to dry the ink.

"Just an idea." He gestured at the open square in the wall. "Sometimes I get them from the view." Despite the ferm his words were clear, unslurred.

She stalked to the opening. Wind tugged at her hair. Below, the main road led from the Church doors to the city, an avenue among the buildings that had long since fallen to ruin. The forcewall, invisible even to her from this distance, curved all the way around the city, beyond the inhabited edges. East, the sludgy remains of the river reflected flat black, like a streak of dried blood.

But her eyes, as always, were drawn to the west, where the dish and panels atop the Church spire flashed in the sun. She had flown higher in aircars, of course, but never stood anchored at a height that gave her such a viewpoint. The streets and buildings, alleyways and ruins wove a regular design, filigreed light and shadow like the patterns on the priests' boards. Perhaps this was how the Saint saw the city, everything known to her at once. A yearning pierced Echo's heart. *Do you see me?*

Exey came up behind her. She turned enough that

a stumble, or push, would not send her through the gap. He didn't appear to notice. The gold bauble in his hair sparked like a bit of spire broken off. "I don't suppose you chased me here to see where I get my inspiration."

"The priests need you."

"Can you people not just leave me alone? You've rousted my customers, and half the city probably thinks I'm spying for the Church. Not to mention—" Exey stopped himself, but Echo knew what he had been about to say. He ducked his head to hide his expression. The paper crumpled in his fist. "Would I have to see her?"

She loomed over him, and now he had to think about somebody getting pushed. "If you can help her, you will."

He stared at her a moment more, then whirled with a violent jerk of his arm to fling the wadded paper through the gap. The wind caught it and carried it up, out of sight.

She didn't have time for his anger, or his fear. She had already delayed enough in her weakness. "Do you still have that charge splitter?"

"The one your lovely friend broke into a hundred pieces? I melted them for scrap."

She didn't have time for his games, either. "I know you. You did not make only the one."

He laughed shortly. "Of course not."

Back in his shop, he pulled open a drawer. Echo

tensed, ready to strike, but it wasn't a weapon he withdrew, only a flat metal box with a tangle of wire connectors at each end. "This is the new improved version. Divides the charges, directs them in any combination you want. Very handy if you choose not to depend on the Church for all your power. Though certainly there's plenty to go around these days. The new Saint . . ." Voice trailing off, he lowered his gaze again.

"I need that splitter, Exey. She does. Right now."

His head jerked up. "What for?"

"I'll explain as we go." She thought she might have to force him, but he was grabbing his satchel already, curiosity lightening the shadow in his eyes. He packed the charge splitter, then, after a moment's swift thought, rolled a selection of delicate tools into a cloth.

At the top of the stairs he made to lock the door, then gave up when he saw the damage.

"It holds against most people other than you. Now tell me why you're abducting me, and why Lia needs a charge splitter."

He understood better than she did. By the time they arrived at the Church, he had questioned her as thoroughly as a priest, and it was concentration, not anger, that drew his brows together. He paused on the Church steps, head tilted back to take in the doors soaring three time his height, great planks with worked-metal bindings and a panel where the handle should be. "I've never been inside," he said. He raised a hand tentatively towards the panel.

"It's set only to open to hunters." She laid a palm on the warm metal. The doors could tell more than hunter from cityen, a great deal more. They could choose not to react at all, or to kill with a single charge. Like everything else in the city, some fragment of the Saint's consciousness controlled them, choosing. Judging.

She remembered Lia's lips, warm against her palm. Her fist clenched.

The massive door swung open onto darkness. "Exey. Don't call her Lia. Not here."

CHAPTER 16

Exey was so shocked to find himself face to face with the stranger from beyond the city that he actually fell silent for a moment before bursting into a stream of interrogatives that made Khyn laugh. Dalto was nearly as surprised, though he controlled it better. His eyes grew wide at the sight of the charge splitter, and the citizen who had created it, but he only shook his head. "If a stranger from somewhere we didn't even know existed until a few days ago can help, why not a citizen of our own? And I suppose I should be used to the strange things Echo brings us . . ."

Ignoring the curious priests, Echo sought a place out of the way by the altar. Exey's presence in the sanctuary unsettled her, and not only because he was a citizen. He must suffer the same confusion she had, seeing Lia where there could only be the Saint. After one quickly averted glance, he did not look toward the altar again. But Echo sat by the Saint, counting her breath silently, seeking the calm the Saint deserved of her. Before she could achieve it, Gem interrupted with a summons.

"Nyree wishes to see you. She is at the training ground."

"I have no wish to see her."

The line appeared between Gem's brows. "It is not advantageous to oppose her at every opportunity."

"If you seek some advantage with Nyree that is your affair, but I have no such ambition. I know my place."

"I do not doubt that." Gem's eyes rested a moment on the Saint. "Nyree is waiting."

The training ground was at the farthest edge of the Church compound, where the hunters' activities would not disturb, or endanger, the nuns and priests. The modeled ruins of a city block had been assembled there to allow the practice of maneuvers; both buildings and practice seemed a paltry imitation now that hunters had faced real fighting during the rebellion. Beyond the ruins lay an expanse of flat ground, a rare area with no evidence of previous construction. It was clear enough what it had been; beneath the accumulated dust lay many polished stone panels, traces of letters and numbers still visible on some; and the occasional bone still worked its way to the surface.

Nyree faced the expanse from atop a broken rock wall, shading her eyes to watch a group of juveniles whom Gem went to join. "Why did you bring the fabricator to the Church?"

"Dalto sought his expertise." The juveniles were working in groups to drag the heavy stone blocks into a pile that stood waist high and as wide as a hunter's outstretched arms. Each time a panel fell on top of the pile there was a dull, hollow thud, like a giant heart beating. Not far beyond, another group was setting up tripods made of recovered scraps of metal, legs spread wide at the bottom, the tops bound together with wire wrappings. Gem affixed something to the top of the first tripod, attached a long wire to it, and motioned the juveniles behind her. The object was too small for Echo to make out from here, but a sense of foreboding overtook her.

Nyree said, "A trade shop on the edge of North was broken into last night. The trader was sleeping in the back and heard the noise. When he came out to investigate, he was fired upon by a man with a projectile weapon. He was not injured, and the man escaped. Marin was on patrol; she found the discarded weapon nearby." She jumped lightly from her perch. "The fabricator is known to sympathize with the Ward."

"The rebellion is over, Nyree."

"Tell that to the cityens who have been attacked."

"The city has never been altogether safe. There are not enough of us to patrol every alley, and the fringes—"

"I am not concerned about random crimes. Projectile weapons are different. They made cityens"—Nyree's lips puckered as if the word tasted sour—"a threat to the Church. That threat originated in the Ward. I will not forget. The Church will not."

"I know what happened. I was there."

"With the Wardmen."

Anger rose in a wave, like the heat reflecting from the rock they stood on. "I went where the Patri sent me."

"*Sent* you? The Patri cast you out for doubting him. What service was that?"

"I returned with the Saint. Her ascension ended the rebellion. That danger is past, Nyree. If you cannot see that, you will not be able to see whatever new arises."

"I see trouble enough." Nyree's eyes bored into her. "Much of what is new comes back to you, one way or another. Cityens with weapons more powerful than hunters have. An excommunicated hunter who never meant to return and ran again before anyone had the sense to stop her, who brings a *stranger* to the Church, and who knows how many other enemies on her tail. A Saint claimed by a clave as their own. By the Ward."

"It is blasphemy to question the Saint, Nyree. After everything she—" Echo bit off the words before she revealed too much. If she gave Nyree the slightest reason to suspect her fears, her hopes— *"Blasphemy."*

A sharp *crack* split the air, followed by an explosion of splinters from the pile of stones the juveniles had made. Echo ducked into the cover of the broken wall, searching wildly for an assailant, before she realized that neither Nyree nor the hunters across the way had moved. A thread of smoke rose from one of the objects Gem had affixed to the tripods. The young hunter studied the weapon closely. Echo straightened from her defensive crouch, refusing to acknowledge the juveniles' poorly disguised amusement.

Nyree's lips thinned as she drew them back in something not at all a smile. "It is not the Saint I question."

The wave of anger threatened to sweep Echo over the cliff. "Take your doubts to the Patri, if you have evidence for them. Otherwise let me be." Then she turned on her heel and left Nyree there, watching the young hunters steal stones from the dead.

The confrontation with Nyree left Echo even more unsettled. For all their differences, their worries about the cityens, the weapons, had too much in common. *Hurry,* she silently urged Exey and the priests as they worked to connect the charge splitter. Every moment the Saint was vulnerable felt like a step closer to a cliff's edge in the dark. But the manipulations in the sanctuary made Echo anxious too. "Could the charge splitter harm the Sai—the systems?" she asked Khyn as the Preserver studied the panels.

"It's pretty primitive." Khyn grimaced. "About like hitting someone over the head to help them sleep. At least it should let the priests override whatever power flows from the Saint's side of the circuit. It's a good thing. Surges like that would cook a steward's brain. The Saint seems to be okay so far, but I wouldn't count on it staying that way if the splitter doesn't work."

Echo sat by the altar as if that would somehow help. The instinct was foolish; a hunter could only protect against outward dangers, and those were not what the Saint faced. She could not help wishing that it was Stigir, with his greater understanding, who oversaw the installation. She thought again about the distance to the Preserve, the chances that she could find it again, and what she would do to persuade the Patri, if it came to that . . .

Marin's report at the noon meal did nothing to ease her mind. A Norther's habitation had been burned by a Wardman whose daughter had been wooed then spurned; and the Norther and his friends had chased the arsonist almost all the way to the Ward. Fortunately a hunter patrol had intervened in time to prevent another murder. "I don't know why they were all so angry," Marin said. "The young woman will have a child, which is a desirable outcome for the city as a whole; and the Church will compensate the Norther for the loss of his habitation."

"You forget your lessons," Indine said, taking a portion of greens and arranging them so the stems lined up in parallel across her plate. "The citizens are sensitive to slights, and they hold grudges. Not like hunters."

"That was the reason for the rebellion," Brit concurred. "They were so angry about the nun tithe."

"Not only the tithe," Gem said. "Some of them had visions of a greater change."

"That is not a cityen's business," Indine declared.

Marin passed the platter of greens to Echo. "Finish these, you like them better than I do." Her frown was not for the food. "Cityens have some strong points. They're clever and adaptable; their problem-solving is often quite creative. It is unfortunate that at this moment they are spending so much energy on their disagreements. Do the Preservers have similar difficulties?" she asked Khyn.

Khyn's troubled frown matched Marin's. "Not exactly. Our population is so much smaller, and we're not divided like you into different groups . . . Of course we don't always get along. That's how I ended up here. With some help from Echo of course. But attacking each other, burning habitations—" Khyn shuddered. "Exey told me how awful it was during your rebellion. I can't even imagine. Preservers don't settle their differences like that."

Perhaps not with each other, Echo thought, but they had sent the vektere for her that last day.

The young hunter's gaze was far away. "It is difficult to envision a place so peaceful."

"Marin's not so bad when Nyree's not around," Khyn said later. "She kind of reminds me of Taavi."

Echo nodded without listening, her thoughts still occupied by Marin's report. If the cityens went too far, the Patri would have no choice but to teach a lesson no one would soon forget. And the hunters were arming themselves now as the rebels had done. It would not only be a matter of stunners and projtrodes. Even small disruptions in the city had strained the old Saint, but she had already been failing. Surely this Saint was too strong to be affected by such things. But if real violence broke out . . .

"Do you have a few minutes? Maybe we could go to that little grove." Something in Khyn's tone captured Echo's full attention.

The Preserver paced beneath the small trees, tugging occasionally at twigs. Echo drew a slow breath, trying to pick up the scent of pomme, but the priests had been back through; there were no fruits at all remaining on the limbs. The trees would not bear again until after the vernal rains. At least there was still shade, though the wind had thinned the leaves. "I don't know how you can stand this heat all the time," Khyn said.

Echo waited.

"I've been thinking . . . You know, when I first heard you describe the city . . . I guess I thought it would be like the Preserve, only bigger. But it's so strange here." She pulled a branch closer to inspect a dead twig at the end. "Dalto's told me how the Church used to arrange the most advantageous pairings among the cityens, and he'll explain more as soon as the splitter's in place. After that . . ." The twig broke with a snap; the branch sprang back into place. "Maybe it will be time to figure out how I might get home."

Back to the Preserve. That request would bring its own considerations: whether Khyn could reveal too much now, and what the Church might gain from access to the Preserve, against how much it might cost. What Khyn wanted—what Echo had promised—would count for little, in the end, only what would serve. One way or another, the Patri would have to decide. And Echo remembered the look on the vekteres' faces, when they had come for her after the Preservers made a similar calculation.

Perhaps the same thought occurred to Khyn. "You'll help me, won't you?" she asked, searching Echo's face.

Echo pictured Stigir, taking off the crown.

"Yes," she said.

Khyn snapped another twig. "They're bringing the charge splitter online this afternoon."

The sun felt too hot all at once; sweat trickled beneath Echo's shirt. She and Khyn crossed the compound in separate silences.

The priests sat in their orderly rank at the panels, hands busy with switches and dials, Exey standing a little apart, Dalto giving clipped orders while the machines hummed their soft counterpoint. The familiar sounds seemed only to deepen the silence. Against it Khyn's footsteps tapped a syncopated rhythm. Exey turned their way. "So nice to have someone who gives you warning. Hunters are always sneaking up on people. And the rest of them are just as bad. These priest fellows are happy to let me work in their shop—and what a shop it is!—but they certainly have a knack for not answering a question. Shows you what kind of trader I am, giving away my baubles for free." He touched a hand to his hair, but it was tied back with a bit of string. "Ah, well, lost that one too. I'll make another, when I get a chance . . ."

He had always talked too much when he was nervous. The anxiety was contagious. Echo's belly churned as she left him and Khyn alone. The charge splitter made a gleaming ornament amidst the dull patina of the ancient wiring. New connections ran from it to the boards, and in the other direction back towards the altar. The Saint herself was lost in shadow.

Dalto had stopped giving orders. The pattern on his board pulsed steadily, blue and green and yellow. He watched, face a mask of hunterlike concentration.

Echo peered over his shoulder, trying to understand what he saw. *It is for the Saint's good*, she told herself; but her heart was pounding. "All is in order," Dalto said at last. "The circuit is stable in isolation. Now we must see if it is compatible with the Saint. Toler, confirm your boards."

The priest on the far right nodded. "Ready, Dalto."

"Radnish?"

"Ready."

"Stepan?"

The young priest in the middle did not answer immediately. The orange and yellow light from his panel reflected like firelight across his high cheekbones.

"Stepan, confirm your readiness."

"A moment, Dalto." His thin fingers made the barest adjustment to a dial, and the panel's colors cooled. "I confirm my board."

"Merick?"

"My board is ready, Dalto."

"Very well." Dalto took a deep breath. Echo's chest tightened.

And then, for an instant, she almost had it: the pattern flickering as the priests tuned their panels, the balance, the unspoken language of the Saint's mind as she lay, not sleeping at all, but casting her awareness all across the city she loved—

Do you see me?

"Switch the circuit over."

The alarm whooped as power surged.

"Quickly!" Dalto ordered. "Activate the splitter!"

The pattern flew apart. What had been a single note divided, like the wind whistling through wires, sliding up into a grating dissonance that made Echo's whole body clench. Exey turned wide-eyed to Khyn. "What's wrong?" he whispered urgently. "It's not supposed to hurt her!" She put a finger to her lips, shushing him.

Stepan's board flared into orange, then red. "I have it," Stepan said, tuning a dial before Dalto could speak. "I have it." The red faded, and the machine hum softened, the dissonance fading.

Dalto traced a pattern on his own panel. "Your board is steady," he confirmed. "Radnish, decrease your input. Merick, turn yours up two clicks."

"Yes, Dalto," the priests chorused.

Then it was quiet for a long time while the priests worked, Dalto occasionally calling instructions, but softly, and the fluctuations in the panels no worse than the usual flickers. Echo's breathing slowed in tandem with the pattern, though something in her gut still tensed. Finally Dalto's shoulders lifted and fell, and he pushed his chair back from his panel. Damp patches darkened his robes under his arms. "It is working," he said. "Thank the Saint. Her output is stable, and we can divide it among the circuits as needed." He shook his head to himself, his pale face creasing in a half-disbelieving smile at the board he watched. Khyn stood tugging her braid, lips quirked to one side in an odd expression of relief touched by sadness.

Exey glanced towards the altar, biting his lip.

Echo drew him that way. The Saint lay still in the shadows; the machines droned steadily. Echo imagined something heavy about the quiet, a muffled quality that had not been there before the splitter. *That is as it should be*, she told herself, but a weight seemed to sit on her heart too. "Look, Exey, she is at peace."

The fabricator stood, head bowed, pinching the bridge of his nose. Echo hesitated, then moved back a respectful distance from his grief. She tried not to look, but her eyes kept stealing to the Saint. It was foolish, she knew, as if she watched someone who had been ill fall into a restful sleep, and kept checking needlessly to see if she still breathed. But the Saint's face was so distant, empty . . . And then Exey gave a stifled cry, and fled from the sanctuary. "Let him go," Dalto said. "He has given us what we need. We can control the Saint."

Echo told herself that she was glad.

The next morning the Patri came to see the splitter. The look in Jozef's eye reminded Echo of the time she had watched him in his laboratory, deftly maneuvering tiny instruments to harvest the eggs that would become the next batches of hunters. The old Patri had made him let her look through his magnifier. The small nubbin of flesh beneath the lenses became the whole world when she stared through the eyepiece. Perhaps Jozef saw everything that way. Now, as he studied the Saint, his fingers twitched, as if they manipulated instruments still.

It was the only part of her that mattered, Echo had said to herself, watching them dissect Ela's ovaries.

She had not believed it even then.

CHAPTER 17

The splitter's installation came not a moment too soon. The city trembled above the precipice. First a shop in the Ward burned, which might have been an accident, or revenge. Then another body appeared on the fringes between the claves; it belonged to a man from North known to have unsavory associations in other claves. The projectile wound in his chest could not have been an accident. And the hunters were no closer to eliminating the threat. They checked every smithy, but found no sign of weapons being forged. "You might wouldn't," Tren told them when they stopped in North. "Know you're coming, a smith could as hide anything he wanted. But look around my shop, all as you think fit."

"We have no reason to suspect you," Nyree said.

"Look anyway, esteemed hunter. I won't have

the other claves say as North got special treatment."
They found nothing, of course.

Now it was a market day, when all the cityens
would rub up against each other. That might spark
any manner of trouble. The hunters planned to patrol
in enough force to discourage trouble, yet not so
much that their presence itself provoked it. The juveniles would be there too, to give the appearance of an
exercise and not a threat.

But Fury was missing. No one had seen her, Indine
reported, since last evening's meal, when her penance
for killing the cityen had ended. "If she's run off, all
the better for her."

Echo, fighting a surge of panic, thought of all the
accidents that could happen, even inside the Church
compound; of the time she had seen a young hunter
kill another, near this very spot, in a training exercise
gone wrong. And Fury had made no friends among
the juveniles . . . "She wouldn't just run."

"Why not?" Indine asked sensibly.

"Because—" All at once Echo knew where to
look. She ran for the priests' domicile without explanation. There, in an empty room near the laboratories, she found the boy sounding out the letters from
a print, Fury curled up at his side, listening with her
eyes aglow. "Then the base pairs match up in two
comple—comple—"

"Complementary," Echo said from the doorway.
Both children jumped; a juvenile hunter would have

heard her. "Come Fury. Your batch is assembling to help patrol the market. You are late."

"I want t'hear about the denas," the girl objected.

"Another time. You must fulfill your duty."

"Go on," the boy said. "Don't want no more trouble with them. Send you away for good."

"Who told you that?" Indine, it must have been. She was only looking for an excuse.

He only shrugged. Fury hugged him, so hard he squeaked, then punched him lightly on the arm. "More later," she ordered, and scurried past Echo up the steps.

The boy's face crooked into a worried grin as he watched her go, but it turned hard again when he looked at Echo. "What d'you want?" he asked when she did not follow Fury away.

"Nothing," she almost answered, as she had in the desert when she had first found the children, but it was no more true now than it had been then. "What do they call you here?" she asked instead.

"Andrik."

"That's a cityen's name. Who gave it to you, the priests?" Her heart sank at the thought that he fit in no better than Fury.

"My patr'. Fore he died."

All the time in the desert, she had never asked. It was the one thing Lia had been truly angry with her about. "I'm sorry," she said, to the boy, to the memory.

"Won't matter when you go 'way again."

Now she understood. Twice she had abandoned them, once in the desert, then again here. "I'm sorry," she said again. "Andrik. If I could have—" But she could have, and they both knew it. That she had chosen duty made it no less a choice.

He flipped the print open again, eyes fixing on the page. The stony silence followed her up the stairs and out into the yard. For once she did not seek comfort from the Saint.

The sky over the market square shone metallic gray. The priests predicted worsening wind, but this morning there was nothing more than a steady breeze, welcome in the heat. Echo crouched in concealment on a high fragment of cemented stone, all that remained of a building that had fallen to ruin long ago. The market was neutral territory, sacrosanct among the three claves, but tension stretched the city tight.

Despite the violence, no one appeared to have stayed home. The square was packed. Vendors called out, enticing cityens to try their wares; buyers haggled with sellers, enjoying the sport as much as the exchange of chits and merchandise. Carts were loaded with small sacks of grain; whatever shortages Kennit and the councilors feared, it wasn't stopping ordinary cityens from trading their portions for goods they wanted more right now. Echo wondered if they'd regret those trades in the hungry days of winter, before the vernal rains brought the next flush of green to the fields. Likely not: the long view had always been the Church's domain.

A twist of smoke, carrying the delicious smell of roasted bovine, rose from a group of wheeled metal boxes set apart from the more flammable parts of market. The customers clustered there were fewer, and better dressed. Bovine meat remained a delicacy; most of the animals that grazed in the fields by the stads were kept for milk and the hard cheese that made Khyn wrinkle her nose. Across the square, long wires were strung with a variety of the skirts and trousers and shirts that cityens wore. The vendors who dealt in polymer had set their stalls just beyond, providing rolls of combed-fiber cloth, various thicknesses of thread, and other goods that those who made their own clothing would need. At the very end of that row a woman had set out a small tray of cutting tools, the reclaimed metal gleaming in the sun.

Tools meant a smithy. Or a shop. Echo searched among the Benders' stalls for Exey's cart. From this height she should be able to recognize the sun-charging panels he had mounted on top. But either he wasn't here, or he no longer had the panels; in any event, she saw no sign of him, nor had she since he'd fled the sanctuary after the splitter was installed. The priests were asking about him; apparently his estimation of his skills was not entirely exaggerated. She stifled a flash of anger. His pain was a poor excuse to deprive the Saint of a resource. She would find him again.

The morning wore on without incident. She was just starting to think the hunters' precautions were wasted when she saw it: an eddy in the crowd around the food stalls, where the steady flow of cityens was becoming turbulent in one corner. An argument, perhaps haggling gone too far; as she watched, a hand shading her eyes, the turbulence spread.

She leapt down from her perch, angling towards the trouble. She didn't run; a panic in the market could turn into a deadly stampede. But already the voice of the crowd was changing. The cheerful babble developed an anxious overtone, and cityens left off their purchases to look around in puzzlement as more and more of their fellows pushed their way down the narrow aisles, away from whatever was going on. They weren't running either, and they hadn't yet decided to abandon the baskets and heavy bags that were impeding their progress; but the sense of flight from danger grew more acute. Echo slipped upstream against the flow, until she met a wall of cityens, mostly young men, many of them stinking of ferm. They were not fleeing but pushing and shoving each other to get a better view. Most likely they had nothing to do with whatever was happening up ahead, but they were already beginning to glower at each other and curse. She had to put an end to this quickly.

"I told you as to get away from here!" A burly man had a club out from behind his cart and was waving it in a practiced arc back and forth across his body. A few pommes had spilled from his cart; Echo smelled the fruity sweetness where one had split open on the stone. Memory stabbed at her, another market, a pomme shared with Lia—she took a quick breath to dispel it and focused on the men in front of her. "I'm not selling to any the likes of you," the vendor told someone. "I don't care how many chits as you offer. It'll never be enough." Beside him, a few of his fellow traders, similarly armed, nodded agreement.

"Market's neutral ground," the object of his ire said. That man had a larger group of friends, but they were empty-handed. "You got no right to refuse my custom."

"Is there a problem, cityens?" Echo stepped forward with a suddenness that made them all take notice. She stood feet spread and shoulders square, hand resting lightly on the projtrodes at her belt. She hoped these men hadn't yet got into their ferm. If she had to use her weapon, she could trigger the panic she sought to prevent.

The crowd eased back a bit, but the trader only pointed with his club. "Wardmen thieves as want to buy my grain? I'm thinking not. They've already taken as more'n their share."

"That's right, Rolt," one of his comrades said. "Remember the grain count."

"There was a misunderstanding," Echo said, trying to keep her voice light. "The Church sorted it out."

"And thanks for that," the Norther said. "But I'm still not selling to them."

"He's got no right," the Wardman complained. "Look." Something flashed in his palm. Echo had the projtrodes out even faster, pointed at his chest. Gasps and exclamations sounded all around. The man's hands flew up in panic; gold and copper scattered at his feet. "It's only chits!" he cried.

Taking a deep breath, she lowered the trodes. "Here is what I want," she said, loud enough for everyone to hear. "You cityens"—she turned a hard hunter stare on the restive observers, in case they thought they'd escaped her attention—"clear this area. You Wardmen can find another place to make your purchase. The rest of you pack up your stalls. This part of market is closed."

"How's that as fair?" the vendor asked, outraged. "We aren't the ones as started the trouble."

"Then do not be the ones to make it worse."

"See?" the Wardman said, sneering. He stooped to gather his chits back into his pouch, snatching up one of the fallen pommes as well. "Should've just sold me my grain like I asked."

"Pay him for the pomme, cityen," Echo said.

"It was going to waste," the Wardman complained,

but he tossed a bit of copper to the vendor, who caught it with a practiced hand. Then he held it up between thumb and forefingers so everyone could see.

"Ward's chit? I wouldn't take that rebel trash no matter as who was paying." He spat on it and flipped the disc, spittle and all, right into the Wardman's face.

The Wardman leapt forward. Echo caught him with a foot behind the ankle and a quick tug on his sleeve that tumbled him to the ground. The Norther was already scrambling over his cart, club raised; she stripped it from him as she knocked him back with a flat hand to the chest. He clutched himself, eyes wide with surprise, then stumbled into his cart, falling heavily. The crowd, which had been trickling away down the main aisle, paused with renewed interest.

"All of you," Echo ordered, "sit down where you are. Now."

Cityens had killed hunters in the rebellion. Only a few, and the price had been great; but now they knew it was possible. A man raised his chin a little, sniffing the air like a predator deciding if its larger prey were weak enough yet to take down. She focused a hard stare squarely at him, raising the trodes for good measure. Self-preservation prevailed; he folded to the ground, hands in the air.

No one else objected to her order. She slipped the projtrodes back in her belt. The market-goers would sense the trouble abating, return to their business, panic averted. But it had been far closer than Echo liked. The vendor from North still lay where he had fallen by his cart. One of his friends knelt next to him, white-faced. "He's dead!"

"Dead?" Echo reached down, feeling his neck for a pulse, found none. She stepped back, dismayed.

"You killed him!"

A shocked silence spread over the circle of sitting men. It was one thing for them to fight each other. But for a hunter to intervene, and a cityen end up dead, when it was the hunters who were supposed to save them from themselves—

The high, flat *crack* echoed across the square. The cityens whirled, wild-eyed. They knew that sound as well as she did. "Get down," she snapped at them, and raced in the direction the noise had come from, ignoring the stab of pain from her ankle. Folly to run at danger, but there was no choice. She couldn't let whoever had fired that weapon get away. Her whole body tensed, bracing itself against the invisible blow that could fall any second. Then she heard a different noise: footfalls up ahead, quick and light. Moving towards her. She froze, hugged tight against a wall. Closer. She eased the projtrodes from her belt. Closer. Around the corner and—

She jerked her hand aside just in time to send the trodes into the ground instead of the girl. "Fury! What in the Saint's name are you doing here?"

"Caught th' hunter!" The girl put on a triumphant grin, but her wide eyes followed the trodes as Echo rewound them. "Supposed t' be with Deann, but heard a noise. That weapon, like before." Fury had been in the city alone at the start of the rebellion. Alone because Echo, to her shame, had used her as a decoy while she escaped with Lia. "Knew was you running. Wanted to warn."

"Do you know where the noise came from?"

"Th' mill. Show you."

"No!" Echo caught the girl back roughly. "Get Deann. Tell her"—a juvenile might be useful as a distraction, two juveniles could certainly aid in a fight, but against projectile weapons—"tell her to bring reinforcements."

Echo knew the mill Fury meant. Each clave had small towers repurposed from grander structures that no longer functioned in the curtailed world, polymer vanes using wind to drive the gears. The Ward's was just ahead. Exey had designed its new mechanism, and its fine-ground flour made the best bread in the city. Echo had shared that bread at many a meal with Lia.

Why someone would fire a weapon there . . .

A minute later Echo sheltered behind an empty cart outside the mill. Most days at this time the place would be bustling with activity. Today, with everyone at market, it appeared to be deserted. The windwheel on its tower still hummed, wings ablur, and the long jackscrew turned, but inside the squat building, all was silent. White-powdered bootprints tracked out from the single door, mingling with the dust. Echo crept forward noiselessly, making herself as small a target as she could.

The door stood ajar. She paused, a hand on the latch, listening, but still heard nothing. With a single motion she flung the door open and threw herself in a roll across the floor. The roll ended in a leap upright, her knees bent in a fighting crouch, trodes in hand.

Nothing happened. The silence was broken only by steady whir of the turning screw; she heard nothing else. No one so much as breathing. The mill's gearing had been disengaged, the great stones motionless. Empty grain sacks lay piled on a table, their former contents no doubt among the goods being sold at market today. White dust, disturbed by her skidding roll, hung in the air. Straightening, Echo blinked flour from her eyelashes. It dropped in tiny flakes, disappearing into the slowly spreading stain on the floor.

She hadn't heard the man breathing because he was not. His blood mixed with the flour in a sticky pink paste, stirred into little mounds were his dying hand had scrabbled in it. The weapon lay nearby.

She squatted to examine the man more closely. There was a small hole in one side of his belly, and a much bigger one higher up on the other flank. The air smelled of offal. She chose not to search through the mess for what might be left of the projectile. Something glinted in the gore, a chit, perhaps, the last trade the dead man would ever make. But no, it was bigger, more delicate. A flat-beaten clasp of golden filigree. She pocketed it, then rose to survey the room again. Her initial impression had been inaccurate. Not all the grain sacks were empty. The one on the table was still half full.

But not of grain.

She heard steps outside now, familiar ones. She tried ineffectively to brush the soft dust from her hands, leaving white streaks down the front of her trousers. A shadow appeared in the door.

Nyree's sharp gaze moved from Echo to the dead man to the weapons on the table. "Caught the hunter," she said.

CHAPTER 18

Gem squatted with her elbows on her knees, studying first the fallen weapon, then the dead man's wounds. "I believe we are meant to believe that he discharged the weapon accidentally. However, the angle suggests otherwise."

"Murdered, then," Nyree said with a hint of satisfaction.

"I did not kill him," Echo said. "Use sense, Nyree. Half the market heard the noise. I was still with the Northers."

"That hardly went any better."

The air reeked. Echo paced, her thoughts just as foul. Without witnesses, the hunters couldn't know all that had happened here, but what they had found was all Nyree would need. Gem examined the weapon, sighting down both barrels and disengaging the trigger mechanisms before dropping it in the sack with the rest. "This is the last of them."

"For now." Nyree stood frowning, hands on hips. "The Wardmen must distribute them from here. The traffic in and out would be good cover. But that still doesn't tell us where they're made."

"I want to take these back to examine further. They appear to be of the new design, but the one that fired is defective. The second mechanism would not have functioned. The others seem to be the same. I think—"

The door swung open to admit Cara, slightly out of breath. "Northers are on their way, Nyree. I don't know how they heard so soon."

"How are they armed?"

"Clubs and knives. No projectile weapons as far as we've heard. If we move now, we can intercept them before they cross into the Ward itself."

"We must stop them," Echo urged. "If North and Ward break into open conflict . . ." It brought back too fresh a memory, mobs of cityens attacking each other before turning on the Church, and too real a fear. The rebellion had damaged the old Saint beyond recovery.

"*We* will," Nyree said. "Not you. Take these weapons back to the Church, if you can manage that without creating a worse incident. Cara and Gem, with me." She was out the door without waiting to see that Echo obeyed.

Anxiety roiled Echo's gut. She came within a breath of following the other hunters to the fight. Then sense prevailed. Her place was with the Saint.

But the knot in her belly grew tighter all the way back to the Church.

"**W**hat is the Church going to do?" Kennit was half out of his chair, leaning towards the Patri with both palms pressed to the table. "North as deserves to know, after all as been done to us!"

"You deserve what the Patri decides, cityen," Nyree said coldly. "More might be dead than just the one in the mill if we had not gotten to the Ward first."

Kennit had the sense to sit back down. "Apologies, Patri," he said, voice brittle. "Our men, they were only so upset as they didn't have time to think what they were doing. I'm grateful as the hunters stopped them from making a terrible mistake. But that leaves the Wardmen still to learn their lesson. We know as what was found in the mill. The rebellion started in the Ward, and it still festers there."

"It's the Church's duty to teach the cityens, Kennit. There can be no doubt of that." Jozef's tone was mild, but tension chiseled the planes of his thin face. For all its progress since the Fall, humanity still teetered on the edge of a cliff. A small push was all it would take to tumble them back into the dark. They might not climb out a second time.

Then Echo thought of the Preserve, and the seed stored in the Vault. For a dislocating moment, she was back there, listening to Stigir speak of the rebirth of the world.

"I understand, Patri." The prominence in Kennit's throat bobbed. "But the old Patri, he used to call us his children from time to time. He said with children so precious, a man loves them all; and he wants them as to have everything easier than he did himself. But without firm direction, they can run themselves into trouble. The more as he loves them, the firmer he needs to be. That's as he said."

The Patri folded his hands. "The miller is in custody. He told us the dead man was a customer of his, who had asked to meet him after market. He claims that he knows nothing of weapons. We are searching the area even now, to be sure there is no other cache." That was mostly for show. The hunters would never be able to clear the city of weapons, not unless they eliminated the source. The gold clasp weighed in Echo's pocket.

"We're glad of that, Patri," Kennit said. "Seems as the Wardmen are bolder every day, there's no knowing what might happen next. And then our man Rolt—" Kennit's voice trembled, but it was as much with anger as with fear.

"The Ward did not kill your man," Nyree interrupted unbidden.

Echo bit back an angry retort. It served no one to

remind North that now they had a grievance against a hunter as well as the Ward. Kennit pointed an accusing finger at her. "And it's not as he was attacking children, or had a weapon either. Rolt was innocent. That's the one as killed him, is it not? The same one as was in with the Wardmen before the rebellion. That's as they say. Asking your forgiveness, Patri, but it would be a terrible thing, wouldn't it, if a hunter as took sides? Favoring the Ward, as maybe it is, against the other claves? In all the nerves, Patri, with people so frightened—a sign from the Church would go a long way."

"A sign?"

"Something as to make us understand the Church still favors North equal as the others, that's all I'm asking, Patri. It seems a small thing, after all as has happened."

The Patri's thumbs chased each other in circles. A coldness spread through Echo's gut. No single hunter was worth more than the Church's interests. Perhaps this was what Nyree intended: a debt easily paid, a way to give North some satisfaction. The old Patri had made many such calculations. Echo forced herself to stand still, equally expressionless. If it kept the peace—a part of her almost hoped that Jozef had the strength. *We are made to serve.* And then, as the Patri still hesitated, she heard herself say, "I regret the man's death. It was an accident."

Kennit's eyes jerked to her, blinking in confusion.

Nyree flashed her a look of plain contempt before the hunter mask closed over her expression. The Patri only leaned back thoughtfully, his thin face telling her nothing. "I understand the man's heart was weak," he said at last.

"Ah, yes, that's as was known," Kennit stammered.

"Yet he tried to attack the Wardman."

"Was only self defense, as was, the Wardman started it all."

"With a weak heart a man's friends might have wanted to keep him out of a fight, I should think."

"Rolt was a stubborn man," Kennit allowed.

The corner of the Patri's mouth drew down. "I understand how that can be. Explain to your friends that the hunter was just trying to protect him. Tell them how sorry she is that she failed." Echo stifled an absurd flash of resentment. The Patri continued, "Remind them too, Kennit, that the man with the projectile weapon ended up dead. *That* is the most important lesson here."

"I—yes, Patri, that's as I will." The heat rose in Kennit's voice again. "But that still leaves the matter of the Ward. Patri, one more thing I want to tell. You know already, but I'm saying so as you hear that we know too. Church as it should be, North remembers. If Wardmen are forgetting, whatever lesson they need, North is willing to help teach. Our men are ready. Howsoever you see fit, we'd do all as you ask."

Saints. He was offering to be the Church's weapon against the Ward.

Jozef smiled grimly. "Thank you, Kennit, but that won't be necessary. I know exactly what to do."

"Cut the power to the Ward?" Dalto, hovering over his board as if to protect it with his body, stared at the Patri in shock. The other priests fixed their eyes on their panels, pretending not to notice; but one bit his lip, and another's hand froze over a dial. Khyn, a fixture among them by now, looked equally appalled, her gaze darting from the Patri to Dalto and back.

"Only for a time." Jozef gestured impatiently. "It can be done, can it not?"

"With the splitter in place, yes, we can control the flow precisely. And with the Saint so strong"—Dalto sounded just like Exey for an instant, before his better sense kicked in—"but cut power to the city, even a part—we have never done such a thing. The cityens will think the Saint is dying. There will be panic."

"Yes. Then we will explain. It will remind them how much they still depend on the Church." Jozef tapped his fingers on the panel, a gesture that made him for a moment seem oddly like Teller. "I thought they had learned the lessons of the rebellion. I wanted to believe it was only a few malcontents. I *hoped*. But we cannot escape the evidence. Claves arming themselves, provoking others to violence—the Saint only knows what they were thinking." He broke off, look-ing towards the altar. "Perhaps she does. There has never been a Saint who was a cityen."

And he would make her punish them, when all her sacrifice had been to save the city. A surge of anger burned in Echo's chest. "Patri, it is too much. The Ward's children, their sick—without power, their lights, their wells won't even run. Even if someone in the Ward is making the weapons—"

"There is no *if.* You yourself found the proof in their mill." Jozef's laugh was mirthless. "'Church as it should be.' What a mess Vanyi gave me to deal with. Can you imagine what he would do in my place? Yes, the Wardmen will be frightened. Some may be hurt. But everyone will learn the lesson." Jozef's boney shoulders rose and fell. "If it is the worst we have to teach, we'll count ourselves lucky. Now do it."

Echo clenched her fists behind her back. Her anger was not all for the Patri. If the Wardmen were not such fools, if she had been quicker to stop the disturbance in the market . . . Dalto worked at his board giving instructions, the priests setting dials and switches, confirming positions. Khyn sat at the board they had rigged by the splitter. It lit her face from be-neath, like the fires she and Echo had shared in the desert, but her eyes were shadowed. By the set of her features, her thoughts were grim. Echo felt a thread of unease. Things that had never been done, tech that was new—what if the power did not come back on?

It seemed a terrible risk. Yet the Patri was right. The cityens—all of them, for this was a lesson for more than the Ward—must learn. The city would not survive another rebellion.

But the Saint did not deserve this.

As Echo watched, the boards changed, a part of the pattern separating from the rest. It was like seeing the city from the tower room, only in colors and flashing lights. She felt a touch of surprise, close to fear. *The Saint's thoughts are not for a hunter to understand.* Then she dismissed the notion. These were not thoughts, only signals in a circuit. When Dalto gave the last order, a priest would move a switch, the splitter would change the flow, and the part of the board that stood for the Ward would go dark.

She would not let the Saint see that alone.

Unnoticed, Echo slipped out of the sanctuary and took the ladder-like stairs that led from the vestibule up to the loft. She would watch with the Saint. At least she could offer that. What it must be like for her— the whole city her body, Ward or Bend or North as close as her own hand, the pumps and power lines her veins and nerves . . . Would it hurt, what the priests were doing?

Echo's eyes stung suddenly. Instead of Khyn she should have brought Stigir, whose expertise was so much greater. He would have known how to control the surges without the splitter, Khyn had said so. Echo should have trusted the hunters to handle the vektere, and the Patri to persuade Stigir. Even if they had simply left the beacon on, giving the vektere a trail to follow, one the hunters could watch, prepared for what might come . . . Instead she had acted in fear, cutting off all chance of contact between the city and the Preserve. Now the Saint was helpless in the hands of the priests, forced to act against cityens, against her own clave . . .

Stop acting like an untrained juvenile, Echo told herself with contempt. To imagine the Saint weak and helpless as a cityen only insulted her. It served no one, the Saint least of all.

The heavy, muffled silence weighed on the air inside the sanctuary, the charge splitter a barrier between the Saint and any disturbance. Yet if there was any chance the Saint could know Echo's thoughts in some strange fashion, as she felt the city need more power here to make a lightstring glow, or there to shape the forceshield keeping out the wilderness . . . Lia was gone, subsumed into that vast consciousness, but Echo knew no other way, and surely the Saint, if she could know at all, would not scorn her offering, little as it was—

Echo fixed the image of Lia in her mind, and thought: *I am here.*

The loft was silent. In the sanctuary below, the priests continued their work; she heard the steady stream of their voices, the occasional counterpoint from Khyn. The process must be difficult; a treacher-

ous part of her hoped they would fail. She cut off the
thought as ruthlessly as the Patri prepared to cut the
power.

I am with you.

The voices below changed, brief questions from
Dalto drawing even shorter answers, call then response, a kind of chant. Then a long, long pause, and
a single word.

Echo must have heard the switch click, though
she didn't register the sound. It was like the shock
after a blow, in the instant before the pain starts.
She felt the systems stagger, balance failing, as when
the expected ground beneath a foot disappeared and
the next step was into air, the body falling, tumbling
over the edge—

No! Not you! I will not let you fall, Saints, Lia, I—

So strong was the instinct that her arm was actually reaching, hand raised to catch Lia's before
she fell, just as she reached for her every night in
the dream. But as in the dream, her fingers closed
on empty air, and she was turning from the rose
window, crying *Lia, Lia,* when, between one beat of
her pounding heart and the next, she heard it.

Echo. Everything stopped, impossibly, even gravity
suspended. She froze, still to her core. If she moved,
even in her mind, the gossamer thread would snap.
Echo, is that you . . .

A high-pitched scream sounded from below.

Echo threw herself down the ladder as a priest

leapt to his feet. In the next instant she realized the sound had been mechanical; but it was followed by a real grunt of pain as a sparking wire snapped against the priest's hand. A thread of smoke floated up from the charge splitter; Khyn stood staring at it, knuckles white in the fingers clutching the end of her braid. The priests sat motionless, eyes fixed on their boards as they awaited Dalto's orders; but he too was frozen, staring not at his boards but at the Saint.

"What is happening?" Echo hissed at Khyn.

The Preserver shook her head. "Dalto made the last input, then there was one big surge, and—"

The door flew open, admitting Gem. "The mast is sparking!" the young hunter reported calmly, but her eyes were wide.

Her words jolted the room back to life. "She's streaming all the excess charge through it," Dalto said, hands flying over his board. "It will hold."

The Patri peered over his shoulder, as wide-eyed as Gem. "It had better," he said through thinned lips. Dalto punched more buttons; the other priests matched with their own responses as he snapped orders, one after another.

None of that mattered to Echo. All she could think was *Lia*. Every other thought was frozen, even her heart seemed not to beat in the infinite time it took to see the panel lights settle, the pattern return to normal as the sanctuary's hum—the Saint's voice— grew whole again. It couldn't have taken more than a minute. The sharp edge of relief cut through her chest with a physical pain, at the same moment that Dalto spoke.

"We have regained control," the priest reported, but his lips pressed thin and white, and the skin around his eyes pulled tight. He shook his head at his board as if he could not believe what it told him. "Or rather, the Saint—" He stopped, took a breath, and said more calmly, "Power is steady—everywhere in the city, including the Ward. The system rejected the command."

"*Rejected the command?*" The Patri's voice rose in disbelief. "How is that possible?" The charge splitter no longer smoked, though the smell of burned polymer lingered. The priests eyed their panels warily, hands poised for quick action. Behind the anger in Jozef's voice Echo heard something else. *They fear her,* Gem had said.

"It should not be," Dalto said. A bead of sweat trickled from his temple down to his jaw; he wiped it, then stared at his fingertips. "The surge must have overwhelmed the inputs. The feedback from that destroyed the splitter, but we have stabilized the flow."

"Are you sure you have control?"

Dalto took a long breath. "This Saint—I am sure of nothing."

His uncertainty terrified Echo. "Patri," she began. Jozef's head jerked around. Before he could speak she said quickly, "The Preservers could help. Khyn says that Stigir knows more than she does. He might know some way of balancing the circuits, some new technology . . ." Khyn nodded, eyes fixed intently on the Patri.

He said, "Speculation helps nothing. They are not here."

"I can find them again, only give me an aircar. Surely it is worth trying." *Anything* was worth trying. Saints, Lia . . . Even as Echo watched, a panel light flickered; Dalto steadied it, but his hand trembled. "Or we could signal them in some way—" Hope surged through her. "Turn on the beacon. If they still are looking for Khyn, if they see—"

"If, if, if. Leave me alone."

Her fists tightened; she forced them open. He was the Patri. He could not simply turn away. Any resource, any slimmest chance to help the Saint . . . the Preservers understood about the crown, and the strain on those who wore it.

Stigir had removed his crown.

Echo tried a final time. "Patri, I am begging you. We must—"

He whirled, and she knew at once that she had gone too far. "Do not say *must* to me, hunter. You have made me too much trouble as it is. Get out of the sanctuary. Speak to no one of what happened here. Go *now*, before I order you out of the Church altogether."

Why couldn't he see? Her jaw clenched as she bit

back her reply. She knew—Belatedly, she realized what the Patri threatened her with. Excommunication, or worse. Once the mere idea would have sent her to her knees. Now all she could think was that she must not give him an excuse. Not when the Saint needed her. The beacon, the Preservers . . . *I swear, if there is any way . . .*

As if in response to her desperation, another panel flared. A priest reached for a dial, but Dalto stopped him, saying "Wait, the systems are balancing themselves. I think it's a—yes, one last bleed-off through the dish. Saints, she is powerful. What would have happened if all that had stayed within the circuits . . ." He shuddered, a swift involuntary motion.

Echo's fingers opened, stretched towards the panel. *Lia . . .* The Patri's pale eyes flashed. "I told you to get *out!*"

Her hand fell to her side. "My service to the Church," Echo said, but inside, she heard a different word.

"As it must be." The reply was automatic; he had turned away already, certain that she would obey this time.

Yet she paused in the nave, a hand on the outer door. *One must serve the Saint. Anything,* she thought. *I will do anything.*

She could still hear the Patri speaking to Dalto within. It was wrong to listen; she did not care. "You must find another way to control the flow or the systems will burn."

"Patri, this Saint's strength . . . In only these few months, the city systems have been repaired, new ones installed. I am not saying I wish it, but even if she were to . . . to be reduced to all but the most basic functions now, it would be enough."

There was a silence, filled only by the pounding of Echo's heart as it raced in confusion and dread. "Stabilize the systems, Dalto. Eliminate the surges. That is all that matters." Dalto must have answered with some gesture; after a moment, the Patri spoke again, so softly she almost did not hear. "We must control her. This proves it beyond all doubt. Find a way, whatever must be done."

Echo stumbled down the steps. Her ears rang as if the alarm in the sanctuary still screamed, but it was all within her mind. Dalto, the Patri, they had given the Saint an order, and the Saint had refused. How that was possible, what circuits and systems had failed—those were matters beyond Echo's understanding.

But she knew she had heard the Saint's voice. And she feared, with the blind terror of the fall within her dreams, that she would never hear it again if she did not serve her now.

Echo knew what the old Patri would have done when his first attempt to punish the Ward failed. Jozef could not, under any circumstances, let the cityens guess that the Saint had refused his order. And worse, what he would do if it happened again . . . Before dawn Echo woke Gem in her cell. "Tell the Patri I have seen to the Ward." She was gone before Gem could question her, and by first light she was at the mill. A Wardman found her there, setting the sack of crop powder against the base of the wall inside. "You have an hour," Echo said.

A crowd gathered, silent with dismay, to watch as cityens hurried to remove the grain and other items that could be carried from the mill. They worked as hard as they could, but in the end it wouldn't matter. The time was nearly up. "If we had a few more minutes," someone begged; she only shook her head and stood cross-armed, watching them scramble, their task made even more difficult by the buffeting wind.

Teller dropped a last sack on a cart and wiped his face. She did not think it was only sweat making channels in the coating of flour dust. His sleeve came away white; beneath the dust, he was white with fury. "How are we supposed to eat? The other mills won't as take up the load. And not like North or Bend will help."

"You should have thought that before you defied the Church," she said.

"This isn't the truce we all agreed to. Take care of each other, that was our oath. The Church to lead us, not to beat us down. Signed in blood, that might as well have been. *Lia's* too, as if you cared." He looked away, lips trembling. "If she knew what you were doing . . ."

"*You* are the ones who betrayed her," she began, then swallowed the rest of it before she could reveal what had happened in the sanctuary, and betray the Saint herself. "The Church won't let you starve. Come to the Patri when you've learned your lesson."

He spat, perilously near her boot. Tralene, weeping openly, drew him away. She had been walking among the crowd, comforting them, assuring them, "It's only as for a little while. We'll rebuild it. The Saint knows we're loyal, and that's as what matters. The Patri will realize soon enough. Come now, go to your homes, let's not as frighten the children . . ."

But her words to Echo were cold. "You know us. You know as this is wrong. How can you let the Church do such a thing?"

"Clear everyone away from here."

Tralene's lips pressed together, trembling with fear and no little anger. Her eyes searched Echo's face, then clouded as she failed to find whatever she sought there. "You never understood a thing she said."

Echo went inside the empty mill and lit the fuse.

She found Exey in the tower room. She made no attempt to hide her approach; there was only one way out, and if he wanted to take it she didn't really care. He was sketching again, cylinders and gears she didn't recognize. She didn't care about that either. She flung the filigreed clasp at him; it skittered across the print like a live thing fleeing her. "Why were you at the mill?"

He started to make one of his insolent rejoinders, then changed his mind at the look on her face. "I had to fix the connection to the vanes. The wind tore some of the wiring loose. If the Wardmen would pay more attention to maintenance I could—" His eyes widened. "Wait, you don't think I had anything to do with—"

She reached down and hauled him to his feet, then off them. His hands clawed at her wrists ineffectually. Two steps and he was framed in the glassless gap. "What were you doing there?"

"Fixing the vanes! I swear that's all!"

"Someone delivered those weapons. Was it you?"

"No!"

She pushed him closer to the drop. "Are you absolutely certain?"

Terror twisted his face. His eyes, lighter than most cityens', were nearly consumed by black, the animal response to fear. Sweat beaded his skin; she saw the pulse pounding in the hollow of his throat. Her hands tightened in his collar, choking him. "I swear! I swear by the Saint!"

She let him go.

He stumbled across the room, hitting the wall

with a dull thud. He clung there, bent over himself, chest heaving in ragged gasps.

She stood on the edge of the fall. The gusting wind made her eyes blur. She wiped them clear. A clang of loose metal far below drew her gaze down. A body falling from here would take a long time to hit the ground. Long enough to know what was coming. As a girl would know, who slipped over the edge of a cliff. Perhaps if you looked up, fixed on something besides the certain end rushing towards you, it wouldn't be too bad. Only a moment's suspension in the air, then nothing at all.

The wind tugged at her, a warning, or an offer.

Her eyes lifted to the spire. *I am not sorry*, she thought defiantly. *I told you I would do anything.*

The crossed panels burned coldly, an impossible distance away.

She stood there a long time, wondering what beacon could guide her home.

And then she saw the aircar come over the horizon.

CHAPTER 19

Echo crouched behind a pile of rubble just inside the forcewall. Khyn's passage had shown that the wall was no barrier to the Preservers, but instinct still drew a line, *in here, out there.* The aircar's instruments must have been able to detect it too. The hull, rocking alarmingly as the engines wheezed, settled a hundred paces beyond the forcewall, spraying sand. The craft was of a size to carry half a dozen or more. It went without saying that they would be vektere. Likely all of them would be carrying energy weapons.

Some of the hunters spread out along the perimeter carried projectile weapons. Echo knew the sense of it; they must take advantage of every resource against a potential enemy. But the sight of the weapons in hunter hands made the old wound in her arm ache. And her heart. Too close a reminder of the rebellion, too much a threat of a slide back down into the dark. And to use them against the Preservers meant the end of all her hopes.

The breeze blew sand with a gentle hiss against the aircar's skin. Echo snugged her collar tighter. She smelled the far desert on the wind's cold edge, warning of the coming storm. Another day and the Preservers might not have made it; nothing could fly through the great windstorms. She could hardly fathom how they had found the city at all. With no beacon, no first-hand knowledge of the desert—it seemed barely possible. She swallowed past a dry throat. When she had pleaded with the Patri to seek their help, she had not imagined that they might arrive unbidden. It shook her in a way that finding the Preserve had not. The other hunters must feel it too: a threat from without instead of within, as there had not been in four hundred annuals; a new predator in the desert.

Perhaps she had made some error, not led them far enough off course, not hidden signs of her passage well enough— She chided herself for wasting energy on such speculation. Blame could be assigned later; Nyree certainly would. It only mattered now that the Preservers were here.

What frightened her most was that she was glad. The memory played over and over in her mind: Stigir removing his crown.

Nyree slipped from position to position along the line, giving orders. "When they open the hatch, we rush. Brit will take left, Gem has right. I will assist you in the middle, since you are inadequately armed. Marin and the others will wait in case a second wave is needed. On my signal."

Echo's fingers clenched on her projtrodes. She forced herself to loosen her grip. "That strategy is faulty. Attacking forces the outcome. We should assess their intentions first."

"If they mean no harm, they can surrender." Nyree lifted her weapon. "I am not seeking opinions. Concur or withdraw."

Echo wondered which of the vektere had come. Jole, perhaps; Taavi. Honor would have compelled her, if the others were going to risk themselves to rescue Khyn, whom she had unknowingly let Echo take. Echo glanced at Nyree, coiled and ready. In a close fight, the young vektere would stand no chance. But energy weapons against projectiles . . . It was a new equation, once Echo had no experience to solve.

"Concur," Echo said. Nyree's eyes flashed at her; then she was gone.

Echo looked over her shoulder towards the Church. The spire winked like a daytime star low in the sky. She could not waste the chance to gain help for the Saint. Then she heard a lock mechanism whir, then the wheeze of hydraulics. Her breath quickened. Nyree would signal when the hatch swung partway up.

Echo launched herself from behind the rock. She ignored the startled exclamation from behind her. She didn't even feel the tingling as she passed through the forcewall, only the prickling between her shoulders as she braced herself for a projectile weapon's crack. It didn't come. *Your problem now*, Nyree's inaction said.

The door stuttered up with an abrasive grinding, sand in the hydraulics. The sound covered her light footsteps; the vektere might not even realize she was there. In this case, surprise was not her ally. She ducked into the low space beneath the aircar's belly, then rapped hard on the metal hull. "Stand down," she called. "I mean you no harm."

The aircar rocked on the landing struts as weight shifted abruptly inside. The door stopped moving. Hunters defending the hatch would crouch high and low on each side, covering the angles while keeping clear of each other's fire. Echo didn't know what the vektere would do. She pressed her back against the aircar's smooth skin, trying to peer up through the narrow gap in the door. Bodies blocked the cabin lights as the vektere moved inside. She heard muffled argument within. "Everyone stay calm. I only want to talk to you."

"We want the same." Stigir's voice, of course. He would never leave anyone behind. *Stigir*. Hope leapt inside her; she thrust it away.

"We must be very careful. My friends are waiting. We need to show them there is no threat."

"How?"

Echo wished she could have explained her plan to the hunters. If not for Nyree, they might even have agreed: the danger in it was primarily to the Preservers, and of course to herself. But there was no point hesitating now. She had been committed the moment she'd abandoned her position. If it didn't work, there was still plenty of time for Nyree to do things her way. And the vektere couldn't know that a hostage hunter would be no shield for them. She crouched in the sand beside the half-open hatch and laid her projtrodes where they could see. "I'm putting down my weapon. Let me in."

"We've seen what you can do empty-handed," Stigir said. Then she heard him expel a heavy breath through his nose. "The hatch is stuck."

She almost laughed. That would have put quite a crimp in Nyree's plan. "I can push it up from beneath."

The aircar rocked slightly again, the vektere redistributing themselves. "If you offer the smallest threat, we'll kill you," Stigir warned. In his place, hunters would have found her mere presence threat enough.

She pushed the protesting hatch up another foot, enough to let her climb through. Eight vektere surrounded her, stun batons on their belts, the red eyes of their energy weapons focused on her. The memory of the smoking holes piercing the dispensary wall came back unnervingly vivid. Taavi met Echo's eyes with the faintest of nods. There was a new hardness in her face, an expression Echo recognized. She knew that she had put it there. She looked around at the

Preservers. "If you hope to see Khyn again, here is what you must do."

Nyree did not gainsay Echo's plan, but her hard stare promised a reckoning later. The Preservers scarcely liked it better.

"How do we know you're not leading us into a trap?" Stigir demanded.

Nyree's lip curled. "You don't."

"We should stay with the aircar," Jole muttered, half to himself.

That had been Nyree's argument as well. But a report would be nothing to the Patri. Echo needed him to see the Preservers himself, hear the evidence that they could help. He would understand. He had to.

"Our word," Echo said as Stigir pressed his weapon to her temple. She tried to meet his eyes without moving her head. "If we wanted you dead, it would have happened already."

She smelled his fear, souring the sweat that dripped into his beard. Taavi and Jole were frightened too, their fingers white around their weapons, their eyes flicking from the aircar to Stigir's face. They knew they had a better chance, scant though it might be, out here than in the heart of the hunters' power. Echo said, "We need your help. The Saint does. I promise that no harm will come to you if you do not provoke it."

It was a strange procession back to the Church:

Echo walking slowly beside Stigir, his weapon at her head; Taavi and Jole armed the same, one in front and one behind; Nyree, Brit, Marin, and Gem encircling the Preservers. The rest of the vektere waited safe in the aircar, or at least as safe as they could be, surrounded by hunters. As long as no one did anything stupid, the truce there should hold. The situation here was more volatile: Nyree would respond to the slightest provocation, and that Echo would certainly be first to die would not cause her the least hesitation.

To get to the Church they had to cross the edge of North clave. Word had spread quickly, and the road was lined with cityens. At first it had been just a few, but as the little party came deeper into the inhabited areas, the crowd swelled, women and men and children, all come to witness what had not been seen in four hundred annuals. The return of a single stranger in a hunter's custody was nothing compared to an aircar full of them arriving on their own. If those watching were disappointed by the sight of a few tired and dusty humans looking about nervously, it didn't show. The crowd stood in eerie silence, amazed; but any trivial event, a shout, an inadvertent stumble, might trigger disaster. Echo felt Stigir's tension in the fingers clamped to her arm. She forced herself to relax, willing him to follow suit.

They came around a corner and found cityens spilled across the road, waiting. The hunters slowed, not showing their weapons yet. "Stand aside," Nyree ordered the crowd.

Once they would have melted away at a hunter's mere glance; but that was before the rebellion. And, Echo thought with a chill, some might be carrying projectile weapons of their own. Stigir's weapon ground against her temple. "Don't let them see," she murmured, keeping her eyes on the crowd. He jammed it into her side instead, high under her arm where the charge would go straight to her heart.

"Who are these, then?" someone called.

"None of your affair," Nyree said. It was not the answer the crowd needed; Echo felt their amazement edge into uncertainty, touched with anger.

The man's voice tightened. "Those aren't cityens as from any clave! They're strangers!" There was a brief moment of silence, overtaken by a rising babble. "Where did they come from? How did they know?"

"They are friends," Echo said, before Nyree could make things worse. "Come at the Patri's bidding."

"Don't look as you're treating them as friends," a woman said, loud enough to be heard by all. "Nor them as you. Are there more?" She squinted up the road as if she expected to see an invading force advance.

But another said, "Old Patri always told us to look for others. One day, he said. Maybe as today's that day."

Then the crowd parted, but not for the hunters.

Kennit hurried through from behind, face as white as if he'd fallen into a bag of his flour. "These strangers have no place as in our city. One's bad enough."

Echo could see the Church spire from here, the dish turning, the arms of the panels outstretched to the morning sun. The Saint's embrace, Lia holding her city. "These are the survivors the Saint commanded us to seek," she said. "Let us pass, cityen."

But Kennit answered, "The council ought to have a say. I'm not questioning the Saint, I would never. Nor the Patri, if it comes to that. But as to what a hunter tells, and one as might even have been excommunicated on a time . . ."

Those near enough to hear murmured agreement. They were still just an attentive crowd, not yet a mob, but the smallest shift in the ground beneath them could send them over that edge. And the delay was unnerving the Preservers. Stigir's fingers dug into Echo's arm. A drop of sweat slid down Taavi's face. Echo sensed the fighting hormones rising in their blood. Nyree felt it too; she spread her feet and let the stunner on her belt show. Her projectile weapon, still hidden, was just as close at hand.

The crowd edged back, but only a little. They scowled now, and some of them mirrored Nyree's stance. Brit took a casual step left, making herself a separate target. It was standard procedure: if they needed to fight through the crowd, she would take that flank, leaving Gem and Nyree to split right and middle. The numbers were unfavorable, but the city-ens were untrained; the hunters would not normally have to do lethal damage to pass. But the Preservers were a burden; they could not be left behind with their energy weapons to wreak havoc on the cityens before they were overwhelmed.

If it came to that, Echo's duty was clear. She shifted her weight, too subtly for Stigir to feel, but enough that if he killed her, her body would fall into him. The hunters would ensure that he didn't have time for a second discharge. But she couldn't let it come to that. The Saint depended on her. *Think*, she told herself, *think of something*.

Nyree put her hand on her weapon. The crowd teetered on the cliff's edge; the next action would decide everything.

Into that gap Gem stepped forward. She raised her empty hands in a gesture that included all the city-ens. Her gaze lifted towards the shining spire; despite the distance, the same glow seemed to touch her face. Her eyes shone in it, and she smiled. Echo's breath caught. To the spire Gem called, "Our service to the Church in all things." Then she dropped her gaze to the cityens, letting it play over all of them, slow and certain. "The Saint preserves the Church, the Church the city. Thank the Saint." There was only silence. She said again, with utter hunter command, "Thank the Saint."

Another moment of silence, and then a voice from

the crowd called, "Thank the Saint." Another took it up, and another, and it carried until even Kennit had no choice. "Thank the Saint," he gritted, stepping aside, and the crowd parted, letting the hunters and vektere pass through.

Echo wiped sweat from her eyes with a hand she refused to let tremble.

"Clever," Nyree said when they were out of earshot of the crowd. Gem did not reply, and all the rest of the way her gaze was focused on the spire.

Tension leapt anew in the Preservers as Nyree took the side road that funneled them towards the secondary gate. Once within the walls they had no hope of fighting their way out. "Tell me again why we should trust you," Stigir demanded.

"I serve the Saint," Echo said. It explained nothing, and everything.

Nyree slapped her palm on the gate panel without waiting for Stigir's reply. It swung open ponderously. Stigir's fingers tried to meet through Echo's arm. She wondered if she would feel the energy weapon's bolt or simply cease to exist between one breath and the next. She raised her eyes to the spire. The mast turned, its rhythm slow and steady. She tried to slow her racing pulse to match. Her heart beating with the Saint's, with Lia's . . .that would be enough, between now and the end, if only she could know that the Saint were safe.

Stigir jerked her forward, through the gate.

Hunters waited inside, arrayed just like the city-ens along the road. The Preservers' passage through the forcewall had showed on the priests' panels, of course. Even the juveniles were there, unarmed but still a weapon to defend the Church. Fury stood a little apart from the rest of the 384s. Thunder gathered in her face at the sight of Echo captive in Stigir's grasp. She took a step forward, then another. Indine gave a sharp order; Fury, all her attention on Echo, didn't even glance her way. Echo shook her head, eyes boring into Fury's, willing the girl to be still. Small fists knotting, Fury glared a long moment in Stigir's direction before retreating to her place.

Nyree led them on. More and more hunters attached themselves to the group as it passed, until by the time they approached the heart of the compound, the tiny group of Preservers was completely surrounded, with Echo at their center.

And then, finally, they were there.

CHAPTER 20

"**F**our hundred annuals since we've had visitors, and you choose this moment to arrive." The Patri's thin lips quirked into a smile that for once contained real humor, though not of a kind that would be enjoyable to share. Despite Nyree's objections, he had ordered Stigir brought to him immediately. "I will see these strangers come to call on us. Vanyi left me so many gifts. Surely this is the one he would rather have had for himself." There had been a brief but fraught nego-tiation over the circumstances: the hunters would not permit armed vektere near the Patri, and the vektere would not give up what they thought was their only advantage. Finally a compromise had been reached, and now Stigir sat in the Patri's office, Jole standing directly behind him. Nyree took her usual place by the window, and Echo was seated beside Taavi, who held the Preservers' single weapon, a stun baton she held against the base of Echo's neck. Echo hoped nothing tempted Taavi to use it; she needed everyone to live long enough for her plan to work.

"We came to get our citizen back," Stigir said. "If your *hunter*"—Stigir spoke the word with a touch of disdain—"told you anything true about us, you would understand that we would never stop trying to find her."

Echo could imagine Khyn's consternation when she heard that they had succeeded. She would be apprehensive, yes, in case of Stigir's lingering anger; but she had been away from her home for many days now, living among strangers, and that grated inside like sand inside boots, an irritant that could be tolerated, until the sudden prospect of relief rendered it nearly unbearable. Gem had her somewhere under guard.

"You seek her well prepared," the Patri said. "We do not have weapons like yours. You could certainly make plenty of trouble for us if you chose." Nyree stirred, disturbed that he had given away even that much; it was an error the old Patri never would have made.

Stigir said, "We're peaceful people. We do not seek trouble. When your citizen came to us, we offered kindness. We saved her life. In payment she stole Khyn from us."

"Echo Hunter 367 has been known to act in haste," the Patri said dryly. "Let me be plain with you. When she returned with news of your existence, I saw no hurry to seek you out. We have waited all these annuals; we could wait a little longer. So I thought. But now here you are. After all—ah, thank you, Luida." A nun came in, bearing a tray with a pitcher, some glasses, and a cut loaf of bread with cheese. Echo recognized her, the girl who had always been laughing; but some recent grief had driven the smile from her eyes. Echo felt a pang of regret, then set it aside. There was little enough for anyone to laugh about. "I thought refreshments would be welcome after your dusty walk," the Patri said. "Though I understand that our choices are meager compared with yours."

"You are kind," Stigir said. Luida served him first, a gesture of respect, then the Patri, then the rest of the vektere. There was a moment of awkwardness with Taavi, who could not put down her stunner to accept both water and food; Luida settled for balancing the plate on the young vektere's knee.

"Please," the Patri said. "Enjoy."

Stigir lifted the cheese to his mouth, then stopped, nostrils flaring.

"Do you wish me to taste it for you?" Nyree asked.

The little space the Patri's casual welcome had bought contracted into a tight silence.

Taavi handed her cup to Echo as if they were back sharing a meal in the glasshouse. Echo accepted it automatically, and the vektere took a bite of the bread and cheese. "It's delicious," she said, in a tone close to her old lightness. "You must have a different kind of capri here."

"It is bovine," Echo said stupidly.

The rest of them ate then, silent until Stigir finally set down his plate. "Your hospitality is generous. I hope you take no offense at what I'm about to say. I'm sure that you know something about us by now. I believe"—Stigir cast a hard glance at Echo—"that we know something about you as well. We won't be so foolish as to give any of you a reason to consider harming us. But your citizens along the road were not exactly welcoming. We left our friends in the aircar on Echo's word that they would be safe there. But now I wonder—"

"The hunters there will watch them," the Patri said. "To protect everyone from any misunderstandings that we would all regret after."

Stigir said, "Give us back our citizen and we will go. That's the surest way to avoid such difficulties."

The Patri's thumbs wrestled each other. Echo's heart pounded, but not from fear of the stunner Taavi still held steady. Jozef was the Patri. Vanyi had to have chosen him for some reason. He bore many burdens; in that regard, the Preservers were only another problem he had to deal with. But in bringing Stigir to him she had given him an answer to a problem as well. She only had to help him take it.

She said to Stigir, "I regret causing you so much worry over Khyn. Thank the Saint you arrived here safely."

Stigir's nod was stiff. "It was a long journey. It's a

relief to know that it wasn't wasted. If your Saint is to thank for that, then I am grateful."

The Patri's hands stilled. "I understand that your aircar needs repair. While that is taking place, we might as well make use of the time. You have come all this way. I confess that I am curious. Are you not?"

"Our duties are enough for us," Stigir said. Then he looked around the room, at the hunters, the Patri, and last at Echo. His shoulders rose and fell. "But it is our custom to study and confer, not to resolve our differences with violence." He gestured, and Taavi set aside the stunner with obvious relief. "I'd like to see Khyn now, please."

Granting his wish would be premature. Keeping the newcomers separate from Khyn provided leverage, and split three ways, none of the Preservers could afford to make trouble that might endanger the others. The prospect of reunion with Khyn could be dangled in front of Stigir as motivation should the Patri decide he needed it. Whether the Patri had thought all that through was doubtful; Nyree certainly had. But there was a better way to gain Stigir's cooperation. Before the other hunter could speak, Echo pushed back her chair. "I will bring her to you."

Khyn stopped short, her hand on the door. A classroom in the hunters' domicile had been hastily rearranged as quarters for the Preservers. "How did they seem?" she asked for the third time.

"They came for you. That says enough."

"Maybe." Eagerness and anxiety warred in Khyn's expression. She patted her braid, poking at the escaped strands with trembling fingers, then gave up. "Might as well find out." She pushed open the door.

Stigir rose slowly, eyes raking Khyn. She stood still, biting her lip. Taavi and Jole exchanged an uncertain glance. Then Stigir opened his arms, and Khyn flung herself into them. Taavi and Jole joined the embrace, and they all clung to each other for a long moment, until Stigir set Khyn back, hands on her shoulders. His cheeks creased above the trimmed beard. "Are you well? Have they hurt you?"

Khyn shook her head, wiping her eyes. "They've been as good as they know how, I think. I'll tell you all about it later. Stigir, I'm so sorry, I didn't mean for things to turn out the way they did. You have to believe me, no matter how it looked, I only wanted to help. I should have listened to you. I kept thinking how angry at me you must be . . ." The words tumbled out in a rush, as if she'd been holding them back a long time.

"It only matters that we've found you." Stigir embraced her again. "Thank the Preservers. Here, sit by me." He wrapped an arm around Khyn's shoulders; she leaned into him with a sigh. "We'd practically given up hope."

"I knew you would keep looking," Khyn said. "But all this time I've thought . . . I wondered if I'd ever see the Preserve again. And now you're here . . ." Voice trailing off, she wiped her eyes again. "I don't know what to say. This city—it's not like anything we could imagine. Everything's so strange, but I've learned so much." A hint of defiance crept into her voice. "The population here used to have problems like ours with the babies, but they figured them out. They have children—wait until you see! I've made their priests teach me part of how they do it, how to tell which women are most fertile—I still don't know enough, but it's a good start."

Stigir's smiled faded. "You do want to come home?"

"Preservers, yes!" Khyn sobered. "But what about Birn?"

"Birn's anger was nothing," Stigir said, a hint of reproach in his voice. "He'll be first to welcome you."

"I still can't believe you're really here. I want to know everything that's happened! Where you've been, how you found us, when we're leaving . . . all of it!"

Stigir looked at Echo. "Would it be possible for us to have some time alone?"

"I am sorry." Echo settled her back against the door.

"She's not," Khyn said with a shaky laugh. "They're all just like her. I still don't know quite how they do that part, but it takes some getting used to, I can tell you. Everything here does."

"We've tasted the cheese," Taavi said with a shudder. "No wonder you're so thin."

"That's the heat," Khyn said. "You get accustomed to the cheese after a while." Perhaps that reminded her of capri, for she asked, "How's Netje?"

Taavi lifted a shoulder, her expression clouding. "It's been hard on her. I wish we had a way to get word back." She pursed her lips. "Do you think we could—"

"We have no way to communicate with the Preserve," Echo said.

"But I thought the beacon—" Taavi broke off in confusion. "Well, Netje can wait a little longer. We'll be home soon enough."

They all fell silent then, the relief of finding Khyn alive and well fading as they considered the danger they were still in. "I ask you plainly," Stigir said. "What will happen next?"

Everything Echo had done from the instant she saw the aircar come over the horizon was aimed at this moment. No, earlier than that. From the time she saw Stigir remove his crown, and began to hope . . . And yet she hesitated. She was a hunter. The promises she had made to the Preservers were bad enough already. What she was about to do was a betrayal of every trust.

But one.

I serve the Saint.

She took a deep breath. "The hunters will want to know more about the Preserve. Whether you are a threat to the city. They will question you until they are completely certain."

"But I've told them everything I know already," Khyn objected.

"Vektere are a different matter."

Stigir rose again, face hard. In the small room she could smell the Preserve on him, even after long days of hard travel, the resiny sweetness out of place amidst the hot stone and flint of the Church. "You promised us safe passage. We took you at your word."

"That was wise. It saved all your lives. You must listen to me again now. The hunters will not let you leave without the Patri's permission, but they cannot hold you longer than he wishes. You must bargain with him for your release."

"And you think we have something that he wants." Stigir's voice held hope, more than at any time since she had entered the aircar, and a hint of the same disdain she had heard in the Patri's office. Let him judge her; she answered elsewhere.

"Tell them about the Saint," she said to Khyn.

Stigir listened intently. When Khyn was finished at last, he stroked his beard, silent for a time, lost in thought. "So this saint is a kind of steward, but there is only one, and these power surges could destroy her at any time."

The plain words burned through Echo's nerves as if she felt the surges herself. For an instant, fear threatened to overwhelm her. *Saints, Lia!*

Khyn nodded, unnoticing. "I did what I could to help stabilize the systems, but it wasn't enough."

Taavi said, "Your whole city will die without her?"

"If you can help," Echo said, ignoring her pounding heart, "the Patri would be grateful."

Stigir crossed his arms. "I would ask more than gratitude in exchange."

His bravado was admirable. The Preservers' position was still weak; they were reunited with Khyn, but separated from the others, and more importantly, from their only means of escape. Hunters, in the unlikely event that they wanted to rescue one of their own from an enemy, would never have taken such a foolish risk. Even in a desperate situation they would have scouted the area first, marking strengths and weaknesses, developing whatever plan had the best chance of success. If they judged the risk greater than the reward, they would not hesitate to abort the mission. Better to lose one than all.

But the Preservers were not hunters, Echo told herself once again. She had persuaded Stigir he had something to bargain with. She must not let him get too greedy. If she maneuvered properly, the Patri would give Stigir something he intended to give him anyway, and the Church would get something of value.

It all seemed too easy.

"You should be glad there is a prospect for your lives," she told Stigir. "What more do you wish to obtain?"

The answer came as no surprise.

"Leave you alone?" The Patri laughed his humorless laugh. He had received the Preservers on a balcony above the yard. The choice seemed odd. The balustrade formed a series of pointed arches; peculiar creatures with wings and wide, fanged mouths projected from the wall. Perhaps they were modeled from predators that had existed before the Fall. Echo wondered irrelevantly if the Vault in the Preserve contained their seed. "That is hardly a grand reward for sharing with us your knowledge of the systems."

"We only want to live as we have been, undisturbed. It means little to you, perhaps, but a great deal to us."

The Patri looked down across the Churchyard. The compound bustled with morning activity, the 388s at play in the side yard as usual, nuns and priests walking, some arm in arm, in the shade of the wall. A group of 382s practiced unarmed combat off to one side, Nyree overseeing them. That was not usual, and Nyree would not have arranged it without reason. *These are only our juveniles*, the display told the Preservers, if they were able to notice. *Imagine what the rest of us can do.* The old Patri, Vanyi, would have understood in an instant, perhaps would have put Nyree up to it. He had read the Church and the city as the sanctuary priests read the boards. The Preservers would have been only another part of the pattern to him.

Echo felt dizzy a moment, as if the height were greater than it was. She clutched the stone rail; it passed.

"I envy you," Jozef said, watching the yard. Something dark touched his eyes, the shadow of the burden he carried. For an instant he looked like the Patri Echo remembered. Then he straightened. "We have enough trouble; I am happy not to add to it. I will make you this bargain: assist us with the systems, to the best of your abilities, and we will let you go. I cannot speak for some next Patri any more than the last spoke for me, but this I will give you: as long as I am Patri we will leave you to your solitude."

Vanyi would have been lying.

High-pitched laughter erupted below, the 388s squealing at each other in fierce delight. Stigir's eyes widened at the sound, a yearning flickering through them. Then his gaze slid to the other girls, who practiced in silent concentration. He sighed, his face damp in the heat. "Let us see how we can help your Saint."

CHAPTER 21

Nyree slammed Echo back against the wall. "What right do you have to strike bargains for the Patri?"

Echo caught her own hand back before the retaliatory blow connected. The other hunters were out of sight, escorting Stigir and Khyn to the sanctuary. Around the corner, one of the 382s was counting out loud, marking time for the others as they stepped through their drill, and shoes scuffed as someone hurried by. "He accepted Stigir's proposal. That is sufficient."

"You manipulated the situation so he had no choice! You are arrogant, Echo Hunter 367. You forget your place."

She must not let Nyree goad her into a fight. "What is your complaint? The threat is neutralized. With hunters guarding the landing site there is little opportunity for the Preservers to take aggressive action, even if that were their intent."

"What other intent would they have?" Nyree asked. "They came armed to the city, demanding the return of their cityen. And you told us yourself they tried to keep you prisoner when you stumbled upon their city."

"They thought *I* was a threat." And she had been. But she was a hunter, and they were not. "Think, Nyree. If they truly meant ill, would they come with so little force? They could not have expected to defeat us, or even to defend themselves if we meant to repel them."

"Then why would they come at all? It is only one cityen. They must have a better reason."

Nyree still gripped her shirt front. Their faces were very close. It wasn't only anger in Nyree's eyes. "They take care of each other," Echo said. "Is it so difficult to understand?" But it was, for a hunter. Only from the cityens had Echo learned that lesson. From Lia.

"It is you who are difficult to understand. You disobeyed my order at the aircar. You brought strangers into the Church—not one foolish woman, but armed fighters. It was an unconscionable risk."

"Your plan would have deprived the Church of resources. I was correct." But Echo remembered what she had said to Deann. *Even if you decide correctly, you must still accept the consequences of your disobedience.* She remembered too the old Patri's words, spoken as she had stood near this exact spot, long ago. Before she had challenged him and earned exile. *Obedience is the foundation of service, Echo*. If she were wrong about the Preservers . . . but no. She served the Saint.

Nyree's grip tightened. "You—you are a worse danger to the Church than the Preservers. And I am not the only hunter who thinks so."

Echo struck Nyree's hand away. "Let them say so to my face then. I have no interest in the games of juveniles who send one to do the others' bidding."

Nyree stepped back, face tight with anger, but her voice was hunter cold. "You presume too much, Echo Hunter 367."

"I live to serve." With that she shouldered past the other hunter into the yard. The wind was gusting again, stronger than before; dust swirled along the ground, blurring the spire's shadow. She had to focus. She looked up at the spire. The bargain she had made with the Preservers—*the Patri's bargain*, she told herself fiercely—balanced on the thinnest edge.

She would not let anything tip it over.

Stigir ran a reverent palm over the Saint's body, then the wire crown. Echo clasped her wrists behind her back, restraining the brute desire to strike his hand away. Dalto and Khyn looked on, while Gem stood silent guard in the shadows. Even the Patri had come to watch. "I did not imagine what you said was really possible," Stigir said, his voice touched with something approaching wonder. "Our procedures say this was tried many times, but I never truly believed it. How desperate they must have been . . ."

"Many?" Dalto's face reflected the same shock Echo had felt when she saw the six stewards connected to the Preserve's systems. "There is only one Church. One Saint."

"This must be the only one that ever worked. There is no record of it in our procedures. None of those who tried succeeded before the world forgot about us." Stigir stepped back from the altar, looking about the sanctuary in a kind of troubled amazement. "It has preserved your city all these centuries."

"It's horrible," Khyn muttered. "Alone like that, forever . . ."

Stigir pulled his gaze down from the rose window to fix on Echo. "There was much you chose not to reveal to us. But I am beginning to understand."

"Can you help her?" Echo asked. "That is all that matters now."

Stigir scrubbed his beard. The small rasping sound was loud in the vaulted space. "I do not know for certain."

A knot of fear coiled in Echo's gut. If he could not—if the surges continued—she heard Dalto's words again. *Reduced to basic systems . . .* She did not need to understand the details of panels and links to know what that meant. What would happen to the Saint. And as for that other dream . . . Echo's belly turned hollow, dropping, as if she fell from a great height. "You have the stewards," she insisted. "They control your systems. They wear a crown and . . ." *Take it off.* "Is it not the same thing?"

"Oh, no. Our interface is like your priests' panels—a way of guiding inputs, translating output. The rest is machinery. But this—this is something else entirely. She *is* the machinery. A mind, controlling the entire city, the same as yours controls your body . . ." Stigir traced the crown again with a finger, brushing a limp lock of Lia's hair from her forehead, then turned to Dalto. "You say your prints contain procedures that describe the wiring?"

"Yes, but . . ." Dalto shuddered. "It is certain death for anyone but the Saint to don the crown. Her mind, to be able to accept the load—that is where the complexity lies, not the crown itself."

"I can't imagine," Stigir said, shaking his head. "But if the interface connected to the panels, and then from the panels to the Saint, rather than directly to the city systems . . . That would be like what the stewards do."

Khyn's head swung in an arc of negation. "You can't be talking about trying to join their link yourself! An untested interface . . . And there's no way I could monitor you. It's not like home, Stigir. Nothing here is."

"It may not even be possible," Stigir said. "Let's see if we can make an interface first. I make no promises."

"You must try," Echo said. It came out harsh; she controlled her voice with an effort. "That was the Patri's bargain."

Word of the Preservers' arrival spread through the city like wind-blown sand. Half of North had seen them on the road, and the whole Church had watched them arrive in the compound; there was no point, the Patri said wryly, in trying to hide them away now. Nor, under the terms of the bargain, were they precisely prisoners, to Nyree's chagrin. They took the evening meal in the refectory, at a table separate from the rest; but Taavi, eyes alight with curiosity, went under a hunter's guard to speak with Luida and a few nuns and priests, and lingered until Stigir, noticing the priests' eager questioning, called her back. Taavi returned still grinning, but Stigir's expression was set.

The next morning cityens gathered outside the Church compound, and by noon there was a crowd as big as in the square on a market day. It was impossible to tell from here which clave the individuals were from; for the moment, they were united in their intent, which appeared mainly to be to try to catch a glimpse of the strangers. The babble of voices floated up the wall; so did the smell of excitement and sweaty bodies as more and more cityens arrived. The hunters chose not to interfere, instead only monitoring from the platforms along the Church side of the wall, and keeping carefully out of sight. Cityens got bored as quickly as they became aroused; if nothing further excited them, they should disperse on their own. The weather should help too; between the heat and the rising wind, there was little comfort for them as they milled about the road.

So far they offered no threat, but Echo remembered all too well a day when an angry crowd, armed with crop-powder explosives and projectile weapons, had rushed this very wall. The day of the Saint's ascension.

So did the other hunters. They gave no outward sign of concern, but their faces were intent, their sharp eyes constantly roving over the crowd.

"What do they think they're going to see?" Brit wondered. "A Preserver could walk right past them and they wouldn't be able to tell, except by the clothes."

"They are curious nonetheless," Marin said. "We would be too. It is a chance to observe something that has not been seen in many lifetimes."

"Look how many there are!" Excitement tinged Taavi's voice, though she made an effort to comport herself calmly. Marin had escorted her here, while Khyn and Stigir worked in the sanctuary. Echo hoped they did not know about the cityens clamoring outside; she wanted nothing to distract them from creating the interface. Her chest constricted with fear of what might happen if the cityens lost control before the Saint was safe from the surges.

Indine turned to the 382s, whom she had brought to observe the extraordinary event. "What is your estimate of the crowd's size?"

Deann arrived at an answer first. "Approximately two thousand, based on the number in the section immediately below the steps."

"Two thousand!" Taavi surveyed the crowd again. "That's almost as many as the whole Preserve."

"I could be more accurate if they did not move around so much," Deann said, squinting over the wall.

"Conditions are seldom optimal," Indine said. "You must be able to adapt. Nonetheless, your number is adequate for tactical purposes. Develop a plan to disperse them, with options for various proportions who are uncooperative. We will meet at the training ground in one hour. Set up a section of wall, and tell Flo to gather the 384s to act as cityens." The juveniles scrambled down from their posts. Echo wondered what they would come up with. The full force of the Church might not have stopped the rebellion, if the Saint had not ascended.

Taavi said, "Echo told us there were a lot of you, but I didn't really believe it until now."

"What else did Echo Hunter 367 reveal?" Indine

asked, in the same dry tone she had used with Deann, but Echo went still inside. *You are the danger*, Nyree had said. *I am not the only hunter who thinks so.*

"What do you mean?"

Now Brit looked at the young vektere. "Surely you perform your own tactical exercises. Opportunities to practice with completely unfamiliar scenarios are rare. Any information Echo disclosed to you would have been valuable."

Taavi worked to meet Brit's gaze. She edged back a little, perhaps unconsciously. She kept her face admirably blank, but all the hunters would see the tightening of her jaw, note the fresh sweat beading along her hairline. "Echo was our guest," she said. "At least until the end." Then she managed a tight laugh. "The vektere are still talking about how you managed to overcome three armed men. But other than that . . ." She squared her shoulders, facing the hunters. "She told us enough that I wanted to see for myself."

"To assess the threat."

"To see the place she made sound so beautiful."

There was a little silence. Echo fixed her gaze on the cityens milling about below. Then Marin smiled. "Khyn makes the Preserve sound that way as well. I hope for a chance to evaluate her accuracy one day myself. Now, though, I should return you to your quarters. You are not accustomed to our heat, and it would not further relations among us if you fell from the wall."

Taavi's laugh was less forced this time, and it held something of relief. She disappeared down the ladder with Marin. Indine said, "The Preservers are not hunters, but neither are they fools."

"I was aware of that from the beginning," Echo said.

"Perhaps you did not cover your trail as well as you thought." Indine only appeared to be focused on the crowd.

"I did not lead them here." But now Echo wondered. Perhaps somehow, unbeknownst to herself, she had wished it even then. A small mistake, an unconscious clue . . . "No," she said aloud.

"Yet they managed to find us."

Echo shifted to take the weight off her weak ankle, more habit than necessity by now. "The priests failed to turn off the beacon until after I arrived. Perhaps—"

"The beacon was not strong enough to travel so far. You yourself told us that."

"Then I don't know." The sun, glinting off the turning dish atop the mast, sparked in her eye. The after-image left a dark spot in her vision. She rubbed her lid, then stopped, looking up again.

The dish. The huge surge, that day in the sanctuary, and Dalto's voice: *One last bleed-off through the dish. Saints, she is strong.*

Echo's whole body went cold despite the heat. She stared, unseeing, at the faceless cityens below. She barely noticed the crowd parting, or the cityens who marched right up to the wall. She remembered herself pleading, and the Patri's denial, and then the Saint flaring, beyond control.

Sending the signal to the Preservers.

For a dizzy moment the shock nearly sent Echo tumbling off the platform. She clutched the rail to catch her balance. The Saint had brought the Preservers, because Echo wished for it. She had refused the Patri's order, yet answered Echo's plea.

Saints. Saints.

"What is she up to?" Echo drew a breath, but Indine was pointing down at the crowd.

A cityen had clambered up on some high point and was shouting and gesticulating at the crowd. She succeeded in capturing the attention of those nearby; they quieted enough for her words to rise over the other voices and up to the hunters on the wall. "Strangers as ought not be here," she shouted, and the quiet spread, more of the cityens turning to listen. "Who knows as what they want?"

"*We* don't want *them!*" someone called back, and then another shouted, "No." Cityens nearby gathered around the woman in an irregular circle that grew as others, attracted by the shouting, pushed closer to see what they were missing. One tried to climb up beside the woman. Echo saw now what she stood on: a piece of plank balanced precariously across two piles of stone. The woman wobbled as a man leapt onto the plank. "Send them back!" he yelled, and others took it up until it grew into an unsynchronized chant. "Send them back. Send them back."

Echo's belly knotted. "We must disperse them."

Indine scowled down at the crowd as if they were unruly juveniles. "Let them shout themselves hoarse. They will tire soon enough."

"Indine—"

"It is only words," Brit said, but her voice held a trace of unease.

Echo had seen what words could do. And she had another fear as well. "The Preservers will hear."

"So? They already know they are not equally welcomed by all." Indine was not referring only to city-ens. "It is just as well. It will give them incentive to keep their end of the bargain."

"How will hostility encourage Stigir to work with the Saint?"

"I was speaking of their departure after."

By now the crowd had packed closer, trying to hear what all the yelling was about. Some were shouting themselves, others trying to quiet them. Within the concentric circles around the woman, little knots developed as smaller groups took up the argument.

Another bunch shoved their way towards the center. They were yelling too, words barely intelligible from here. "Don't speak for us," Echo made out, then there was something indistinct, then "Northers." Now the groups were coalescing into sides, and the shouting took on an ominous tone.

One of the newcomers approached the pair already on the plank. As he tried to climb up himself, someone grabbed him and pulled him back, with a shout of, "Get the scum off of there!" The man fell, disappearing from view amidst those standing all around. His friends tried to pull him up, and the chanting broke apart into angry argument as the cityens nearest pushed and shoved each other. Someone bumped against the makeshift platform, and the woman leading the protest fell too.

A man bent to help her, and someone pushed him away. He staggered, then turned back, arm swinging wildly. In another moment it would be a brawl.

Echo flung herself down the ladder, palms burning on the rails. Indine, cursing, followed after, and Brit behind her. They were out the gate and wading through the crowd before the cityens saw them coming. It was not the organized force of the rebellion; the cityens nearest pulled back, dragging their comrades with them, giving way in a panicked retreat that separated the factions as the hunters made for the fight at the crowd's core.

"Get back," Echo ordered, wrestling two men apart. Brit sent another man to the ground and Indine pinned a fourth, and then it was over, the punches subsiding to pushes and shoves, and then to angry glares and muttering as Echo hopped up onto the platform. "Go home, all of you," she ordered, pitching her voice to carry to the fringes of the crowd. "Make no more foolish trouble."

"Wardmen scum as started it," one more foolish than the others called, but his friends cuffed him to sensible silence.

"Go," Echo said again. By now more hunters had come through the gate, arraying themselves along the wall in a show of force that did not need to engage the cityens to discourage any further thought of violence. The fringes of the crowd peeled back, cityens starting away down the road, and the center began to unwind.

But then another voice, cooler, rose in a question. "What about the strangers, then?" And some who had been departing paused, waiting to hear the answer.

"They are the Patri's welcome guests," Echo said, pulse spiking anew. "And you have disgraced him in their eyes. Now go, all of you, and thank the Saint that no worse harm has come of this." The cityens looked at one another, and the hunters, and decided not to take their chances.

But Echo was wrong, as it turned out. For as the cityens withdrew, a murmur started up again near where she stood, and cityens were staring at something on the ground. It was the woman who had started the chanting, lying still where she had fallen, trampled by the crowd.

Hunters brought the councilors to the windowless room at the end of the hall. The Patri looked calm enough, leaning back in his chair; but his thumbs tapped a rapid rhythm. The councilors were nearly as disorderly as the cityens had been. "How could such a thing happen?" Kennit cried. He was still sweating from the long walk from North, and the hard faces of the hunters weren't helping. His shirt was damp at the neck, and the white was yellowing beneath the arms. Despite all that, he managed to look the Patri in the eye. "I have word from the Northers who were there. Sira didn't do anything as to deserve it. She was just talking, and not even against the Church, not as I hear."

"She was speaking against the Preservers," Echo said out of turn. The Patri flicked a glance at her, but she continued, "They are the Patri's guests. She was wrong to stir the crowd against them."

Kennit swung on her. "Always you as in the middle when something happens to my people. Trampled, that's as they say. Where were you when the crowd was getting out of hand? And then it's as no one would have panicked if hunters hadn't attacked."

"It was cityens who started the trouble," the Patri said, voice hard. "And I want no more of it. Is there anyone here who does not understand?"

"That woman didn't speak for us," Tralene said. "If these strangers offer help—" She looked down for a moment, then lifted her face again with a determined look. "I heard the one told Luida they had more grain than they know what to do with, and there's never a hungry child as in the winter. If that's so, there's no cityen should be complaining."

"I don't see as they brought us any gifts," Kennit said. "And even if they did—it's just as this, Patri. Everything that's happened . . . the people are nervous enough. It's not so long since the rebellion, and so many things as different now to how they used to be. One stranger, that we could as much as see, but so many, and all of them here . . . and some of them were like as hunters, I saw that on the road."

"They are not hunters," Echo said.

Teller, looked at her, lip curling in disdain. "We heard it was you that brought them. That's extra reason to send them on their way. There's nothing you do ends up to have a right reason."

"You see?" Kennit said. "The next thing will happen is some fool Wardman gets it in his head as he knows better than the Church, and it all starts again. North is loyal, Patri, you know that; but there's those in the city as don't know to listen, to you or me or anyone. What they might do, as they get frightened, or too much ferm . . . Send the strangers away, Patri, I beg you."

His argument held sense. Echo saw it suddenly from the cityens' point of view: the memory fresh of a time they had turned against each other, and some of them against the Church; the terror of the old Saint's death, that might have taken them all over the edge with it; a new Saint, and a new Patri, who reasoned with them even when they wished to be commanded. They must be feeling the ground shift as they walked.

And now, in the shape of one aircar with half a dozen passengers, the dawning sense that they might have many more things to fear than they had known.

Echo watched the Patri, scarcely breathing. Jozef said nothing, his hands for once still. *Don't listen*, she thought. *Please. The Saint needs the Preservers.* Through the thick walls she heard the wind; the lights dimmed fractionally, then held.

The Patri stood abruptly. "I will not debate you. Go back to your claves, all of you, and tell your city-ens this: trust the Church as you should have done from the beginning. Your understanding is not required, in this matter, only your obedience. Do not forget the lesson of the mill." His hard gaze traveled from councilor to councilor, and one by one they dropped their eyes, even, at last, Teller.

That should have been the end of it. But as the hunters were escorting the councilors to the gate, Khyn and Stigir emerged from the sanctuary not twenty paces away. Kennit stepped towards them. "You are not welcome here," he called, loud enough for all to hear. "Go back to your own city, where you're as wanted."

Echo jerked him back, nearly off his feet. He

clutched his arm, lips compressed in pain; but the fear in his eyes was not for her, who deserved it, but the Preservers, who could do him no harm at all. She dragged him to the gate and shoved him stumbling out.

When she turned back, Stigir was watching, and by his look his thoughts were dark.

"I want Taavi and Jole back at the aircar," Stigir said to the Patri. His crossed arms were the only outward sign of his anger, but Echo had no doubt what he would do if the Patri did not agree.

Jozef knew too; his pale eyes were cool but he only said, "It is an unnecessary precaution, but if it is a condition for finishing your work . . ."

"I don't like leaving you here without us," Jole objected, looking darkly on the hunters.

"Make the aircar ready," Stigir said, clapping him on the shoulder. "I will finish as quickly as I can, and we will all get away from this place. I expect," he added for Nyree, "that you will maintain a guard around the aircar, in case any of your cityens attempt to confront my people there."

"They do not cross the forcewall," Nyree said, "but if it will make you feel more comfortable, we will be happy to watch over you." She managed somehow to convey both indifference to Stigir's concern and contempt for his weakness in the same few words. Stigir nodded curtly and left without saying any more.

A few cityens returned to the wall that day, but the hunters dispersed them, as they turned away those who came to visit the nuns. So easily erased, the small gains made after the rebellion. Echo wondered what the councilors had told their claves. Kennit's fear and Teller's anger made a bad combination, more volatile than a pure strain of either; and she knew from bitter experience that a small spark was all it took when the cityens were already primed for violence. Even Patri Vanyi, farseeing as he had been, had nearly lost the city. If the cityens had any idea how close Jozef allowed the strangers to the heart of the Church . . .

But it was Echo who had brought them here.

The sanctuary offered no respite from her worries. Though the priests sat at their panels as always, lights flickering and machines humming softly, there was unaccustomed activity by the altar. A low pallet, like the stewards' couches in the vault, had been set not far away, and lengths of cable, not yet connected, ran from there back to the priests' main panels, where Dalto worked. Stigir bent again above the Saint, not touching, but his eyes traced every detail with an intimacy that made the shroud too thin a cover. Gem stood nearby, watching it all, whatever she thought well hidden behind the featureless hunter mask. Tools and extra wire were strewn across the bench where Echo usually sat; she turned away after a minute, back to the panels.

"How is the work progressing?" Echo asked Dalto.

The priest started, so engrossed in his work that he hadn't noticed her approach. Lights chased each other in an intricate pattern across the panel. "Well enough. We will create an effect somewhat like the charge splitter, only permanent." A strange expression flashed across Dalto's face, sorrow mixed with satisfaction. It was gone before Echo could be sure she had seen it, but it left her shaken.

She studied the lights, willing herself to understand the patterns. Hunters knew the basics of a body's working, enough to treat their own wounds and maintain their usefulness in an emergency; she supposed that the panels were something like that to a priest. The blinking there could be a kind of pulse, and the lines connecting one area to another the blood vessels, or the nerves, the net that carried the Saint's awareness through the crown, beyond the spire and out across the city . . . She saw the gap Dalto had pointed out to Khyn that first day, the incompleteness where a vital piece was missing. The board blurred, and she closed her eyes; when she opened them, Stigir was tapping a finger on the panel.

"This discontinuity in the circuit, that's why you get the surges. If the interface works, I'll be able to tune the flow just long enough to close it," Stigir said.

Dalto nodded. "That will keep the systems in perfect isolation."

"Will the interface process be dangerous?" Echo asked, seeing not the small dark space in the pattern but a cliff's edge, and a hand scrabbling desperately for any grip to stop the fall . . .

"I'm sure my head will ache for days," Stigir said with a rueful smile. Echo felt a stab of guilt. She had not spared the slightest thought for his safety, or his courage. "But other than that I don't think so. This is close enough to what a steward does. With Dalto keeping the power to a minimum, and Khyn ready to extract me from the link if there's any problem, I should be safe. Reasonably," he added.

It was worth any risk, any risk at all. And he would be in the interface with the Saint. Echo's eyes blurred again. Before she could stop herself she whispered, "Will you be able to hear her thoughts?"

"It's only circuitry on our side," Dalto said. She was glad that in the dimness he could not see the shame that flooded her face. But Gem was watching too, and there was plenty of light for a hunter to see. The line formed again between Gem's brows, and she studied Echo for a long moment before she finally turned away.

Echo dreamed of the cliff again that night, and woke long before dawn. She could not seek comfort in the sanctuary, center of her greatest fears. Instead she found a place in the yard out of the wind, where she could see the spire. She tucked up her knees and leaned her back against the stone as she used to long ago, before she knew anything of panels and circuitry, before the hopes and schemes that brought the Preservers here—before Lia—and watched the pulsing spire turn. If Stigir's interface worked, there would be no more surges. The Saint would be saved. And she would preserve the Church, and the Church, the city.

That was all that mattered.

The gap in the circuit closed. The Saint safe, in perfect isolation.

But nothing would ever close the gap in Echo's heart.

The winds steadily increased, putting everyone on edge. Hunters were dispatched to each clave, carrying the priests' warning that this storm looked to be a bad one, and helping to oversee the preparations. "Everyone sensible knows to be off the streets when it hits," they reported on their return. "Some of the fools in the fringes seem to think ferm will protect them, but otherwise it's the best we can expect."

Echo worked with the others around the compound, securing loose objects, covering equipment as best they could to protect against the blowing sand. The Church had withstood many windstorms; the hewn stone buildings and underground warrens were proof against the worst weather. But it wasn't only structure they had to worry about. A weak connection brought a wire down, the end sparking and snapping in the middle of the yard. It only took a moment for the power to reroute, eliminating the danger. "Thank the Saint," a priest said; but Echo thought of the strain to keep all the city systems running, and her anxiety grew more acute.

She went to the sanctuary then, despite her vow, but only as far as the nave door, where she could watch unseen. Stigir sat beside Dalto, the panel lighting their faces from below, as if they sat by a fire burning green. "The systems adjust remarkably fast," the Preserver said. "But what if the main power lines come down?"

"Those lines are buried," Dalto said, but Echo heard the worry in his voice. "But I'm afraid we might see worse surges. We must complete the interface quickly."

"I want that as much as you," Stigir said.

Echo couldn't see his face, but something in his tone sent a grating hum through her nerves, like the wind whistling through the wires.

Gem appeared at the door from within. "You have been avoiding the sanctuary."

"My services have been required for storm preparations."

"If your other duties permit, perhaps you could assist here as well."

The request sounded strange coming from the girl who had been so arrogant. "You have always performed adequately without my assistance."

A pause, then: "Perhaps you are right. One can watch as well as two; there is no sense wasting a resource."

Echo remembered what Indine had said, about

Gem's wanting to set patrols to look for Echo's return. She remembered too Gem's justification. "Is that all it is to you? A matter of resources?"

Gem cocked her head. "What else should a hunter consider?"

Friendship. That we matter to one another. But hunters did not speak of such things. Then Echo saw in Gem's face that that was what she offered, like a handhold for a slipping grip, if one dared to reach for it . . . Echo couldn't find her voice. After a moment Gem's lips drew up on one side, a kind of smile that held something besides humor. "About Khyn. I was wrong to think you had any consideration other than the Saint. If I have been unduly—"

The outer doors clanged open. Voices shouted in alarm, a shocking noise in the layered quiet of the sanctuary. Echo sprinted through the nave, wishing that she were armed. "Quickly!" someone shouted.

It was too late for weapons. Nyree stumbled through the doors, covered in blood. That she was still on her feet at all meant that most of it must come from the body she carried in her arms. The woman was still breathing, great irregular gasps accompanied by a bubbling wheeze. Echo tried to take her, but Nyree refused to let go, lumbering towards the priests' domicile, and the laboratories below. Priests scattered out of her way, instruments dangling forgotten in their hands. "In here," one ordered, rushing ahead of Nyree to fling open a door.

Nyree laid the body on a narrow padded table. The woman flailed, struggling for air. "Hold her," the priest commanded. Echo grabbed one arm, Nyree the other and they pinned her while the priest ripped off her shirt.

It was Marin. The wheezing sound was coming from a great gash in her chest, low down on the right. Every time she tried to breathe bubbles came up through the bright oozing blood. Blood came through her mouth, too. It gurgled in the back of her throat, a nightmare drowning sound.

The priest slapped a cloth onto the chest wound. "Hold this."

Echo pressed a palm over the bandage. She could feel the grating of bones underneath. "What happened?"

Nyree's voice was taut with fury. "Warders," was all she said.

Brit came behind, breathing hard, and her face hard, too. "There was a gang of drunk cityens roaming the streets, agitating about the Preservers and blaming the Ward for bringing them. It didn't have to make sense for the Wardmen to take exception. We got them apart, but a couple ran a Wardman into the fringes. Marin had them stopped, but the idiot Wardman pulled something out of his pocket. It wasn't a weapon, he was faking, but everyone panicked, and the gang must have had friends waiting, because then there *was* projectile fire."

"They fired at a hunter?" Echo said in horror.

"At the Wardman," Nyree gritted. "She took it. The rest of them ran. When I find them—"

The priest pushed to the top of the bed, a thin tube in his hand. "Tip her head back and hold it steady." Nyree took Marin's face in her hands, and the priest slid the tube down her nose. She bucked weakly. He hooked the tube to a glass-walled machine, adjusted a dial. Inside the machine a piston stroked; Marin's chest rose, then fell. The priest tipped a few drops of liquid into the piston chamber. Echo smelled something sickly sweet. "The Saint will breathe for her, and ease the pain. If I can fix the damage . . ."

His hands were quick, deft as a hunter's with weapons. Deft as Lia's had been, when Echo used to watch her tend injured cityens in her clinic. She envisioned the Saint on the altar now, knew that the consciousness spread all through the city would not neglect one life, however insignificant. But the med had never been able to save everyone. Though the priest worked furiously, Echo soon saw that it would not matter. She did not need to hold Marin still now; the young woman's hand was limp in hers. The air the Saint pumped still leaked out through the gash the priest could not close. Sometime in the action, a crowd had gathered to watch from the doorway; they were silent now, as still as the body on the bed. Echo felt the pulse in Marin's throat. It beat thin, irregular, and the pauses grew longer. "She is not going to survive."

"No," the priest said. His busy hands paused.

"It is too soon to stop," Nyree objected, still cradling the hunter's bloodless face.

"Do what must be done," Echo ordered the priest. Then to Nyree she said, "I will assist. You need not stay."

Nyree crouched there a moment longer, breathing harsh. Echo shifted, ready to move between her and the priest if Nyree's control failed.

It did not. The hunter straightened, her hands painting Marin's cheeks with blood as they withdrew. "Her service to the Church," Nyree said, and shouldered her way out the door.

Echo held the vials of preservative as the priest, no longer concerned with the damage, sliced through to the ovaries. The thumb-size blobs of flesh floated in the glass. Another priest came forward to take them reverently. "I will begin at once," he said.

The medical priest turned a dial, and the piston stopped. He slid the breathing tube free. There was one more wet gasp, then nothing. Echo looked down at the blood-streaked face. It had been Marin; now it was not. Somehow Echo was always surprised.

A choking sound came from the doorway. Khyn stood there, a hand clamped over her mouth, and a look of horror on her face.

Khyn sat on the edge of the bed in the Preservers' quarters, hands folded between her knees. "Alive," she whispered, eyes welling. "You take their seed while they're alive."

"There is not usually the opportunity," Echo said, tamping down a spark of anger. Often when a hunter died the ovaries could not be recovered in time, a waste that cost many potential batches. There were never enough hunters—not even enough to find the projectile weapons, so a fool could not frighten other fools with the mere idea of one. "The priests say the process works better when the material is fresh."

"Opportunity? You might as well have killed her with your own hands."

Ela, dead at the bottom of the cliff.

"You eat the capri you cull. Surely you must understand."

"Those are capri," Khyn said. A violent shudder shook her body. "Netje saw this in you, when you killed the one in the flood. I know, you're going to say you saved her life. It's not that. It's the way—you didn't care. Not about the capri, not about Marin. It's all the same to you, what happens to anyone, isn't it?"

That Marin should have died for something so stupid as the imitation of a weapon . . . Echo felt a touch of Nyree's fury. She struggled to keep it out of her voice. "We are made to serve. Marin Hunter 373 would have made the same choice."

"If you say so." Khyn dragged a sleeve across her face, looking so much like Netje that they might have been batchmates. She stared at the floor. "I'm sorry. It's just—I don't know. I don't know."

A flood of weariness overtook Echo. She made to sit, but Khyn stiffened. "Perhaps some time alone will help you compose yourself."

Khyn finally met Echo's eyes. "Yes," she said, her face settling into new, strange lines. "That's exactly what I need."

CHAPTER 22

The hunters did not have to search for the Wardman Marin had died to save. Teller brought him to the gate only hours later, a youth barely out of boyhood, one eye blackened and his face contorted with tears. "He's sorry," Teller snarled, and threw the boy at the hunters there, leaving him alone. They held him until Nyree arrived. Echo, hearing the disturbance, followed with her heart in her throat. But Nyree only studied him, her face an empty mask, while he blubbered and begged for his life. "Find out what he knows, then lock him with the others," she said at last, and turned and stalked across the yard.

Soon after Kennit came, alone. He looked almost as bad as the boy, shadowed eyes darting around the office. "Tell the Patri," Kennit begged. "We heard as what happened, and we're sorry, North is, truly. This

is what I warned of, what I feared. I know the hunters will search, maybe they'll even find who as did
this, but after that there will be others, and others
more . . . But he can stop it, the Patri, please, he must.
He must send the strangers away, now, before they
provoke worse. Before it all happens again."

The Patri refused to see him. Echo took Kennit
back to the gate, a hand on his arm. It trembled beneath the fine-woven polymer. "Calm yourself," she
said. "You have nothing to fear from the Preservers."

"It isn't only them." He looked at her with a ghost
of his old disdain. "I've heard as hunters aren't afraid
of anything. It must be true, or you'd know fear's not
a thing as telling makes a difference." His voice began
to shake again. "The old Patri started before as I was
born, and all those annuals I never even saw him.
Strange things as make a man afraid."

She watched from the gate until the wind-blown
dust obscured him from view. Then she went in
search of Nyree.

Echo found her in the refectory, directing preparations to convert the huge room to a shelter for when
the wind made it unsafe to cross the open yard. The
place was crowded already, and soon would be packed
with all the nuns and priests and juveniles who would
normally be out about the compound. Pallets had been
brought to let the nuns rest comfortably; the juveniles
would sleep on the floor. The smaller ones were already making a game of it, curled up under the tables

as if they camped among the desert ruins. Brit and Gem worked at one end, stacking large containers of water that Indine and the older juveniles passed from outside in a hand to hand chain. On the far side Nyree was arranging chairs, lining them up against the wall with greater concentration than the task deserved.

Echo took a chair in each hand and carried them over. Nyree took them wordlessly and fit them into place. When she noticed Echo still standing there, she asked, "Is there something you require?"

"No. Yes. I wanted to say—" Echo stopped, like a juvenile without a satisfactory answer in a drill.

Nyree looked at her coldly. "I am not interested in your thoughts about duty or service."

"We will find the weapons makers. When the storm has passed, when the Preservers have finished their work—"

"It is good to know that you place such a priority on the search."

"That isn't what I meant."

"I am not interested in parsing your words either. The hunters who could be spared are searching. There is likely insufficient time for them to find anything. I have ordered them to pull back well before the storm hits."

Echo took a deep breath. "We should bring the Preservers in from the desert as well."

"The aircar will provide adequate shelter."

"Even if it does, the hunters guarding them will

have to withdraw." Gem and Brit were bringing more chairs this way. "Kennit was here again. There is more unrest within the city than just a few trouble-makers."

"I know that," Nyree said. "That is why I want the Preservers as far away from them as possible."

"If we bring them back to the Church, they will not be exposed to the cityens," Echo insisted.

Brit slid the chair she carried into place. "Do you think they would give up their weapons?"

"No," Echo admitted reluctantly. "Nor would we, if the situation were reversed. But if we leave them unguarded—" She broke off as the lights dimmed, then came back. *That is normal in the wind*, she told herself. *The wires shake. It does not mean a difficulty with the Saint*. But Gem's eyes flicked towards the sanctuary too. "We cannot risk any confrontation between them and the cityens. We have seen what happens when passions run high. Many on both sides could be killed."

"There are not that many Preservers," Gem said reasonably.

"You sound like Indine," Echo snapped. As if she heard, Indine looked toward them, frowning at what she saw.

Echo said to Nyree, "If you care about nothing else, consider the cityens. Even one Preserver with an energy weapon could do great damage."

"Are you saying they are the danger now?"

"You twist my words, Nyree. I am only considering every possibility, no matter how unlikely. That is what a hunter does."

"Then consider this: if the Preservers do endanger cityens, it is you who put them in position to do it. If you had obeyed me to begin with, they would have been neutralized at the aircar the instant they arrived. There would be no threat to the cityens—no threat to the city at all." She did not add, "Marin would be alive." The words rang in Echo's ears louder than if she'd spoken.

Echo gripped the back of a chair, struggling to keep her tone reasonable. "We need Stigir. He must complete his work. If not, the city will be in greater danger than any weapon could bring."

"The Church preserves the city," Nyree said. Indine stood at her shoulder now, and Brit by Echo. "The *Church* does. Not strangers. Not a hunter who has never obeyed an order that didn't suit her. Even back to the days of the old Patri—if you had carried out your mission, if you had eliminated the threat from the Ward *before* they rebelled—but you thought you knew better. You always think you know better. You question, you doubt—the old Patri was right to cast you out. You disgrace the Church." She made a sound of disgust, deep in her throat. "You disgrace the Saint."

"Do not speak to me of the Saint," Echo said, too loudly.

A sudden silence fell across the refectory, making the wind outside sound very loud. Nuns and priests turned in unison towards the disturbance. The juveniles froze in the midst of their games. Adult hunters, confronting each other in public—it was unheard of. They waited to see what calamity must unfold.

Nyree drew herself up, balanced light and easy on the balls of her feet. "It's time that someone did. That is the heart of the matter, isn't it? The Patri sent you, but it was Gem who brought her. You would have run. You would have sacrificed everyone else, as long as you had what you wanted."

The fighting hormones surged through Echo, her pulse thrumming in her ears like a sanctuary alarm. "You know nothing about it, Nyree. I have had enough of you, questioning my every move, poisoning the other hunters against me. Casting doubt on all my service."

They were there now, those other hunters, a loose handful scattered around the perimeter of the room. Everyone watching, hunters and priests and nuns, and the whole room so silent that the water trickling from a forgotten container bubbled loud as a drowning breath. All watching Echo. Waiting to see what she would do. Her fists bunched.

Nyree's lip curled. "Is this what you want to show them, Echo Hunter 367? A hunter unable to control her anger? Is that how you serve?"

The moment stretched to breaking. Then, without haste, Gem stepped between Echo and Nyree. She gestured to Brit. "If you could bring a few more chairs? We must complete our preparations before the storm hits."

"I concur. There is much work to do." Brit didn't move. "Indine?"

Indine's heavy-lidded look transferred itself from Echo to Nyree, and back. "I concur."

There was a tight silence. Then Nyree said, "I too." She smiled for the nuns and priests, a mere baring of her teeth. Her voice was calm; her face expressionless, but the skin around her eyes was tight, the bones' sharp edges showing through. "If you wish to endanger yourself guarding the Preservers, I have no objection. I will not risk anyone else. Otherwise—I suggest that you return to your cell, Echo Hunter 367. I suggest it very strongly."

Everyone still watched, waiting. Echo forced her fingers open, drew a blank hunter mask across her features. "I live to serve," she said for all to hear. Her words rippled through the silence, joined by more, the watchers resuming their conversations, relieved voices too loud as they tried to drown out uncomfortable thoughts. The juveniles resumed their activities with greater vigor than before, to demonstrate that they had not been frightened. Echo spun on her heel and left.

In the doorway she nearly walked into Khyn and Stigir. A shadow of the earlier horror crossed Khyn's face again, and by Stigir's expression Echo knew Khyn had told him everything. But the look in his eyes was not horror, only a weary confirmation, as if he had known it all along.

She stepped aside for them to pass.

Her hand, poised to knock, hesitated as if some force-wall came between it and the Patri's door. *Don't be a fool*, she told herself. *You have faced him before, and the old Patri as well. You must make him understand.*

Her knuckles fell against the wood with a hollow thump. "Enter," came the curt response.

Jozef sat alone, surrounded by prints that were organized into neat stacks, and the shelves were full of them too. Most had been collected by the priests, perhaps even before the Fall; others had been unearthed from the vaults beneath the domicile. Some had even been brought on Lia's orders from the Ward, in the hope that they contained information that might save the old Saint. Those pages might as well have been blank, for all the good they'd done.

"What do you want?" Jozef asked.

She had carefully rehearsed what she would tell him. Her worry about Kennit's words, and Nyree's plan to withdraw the hunters from the aircar. Her concern about the unrest in the city, about Stigir and Khyn's disgust. Her fear that a balance might tip at any moment, and what that would do to the city, and the Saint. She opened her mouth to speak, then closed it again. Those were words for another Patri. The man who had towered over the Church, and her life. Who had seen his place in a great order stretching from the forebears to a future he dedicated his life to assuring, though he would never see it.

Who had, in the end, found his comfort in the presence of the Saint.

But this was Jozef. For him, she needed evidence.

"Well? As you can see, I'm busy."

The fighting hormones had not entirely dissipated. She drew a calming breath, then said, "I believe that our tactical approach to the Preservers may require adjustment."

"Speak with Nyree. Such things are her responsibility."

"Nyree does not see—" She caught herself, finished instead, "Share my concerns. But Patri, I believe that my experiences with the Preservers, and the cityens, gives me perspective that might be valuable."

"I have no doubt that you've expressed your point of view clearly. And I am equally certain that Nyree has weighed the evidence and drawn her own conclusions. That is sufficient for me." He did not have to add that he expected his answer to be sufficient for her; his eyes had already returned to the print she had distracted him from, clear enough dismissal.

Yet she delayed. She must find a way to make him understand why it mattered. Past his shoulder she could see the sanctuary framed in the office window. She wondered if he ever looked out. "Patri," she asked, dreading the answer, "what if Stigir fails?"

His thumbs tapped lightly, then stilled. "We will find another solution."

She took a breath. "And the Saint, is she . . ." Again the words trailed off. "Has the wind caused any difficulties?"

He did glance through the darkening window then, one corner of his mouth curving up in the motion that passed for his smile. "You know, when I was a priest in the laboratory, I hardly even noticed the windstorms. They were just an irritation sometimes when I had to come up for meals. Dealing with them was for the Patri. I had no idea Vanyi would be handing me all his troubles."

The wind was the least of those. Fractious cityens, strangers, weapons . . . "We will find out who is responsible for Marin's death," Echo vowed.

"Marin?" His brows drew up. "Ah, yes, the hunter. Once I thought Vanyi's methods too harsh, but the evidence has proven me wrong. Reason does not work with the Ward, or they would have learned their lesson by now. But we will make them understand. When Stigir's finished with his work, we'll see to that."

Her belly clenched at the memory of the enormous surge burning through the systems, melting the charge splitter to slag, and of the Patri's fear, knowing the Saint had rejected his command.

"If cityens require punishment, Patri, send the hunters. Please don't ask the Saint to—" She broke off all at once, but it was too late.

He leaned forward suddenly, studying her with the intensity of a priest examining a specimen beneath his magnifier. Under that sharp scrutiny she remembered again that the old Patri had picked him for a reason. "Is that why you destroyed the mill yourself?" He frowned, perplexed. "Why do you care so much about the Saint?"

Her breath hitched, but she forced her voice to come out steady. "I live to serve." They were the right words. They explained nothing.

He knew there was more. She saw it in the expansion of the dark pupils within his pale eyes, the faint whitening of the lines beside his nose. If he realized, if he even began to understand—Nyree's accusations against her would be as nothing. She made her face the hunter mask, empty, blank.

She was not certain what it covered anymore.

After a moment he sat back, frowning. "I've been told that you knew the woman before. Perhaps you feel some strange attachment because of it. If so, then it's obvious that you don't understand. Think of it like the hunters' eggs. What is important is passed on, into the systems. The rest is waste, discarded." The words stabbed like the instruments through Marin's belly. Not Lia. *No*. The Patri continued, "Nothing remains but the systems now. Managing them is a matter for the priests. Not for a hunter. Not for you. Let me make it simple: stay away from the sanctuary. Stay away from the Saint, and trouble me no more with childish fantasies."

Shadow lay heavy across the compound, except where the juveniles playing in the gated yard triggered the motion-sensing lights. Echo didn't want them; the brightness made it hard to see the stars. She looked up anyway. The twinkling sparks must be incalculably distant to remain the same here, in the desert, in the Preserve. Priests studied such things; hunters needed only to know the patterns, a guide no matter where their duties took them.

Marin's eyes had gathered that light, and now saw nothing.

The Patri hadn't even known her name.

Far brighter than the stars, the spire glowed against the coming night. *That* had ever been Echo's guide, even when it was too dark to see. Her feet found their way unerringly. They knew where duty lay, regardless of the Patri's order.

Echo pushed aside tools and cable to make space on the bench in the cool dimness by the altar. Marin had simply had bad luck. Most hunters would, eventually. At least hers had come in the performance of her duty, protecting a cityen on behalf of the Church. Better that than an aircar crash, or a misstep over the edge of a cliff. And far better than the slow descent of illness that so often took cityens. Most often there was no stopping that. Lia had hated her helplessness, the sorrow fresh each time.

But even the Saint was helpless sometimes. The priests whispered over their blinking boards, things about power, and relays, and protocols that must be invoked. They seemed untroubled, so Echo ignored them, letting the sound fade into the background along with the noises of the machines. So many wires in the crown, and the tubes to carry nutrition and waste; perhaps one of them even breathed for the Saint somehow, as the Saint had tried to breathe for Marin.

What lay before her was not Lia anymore. It was not so simple as putting the crown on or off. Only a child or a fool would imagine that the Saint, transformed as she was into something so much greater than human, felt anything at all that a mere hunter could comprehend. Sorrow, grief, love—none of it could matter to her now.

Yet Lia had asked her once, *Don't you even know when something hurts?* Maybe the Patri was right, and nothing remained but the systems. The Saint's voice might be no more than an echo in the patterns. That could not matter. Echo knew her duty. She reached towards the Saint, all her senses extended into the sanctuary as they would be in the desert when her life depended on the faintest hint of danger. Her vision, unfocused, sought to penetrate the shadowed vaults. She absorbed the sounds around her, the hum of the machines, the priests' soft murmuring, feeling the vibrations with her skin as much as in the membranes of her ears, reaching with every sense towards the part of the Saint that lay beyond the altar.

I am still here, she said into the silence. *While I breathe I will never leave you.* Then, not to the Saint, but to the woman who had given herself up to become Saint: *Lia. I love you.*

For an instant, between one heartbeat and the next, she heard a whisper: *Echo.* Then the too-familiar alarm began its cry, the sound of systems straining, trying to bridge a gap and failing, falling—

"No!" Echo jerked back from the Saint, in the room and in her mind. The alarm went silent in midwail.

"What was that?" Urgency laced through the priest's voice; a pattern changed on his panel, throwing a flicker like flame into the darkness around the altar.

"Another fluctuation," a second priest began, "but I don't see—"

"No, wait," the first priest said, with a low whistle of relief. "It was just the wind. There's nothing there."

But he was wrong. Echo knew. She had called to the Saint, and the Saint had tried to answer. And the power had surged.

She had done that.

She had.

Every time. Every time she had spoken to Lia, and heard the beginnings of an answer in the closeness of her heart.

Dalto said it was impossible, the Patri did not believe, but Echo knew the truth.

The ache inside swelled until her whole body pounded with it. The Saint could preserve the city, her strength as profligate as a hunter's; but Echo's lightest touch perturbed the systems. And when the Saint responded, the power surged, uncontrolled.

Even if Stigir repaired the circuit, stopped the surges, that might not be enough. If the Patri ever found out, if he had the slightest suspicion that Echo could affect the Saint—it was not only Echo who would suffer. *We must control her. Whatever must be done.*

Then an even worse fear stole Echo's breath: what if, despite the Patri's conviction, some remnant of Lia *did* sleep within the Saint's great mind, dreaming peacefully as her thoughts parsed inputs, flowed without effort into the myriad outputs, calm, quiet, until Echo's presence disturbed her, and she struggled as a sleeper who could not awaken, trapped within a nightmare . . . .

Once sleep was disturbed, every sound was louder, every touch made it harder to slip back into the sanctuary of rest. What if, instead of comfort, Echo's very presence *was* the nightmare?

The thought filled her with horror.

Echo's mind reeled. *Think*, she commanded herself. Not like a hunter, not this time, but like the woman who had stood in this sanctuary in the midst of the rebellion, the old Saint dying, the world about to tumble to its death, and made a choice.

Echo knew what she must do. For a last moment her heart clung to the woman she had loved. Lia, who was more than the Saint. Who would not let go of Echo, if Echo were the one condemned to the shadows, alone . . .

But: Lia *had* let go, a traitorous voice whispered in the back of her mind. A splinter of anger shot through the pain. *How could you leave me?*

No. That was not what had happened. Lia had given up all she loved to ascend as Saint, to serve as she was meant to. It was Echo, even now, who grasped at what she wanted. That her mere presence might endanger the Saint—might, somehow, hurt Lia—the enormity of that would reach her anywhere, would penetrate any hiding place, follow her as far as she might ever run. She could not even recognize her own feeling as pain; it was, instead, as if she had empty stumps where her hands should be, and still tried to grasp for a last hold as she tumbled over a cliff . . .

But Echo knew. Until she let go of Lia, she would always be a danger to the Saint. She must give up that connection. She must never try to reach Lia again.

It was like telling herself not to breathe.

She shut her eyes and stared into the empty dark. Empty, that was it. She knew what she must do. Lia was a memory, a sensation, like hunger, like the pain that shook Echo now. She took the pain and squeezed it into a tiny ball, then wrapped it in the emptiness, layer upon layer, like something fragile she must not break, or the shards would pierce her heart. She breathed in and out, carefully, adding layers of nothing until the feeling was far away. It seemed to take a long time. When she was done, she felt weak as after a long illness, when the fever had barely passed.

The Saint lay there still, peaceful, remote. Echo would serve her. Only her. Without expectation, or hope. That was where duty lay. That was what the words meant: *I serve the Saint.*

It was not enough. It would never be enough.

The shadows deepened as the priests clicked through their rituals. Beyond the panels, the dials and switches, there was no response.

Echo stood to go. The lights came on brighter; the disciplined voices filled the silence. She waited one last moment for a voice to call her back. The silence only echoed louder. Then she turned and walked away.

Halfway down the steps she had to stop as the leaden sky whirled above her. The juveniles were still out here, nuns watching over them, hoping they would burn off the excess energy in this last little while they could be out before the storm chased them inside. The wind made the nuns' robes flap and sent bits of plant material and dust swirling unpredictably across the yard. The juveniles had invented some kind of practice that involved stalking bits of blown debris and pouncing when they stopped moving for more than a second. Snippets of the nuns' chatter, less animated than usual, carried to Echo on the wind. She heard the words but hardly processed them. "There, there, Luida," someone said. "You still have all of us."

"I knew he wasn't really just hiding in the desert after the rebellion," the girl said, voice catching the way cityens' did when they were not quite done crying. "But I always hoped one day, maybe I could see him once again. I just didn't want to believe as he could really be gone . . . Oh, Loro, my poor brother . . ." Her words dissolved into quiet sobs.

Echo closed her eyes, willing the dizziness to pass.

Something slammed low into her, wrenching her weak ankle with a stab of pain. Losing her balance, she tumbled into the yard amidst the laughter of the juveniles, the alarmed cries of the nuns. She landed on top of something that wriggled and poked her with a sharp elbow. She rolled off the child and onto her feet, hauling the girl up with a fist bunched in her shirt. Fury bared her teeth at her, eyes glinting in triumph.

"What do you think you're doing?" Echo demanded, shaking her hard.

"Caught th' hunter," Fury answered, the shaking snapping her teeth together. The other juveniles stared at her in stunned admiration.

Echo let go so suddenly the girl nearly fell. "Get back to your place and leave me alone."

Fury's expression froze. She wiped a bit of blood from her mouth where she'd bitten her tongue. She turned her head, barely, and spat, the red-tinged glob landing an inch from Echo's boot. Then she spun away, running out of the side yard, the gate clanging behind her. The other juveniles whooped and gave chase.

The nuns rose wearily to follow, their rest spoiled. Luida, last of them, paused at the gate. "She didn't mean to hurt you."

"It does not matter what she meant," Echo snapped. Luida turned away, not before Echo saw the tears start down her face again.

She tested the ankle with a cautious step. It held; she didn't care about the pain. She bent to re-tie her boot. As she knelt, she saw Stigir and Dalto on the landing at the top of the stairs. She didn't have to wonder how much they had seen: the Preserver's lips thinned; he shook his head in a faint motion of disgust. Dalto drew him away, towards the laboratories. He glanced back once over his shoulder as they left.

She snapped the laces tight. Then she forced herself to straighten. She tried to think the way a hunter should, assembling the facts she had barely attended to in her distraction. The weapons she had found in the mill, that Gem had said were all defective. The unrest in the city, and Kennit's fear of it. The Preservers. The Patri's determination to punish the Ward for its defiance. Her own fear that he would try to use the Saint to do it, and she would reject the command . . .

The pieces meshed together like Exey's gears, turning in some in explicable pattern whose purpose she could not see. Echo had set much of it in motion, one way or the other. She must stop it, to serve the Saint.

She limped down the stairs as fast as her ankle would let her. The confiscated projectile weapons sat in the locker, some intact and others disassembled in Gem's investigations. Handholds, cylinders, a few tiny gears . . . The actual projectiles were no more than metal pebbles. Such small things to cause so much destruction, and so few. Echo touched the puckered skin where Lia had cut one from her arm. It was not the weapons themselves that created the danger. It was the illusion of power they gave the men who held them. A cityen had dared attack a hunter; the Wardmen had dared rebel against the Church. And now another hunter dead. But something did not make sense. The Ward was making weapons, so everyone believed; but the Wardmen had nothing to gain from another war, and everything to lose. They had not even tried to defend their mill when she destroyed it, only gathered up the pieces and started over with the machinery, which was not so different from the parts scattered on the tray in front of Echo now.

Cylinders and gears. All her attention snapped back to the weapons before her. Cylinders and gears. She had seen them before. And she knew where.

CHAPTER 23

A few cityens were still out in the streets under the lightstrings, struggling with their baskets and handcarts as they tried to ready themselves for the storm. The wind caught a stooped old woman as she stepped out of the shelter of a wall to cross the street. Fighting her own impatience, Echo spared a moment to assist her, righting her cart and stuffing the goods that had not blown away back into it. The woman started to chase after a bag that was scudding down the alley. Echo caught her arm. "It is not worth it. Take what you have and go home, quickly." She raised her voice so the other cityens would hear. "All of you, go back to your domiciles. Seek shelter before it gets worse." An inopportune gust blew away her words. She could not tell if the cityens had heard her; a few looked her way, hesitating. Then, as if to belie her warning, the wind died suddenly. The calm seemed more ominous. The cityens shrugged and continued on as they had been.

She left them to their foolishness, debating where to search first. The tower seemed unlikely in the night and wind. She would have chosen the shop. A cityen, though, facing the prospect of long days isolated and confined . . . she found him at his brother's small habitation in the Bend. He was sitting at the single table, making odd noises and contorting his face at the baby in his arms. It appeared to be amused rather than alarmed, drooling toothlessly and trying to pluck the shiny yellow bauble from his hair. The expression dropped off his face when he saw her.

"Now you're breaking into my brother's house?"

She moved aside to let him see the woman behind her. "Perhaps"—she searched for the name; Mari, it came to her from long ago. A time with Lia. She shook herself. "Perhaps Mari would like to take the child."

The baby squalled in protest as Mari drew it away. Exey's brother poked his head out of the back room at the noise; his eyes met Mari's and the worried faces turned to her as one. Before they could ask Exey said, "Give us a few minutes, if you don't mind. It's old business, nothing to worry about. Just cover your ears if you hear screaming." His weak smile could not have reassured them, but after a moment they withdrew. The curtain did nothing to mute the baby's cries.

"I see you made another hairclasp."

"There's nothing to them." Exey's face contracted. "I took the design from a print Lia gave me."

Echo remembered the way Lia set prints aside for Exey, mechanical designs or simply pretty things she thought he'd like. She had given one of his ornaments to Echo once, a gold ring for her ear. Echo had lost it during the rebellion, a tiny failure that stung unexpectedly now. "What was the drawing you made in the tower?"

"Who knows? I draw all the time up there, I told you that before. Probably just some random design, something to sell at market. You know me, always fooling with my baubles."

"You were designing weapons. Why?"

"I have no idea what you're talking about. Hardly surprising, though, you always think the worst—"

"You know who's making them. Tell me." She took a step towards him, looked at the curtain, stopped. "I'll do anything," she said.

His face changed, and so did his voice. "Let's go outside."

He wasn't stupid enough to try to run from her, but she stood close to him anyway, backing him against the habitation's rough wall. The wind plucked a few strands of his hair free of the new clasp. "Tell me," she demanded.

"You don't know what you're asking." His eyes flickered towards the door.

"Who?"

His voice shook. "I don't know. I swear, I don't know. It was only ever messages. I never saw anyone. But they knew where my brother and Mari lived, and they said . . . I only left some prints, and a key I copied from the mill . . ."

"Saints, Exey! Have you learned nothing? Why didn't you come to the Church? We would have protected you. *I* would have."

"Like you protected *her*?"

She jerked her fist aside at the last second, splintering the doorframe instead of his bones. Someone inside cried out at the noise. "A hunter is dead! If the Church does not find the source of the weapons, what happens to the Ward will make the mill look like nothing."

"The Ward deserves it!" She stared at him dumbfounded. "Don't you see? It's all their fault. If they hadn't started talking about change, goading the cityens to rebel . . . None of this had to happen! The Church would never have sent you to the Ward. You would never have found Lia. And she would still— she would still be— Saints. Saints." Exey slid to the ground, back against the wall. His face dropped into his hands. "Lia. I've made a terrible mistake."

Echo squatted by him. "Who is making the weapons?"

"North," he whispered. "It's North. They just wanted to make it look like the Ward."

The mill, that she had destroyed with her own hands. The Saint's anguish, the order she had refused. And the surge that followed, and the Patri's threats. Echo clasped her hands together before they could close on Exey's throat. "You're passing weapon designs to North?"

"No! Yes, but it's not what you think. I swear by—"

"*Don't*," she hissed. "Don't you dare."

"You have to believe me. What I've given them— the weapons wouldn't work. Not any better than the old kind, anyway. What's the difference? They have them already. Everyone does . . ." His head rolled slowly back and forth. "Lia will never forgive me."

She hauled him to his feet. "Stop your nonsense and listen to me. Go to the Church now. Tell them what you just told me."

"They'll kill me," he wept.

He deserved it. That's what Nyree would say. For Marin alone . . . "Ask for Gem. Gem, no one else. Tell her everything. I swear to you, Exey—if you fail the Saint again, I will kill you myself."

Swirling dust and debris triggered the glowlights in random bursts that ruined her night vision, more troublesome than if it had merely been dark. At least she did not have to worry about the lights giving warning of her approach. By now everyone would be ignoring them. She saw no one else on the road to North, but that meant little. The same conditions that made it easy for her to cross the city unnoticed would favor others as well.

She arrived at the smithy at last. It was a squat building, sensible stone against the risk of fire, all but the shutters and the wooden door that creaked and rattled in its frame. Unsurprisingly, it was locked. She broke the handle with a hard jerk, the noise scarcely audible above the din of the storm. Inside the big main room it was warm, the fire banked in the forge. A pot sat atop the still-hot metal; absurdly, the sweet smell of slow-cooking grain made her mouth water. Tren slept on a pallet in a side room. Some sense warned him as she looked in; he stirred, reaching for a long metal bar that lay beside him. She evaded its swing easily and left the smith sleeping more soundly.

Then she tore the smithy systematically to pieces. It took an hour, and when she was done she had emptied every drawer, upended every box, checked every square of the floor for a false chamber. She even dumped out the container of grain he kept near the forge for his meals.

She found nothing.

She stood amidst the debris, feeling a gray sinking in her gut. If she accused North without evidence, it only showed that Kennit was right about her. Exey's word would be nothing to the Church; he had sided with the Ward once, and they would assume that he still did. And whatever he said about North, that he was involved with weapons at all—it was just further proof that the Wardmen must be punished.

And Jozef would make the Saint do it.

She thought quickly. Even with the storm, someone would show up at the smithy eventually. No one must suspect that a hunter had done this damage. Echo scattered the wreckage into a more disorderly pattern, then, after a moment's consideration, pocketed Tren's pouch of gold chits, small but heavy. He'd been doing well enough for himself. When she was finished, she peered through the shutters. It must be close to dawn, but the sky was still an opaque black. Tren would be sleeping late, thanks to her. She moved the pot off the forge so his breakfast wouldn't set the place on fire before he woke. That wasn't the kind of thing a thief would do, but the smith would be too upset to notice. He would need a good meal, to face the mess she was leaving. And he was obviously a man who enjoyed his grain: a pile of empty sacks lay folded in the corner, waiting to be taken back to the storehouse for refilling.

The storehouse. She stood for a moment, eyeing the sacks. They were the small kind that the grain was portioned into when an individual was allotted grain from storage, or bought extra at the market. A bit of red thread had been sewn into a corner of each, perhaps to mark them for Tren. She rubbed the fabric between her fingers, feeling the roughness of the weave. And something else, small and hard and flat, stuck in the corner. A bit of grain, maybe.

She flipped the bag inside out. The small object fell to the floor, where it landed with a faint clink. Heart pounding, she reached for it, held it close to the forge to see better. The light from the banked coals gave its sharp edges a reddish cast, like fresh blood staining a predator's teeth.

What she held was a tiny gear.

Echo broke a window out of the back of the store-house with the first heavy thing that came to her hand. Tren's pouch of chits, as it happened. The room she climbed into was full of old bones. She pulled her-self up a ladder of ribs and came face to face with a giant skull, teeth the size of her fingers bristling in a deadly grin. She slid quickly down the other side. She had little time; when the alarm was raised at the smithy, the Northers might think to check elsewhere, just in case Tren wasn't the victim of a random thief. If her guess was right, the storehouse would be high on their list.

She ignored the piles of grain sacks the juveniles had worked so hard to count. If the weapons were hidden among those, she had no hope of finding them, not by herself in what remained of the night. The front area, where the individual allocations were made. She had to hope the weapons were hidden there.

Hope won't make it happen or not happen, she had told Lia once long ago, when Echo still judged her a cityen, soft. Before Lia had become her world. Pain lanced through her. She stopped where she stood, wasting a precious moment to catch her breath. Then she set about her task.

She had to admire the Northers' foresight. Cityens, nervous about having enough grain to last through the storm, would have been picking up their allotments of grain right up until the weather forced the storehouse to close. Yet fresh bags were stacked in neat piles in the front room, ready to pass out as soon as the wind abated enough. She held her lightstick to the sacks. Plain, mostly, ones for sale; but some were marked as paid already, with a scrap of colored thread sewn through.

She pawed through the piles until she found red. Five sacks, far too much grain for one man's breakfast, even Tren's. She hefted them one by one, heart in her throat. If she was wrong about this . . .

The fourth sack was heavier than the others. She ripped the drawstring open, spilling grain across the floor like sand. Her hand dug through the bag, spilling more, and then closed around something hard.

Slowly she drew the weapon out. It fit in her hand with loathsome ease. The twinned cylinders gleamed dully in her lightstick's glow. She set it down, barrel aimed away from her, and dug out two more just like it. Then she tore open the fifth sack, dumping its contents onto the floor with a ringing clang. Hundreds of small metal balls poured out and chased each other around the floor.

Here was her evidence.

She should feel triumph, North's deception uncovered, the Ward shown innocent. The Saint, safe from being asked to punish her own people unjustly. Mostly Echo just felt sick. Cityens used these on each other. On hunters, like her.

One of the balls had rolled into the socket of a discarded skull. It stared up at her, a blind metal eye. The world ends over and over, it told her. The Fall happened to us. It will happen to you. The Church could find every weapon, punish everyone who touched one, but no one could make that instinct to use them go away. Men had been like that long before the Fall. Echo had told Lia as much, that long ago day.

But: *We don't have to be like that forever*, Lia had answered.

She swept the weapons back into the empty sack.

The lights came on, blinding her.

"Echo Hunter 367," a familiar voice said out of the glare. "What do you have there?"

Echo lifted the sack. "Slowly!" Nyree ordered. Gem must have told her. Amidst everything else, Echo felt the unexpected pang of something lost, almost before she knew she had it. "Set it down."

Echo did, with a metallic clank. And as her eyes adjusted to the brightness, she saw Nyree in the doorway, Kennit behind her, flanked by Brit and Cara. And she saw the weapons the hunters held. "Saints, Nyree!"

The woman's teeth gleamed in the bright light. "There is no sense in wasting a resource. But you haven't answered my question."

"The answer is obvious. I have found the cityens' weapons. The cache we were looking for. Tren is making them in his shop. North planned it all along; they only made it look like the Ward."

"She's a liar!" Kennit said.

"It seems likely," Nyree agreed, but Brit held Kennit's arm.

"Look for yourself," Echo said. "You can see what's happening. Tren makes the weapons, then they hide them in with the grain. You were right: they can move them anywhere in the city that way. But it's North, not Ward, that's doing it." She paused, another realization dawning. "They planted the weapons in the mill. The dead man—they killed him to be sure we would investigate." And she had fallen for their trick. "We thought exactly what they wanted us to."

"*She's* the one as been planting weapons," Kennit said. Sweat glistened on his throat; the prominence there worked. "She's been favoring the Wardmen all this time."

"Finish the search here," Echo said. "I must report to the Patri at once."

Nyree's weapon did not waver. "I do not take orders from you, Echo Hunter 367."

"Then listen to me and think, Nyree. We do not know how many of North are armed, or what they plan to do. They have already tricked the Patri into moving against the Ward. It will be a terrible mistake."

"You not only know better than me, you wish to correct the Patri as well? Your arrogance is breathtaking."

"Nyree, please. This is not about our differences. There is danger to the city. Maybe even to the Church. We must tell the Patri. Let him decide."

"He will want to know about the weapons," Brit said. Then, as Nyree stood stubbornly silent, she added, "Regardless of who planted them."

Nyree's face was hard. "I concur."

Brit, still holding Kennit's arm, gestured at Echo with her weapon. "No," Nyree said. "You stay here. Maintain the watch, in case the Wardmen try something under cover of the storm. I will take her myself."

"What about this man?" Brit asked.

Nyree cast Kennit a withering glance. "The Patri will decide what to do with him. With both of them."

The sky was the yellowing green of an old bruise, the rising sun's disk blurred, edges sanded away by the wind-borne grains. They found the Patri in the sanctuary, studying the panels. Gem was there too, holding Exey off to one side. Her grip on his arm looked as likely to be for support as to keep him under control; the fabricator's face was pale, his eyes wide and frightened. His gaze kept darting to the altar, where Khyn had threaded more cable to the wire circlet while Dalto made adjustments. The three of them barely acknowledged the odd gathering over by the panels, before returning to their work with feverish concentration.

"Is there evidence either way?" the Patri asked when Nyree finished her report.

"No," Nyree said. "I have been following her all night." Echo cast a shamed look at Gem, who answered with a wry quirk of her lips. "There were weapons in the storehouse, but Echo could have placed them there another time. The fabricator is known to have sympathized with the Ward. The two of them could be working together to cast the blame on North."

"You must believe me, Patri," Echo urged. "The Ward is not at fault. It was always North."

"We found no weapons the first time we searched the metalsmith's shop," Nyree said.

Another piece fell into place. "Tren invited us to search there."

"Yes. Because he knew he was innocent."

"No," Echo said slowly. "Exey told us to look in the smithies. But the other cityens did not know yet that

we were looking for newly made weapons. Old ones
could have come from anywhere. Tren wanted us to
search his shop so we wouldn't look there again. And
the weapons I found last night were new."

"You still could have planted them," Nyree said.

Echo shook her head in mute frustration. All the
things she was guilty of, and Nyree pursued the one
that she was not. "Why *would* I?" she asked.

No, that was not the question. Why would North?
Why would they make weapons at all? The Ward was
effectively disarmed, and North were hardly rebels . . .
The answer tried to shape itself, a handhold on the
truth. She could not grasp it. The work at the altar
distracted her; the glinting wire and the occasional
clink of metal sounded unnatural in the shadowy silence where the Preservers prepared the changes that
would save the Saint.

It's time for everything to change, Lia had said, here,
in this room, on that altar. She had meant the city,
and the Church. Even the change that was forced on
her, when she ascended as the Saint.

That was the answer. Change.

Echo bit back the sound that came to her lips.

Kennit, hearing, pointed a shaking finger at her.
"Patri, I've said it all along. She as hates North. She
was with the Ward from the beginning." His eyes
darted to Stigir and Khyn at the altar. "And strangers now, here as in the Church itself, ones as *she*
brought . . . It's as I feared. It's all as I feared."

"I don't have time for this trouble now," the Patri said. "Take them both away."

"No," Echo said. Now she realized Kennit was telling the truth. But not about her.

Nyree's hand closed hard on her arm. Her voice tightened with anger. "You have disobeyed the Patri for the last time. Even if you are innocent of planting the weapons—and we *will* find out your part in that—you are guilty of far worse. It is not only your actions that betray the Church. It is your heart. You know nothing of duty. You do not serve the Church. You are no hunter." Her lip curled in familiar disdain. "Only give your order, Patri, and I will cast her out myself."

Once the words would have shaken Echo to her very core. Somewhere inside the fear still clawed at her, but distantly. If they cast her out—she had to make them understand. But not for herself. The Saint preserved the city. All of it: Church and Ward and Bend and North. Hunters and priests and cityens. Even this cityen who stood in the sanctuary, his face twisted, fury and terror darkening his eyes. And now Echo knew why he wore that look.

"It *is* as you feared," she said to Kennit. There was a softness in her voice she did not recognize. "But your fear is not of me. It is not of the Preservers either. You've told us all along, but we failed to hear. Patri, don't you see? He fears the *change*."

The Patri's eyes narrowed. The pale gaze weighed

heavy on her, then shifted to Kennit, and under that scrutiny the Norther's face lost its last color. His eyes screwed shut, and he began to weep. "We only wanted as to help the Church. We're loyal, Patri, North has always been. But the Ward was never properly as punished, you were too kind to teach them the lessons as they deserved—" He drew a huge sobbing breath. "We never passed a weapon but was faulty, we never as armed the Church's enemies . . . If they tried to use them, that only showed that we were right. And then the strangers came, and all of us as arguing again, even some of my own too angry to obey . . . It's not as right, Patri. We must go back to how it was."

The Patri's voice rose in disbelief. "You have done these things because today is not the same as yesterday?"

"We only wanted a strong arm as was before, that's all. We serve the Church. The Church as it should be, and the city. We only wanted as to help you see it, Patri."

Jozef shook his head in slow disgust. "This is not service."

Echo closed her eyes as they took Kennit away. There was still work to do, to find the rest of the weapons, to close the gaps dividing the cityens. Part of her still burned with anger. The Ward had suffered for Kennit's lies, and some of that at Echo's hands. But the mill could be rebuilt. The Saint had suffered too. So many dead. So much pain. For men's fear, that they brought on themselves. Echo felt a twist of her own fear still, that the Preservers might fail. Some other thought tried to form as well. A loose connection, something she had missed . . . But all that barely penetrated the deep weariness inside. Now she only wanted to sit by the altar, by the Saint. To find the way to serve.

Nyree shifted, her hand still clamped on Echo's arm. Echo opened her eyes to see Stigir approaching from the altar, Khyn trailing behind him. "We could not help but overhear." The Preserver's voice was cool. "We've kept our part of the bargain until now. If your people do not want our help, only say so. We will join our friends at the aircar and leave as soon as the wind permits."

Fear jolted Echo back to full awareness. Nyree felt the change; her fingers dug deeper into Echo's arm. But the Patri only said, "The man did not speak for the Church. Please, continue as you were."

But Khyn was looking at Echo. "I wanted to see the reborn city you described. This place with people working together, growing, full of children. I wanted to bring that future back to the Preserve. That's why I came with you. But how you treat each other— what you *are*—there is nothing here for us." Her eyes swam, but the tears did not fall.

"Come," Stigir said, resting a hand on Khyn's shoulder. "The sooner we finish the sooner we can go home." He looked around the sanctuary, his face as weary as Echo felt. "I will be happy to be away from here. And happier still if you keep your promise, Patri Jozef."

The Patri smiled without humor. "We'll leave you alone, you needn't fear. We've brought each other enough trouble for a lifetime." Stigir searched Jozef's eyes. Echo wondered if he found what he sought. The Preserver only turned away after a moment and went back to the altar.

Echo made to follow, but Nyree jerked her back. "I have not finished with you."

"We will settle our differences later. I want to see her." Something in her voice, or in her face, made Nyree let go. Echo turned towards the altar. Gem stepped back to let her pass, but Echo stopped before the young hunter. An offer had been made, just before Marin died; Echo still owed an answer. It took a moment to find the words. "It has never been only a matter of resources, has it, Gem?"

A tiny pause, not even the space of a breath. Then: "You and the Saint showed me that."

Echo shook her head. "She taught us both." Echo extended her hand, a cityen's gesture, for hunters had none suitable.

Gem's lips quirked into the familiar half curve, but above it her eyes were warm. Her hand closed around Echo's in a grip that was strong and sure.

Then Echo limped the rest of the way to the altar. There the weariness and sorrow overtook her, and she

dropped to her knees. The circlet lay on the temporary couch, empty, waiting. Light gleamed off the cold
metal. Echo imagined the simple crown settling on Stigir's forehead, the moment when his eyes went wide
and empty, and his human mind danced through the
wires—he would not be connecting truly to the Saint,
he had explained that once, but touching, still . . . A
touch that was far beyond anything Echo could dream
of now.

Up so close, the light was merciless. It glinted
harshly off the Saint's metallic shroud and turned her
face into a bloodless mask, like a poor copy made in
pallid wax. Her lips still held their fullness, but the
lines beside them cut deeper, and her brows were
drawn slightly together, as if even in this deep sleep
something troubled her. That faint pain was the only
sign of life at all.

The pain burst in Echo's heart.

Saints. Lia.

Echo could not help herself. She reached out,
cupped Lia's cheek beneath the crown that bound
her to the Church. The skin was warm, as soft as she
remembered. Her whole body ached to crawl up on
the altar, despite the crown and tubes and shroud,
take Lia in her arms, hold her again as she had barely
learned to do before Lia sacrificed herself. Echo's
skin, her very bones could feel that embrace, soft and
warm and so real, so true that nothing else could
matter. She willed herself to Lia, the air in her lungs,

the blood pumping through her veins, the lightning surging through the circuits of her human mind . . . *Lia*, she wept inside. *Lia*.

Beneath her hands the Saint's lips moved. *Echo*, she heard Lia whisper, far away in the cage of wires. *Echo, my love*.

Then the background hum rose, machine pain screaming up through the scale until Echo clamped her hands over her ears. The priest holding the wire circlet screamed and fell away. An alarm shrieked through the sanctuary. Now the other priests were shouting, and she smelled hot metal. The Patri sprinted towards the panels, where Dalto called orders in a staccato burst. Something caught fire; the stench of smoke and burned flesh filled the room. She was dimly aware of Gem and Nyree batting at flames, shouting orders, Exey with the Preservers by the makeshift pallet. Forgotten, Echo crouched over the Saint's body, all she could do to protect her amidst the chaos. The priest thrashing about the floor knocked over a light stand. Echo tried to fend it off as it fell towards the altar, caught a blow to her head that made her senses swim. *Shh*, she whispered. *I have you. I have you*.

The alarm cut off abruptly. The other sounds died down more gradually; the lights steadying, the flurry of action slowing. "Flow contained," a priest called in a voice shaking with relief. "I concur," another said, and another.

Priests swarmed around the altar checking connections and cables. "Intact," someone said, and she sagged with relief. Strong hands eased Echo away. She let go reluctantly, the Saint's empty face swimming in her vision. The hands steadied her, then withdrew. Gem.

Someone had opened the door. Wind swept through the sanctuary, clearing the smoke, though an acrid haze clung high in the vaults, obscuring the rose window. The burned priest slumped in a chair, attended by others. The priests at the panels still worked, but deliberately now, and Dalto was nodding over his own boards. Finally he let out a huge breath. "Stable," he said. "But it was too close. Much too close. You must hurry, Stigir."

Stigir's eyes flicked from one board to the other. "What in the Preservers' name caused that?"

Dalto rubbed his face. "I don't know. All the flows were stable, then they all surged at once. But nothing else changed; there was no input from the boards. It started with the Saint."

The Patri said, "If it was something in the interface process . . ."

Dalto shook his head. "No. It came from the Saint herself."

Dread weighed in Echo's chest, making it hard to breathe. Dalto, the Patri, all of them looked to the altar.

But Exey looked at her.

"It's Echo," he said.

CHAPTER 24

"**N**o!" Echo backed until her hip bumped up against the hard edge of a panel. She stopped there, trapped, all of them staring at her. Gem, white-faced, took an almost imperceptible step, putting herself between Echo and the altar.

Defending the Saint against her.

But it was not the Saint who had called to her.

It was not the circuits screaming.

Dalto's eyes were wide with shock and recognition. "Saints. Saints, yes. Of course."

"That's impossible," the Patri said flatly. "She is a hunter. She cannot even read the boards, let alone input a signal to the Saint."

"There were small fluctuations before, but that first big surge was on the day she returned." Dalto's gaze fixed on Echo, and he nodded to himself. "All the others, she has been here—inside the sanctuary. All of them. And every time, the boards have shown an unexplained input. The pattern is clear. Why I didn't see before . . ."

Exey stared at her in something close to wonder. Soot streaked his face like a predator's claw marks. "Echo. Saints. She *knows* you."

"She causes the danger to the Saint?" Nyree's sharp tone cut through the sanctuary.

"She would not," Gem said, her certainty a rock beneath Echo's wobbling feet, and then her face changed, and the sliding sand carried Echo towards the edge. "Not knowingly."

"No," Echo whispered. Her breath came quick, pulse pounding with panic, as if some uncontrollable surge shot through her own nerves.

Nyree whipped out her projectile weapon, aiming it square at Echo's face. With her heightened senses Echo could see the firing level begin to move. She wondered if she would see the projectile before it tore through her brain.

Lia.

A panel shrieked new warning. "Stop!" Dalto ordered. "Lower the weapon."

Nyree only turned her head slightly, the cylinder still pointed straight at Echo. "Patri?" she asked calmly.

Jozef bared his teeth at the panels. "Do it."

For a moment Echo thought Nyree would disobey.

Her knuckle whitened on the lever. There could not be much more play before the mechanism fired. *I serve*—Nyree laid the weapon aside.

The alarm quieted. "She recognizes you," Exey said, his voice a shaking whisper. "The Saint remembers."

Gem looked down at the shrouded figure, then back to Echo. The corner of her mouth drew up in a faint smile, but the line cut deep between her brows. The boards' lights swam in her dark eyes. "She said she would. Before she ascended, she told us she would know if any harm came to her."

For one moment, a wild exhilaration shot through Echo. Not the Saint. Not the Saint alone. *Lia* still felt her, responded to her—*knew* her. It was not too late. If Lia still lived then somehow, one day, like Stigir she could—in the next moment, pain ripped through Echo's chest, so sharp that for an instant she thought Nyree had fired after all. The power surges, the feedback loops that threatened to destroy the Saint—it was Lia who suffered, deep within.

Saints, no!

Echo could not help herself; she turned to the board behind her, watched the input readout flicker. *No!* A fresh pain stabbed through her; the readout spiked.

Jozef closed on her. For all his slight build, he seemed to tower over her. Once before she had stood before the Patri—a different man, then, but she felt the same weight in the look upon her now, the same balance as her life turned upon his next words. Vanyi had excommunicated her from the Church, the greatest pain she had ever known. Until Lia's ascension.

What, she wondered, could Jozef do to her now? She was as afraid as she ever had been. But not of the Patri. She heard Vanyi's words again, coming from Gem's lips. *One must serve the Saint.* She thought she had been. *Oh, Lia, what have I done . . .*

The Patri's pale eyes pierced her. She stood pinned through, utterly helpless. He was thin beneath his robes, almost as fragile as the Saint; the bony points of his collarbones stuck out. But his irises were hard and metallic, projectiles staring at her from empty sockets. She saw no emotion in them at all, only the cold evaluation of the answer to a problem. Then he turned away, one last dismissal. "Finish your work, Stigir. When the gap in the circuit is closed, this will all be over."

Echo barely felt Nyree's grip digging into her arm as she dragged her across the wind-swept yard. Terror squeezed her gut. If the Saint could not control herself—if the Patri thought his fears were realized—

Stigir must complete the repair. The surges must be stopped. There was no other hope for the Saint.

For Lia.

Echo stumbled over some piece of debris in the yard. The weak ankle gave; Nyree pulled her upright with a punishing jerk. "You knew. You knew you were causing the surges." Nyree's nostrils flared. "I said all along you were a danger to the Church, but I never imagined—it is time to put a stop to this for good." Nyree dragged her forward again into a stumbling walk.

The Saint—Echo took a breath, forcing herself to think only of the air passing between her lips, trickling past the swelling in her throat. She jerked free of Nyree's grip. "That will make it worse! She'll know. You can't just—" But Nyree had drawn her stunwand.

"For once I find your reasoning sound." The wand hummed up to full charge. "I will take you past the forcewall. It will be as if you left again in search of other cities. Even the Saint would not doubt that you could be such a fool. And the odds of your survival were always small. She could not expect you to survive a second time. Come."

The wind whipped at them both, spraying sand. The yard was utterly empty; they might have stood in the far wastes, alone, away from everything.

Nyree raised the stunner. "I can carry you if need be."

Echo stood still one more moment, estimating the odds. Nyree, weight centered, one hand holding the stunner raised, the other poised lightly just above waist level. The fighting hormones were well controlled, harnessed to lend her the extra strength, the quickness to anticipate the slightest move from her opponent. It would be suicide to take her on here. A better chance would come, however slim. She must be ready to take it.

Nyree saw the thought; she smiled.

Whatever happens, I will not let go, Echo vowed; but she held the words inside, where they could not hurt Lia.

The yard blurred in her vision. Cloth flapped towards them in the wind. A discarded shirt, Echo thought for an absurd instant. Then she saw the hands emerging from too-long sleeves. And the projectile weapon they held.

Saints.

"Caught th' hunter," Fury said.

CHAPTER 25

"**W**hat are you doing, girl?" Nyree demanded. The stunwand disappeared behind her back, but it could be out again much faster than Echo could overpower her. Not, however, faster than a projectile. Fury's weapon aimed squarely at Nyree.

"Okay?" Fury asked Echo.

"I'm fine," Echo said. Her heart hammered in fear for the girl. It would only take a split second's distraction, and Saints, Nyree against the child . . . "Fine. But you should be in the refectory with the others."

"She hurting you," Fury said, eyes narrow with anger.

"No, she's not. She's helping me. We . . . We have something we need to do, that is all."

"Back soon?"

"As soon as . . ." Echo's voice trailed off. She had

never lied to the girl, not from the first day in the desert so long ago. "I don't know."

Fury scowled at her, a warning of temper to come. "If you are not able to resolve this situation, I will do it," Nyree warned.

"Listen to me." Echo knelt by the girl, shielding Nyree from the weapon. If the child fired now, Nyree would be pleased. Maybe that would be enough for her to show mercy.

"No." Fury's eyes darted to the sanctuary. "Back to your place."

"It isn't my place now." The words hurt even to speak.

An inarticulate pain welled in Fury's eyes. Her face twisted on itself. "Go with you," she said in a muffled voice.

Echo grasped the small shoulders. They were shaking, from the weight of the weapon or the effort to hold back the tears. "You can't go where I'm going. No, listen. You have to let me go." She tried to think. What would happen to the child if Echo never returned? "I know: go to your brother. You can stay with him. That's the place you want, isn't it?" The girl's eyes widened, tears spilling over. "Then go. You don't have to try to be a hunter anymore. The priests won't care, as long as you don't make trouble. And Indine won't be angry. Nyree will see to it." Echo twisted to look over her shoulder. "Isn't that right, Nyree?"

The woman was silent for so long that Echo thought she would refuse out of sheer spite. Finally Nyree stretched out a hand. "Give me the weapon."

Fury shrugged out of Echo's gasp. She walked right up to Nyree, but she didn't lower the barrel. Nyree stood still, waiting. Echo's pulse raced. Then Fury slammed the weapon into Nyree's palm. She grabbed Echo in one more fierce hug, so tight it squeezed the breath from Echo's lungs, leaving her mute. Then the girl took off, flying towards the priests' domicile.

After a minute Echo rose. "Promise me, Nyree."

Nyree looked past her. "She was never a hunter."

They stood at the edge of the city. Nyree had bound her wrists with a scrap of wire from the sanctuary, never giving her the smallest opening to resist. The windstorm had erased the horizon, leaving nothing but a red-brown fog, as if the world were being eaten away from the edges first. Echo had crossed the force-wall more times than she could count. Each time before—even on that horrible day the old Patri had excommunicated her, cutting her off from all the life she had ever known—even then she had harbored, deep within, some faint spark of hope that she would find a way home. Now the next step she took would be onto the road that led only to one end.

Even at this distance she dare not think of Lia. She must not say goodbye.

She turned for a last look at the spire, but it was lost in the haze.

When she turned back, Nyree had the projectile weapon in her hand again, squared at Echo's chest. Echo summoned all her strength. The effort would be futile, but she would make it anyway. She served the Saint.

Before she could move she heard a muffled noise, far away, dull, like a heart bursting. *The journey will be short*, she thought with a kind of relieved surprise.

Then Nyree's head swung abruptly to the north as the other hunter heard it too. The hollow *bang* sounded again. *Saints!* It was coming from the aircar.

"Nyree, we have to—"

The other hunter spun back. "Cross the forcewall now, or I will kill you inside whether the Saint knows it or not!"

A last choice how to serve. Echo's shoulders slumped. She turned slowly away from Nyree, taking half a step towards the desert. Her ankle twisted and she slipped to a knee. Her fists clenched in the gritty dirt. Nyree raised the weapon.

Then Echo thrust herself to her feet, whirling in the same moment to fling the double handful of sand into Nyree's face. And then she sprinted hard in the direction of the aircar.

A searing pain creased her hip at the same time the sharp crack of the weapon hit her ears. How many cylinders? She hadn't paid attention. One, two, how many times could Nyree possibly miss?

The wind helped. She let it buffet her in zigs and zags while she ran. She heard another *crack* and flinched, anticipating impact, but the projectile whined off a rock. No third shot followed. Nyree would have to slow down to reload. Echo forced herself to run faster, despite the pain in her hip and the old ache in her ankle. She cut towards the road, where the footing would be better. She listened for the sound of pursuit as best she could above the howling wind, but all she could hear was her own heaving breath, and the whine of engines.

There, just over the crest of the hill, was the aircar. In the blur of whirling sand and wind-drawn tears, Echo could see only the outlines of figures crouched in twos and threes in sheltered positions opposite the aircar. And the one on the ground, lying still. They caught sight of her at the exact same moment. One of the figures straightened, raising an arm. She saw a bright spark, heard the familiar crack. And something slammed into her, knocking her off her feet with a crushing blow.

She landed in the ditch alongside the road, breath driven from her body, vision dark. She gasped for air, but a weight compressed her chest, and something closed around her throat. She thrashed in an instant of animal terror. Then: *Think like a hunter,* her own voice hissed savagely in her mind. It was a knee in her chest, and hands choking her. She thrust up with both fists to break the grip, and froze.

"Brit!" she rasped.

"Echo Hunter 367." Brit rolled off her, then shoved her back down as she tried to rise. "Do not expose your head. Report."

"I had a disagreement with Nyree. What is happening here? The Preservers—"

Brit made a noise of disgust. "We overestimated the Northers' common sense. A group of Kennit's friends came looking for him. We persuaded them that confrontation with us would be foolish. We believed they had withdrawn, but unfortunately someone got the even more foolish idea that they could take the Preservers hostage to trade for him." She gestured towards the aircar. "As long as the Preservers keep their heads, nothing will come of it. We could counterattack, of course, but it seems safer for all concerned to wait them out."

Echo raised her head cautiously over the edge of the ditch. The jammed hatch still hung partway open, but otherwise the aircar did not show the damage she feared. But there was a cable wrapped around one of the landing struts, tied off to something in the rubble. The cable stretched taut as the aircar tried to lift, the straining engines sounding oddly weak. That was the windstorm: there hadn't been enough sun in days to restore the power. The cable held; the aircar bounced back down with a thump.

"I heard explosions."

"The projectile weapons remain unreliable. Projtrodes are not much more accurate in this wind, but at least they do not blow up."

That explained the downed cityen. Echo could only imagine what the Preservers must be thinking, trapped in their aircar, the sounds of a battle around them, no idea who their assailants were, or that the hunters were trying to protect them. "Untie me."

Brit took in the wire binding her wrists, the blood staining one whole leg of Echo's pants. Her brows drew together. "What was the nature of your disagreement with Nyree?"

"The Patri guaranteed the Preservers' safety. We cannot break his bargain! Stigir will stop his work on the Saint." And when the other hunter still hesitated: "The Saint is in danger, Brit. I need to get to the aircar."

Brit unwound the cable from Echo's wrists. "What do you propose?"

"Draw the cityens' attention long enough for me to get to the Preservers. We must make them understand it was not the Church that attacked them."

Brit asked no foolish questions, only nodded and slipped away. In a few minutes, there was a shout from beyond the aircar, and sand erupting as a flurry of projectiles struck near the cityens. Brit throwing pebbles, but the cityens ducked deeper into cover. Echo shot out of the ditch and dove towards the aircar. The cityens figured it out too late; she had ducked beneath the car, crouching in the shelter of a landing strut, before they could bring their weapons to bear. A few projectiles struck the strut, sparking; but they only scratched the metal.

"Taavi," Echo shouted up towards the hatch. "Taavi, it's me, Echo. I mean you no harm, I just want to talk to you." She couldn't tell if they heard. "It's me!" The aircar engines revved again. The wind sang across the taut cable. Metal creaked, but the cable still held. An energy weapon poked out of the hatch, seeking Echo blindly. Its eye flashed once, twice; red beams reflected chaotically around her. "Taavi!" Echo screamed again.

She flung herself back just in time to avoid being crushed by the strut as the aircar thumped back to the ground. It bounced, pulling at the cable. The weapon flashed again. The beam missed Echo and ricocheted off the strut. By some fluke of geometry it cut through the cable, which snapped with an enormous twang.

The broken cable whipped through the air. The aircar, its back end suddenly sprung free, tipped tail up. Echo threw herself flat as the nose of the craft nearly hit the ground in front of her. For one brief moment, the open hatch was in reach. She sprang up, grabbed the lip, and was swung into the air as the craft leveled again.

For an instant she hung there by her fingertips, body buffeted by the wind and shoulders creaking with strain. The weapon protruded over her head. Instinct screamed at her to drop while she had a chance, however tiny, to survive the fall. Instead, she gathered her breath, made one enormous effort, and flung herself up and over the lip of the hatch. She kicked at the Preserver holding the weapon, knocking it out of the vektere's hands. It tumbled away through the air. In the same moment her hands slipped, scrabbling vainly for purchase on the smooth metal, and her legs went back over the edge. All that held her were the fingertips of her left hand, caught in the hinge between the hatch and the frame. The craft bounced in the wind; one of her fingers broke with a sickening crack. The pain shot clear to her shoulder.

She was going to fall, surely as a girl sliding over the edge of a cliff. Time hung, suspended in the air like her body. The aircar was still scudding forward, towards the city. Her grip wasn't going to last long enough for it to matter to her. She twisted a little as she dangled there, searching one last time for the spire. The distant panels still turned, arms spread for a final embrace. The power flashed, as fast as Echo's pulse, the Saint's heartbeat matched to hers. For an instant she imagined Lia's golden eyes opening to look on her a last time. Heard her voice whisper, *Echo. Echo, my love.*

It was all she wanted. She felt her fingers loosen.

She didn't care. She would stare into those eyes all the way down. She would never feel the last blow.

But Lia would. Echo flung her other hand up, flailing for any grip. Her fingers closed around flesh, sheer reflex as something clamped around her wrist. Then she was being pulled back over the edge of the hatch and into the arms of the vektere who'd caught her. The two of them tumbled into the aircar. Echo had a confused view of weapons swinging to aim as the aircar bucked with the sudden shift in weight. She clutched the vektere in a tight hug, holding him close to shield her body from the beams as they fell together half upright across a seat.

Not him, her. Taavi.

"Don't fire in here!" one of the vektere shouted.

The craft bounced again, turbulent with the wind gusting in through the open hatch. Somehow the pilot wrestled it into a semblance of controlled flight. "Listen to me," Echo gasped. "It wasn't the Church."

"Let Taavi go!"

She had little to lose, and maybe it would calm them. She pushed the young vektere away, not roughly. Others pinned Echo's arms over the back of the seat. One jammed the end of his weapon into her ear. His face said he was willing to risk a shot inside the aircar if he had to.

Jole pulled Taavi to her feet. "You should have let her fall." Taavi, white-faced, only shook her head. Jole let her go.

"Land the aircar," Echo said. Her broken hand throbbed in nauseating waves. The scent of the vekteres' fear was overwhelming. They were not hunters. They did not want to die. That was useful. "You don't have to get yourselves killed." The pilot looked back over his shoulder at Jole. "That's right. We can talk. Just land the aircar."

"So your friends can finish what they started?" Jole said. His voice shook.

"It was cityens, not the Church. They aren't—" She realized the hopelessness of trying to explain. Saints, she barely understood herself, the claves, the rivalries, the fear that made it easier for men to kill each other than face the changes . . . The Preservers did not deserve to die for that. "Taavi, you know me. I'll protect you—but I can't, if you attack the Church. Just land the aircar and—"

"I do know you. I know that we can't trust you. No one's landing anything until Stigir and Khyn are safe."

Echo turned her head, ignoring the weapon digging into her ear. Through the forward windows she saw the forceshield shimmering, invisible to cityen eyes. The vektere had forgotten about it in their panic. Another few seconds, and it would do her job for her.

The forceshield glimmered. Three more heartbeats. Two. One.

Nothing.

The barrier flicked and died. Through the rear windows she caught a glimpse as it came up again behind them, letting the aircar pass untouched.

Saints. Lia, no.

The car jostled in the wind, but the pilot steered it right down the main road toward the Church. The spire flashed ahead.

"Set down by the steps," Jole ordered. "She can get us through the doors."

She would never let them into the Church.

Now she had only one choice. She closed her mind before Lia could hear the thought.

"Saints help us!" she cried. "Look! They're after us!"

Frightened, all senses primed for action, the vektere could not prevent the instinctive response. For the space of an indrawn breath their attention followed her terrified gaze out the back windows. It was just long enough.

She slammed a boot into the knee of the vektere holding the weapon at her ear, jerking her head back hard against the seat in the same moment. The bolt sizzled past her face so close she smelled the burning air. She sank farther into the seat, and as the vektere holding her arms instinctively pulled up against her, she thrust up and back with all the strength in her legs and hips. The seat back broke; the vektere pinning her arms lost their leverage. Instead of pulling away she pushed back again, into them. They stumbled off balance, all the opening she needed to jerk herself free.

She saw the road passing beneath the open hatch, close enough for her to risk a jump. That wasn't her goal. She leapt across the gap towards the pilot. Her fist slammed into his face at the same time she rammed the lever to pitch the nose of the craft straight down into the road.

There was a screech of metal as the nose skidded along the stone. Somehow the aircar held together. They had not had much forward speed to begin with, and it was a sturdy little craft. As the nose dug in, the tail rose, sending everyone rolling forward. They were going to flip, hit upside down. Echo nodded to herself. That would be good enough. She strained for a last look up at the spire.

The craft kept tipping, tail up and up, nearly vertical now, spinning in a half circle as the wind blew it in a pirouette around its dragging nose. And then Echo saw the curtain of sand, rising on the wind in front of them as solid as a wall. The blowing grains struck the hull with a noise like innumerable projectile weapons fired all at once.

Everything slowed. Then, absurdly, another gust blew the tail back down flat. The craft skidded right up the steps, metal and vektere screaming. Echo took one last breath. Closing her eyes, she fixed Lia's face in her mind. *Forgive me. Forgive me for everything. I love you.* Then the aircar hit the cathedral wall, and everything went black.

CHAPTER 26

She woke abruptly, facing a wall. Every part of her body hurt, so much that she could barely draw breath. *This has happened before*, she thought, and then, as someone laughed far away, *Gem. She is laughing at me.*

It took a little while to get any farther. She eventually opened her eyes onto a dimness that was intermittently lit by something flashing. The flashes hurt her head; she let her eyes drift closed again. She heard noises: the hum of machinery, and voices arguing, and a pulsing sound that must be some kind of alarm she had never heard before. Metal creaked ominously nearby; while she pondered that, something fell, rattling the floor she lay on.

There was a curse, and more laughter. Out of the babble one word coalesced: *Saint.*

She snapped abruptly conscious.

The wall in front of her was stone. The machine hum, the dim light—she was in the sanctuary. She must have been thrown clear when the aircar crashed. She let her head fall to the side, hoping that if anyone noticed, it would seem the boneless movement of someone still unconscious. Even fully awake, it took her a moment to understand what she was seeing: the broken nose of the aircar, metal peeled back like one of Gem's exploded weapon cylinders. It jutted through the cathedral's stone wall, next to the huge metal doors, which stood defiantly intact. Blowing sand trickled through the gaps; outside the wind howled like the fear in Echo's heart. She lay unguarded. Either the others in the sanctuary hadn't seen her, or they thought she was dead.

At least some of the Preservers had survived as well. Jole said something sharp and angry. It made Gem laugh again. The sharp *slap* of a hand on flesh stopped her. Echo could not imagine why Gem had let him live so long.

Echo rolled in a slow movement that would not draw attention. Then she saw, and her stomach dropped, as in an aircar that had lost thrust.

Gem stood by the Saint. Her hands were raised wide from her body, and she stood nearly as still as the figure on the altar. Jole held a projectile weapon that he must have taken from her. He had been able to because Taavi perched at the top of the altar, her energy weapon clenched in both fists. Its ugly eye stared down at the Saint. She only had to press the button. It would mean the end of everything. Priests sat at their panels, frozen in dismay. Stigir stood by the Saint, the circlet of the new interface dangling from one hand. So close. If Echo had done something, anything, to delay the aircar . . .

She closed her eyes again. Pain washed through her. *Lia*.

The alarm pulsed louder. "The storm is making things worse," someone said in a voice tight with fear. Dalto. "It's taxing the city circuits. If the systems overload now, the whole sanctuary may go up." Wind whistled through the gap in the broken wall. "We don't have much time."

Echo tried to calculate angles, lines of attack. She could barely focus; the alarm seemed to pulse inside her head. She forced herself to think. By now the hunters would be positioned outside, planning to retake the sanctuary; but they did not dare any action that would endanger the Saint. Taavi was the immediate threat. If Echo could somehow wrestle her away from the Saint before she had time to fire . . . Gem caught her eye, shook her head fractionally, *No*.

The Patri, by the panels, said, "Please finish your work, Stigir."

"Finish?" Khyn's voice was incredulous. "If you think he would ever do anything to help you after you—"

"Hunters would not have attacked the aircar," the

Patri said. It was the tone he would use with the councilors, or anyone else he was trying hard to make see sense. "You are doing what we agreed. We have no reason to break our bargain."

"And we would have succeeded if we meant to destroy you," Gem said. Jole raised his hand again, but she only looked at him, and this time he decided to hold it.

"It is what you are best at," Stigir said, but it was sorrow more than bitterness that weighted his words.

"*She* tried," Jole spat. His weapon swung to cover Echo. "I know you're awake. Get up."

Echo climbed shakily to her feet. Partway up she had to stop, hands on knees, until the sanctuary stopped spinning around her. Her pant leg was soaked in blood. It was a struggle to put words together. "It was North. The hunters were trying to protect you. I tried to tell you—I just wanted Stigir to help the Saint." She turned to the Preserver. *"Please."*

Stigir's look burned into her like the hot beam of an energy weapon. Then he settled the circlet over his head. "I am thankful that we are not like you."

"Stigir," Khyn whispered.

"We are *Preservers*," he said, leaning back on the makeshift couch. A length of wire ran from the circlet to a panel; it would bring him closer to the Saint than Echo had ever been. Her fists tried to clench, sending a bolt of pain up her arm from the broken finger.

Stigir nodded at Dalto. "Let us finish this. Begin the sequence."

The priest folded his hands together for a moment, head bowed, then reached for his board.

"How long to interface?" Stigir asked in a distant voice. His eyes were already losing focus, body slackening as his mind fell towards the link.

"Coming online in ten seconds. Nine, eight, seven—"

Lia. Please. Let them help you. Even if it means we can never—

Dalto's fingers seemed awkward as Echo had never seen them. His movements were hesitant, jerky. Something was wrong, something even Dalto feared . . .

"Wait," Echo said.

"It is too late," Dalto said. Sorrow gathered in his eyes, spilled down his face. His hands trembled as they played across his panel. He adjusted a dial, and Stigir's body stiffened in the chair. Every muscle in Echo's body jerked as if the panel fired her nerves too. On the altar, the Saint's lips parted in a tiny, human gasp.

The alarm shrieked. "Cut the sound, Dalto," the Patri said. The silence thundered in Echo's ears, answering the thunder in her heart.

Stop them, the Saint said in her mind. In Lia's voice. Echo's head jerked to the altar, where the Saint lay in her eternal silence. Then her gaze dropped to Dalto's board. She saw the Saint there too, in the dials and readouts, the light playing across the screen, shining

like the constellations that guided hunters home . . .
The pattern fractured in her vision. She blinked furiously, and it cleared. And she saw. That line, that
curve—a gap where it didn't belong. A step that led
to an endless drop—

Dalto's fingers hovered above the button.

"Four, three, two—"

Saints, Lia, what have I done . . .

Stop them.

Echo's hand clamped over Dalto's wrist. She
twisted, flinging him half out of his chair.

Jole swung his weapon to her. Echo crouched over
the panel as if she could shield the Saint that way. "No
one fire!" Gem ordered with twenty generations of
hunter authority in her calm voice, and by some miracle, it worked, everyone freezing in place for the split
second it took Stigir to open his eyes.

Khyn ran to him, helping him sit. "I'm all right,"
he murmured. The circlet gleamed against his hair.

The Patri advanced on Echo. "What do you think
you're doing?" His voice was icy, but it held more
death than Vanyi's ever had.

"Patri," she choked out, pointing a shaking hand
a Dalto. "He has betrayed the Church. I heard him
talking that day. When you told him to find a way
to stabilize the Saint—'reduce her to basic systems,'
he said. Somehow when Stigir is in the link—Dalto
means to make it happen now—something terrible,
something that will hurt the Saint—"

"I'm afraid you misunderstand," the Patri said. His hands wove together, thumbs tapping a thoughtful rhythm. "Dalto serves the Church most loyally." He turned to the priest, who was settling himself back at his board. Echo's heart slammed against her chest. She was missing something still, something of utmost importance to the Saint.

Dalto was not afraid, not as he should have been, his plan exposed. Instead the priest only indicated a pattern on the panel. "It is as we expected, Patri."

She looked at Jozef. And saw, in his shadowed gaze, that he knew. Her blood congealed. "Patri, what in the name of the Saint—"

The Patri ignored her. He studied the flashing pattern, the Saint's distress. Then he turned to Stigir. "You, on the other hand—I believe you intended to do more than tune the interface for us. You would have made certain changes, things you thought we wouldn't notice, or at least not until you were gone. It would have been a gradual winding down, until only the most primitive functions were left." His lip curled in an expression Echo could not decipher. "I am correct, am I not?"

All the color had left Stigir's face. His eyes flicked from Dalto to the Patri, and then to the Saint. At last he asked, "How did you know?"

Dalto traced the pattern on his panel. "My life, in service to the Church."

Stigir stood quiet for a moment. Then he said,

"You cannot stop us. If Dalto initiates the circuit with no mind to bridge the interface, she will be destroyed instantly. And if you do not initiate the circuit at all"—he grimaced as an alarm, broken free of Dalto's control, shrieked again—"she does not have long to survive with the surges as they are."

"I'm afraid you misunderstand," the Patri said briskly, "I don't want to stop you. We seek the same thing. Please, continue."

Stigir's face was blank with astonishment. "You *want* me to do it?"

"If we go on as we have been, we risk losing the whole system. This way we have certainty."

The wind howled through the gap in the cathedral wall. It sounded like the city screaming. The force of it pushed Echo a half step forward, towards the edge of the cliff.

"She is the *Saint*!" Echo cried. "That is all the certainty we need!" She struggled desperately for the words that might make them understand. "That day that she rejected your command—it was to save you. She knew the Ward was innocent. That's why she disobeyed. What you were making her do"—*Saints, I brought them the splitter that let them do it*—"it was killing her. But she saved you from making a terrible mistake. And to repay her you would destroy her mind. Make her into nothing more than a piece of machinery . . ." Dalto shook his head. She saw again the sorrow in his eyes. It made no difference. He was in easy reach, his throat exposed, his thin neck waiting for her hands to wrap around it . . .

"It wasn't us killing her," Dalto said. "It was you."

Blood loss grayed Echo's vision. She pressed her palms to her eyes. He was wrong, but it didn't matter. She had wanted Lia back. From the moment she saw Stigir take off his crown, there in the Vault in the Preserver's mountain—that was what she had wanted. Everything else was just an excuse. "Patri, please. Believe this one thing: the Saint knows her duty. She chose to serve. Only help her, and she will do it until the last beat of her heart. But not like this! She sacrificed everything for the city, everything! Do not take that from her. Do not make it all meaningless."

By the altar, Gem drew a breath, sharp enough to hear against the wind. Her face was utterly still. She looked from the Patri to Echo, and then to the Saint. Her head bowed.

The Patri shook his head. "We have lost sight of the reason for her existence, worshipping her too long, thinking of her as a living mystery, a greatness we could never understand. She is not. She is an interface with the systems, no more, as the very first Saint was made to be. And she must be the Saint we need. You have shown me the evidence clearly enough. We will never control her fully as she is." Jozef laughed, but it was touched with sorrow. "I do believe I finally understand why Vanyi chose me." He turned to Stigir, dismissing Echo. "I realize that I can't force you—the mind has to be willing to enter the interface. But it is far and away your most reasonable choice. I am still perfectly willing to keep our bargain. Help us now, and we will let you go, and leave your Preserve in peace. As I said, we want the same thing."

Stigir stood turning the gleaming circlet over and over in his hands. At last he said, "One day the world will be reborn, but it is not now. This city is an ending, not a beginning. You have brought this doom on yourselves, and you have earned it. But for the sake of the Preserve, and only that, I will do as you ask." His stare burned into Echo like the beam of an energy weapon. "We should have left you in the desert to die." He sat down on the edge of the couch. "If anything goes amiss, Taavi, kill the Saint." On the altar, the girl nodded, white-faced.

"Patri," Echo whispered. Pain fired through her nerves, paralyzing her. She heard circuitry sizzle, smelled hot metal and smoke.

"Get Echo away!" Dalto said. "Now!"

Jole raised his weapon. "This will be quicker."

"Don't—" Dalto started, but it was too late. Before Jole could press the trigger, a shower of sparks erupted from a panel, dazzling in the sanctuary's gloom. For the fleeting moment before the tiny stars winked out, everyone turned to watch. Everyone except Gem, who leapt up on the altar in that infinitesimal gap and wrestled Taavi away from the Saint. The struggle only took an instant, but it was long enough for

Echo's fist to connect with Jole's jaw. She reached for his weapon as it fell, but her broken hand missed its grip and the thing clattered away somewhere out of reach.

And then Gem fell too, folding bonelessly across the altar.

Taavi backed away, face twisted with horror. "I didn't mean to—" Her breath caught. Then she steadied, aiming her weapon at the Saint. Her finger whitened on the button.

Echo threw herself forward. She struck Taavi's hands up; the beam stung her cheek on its way to sinking harmlessly into ancient stone. Echo snaked a hand around the back of Taavi's head, grasping the braid at its root; the other, broken finger and all, crushed across her mouth. She felt the vektere's lips move, protesting; their faces were so close together that Echo could see the tiny threaded muscles pulling the blackness across Taavi's blue eyes. "Drop it," Echo pleaded, but instead Taavi twisted, fighting to bring the weapon back to bear. Then there was no other choice. With a swift and practiced motion, Echo snapped her neck.

Khyn screamed something, but the words were distant, meaningless.

"Gem!" Echo caught the young hunter up in her arms. There was far too much blood pulsing from the hole in her chest, soaking Echo's hands, dimming the Saint's glittering shroud. "Gem, no!"

"I promised you I would protect her with my life." Gem's voice bubbled, drowning. Her eyes, wide, already blind, sought the Saint. She saw something, or thought she did; a slow, bloody smile played across her face. "I promised I would remember. . . ." She took a long, rattling breath. "Lia," she whispered on the exhale, and that was all.

For a suspended moment, the sanctuary stilled. Then:

"Lia?" Khyn's voice broke across the name. "Oh, Preservers help us. The Saint is your *Lia*?" She dropped her face into her hands and began to laugh, a lost and bitter sound.

Echo set Gem's body down gently. She rose from the altar. Somehow Taavi's fallen weapon found its way into her hand.

"Put the crown on," Echo ordered Stigir. Her face felt numb. Taavi's last shot must have done something to it. When the Stigir still hesitated she said, "Be willing, or be dead."

Stigir looked at her a long moment, then shrugged. He settled in the seat and lifted the circlet. Keeping her weapon steady on him, she moved to look over Dalto's shoulder. "Set the tuning right to make her whole. I can read the boards. If you hurt her, either of you, I will know. I promise you, I will know."

The priest was brave enough to look to the Patri. Jozef's lips parted slightly, as if he meant to say something, but no words came. He only nodded once, his face unreadable. Dalto's eyes squeezed shut; he inhaled deeply, held it for a moment, then let the air out in a long sigh. His hands moved across his panel. Stigir's face went distant, and his eyes closed. "Interface in five-four-three—"

Echo didn't even have time to turn. There was the familiar *crack*, and something hit her in the back with numbing force. She stumbled forward, falling against the pallet. Alarms shrieked and lights flashed wildly; Dalto scrambled at his board. Khyn stood with Jole's projectile weapon smoking in her hand, a wild grief distorting her face. Echo tried to reach for her and fell, gasping for air that would not come.

Khyn was sobbing. "It's better for us to die here than hand you the future. Look at what you've made of this place! You say you want to serve, but you only serve yourselves. Killing each other, abandoning your children . . . When I saw"—she dragged a gasping breath, as if she too were drowning—"when I saw what you did to poor Marin I knew. If you did that to your own—you'll never keep your bargain. One day you'll decide you want what we have. The Vault, the seed, everything—and nothing will stop you. Nothing. You'll come and take it all, and not think twice. You'll justify it in the name of your own survival. I thought you were bringing us a new beginning. But all you bring is death." Then her voice grew preternaturally calm. "Look at you. How could she ever have loved *you*?"

The words exploded in Echo's heart like projectiles fired from within. For a moment, she almost believed them. But then she remembered: here, in this room, before the altar the Saint now slept on, Lia had wept: *Echo. I love you. Give me that to take with me.*

And Echo had.

Nothing would ever make her doubt that.

Khyn aimed her weapon at Dalto. "Get the crown off Stigir." The priest obeyed silently, helping the dazed Preserver off the couch, while Khyn's free hand scrabbled over Dalto's board. The discarded circlet fell to the couch, wires dangling.

Echo crawled to her knees. "Khyn, please!"

Khyn's hand hovered over the button. She was weeping again, rage and despair. "You should be glad. The city won't be able to hurt her anymore. *You* won't. She would thank me, if she could."

"She would never put her own good first," Echo said. Her vision was blurring, darkness rimming the edges. "She never did. She could have chosen—" *me,* she almost said, but neither of them deserved that thought, continued instead, "She could have lived. She never had to ascend. Please Khyn. You're a Preserver. Don't destroy her."

"This is what your city has made me. What *you* have made me."

Time stretched, but there would never be enough of it. Not enough to stop Khyn. To kneel by the Saint, and say that she was sorry. To say anything at all.

There would only be this one empty moment forever, now.

Khyn's hand moved, slowly, descending towards the button.

Echo was sliding towards the edge, but she didn't try to stop herself. She knew what she had to do. As Khyn pushed the button, Echo snatched up the empty circlet and thrust it onto her own head.

And then she leapt over the edge.

CHAPTER 27

There was an instant where she could have stopped it. Nearly did, the terror of what she'd done so desperate that the bit of her still connected to her body opened her mouth to scream a last protest. Then it was too late. She had taken the nightmare step over the edge, and there was nothing beneath her feet but emptiness and the long, long fall. Her hand flailed, ripping through a thornbush. The pain should wake her, but it did not. She gasped and thrashed, trying to tear herself out of the nightmare as she had so many times since Lia's death. *Echo*, the fading voice that always woke her screamed. But this was no nightmare. There would be no waking.

The terror gripped her, driving all thought from her mind. She was going to hit the bottom, in another moment, the last moment she would have—how long? She twisted mid-fall, searching down, saw nothing but the black abyss beneath. Her body was accelerating towards it even as her arms and legs thrashed, churning the air as if she could pull herself up through nothingness. She heard the thin scream of the air rushing past her, or maybe that was her own voice, she didn't know, couldn't think, could only writhe in animal panic, knowing that any second now she would smash into the rocks beneath, feel her body crush and break. The abyss rose to grip her, blackness filling all her vision. There was a word, echoing past, but she didn't recognize it anymore, and finally the wind ripped even that away, and all she knew was the fall. It would take an eternity to fall, to hit, and in that endless moment she would always be falling, always be hitting, be—

Echo!

Saving Lia.

The darkness exploded into light brighter than the sun. She still fell: not only down, but *out*, all sense of body gone, no arms or legs but somehow still her senses stretching out, spinning through a crown of wire into an infinite net—

Too big. Too far. The crown burned, her mind did, scorching thought. But with thought went the fear, and now there would be only an infinity of—

Echo. I know you're here. I know you hear me.

Something was swimming up out of the light. A

shape, no more than a shadow against the unbearable brightness—

Stay with me. Please. As Lia had asked that night, that single night that they had had together. But:

I can't! I only hurt you. But it doesn't matter. Back there in the sanctuary, they meant to—but I'm stopping them. You'll be whole. That's all that matters now.

The shape took substance, falling up at her, became a body, naked but for its shroud, a crown of fire haloing its head. Beneath it the rocks loomed, suddenly solid, very close. Above—far above—hung the cliff edge she had gone over. The figure's edges streamed indistinct on the burning wind, but Echo saw the face, every detail. She would know it anywhere, in any darkness, after any eternity. Once it had been Lia, but now also something so much more, so much greater. She fixed her streaming eyes on the luminous gaze, the light behind it. It was the last thing she would ever see. She would have that to take with her.

Saint, she called in the fullness of her heart. *Lia. My life, in service to you.* It was enough. It would always be enough.

The Saint flew up, and past her, into the brightness beyond her grasp.

Echo, Lia's voice called. *Stay with me.*

Don't worry. It's not that bad.

You're such a fool. The memory of Lia's laughter as she pulled Echo's face down to hers. *I'm asking for me, not you.*

And then a hand reached down, towards her. The Saint's fingers opened, spread wide, an offering.

Echo reached up and grabbed the arm, but it was her broken hand. Her grip slipped, sliding down to the wrist. The strain was too much, too fast, and that grip failed too, leaving the palms clutching, then only fingertips—

Her body hit with a crushing jolt.

I love you. I will always love you.

And then they had each other.

The weight of her broken human body dropped away, left somewhere on the floor of a room where indistinct figures stood in frozen wonder, watching patterns on screens intertwine and change and complete each other, power surging to close every gap, fill every void, the spire above a burning beacon calling every heart to home. Echo rose, or Lia fell softly; locked in that embrace, they landed together, floating. The shroud billowed like a cloud, dimming the unbearable brightness, then settling softly over the body on the altar. As the sanctuary re-formed around them, Echo hovered one more moment, gazing down upon the Saint. *I love you*, she said.

Lia opened her eyes.

Echo jerked awake with a gasp. A steady, rhythmic sound echoed in her ears, a mechanical sob. She smelled singed hair. For a few minutes she lay there, limp, then dragged her eyes open. A pale oval hovered over her.

"Lia," she croaked.

But it was not. Nyree looked down at her. Then she disappeared. Echo tried to turn her head to follow, could not move. *Paralyzed*, she thought. *The fall*. The medical priest appeared in the narrow cone of her vision. He did something with his hands, and the sobbing sound stopped, and with it, her breath. She felt a pressure in her chest, her throat, and then the tube was out. She still couldn't breathe. She waited for the flurry of motion, the sharp pain as the priest cut out her ovaries, but nothing happened. *They do not want any more of me*, she thought, and laughed, and then she was coughing, breath starting again, and for a few minutes she could only lie there, her breath settling into a pattern, the life returning to her body like power lighting a circuit.

And then she remembered. "Lia," she gasped, and rose, or tried to, but something caught her arm. A tube, the dark blood flowing, connecting her to a machine, and the machine wired to the wall. She felt the faint pressure beating in her vein. The Saint's heart, beating with hers. Lia's.

Always.

"You don't need that anymore," the medical priest said, disconnecting the tube. Her bandaged palm covered the spot, feeling for the pulse. Bandages wrapped her body, too, but she could move, and she sat up, bringing Nyree back into her line of sight. And past Nyree, the other bed, with the body lying still upon it, and blood on the sheet at the chest, and lower down. Death had transformed the smile into a rictus. Echo's breath choked in her throat again. Gem, dead. In service to the Saint. To Lia. *I will remember.*

Echo reached over with a pained effort to clasp the cold hand. After a little while she wiped her eyes. The young hunter's were still open, sightless; vision blurring again, Echo drew them closed.

"I want to see the Saint."

She couldn't walk by herself; Nyree assisted, a hand holding Echo's arm across her shoulders and an arm wrapped around her waist. It was slow going, up the stairs and across the yard. The wind had died down. Nuns and juveniles and priests were at work sweeping away debris. Echo did not have to look up to know the mast atop the spire still turned.

There was debris in the sanctuary too, and wooden planks nailed up to patch the hole the aircar had made. Some of the panels were dark, eyes with the life gone out of them; but Dalto's board glowed, the pattern playing steadily across it. She paused, leaning hard on Nyree, to take it in. She didn't have to ask. Dalto said, "You entered the link. All the way. *Saints*." His voice shook, but not with fear. "Your mind—you should have burned to cinders. The Saint . . . preserved you somehow." His trembling finger traced a pattern. "Whatever you did . . . it saved her too. The power is under control." He adjusted a dial with a little grimace that turned into a pained smile. "Not ours, I think. And the patterns—they've changed, but they are steady. More than steady. Whole. But you know that, don't you."

She didn't say anything, only stood for a moment watching the boards flicker and flash in time to her own thoughts, before finally limping the rest of the way to the altar. The Patri already sat there, fingers laced together in his lap as he contemplated the Saint, face rapt. Nyree eased her down and stepped away.

The empty circlet lay on the couch. The metal was singed, blackened. It didn't matter; she didn't need to enter the link that way again. She didn't need to enter it at all. The pattern was burned into her brain, her heart.

Lia. Her body braced instinctively for the screaming of alarms, but that time was past.

Echo.

After that they had no need for words.

A few days later the Preservers left. Somehow all of them had survived except Taavi. They were taking one of the hunters' last aircars; Echo had expected Nyree to object, but she had merely stripped the craft of everything of tactical value beyond the flight controls and demonstrated the operations. "I am glad to see them go," was all she said.

Echo, still heavily bandaged, stood by the hatch. "The beacon will guide you the shortest way home," she told Stigir. Even as she spoke, she saw it, not with her eyes but the Saint's, in the pattern she shared with Lia. She grasped the ladder, momentarily dizzy. A warm merriment spread through her, as gentle as a touch on her cheek. *You'll become accustomed to it soon.*

Lia, she said, for joy that she could.

Echo.

Time meant nothing inside the link. When she finally narrowed her focus again to the man before her, he seemed unaware of any gap in her attention. "The team will decide whether to open the Vault," Stigir said. "But I would wait another four hundred years before I drew one seed from it. This is not what we have preserved that treasure for. The world is not ready to be reborn." The ladder rattled beneath his boots.

Khyn would not meet her eyes. Echo said anyway, "You have succeeded in your mission. The priests have given you everything that might help with the children, whether or not you use the stored seed." No one had argued with that either, when Echo had ordered it.

"It's my fault that Taavi is dead. That you killed her."

Echo knew that Khyn would be seeing that face in her dreams for a long time to come. It was a burden they shared. "She served as best she knew how. It is up to us to give her sacrifice meaning."

The hatch swung closed on the Preservers.

Echo climbed with difficulty up to the tower room. Exey wasn't there, but she smelled fresh ferm, and scraps of print were scattered everywhere. She studied one of the drawings, baffled at first, then recognized the pattern: vanes, and a power drop tied in, and a huge screw. The Ward's new mill. No doubt Exey was boasting at this very moment about his unmatched design. North, chastened for now, would be complaining soon about being left behind. The fabricator had busy days ahead.

So do we.

Echo smiled. She let the print flutter to the floor and stepped to the window. The city spread before her, her vision and Lia's overlaid in one intricate pattern. It was a market day, and cityens surged towards the square. She could make out hunters scattered here and there among them, ever watchful. Her eyes closed for a moment. Gem's absence made a hollow place that was always going to hurt.

When she looked up again it was to see the spire, flashing bright as the panels turned in the sun. She opened her arms wide to match Lia's embrace. Even from here the connection surged between them. It was the Saint's city, and hers, and together they would preserve it. Stigir had been wrong.

The world was already reborn.

ACKNOWLEDGMENTS

It continues to take a bigger village than I can thank properly here, so I'll just single out a few people: My parents. My brother and sister, who didn't specify a dedication this time and therefore are stuck with "thanks for going fishing with me even when you didn't feel fishy." My agent, Mary C. Moore, who keeps such a good eye out for me. Kelley Eskridge, who told me I could do better and gave me the tools to do it with. Chloe Moffett, Jessie Edwards, Emily Homonoff, and Angela Craft at Harper Voyager Impulse, for the great teamwork. Nicola Griffith, for her support. And most of all my wife, Mary, for saying "Yes, dear" at all the best possible times.

If you liked REGENERATION
make sure to read the first
Echo Hunter 367 novel

DISSENSION

By Stacey Berg
Available now wherever ebooks are sold.

AN EXCERPT FROM *DISSENSION*

CHAPTER 1

The girl Hunter murdered in the desert was only thirteen.

Hunter eased the aircar closer to the cliff's edge, hovering just above the bleached white stone stained bloody by the setting sol. Emptiness spread in every direction, silent and watchful. Hunter felt it pressing down as she studied the cautious tracks she had followed for the last few miles. The girl had tried to obscure them, as she had been taught, but Hunter knew the desert far too well to be deceived. The tracks ended in a patch of scuffed sand. A broken thornbush trailed over the edge where a desperate hand had ripped through it in a last failed grab at salvation. It was obvious now what had happened.

She settled the aircar in the dry creek bed a hundred feet below. Already the cliff cast a long shadow across the canyon. The day's heat still radiated from the stone, but Hunter could feel the chill in the breeze probing for gaps in her clothing, a mild warning of the harsh night to come. She had to hurry; the scavengers would gather quickly once true night fell. Even she did not want to be caught in the open then.

Her boots squeaked a little in the fine layer of dust, though she could have moved silently had it mattered. Glancing up to the torn spot at the edge of the cliff, she estimated the fall line and began to search the bottom in a systematic grid. It was only a few minutes before she spotted the still form crumpled facedown among the rocks.

The ground warmed her as she knelt. She could see why the girl hadn't called out for help: her shoulders rose and fell with desperate effort, no breath to spare. Hunter rolled her gently on her back.

The girl's eyes were open, pupils dilated wide with shock. Her chalk-white face was bathed in sweat despite the chill. Even so, when the girl spoke, her voice, weak as it was, came out calm, controlled. "You came for me. I knew you would."

"We don't waste anyone."

The eyes, dark as Hunter's own, closed briefly, dragged open again with an enormous effort. "The others?"

"Everyone else returned as scheduled." Eight out of nine, a good outcome for this exercise. Ten sols alone in the desert culled the weak quickly, but none of the rest had called for rescue, and the girl had not had time. The 378s were a strong batch; there had only been fourteen to begin with, thirteen annuals ago. When Hunter had been this age only eight were left. The priests always made more, but it was never quite the same as your own batch.

"That's good," the girl whispered breathlessly. Her eyes wandered up the cliff.

"Tell me how it happened," Hunter said, though she already knew. It didn't matter; there was still a little time, and the girl deserved a chance to make her report.

"I was following some canids." She had to stop and gather air. "I thought they'd lead me to water."

"That was a reasonable plan."

"It almost worked. I smelled the spring, but I let myself get too close to the edge, even though you taught us that the rocks there often crumble." Hunter had never taught this batch. The girl's mind was wandering, or maybe it was only the failing light. Snatching what breath she could, the girl continued, "I was so thirsty, and I thought . . . And then I fell. I broke my leg," she added, glancing at the pink and white splinters thrusting out of the torn flesh. Her eyes came back to Hunter's. "It doesn't hurt. I don't feel anything."

"I know." Hunter edged around a little. "Here, let me help you sit up." The girl was a boneless weight against her, arms dangling, a handful of sand trickling between limp fingers as Hunter knelt behind her, holding her close. "It's all right, Ela. You did well." The lie wouldn't hurt anything now.

The girl's head lolled back against Hunter's shoulder, eyes searching her face as if trying to focus across a great distance. Her whisper was barely audible. "Which one are you?"

"Echo."

"Number five, like me."

"Yes, Ela." She eased one palm around to cup the back of the girl's head, the other gently cradling her chin. "Ready?"

The girl's nod was only the barest motion between her hands. Hunter let her lips rest against the girl's dusty hair for a short moment. She felt the girl's mouth move in a smile against her fingers.

Then, with a swift and practiced motion, Hunter snapped her neck.

In a trick of the sunset the spire of the Church glowed, a wire filament burning in a lamp to guide her home. The crossed antennas rose above like a man with arms outstretched to embrace the city. Beneath, the rose window was an eye gazing out at the horizon.

The sky was dark by the time she stood before the massive doors, staring up and up as she always did when she first returned from the desert. The doors faced away from the compound, setting the line between Church and city with an edge not entirely physical; whoever had built them, long before the Fall, had meant the scale to show a greatness far beyond the mere human. Even before the newer defenses had been added, anyone seeking to enter, friend or otherwise, would have to pause here to consider the indifferent power he faced. The great planks were wider than her torso, bolted top and bottom to make the vertical run three times human height, and the worked-metal bindings looked as strong today as the day they were forged. In the center of the doors, just along the seam at chest height, the bindings flattened into a pair of panels. A hand there, and the door knew who sought to enter. Many fates had been decided with a simple touch.

She raised a grimy palm to the panel. Normally there was no wait. Tonight the doors seemed to hesitate, weighing her worth, before the mechanism clicked and they dragged open, permitting her to enter.

Behind its thick walls the cathedral was cool and dim, conditions that changed little day or night. This was the oldest part of the Church, the hewn stone ancient even before the Fall. Stone walls flanked either side of the cathedral for a few hundred paces. Where they left off, the forcewall, invisible but in some ways stronger than the stone, curved to encompass the whole compound. In the other direction, the Saint's thoughts carried the forcewall in a vast circle separating city from desert, and the canids and other dangers that flourished in the absence of men.

Hunter crossed the nave into the sanctuary. Above her head, the vaulted ceilings arched high, a space calculated to awe the men who used to come here in search of something greater than themselves. Now the echoing silence only mirrored the emptiness of the world. Still, it was a miracle of engineering, this huge enclosure constructed from nothing more than small blocks of stone cemented expertly together. The forebears must have glimpsed long into the future to choose this place as their last refuge against the Fall. It was no allegory, the Patri always said, that the ancient cathedral stood intact so long after the metal and glass of newer buildings had fallen into ruins. The Church simply had the capacity to repair the stone.

The altar rose in the center of the sanctuary, surrounded by the panels and stations the priests tended. Lights played across the screens in patterns unreadable to a hunter, the priests' fingers tapping responses with swift precision. Upon the altar lay the Saint. A glittering crown of copper connected her to the machines that preserved the remains of the city, maintaining the forcewall that blocked the wilderness out, the generators that gave the cityens a bit of light in the darkness and heat to keep them from freezing to death in the winter, and more important, powered the crypts where the priests did their work to keep the Church itself alive; for only the Church could preserve what was left of the world. That was the central truth of all life in the four hundred annuals since the Fall: without the Saint, the Church would die; without the Church, the city.

Hunter bowed her head. She envied the priests, who could know the Saint's thoughts, or what passed for thoughts in a mind that was so much greater now than human. The Saint spoke to them through the boards, but no one knew where her awareness began or ended, or if anything about it could be considered awareness, the way men conceived of it.

Once the crown was on, there was no asking.

The Saint had been a girl once, before she ascended to that altar. Hunter hoped for her sake that it was like a deep sleep, undisturbed by any dream.

Hunter had spoken to the girl, before she became the Saint, had received her words and judged her. Wrongly, foolishly. She wished devoutly that she could speak with her now, confess, ask forgiveness. If she listened hard enough she could imagine that she still heard the girl's voice. But that was all it was, imagining, the way a mind would always try to fill a void. To know the Saint's thoughts was not her place, nor any hunter's. That she even wished it made her unworthy.

Yet she lingered, listening, until she knew for certain she would hear no voice answering her from the silence.

The Patri waited for her at the inner gate, sure enough sign of his concern. He must have been standing there for some time; the motion-activated lights glowed softly where he stood, but the path back to the domiciles was lost in darkness. Another man might have wished for less illumination: Hunter hadn't had time to go back to the spring before night fell, and a quick roll in the sand had done little to scrub the blood and gore from her clothes. The Patri only nodded as she came down the steps from the mundane inner doors. "You found her in time, I see."

Hunter nodded, drawing the little vial from her pocket with a sticky hand. "Her ovaries were perfectly intact. I left the rest for the scavengers; there was nothing of value."

The Patri accepted the bottle without hesitation, secreting it in a fold of his loose-flowing robe. "What delayed you? The aircar landed some while ago."

Dust clung to a wet stain across the toe of her boot. "I'm sorry, Patri. I came in through the sanctuary."

She heard the long breath he let out. "Very well. Go bathe. I will have a meal sent to you if you wish."

Hunter's stomach twisted. "Not now, thank you, Patri."

His wise gaze was nearly unbearable. "Rest, then. There will be much to do in the morning."

Hunter let her normally silent footfalls beat a warning down the stone steps to the baths. Two young priests, interrupted in their dalliance, fled flushed and dripping as she came into the chamber. Steam rose gently from pools heated by the same source deep below that also powered systems throughout the Church, even the altar where the Saint lay. But Hunter did not want to think of the Saint, not now.

She stripped quickly, dropping her clothes in a pile for the young nun who tiptoed in silently to collect them. The fabric was another miracle bequeathed by the forebears; by morning it would be washed clean as if never worn, blank and unstained. She caught sight of herself reflected on the calm surface of the pool, a body lean and muscled as all hunters were, marred here and there by blood and grime; the face a dusty mask with two narrow channels washed clean beneath the eyes. Ela stared back at her without accusation.

She closed her eyes and slipped into the water, floating still as death long after the last ripple died away against the stone.

CHAPTER 2

She went down to the laboratory in the morning. Winter or summer, the temperature stayed the same here in the subterranean bowels of the Church, cool and dank. In the two annuals she had spent tending the listening arrays in the desert, she had grown unused to such confining spaces. She felt the rock ribs pressing close just behind the ancient plastered walls, a bone poking through here and there where repairs had been neglected. Long tubes crossed the ceiling like veins on the back of an old man's hand, a bare few still glowing dimly, providing just enough light to let the priests pick their way along the corridor. For a hunter, it was more than enough.

Doors were set at regular intervals along the hall. Most opened, if they opened at all, only onto the mortuary debris of the Fall. Sometimes the juvenile

hunters explored inside those dead rooms, against instructions but well in line with expectations. Hunter
herself had done so once. She had found the desic-
cated remains of two bodies intermingled in a corner,
still wrapped in a few scraps of cloth that might have
been white once. Far more important, beneath the
dead she had spied a rectangular sheaf of prints, fixed
together at one end, with a stiff cover protecting the
bound edge and sides. Nothing in the Church was
worth more than these, save the Saint herself, and she
carried it to the priests with an appreciation border-
ing on awe. That had brought more priests running
to search the room for further treasures. There were
other items still intact and useful to be collected from
the rubble, but it was the papers, burnt and crumbling but still closely covered with the mechanical
writings of the forebears, that brought them up in
reverent silence. They gathered them up tenderly as
children and carried them off to safety, but whether
the brown leaves deigned to give up any of their secrets, Hunter never heard, and though she had tried
other doors after that, she never found anything else
of such value.

She didn't care what any of those rooms might
hold right now. Instead she strode towards the me-
ticulously rebuilt laboratory at the end of the hall.

Not a single priest looked up when she entered,
though rows of them sat evenly spaced along the
pristine tables, bent unmoving over their magnifiers,

giving the illusion that the lenses grew out from their eye sockets. The overhead light was dim as the hallway, but each magnifier was lit from beneath, as if the priests huddled over a dozen tiny fires. Their hands worked tiny, delicate instruments, the ends too fine for even Hunter to see unaided. She knew, though, what they prodded and teased beneath the lenses, and how eagerly the next group of nuns waited for them to finish their work and give it over to be incubated through the long winter. The children would look much like Ela, like Hunter herself.

She stood there for a long time, watching what they wrought with the bloody treasure she had brought them last night. Even when she heard the footsteps coming down the hall, she could not take her eyes off the priests and their work. The Patri stood quietly behind her, waiting patiently, breath even as a metronome. Without a hunter's enhanced senses he could not, she knew, detect the minute irregularity of hers, the tiny increase in heart rate she could not prevent when in his presence, ever since she had something to hide.

Since the Saint.

The Patri let her wait some time before he finally said, "When they told me you missed teachings, I thought I would find you here. Would you like to see?"

"Yes, please."

At the Patri's nod, the priest at the nearest magnifier bowed and stepped aside. Hunter glanced at his face. He was thin and sharp-featured, like all his kind, and his eyes were pale, the better to gather the light in this underground lair. His skin was so white she could see the vessels coursing through it, a map to show where to strike, the unprotected soft parts delivered like an offering. She clasped her hands behind her back. He would never be exposed to danger. He had probably not set foot outside the Church since early childhood, instead spending all his waking moments absorbing the teachings, searching for new truths that might be the difference in the Church's survival. One day he, or one of his brothers, would become the Patri. Hunter could not imagine it.

He did not meet her eyes.

The Patri took the stool first, adjusting the dials with an echo of the priests' skilled delicacy. His hands and face were tinted darker now from the sol he walked in above, but where his loose sleeves fell back the skin showed as white as the priest's. "It's been a long time," he said with a wry smile. The young priest nodded nervous encouragement. The Patri stared down for a long time. When he was satisfied at last, he stood up, holding the stool for Hunter.

She took the seat tentatively and set her eyes to the magnifier. "If it isn't in focus, turn the small ring to adjust. Your eyes are sharper than mine." The lumpy pinkish blob in the viewer gained shape as she dialed the knob. "Do you see those little circles?" She nodded minimally, taking care not to lose her view. "Those are the eggs."

"How many will there be?" Her successors, one day, though most of them would never know her.

"Enough for a few batches, maybe less. Many are lost in the enhancement process. We are not as skilled as our grandfathers, and they were not as skilled as theirs. In the first days after the Fall, the eggs might be taken and the hunter survive. Now we dare not try that. So much easier with priests—pair a priest with a nun, and every child is another priest. But hunters can't bear, so it has to be done this way. And of course we only have so many nuns to carry them." His breath rose and fell in a sigh. She felt acutely how his burdens weighed on him.

The priest cleared his throat. "Speaking of difficulty, Patri," he began, then broke off with a nervous glance at Hunter.

"You may speak in front of Echo, Jozef."

"Yes, Patri. I am sorry to have to tell you, but another magnifier broke today."

"Can you repair it?" There was a sharpness in the Patri's question, quickly smoothed. "If there's a way I'm sure you'll find it."

The priest ran a hand through his thin white hair. "We will try, of course, but I'm afraid not. The lens itself cracked. As you know we've been trying to make more, but there is something missing from our technique. We've been searching the prints, but so far . . ."

Hunter had often seen the priests, dozens of them, pale-eyed and soft as Jozef, hunched over the tables in the nave, where the walls were lined with thousands of volumes, lovingly preserved, like the one Hunter had found. Besides the Saint, those prints were the greatest treasure of the world.

"I understand, Jozef. I thank the forebears who thought to put all those words on paper before the last machine died, of course, but we can wish they had printed us an index, yes?" He laughed ruefully.

Jozef's thin lips curved, without, Hunter thought, much humor. "Yes, Patri. Meanwhile we will try our best with the repairs, of course."

"I know you will, Jozef. We should let you return to your work." He gestured, and Hunter, with a last look through the lenses, surrendered the seat back to the priest.

The Patri laid a hand on her shoulder as they left the laboratory. "You did well to bring her back."

Hunter thought of the broken girl lying in the dust. *It isn't her.*

It is the part of her that mattered, she told herself fiercely. *She knew it too. Do not shame her with your weakness.* "I did what the Church required, no more."

"The Church requires a great deal sometimes."

She stared at the priests manipulating the tiny

plates. "We are made to serve, Patri." It was the earliest truth a hunter learned.

The Patri studied her face. Her heart quickened. He would see, surely he would see. "Do you never wish it could be otherwise, Echo?"

"No, Patri," she said, too quickly. "Of course not. The Church is all world has left. The Saint. Those are the only things that matter. Without them . . ."

"Even with them, I sometimes think."

She stood still, dismayed by heaviness of his tone. In all the annuals she could remember, nothing had shaken him, nothing challenged the calm and clear--eyed judgment that sometimes made him seem as much hunter as priest. He read her expression and smiled. "But not very often. I was sorry to lose Ela, that's all. You are all so precious to me. All those resources that go into your making, and so much we need you for . . . At least you found her in time. It wasn't a total waste; we can make more." He stared into the laboratory for a moment, then shook himself. "Go attend to your duties, Echo. You have a difficult task today, and you are late."

ABOUT THE AUTHOR

STACEY BERG is a medical researcher who writes speculative fiction. Her work as a physician-scientist provides the inspiration for many of her stories. She lives with her wife in Houston and is a member of the Writers' League of Texas. When she's not writing, she practices kung fu and runs half marathons.

http://staceyberg.com
www.harpervoyagerbooks.com

Discover great authors, exclusive offers, and more at hc.com.